Addiction

Kelsey Cole

Published by New Generation Publishing in 2018

Copyright © Kelsey Cole 2018

First Edition

www.newgeneration-publishing.com

 New Generation Publishing

Tuesday, 8 November 2016

Miranda was worried. It was somewhat of a new experience. The net was finally drawing in; a day she had thought would never arrive was now looming. She had always pushed such thoughts to the back of her mind, almost deliberately ignoring the inevitable fact. The past was coming back to haunt her, now it was getting closer. The enormity of what lay ahead was threatening to explode and it was driving her literally insane. She had for some time persuaded herself that the mannerisms that had manifested themselves were just her trying to become more outrageous, to keep outdoing herself and be seen as the hero wildcard; the rags to riches eccentric. The reality was far from that, she needed help but could no longer seek it. She had completely lost her inner soul and was now simply living in a body as a person she herself no longer recognized. It was almost as if she had been possessed and was watching from outside. It reminded her of the time twenty-nine years before when she had an ugly trip on some bad shit in Boston. That had left her in intensive care on a drip for a week whilst the A&E staff pumped the heroin mix out of her blood stream. Just thinking back to that experience made her break out into a sweat and caused her to recount the words of the doctor, "You are one lucky lady, another five minutes and you would have been in a box pushing up the daisies...." As she sat behind her desk staring at the jewel-studded map showing her business empire her only thought was it would have been better if she had been five minutes late.

Her once stunning looks had left her and the multiple surgeries were starting to take their toll. No amount of designer clothes could cover up the fact she was past her prime and actually looked like a third-rate hooker who was down on their luck. The jewelry did little to help. It had just become a comfort blanket and the fact she no longer fitted inside her designer clothes, even from twelve months previously, showed she also had taken comfort from junk food. Her tits, when she sat down, sat on her knees. Her cellulite could not be covered by any amount of tanning process, yet she continued to expose as much flesh as she could. She knew she looked like a dog, but all her assistants and "friends", never wanting to get on her wrong side, continued to lie to her and she continued to believe their lies, even though she knew they were lying. Her hair under the massive wig was sparse and gray and when not worn in her sanctum sanctorum made her look like white trash. The only thing missing was a tattoo, something she had never considered.

As she sat there starting at the map she thought back to how she had got to this point.

Thursday, 20 September 1973

"Fuck you bitch. I ain't interested in your fucking whining. Get back out there and go fuck some stranger and bring me the cash." The door slammed shut as her mother left the house. Miranda knew better than to go down stairs and talk to her father. He was, as normal, drunk, drugged up and wound up. The reason he was wound up seemed irrelevant, it was just a fact of life. She knew what was coming next and steeled herself to being raped by her own father. She had long ago vowed to get even one day and just waited for the inevitable. An hour later and having tried to shower away the brutal invasion she sat there on her bed crying and more determined than ever to put a stop to it. She had considered suicide, but was not brave enough to go through with it. Instead she spent the time going through the multiple ways she was going to make him pay and each time he abused her she mentally went through the options and discarded them one by one, until three days before her fourteenth birthday she had it down to just one. A plan she felt was foolproof and would end the suffering permanently for both her and her broken mother. She had never told her mother of the brutality she suffered at the hands of her father however there was an unspoken understanding that both knew what took place.

The plan was relatively simple, but involved getting her father to take her to a place out of town where few people went. Her father would not be missed. He was a jerk and a second-rate pimp. The only person who would even remotely miss him was his dealer, and she knew that his credit there was shit. Six months previously, on a school trip to New York, she had come across a dealer who had sold her contaminated heroin. She was sure it was not good shit, but her plan didn't require good shit. She wanted it to be the worst shit ever and since then had modified the package to make sure it was going to do the job. Even then as she purchased the shit she had been smart enough to wear gloves so her prints would never be traced to the package. She had tested a small amount on a neighbor's dog, having to inject the animal, and then watched as the poodle had writhed in agony before keeling over dead. Not only was she aroused by the effect of the drug but she felt a swell of emotion that finally she had control over something and she liked the sense of being in control of something else, even if it was a dog.

Wednesday, 24 September 1975

It was an unusually warm day in fall. The temperature was sitting in the low 90s and the sky was still cloudless as Miranda left swimming practice. It had been a tough session but the national championships were coming up and she was determined to show those bastards on the Olympic Committee she was a contender, even if they were still a year away. The criticism that her butterfly stroke was not perfect, and she could never match Wendy Boglioli continued to eat at her, but she would show them. Putting that thought to the back of her mind she focused on putting the false smile on her face and becoming very subversive as her father was waiting outside smoking.

"So are we going to Overmountain Shelter or what? Don't know why you can't give me this 'special' present back home, your bitch mother's working away."

Miranda knew her mother had picked up a potential goldmine, a guy in his early eighties had fallen for her in the strip joint and had whisked her away to Vegas on his private jet. At least she would be safe for a few days and her father had no clue.

"Sorry but it's part of the surprise. The shelter is closed now for the season so no one will be around to bother us."

"Sure, whatever. It had just better be worth it, I should be on the craps table not fucking around out there, there's some fresh meat in town who I am gonna fleece…"

"I promise it will be worth it."

So they got into the lime green Cadillac Eldorado and headed away from the swimming pool. The drive would only take fifteen minutes even with the roads as quiet as they were. Miranda kept up the subversive conversation, hankering to her father and trying to keep him in a 'good' mood yet at the same time looking out for any possible witnesses. Luck was on her side, once they left town they passed no other vehicle and there were no farmers working the fields. As they pulled onto the dirt road leading to the parking lot a mile from the shelter she stilled herself.

There was no turning back now, revenge would happen and it would happen tonight. The hatred burning inside, and the knowledge of what was coming made her start to sweat and she wound down the window slightly to disguise the fact. She had long ago developed this exterior appearance that stopped anyone knowing how she was thinking or feeling. One final look over her shoulder as they pulled closer to the parking lot and not seeing any signs of life gave her a surge of excitement that she had not experienced since the death of the poodle.

The Cadillac side skidded into a parking lot and she sensed her father getting aroused by what was going to happen, at least in his mind. Miranda pulled a rucksack from the trunk and together they walked to the shelter. As they came close to the side door Miranda looked around and pulled a key from her rucksack and took off a padlock she had replaced some weeks before. Putting the padlock in her bag to make sure there was no evidence she could be traced, she entered the shelter. She wasn't sure if the padlock could be traced back to the general store in town, but she was not taking any chances, besides which, it would look more like a break in when eventually the staff returned in spring.

"Hey, I'm just going to get changed, but while I do, I got you a bottle of your favorite, Jack D."

"Fuck me you got something right at last, maybe you're learning after all."

Miranda went into the john and replaced her tracksuit with the leather bondage gear she had found in her mother's wardrobe and slipped into it, making sure to pull on the elbow length leather gloves. There could be no fingerprints. She had done her best to make sure there could be no other evidence, even hair samples and had brought a gimp mask to try and cover all angles. She left her clothes in a pile and went back to the room where her father had already consumed a third of the bottle. He stood there with an evil grin on his face and came towards her.

"I never knew you were into that kinky shit, man I wish

6

I'd known that before."

"Like I said, I wanted to give you a nice surprise. I have something else for you too."

"What?"

Miranda pulled the little package from her panties.

"I've been keeping this warm for you."

"What shit is it?"

"It's coke. I worked extra shifts last month to get you this. Rocca has taken a shine to me and let me have it on the cheap. He promised it was the best quality shit around, the same grade he gets for the governor. I thought you'd like to chill before we got going."

"Fuck me you are full of surprises. Whisky, coke, what the fuck do you want?"

"Nothing, just to pay you back for being my dad."

"Yeah, whatever. Where the fuck is my rolling paper?"

"No worries, I brought some in case you didn't bring yours."

Miranda handed over the pack of reefers and moved back to allow him to fumble the coke joint together. The Jack D was starting to hit and the shakes were subsiding but they never fully went away. *Not long now, get that joint lit you bastard,* she thought. Miranda did some stretching exercises, partly to take the tension out of her body from the swimming session and partly to make it look like she was preparing for what should have been coming.

Finally he had the joint rolled and he flicked open his Zippo ready to light the joint. He suddenly snapped closed the Zippo lid and fear surged through Miranda's body. Surely he was not going to get out of it now. With a huge sense of relief he went for the bottle and took a slug, before re-flicking the Zippo. With a huge cloud of smoke he started to inhale.

Miranda was not sure how long the effects would take. Would it actually work? She thought back to the dog and it was, she seemed to remember, a pretty short time, but it was over a year ago now and quite simply she had not timed the event. At a guess she thought it would take five to ten minutes, however after only a couple of drags she noticed a change. His breathing became challenging and he started to turn a shade of gray. With each passing second the effects grew more and more dramatic. His eyes started to bulge as the toxins raced through his bloodstream. He tried speaking but no words were coming out and then with the joint still to his lips he crashed to the ground and lay still.

Miranda waited and counted. Ten seconds, twenty seconds, thirty seconds, and then a minute. No signs of movement. She could hear no breathing, but still stayed there watching, believing the bastard would get up any minute. It seemed like hours, but in reality ten minutes later she slowly walked across the room. She stripped off her right glove and felt for a pulse. There was none, and the body was already starting to get cold. She had succeeded in her plan and burst out laughing knowing she would no longer endure his vile abuse and deep down vowed that no man would ever have power over her again. They were, in her eyes, evil bastards that should be used and manipulated for her own purposes, nothing more.

She slowly walked back to the john and changed back to her tracksuit, careful to ensure she left no trace. She wiped down the basin she had held onto when steadying herself as she had taken off her boots and without a further look at the body went out through the side door checking for any sights or sounds that might give away a stray walker. There were none and she went to the back of the shelter where she had hidden her bike behind a tarpaulin. It was still there, albeit covered in cobwebs and some rodent shit. She cleaned off the worst with a small towel from her rucksack and then pushed the bike past the car. As she passed she could still hear the sound of the engine cooling down and continued past smiling at the thought of never seeing that or her father again. She was free and she was happy. Miranda mounted her bike and started off down the dirt track to the road. A hundred yards from the road she dismounted and pushed the bike through the undergrowth and trees to a spot which brought her out close to the main road. She waited checking to see if anyone came past. It was 7.13 pm according to her Omega Elephant. It was still warm, but a little breeze had started up and she shivered slightly as she hid in the shade. The plan would not work unless she was home by 8.10 pm. She had to make a move and pushed her bike out of the shade and mounted up heading back to town, not looking behind and just focused directly ahead of her. Again, her luck held out, she saw no traffic, and as she came back to the sign saying "Welcome to Roan Mountain, North Carolina, The Tar Heel State" she turned off the main road and headed around one of the small estates that had grown up over the years, continuing at a fast pace, so anyone seeing her would have thought she was on a training session.

As she pulled up outside her house her watch said 8.02 pm; she had made it. She pushed her bike into the garage and headed inside. Exactly eight minutes later she heard the engine of a car pull up on the drive and switch off, Nancy her mother's step-sister had arrived. She was in town to take care of Miranda whilst her mum was in Vegas.

"Hey, Aunt Nancy. How you doing?"

"Hey sweetheart, I'm doing great. How was swimming practice?"

"Yeah it was OK, but I decided to do a little extra on my bike afterwards and only just got in."

"Any sign of your dad?"

"No, he wasn't here when I got home. He mentioned the other day about some crap game out of town coming up, so I guess it must be today."

"Never mind, probably not a bad thing. I shouldn't say this but that guy gives me the creeps. I really never understood what your mum saw in him."

"No worries, Aunt Nancy, I know he's got issues. What do you want for dinner?"

"How about I treat you at that new Howard Johnson's

that's opened up?"

"Thanks, Aunt Nancy. Can I just go and freshen up? I promise I won't be long."

With that Miranda headed for the stairs barely containing the smile. She was certain she had gotten away with it.

Saturday, 27 September 1975

"Hey Mom, how was Vegas?"

"It was real nice. I just wished you could have been with me. Sorry I was not here to protect you from your father. I felt so guilty all the time, but I hope we may have a way out of this shit life. Where is he, by the way?"

"I don't know, Mom. I haven't seen him since Aunt Nancy arrived. The last thing he said to me was about some crap game out of town, so I guess he's doped up in some shithole staying pissed."

"Better that way, at least it gives us some time together so we can work on my plan. Where's Aunt Nancy?"

"She had to go out to get some groceries, said she'd be back in an hour. She should be back soon. So tell me about Vegas, is it as crazy as it's made out to be?"

"Sure is, it's full on twenty-four hours a day. There was something happening all the time and that trick I was with wanted to make the most of it. He's got a terminal illness. He did say what but I can't remember, and he was going to enjoy every last second he'd got. He wasn't too hot in bed, but at that age, and with that condition I was worried he was going to die on the job, especially when he told me to whip him. Most of the time he just wanted to spend money and be seen with a younger woman. He is kind of just lonely and took a shine to me. Best is, he's asked me to fly to New York to spend time with him there, says it's where he lives. What I can work out is his wife died eight years ago and he never had any kids. He mentioned he had some distant relatives, from his wife's side living in Kansas, but had not even spoken to them since his wife's funeral."

"Guess he has money if he's flying you all over the place?"

"That's the best of it. He made a shit load of money out of the 'Nam war, making bullets for the army. He had some big place out in Michigan which he sold up when his wife died. He was into some way out stuff for a while and even brought a golf place, which was real strange as he has

11

never played the game in his life. Saw it as an investment opportunity to keep his hand in. He did say the name, I think it was Indian Forest, or Indian something… no that was it, Indianwood. No matter, the fact is he's got money, and if I play my cards right we could get out of this shit life and get away from your father. All I need is a signature on a piece of paper and allow nature to take its course."

"Seriously Mom, do you think it's possible?"

"Sure honey, I'm going make it work. Whatever he wants he is going to get until I have that signature. Where the hell is that shit? He should have been back by now. I guess I'd better call Sheriff Reed and ask him if he's seen him."

"Yeah I guess we should but let's wait until the morning. You never know, he may come back tonight and he's only tear the place up if he knew we called the sheriff."

"You're right sweetheart. We'll call in the morning."

The sound of a car pulling up on the drive distracted Miranda and her mom and they watched as Aunt Nancy get out the car.

Sunday, 28 September 1975

The patrol car pulled up on the road outside the house at 09:38 am.

"Hey Sheriff Reed, how you doing?" said Miranda's mother, opening the door

"I'm doing fine thank you, Ma'am. So what's this about Mikey? You not seen him in a few days? Has he been getting himself into trouble again?"

"I hope not, Sheriff, but this is unusual, even for him. You know he's been away before, but normally only a few days and generally word gets back where he is. This time there has been no word. I checked this morning at his normal hangouts and no one has seen him. The regulars seemed almost pleased he had not been there. The last thing he said to Miranda was he was planning on going to some crap game out of town. Did you hear of any game?"

"Well Ma'am, I did hear of a game and will take a ride over there and see if he's there. Is there anything else you can tell me?"

"No Sheriff, that's all we have."

"No worries Ma'am. I'm sure I'll be back in a few hours with Mikey."

"Much obliged, Sheriff."

With that Sheriff Reed left the house and headed back to his patrol car. A minute later he pulled away from the house and headed to the main road.

"Hey Mom, do you think he's OK?"

"Honey, I'm sure he's just had too much drink and is sleeping it off somewhere."

"So Mom, how do you see this New York thing going?"

"He sent me a letter yesterday asking me to go up there in a couple of weeks' time, seems there's some fancy show he wants to take me to. If things go well I'm going to look for a place for us and then will come and get you. We are going to make new lives for ourselves. I've already spoken to Jenny at the club and she's given me her cousin's name who works at a joint in Brooklyn. I should be able to get a job to help make ends meet before the old man kicks the bucket. Either way, we have to get away from your father."

"Mom, what will I do about my swimming? I've only got twelve months before the Olympics and I desperately want to make the team. What about my friends and school?"

"Sweetheart, we will find a good club up in New York and get you set up there. You will make new friends and from what I hear they have the best schools in the country."

"I know you know best, Mom, but I'm worried."

The weather had changed in the past few days. Fall had arrived, but today felt more like winter. Sheriff Reed turned up the heater switch in his patrol car as he headed to the old barn he knew had been used for illegal gambling. His boss turned a bit of a blind eye to it as it was pretty much sure all the scum from the area would be there, and his approach was better they were in one place creating shit than all over the neighborhoods. Whilst Sheriff Reid understood his boss's motivations it still galled him to think of all that scum running around free breaking the law. He was a real by the book officer and everyone knew where they stood. Behind his back his colleagues called him 'BW' or 'Mr. Black & White' and whilst he'd risen through the ranks gradually over the past thirty-two years he was never going to be a high-flyer. He believed he was there to do a job and he was the right man for the job. His private life was much like his work life very regimented and simple. He was married with two grown up kids, who now lived out of the state and had joined the army. He went to church every Sunday and was an established part of the community. The most excitement in his life was to go fishing once a week on the lake with Bill and Toby, two old hands from the Sheriff's Office who had retired some eight years before. He'd only ever un-holstered his weapon three times and only once discharged it in all the years he'd been in the service. That time was to fire a warning shot above some juvenile from out of town who had tried to rob a convenience store. He loved the sense of cracking a case by hard work and persistence and this situation was not really raising his senses.

Sheriff Reed had known Mikey for most his life. They had gone through school together and had been friends all that time. Sheriff Reed had been big on the sports, whereas Mikey was the smart one and the combination had worked well. Sheriff Reed looking out for Mikey in the playground and Mikey helping Sheriff Reed with his grades. All that seemed to change when Mikey turned sixteen. His dad had died in a road traffic accident which left pretty much nothing of the body after the flames had been put out. Mikey, when he did speak about it, talked about the smell of gas and burnt flesh. The driver who caused the accident never stopped and to this day had never been caught, probably a drunk driver as everyone it seemed drank and drove. Sheriff Reed was pretty sure that was the start of it, but his mom quickly moved in with bad news. His name was Walter and he was real nasty piece of work. A Jekyll and Hyde character. On the surface a real charmer, splashing the cash, seeming so caring over his mom's grief. Behind a closed door an evil manipulator who liked to beat up women, and Mikey's mum suffered badly at his hands. When Mikey stepped in he got beat up real bad too and missed a month off school. Walter had told the school he had broken some limbs in a fall, but the reality was Walter had beaten him to within an inch of his life. Everyone was so scared of Walter that the sheriff's office could never get statements to get him into a court, and when Mikey did return to school he was a shadow of his former self. He barely said anything to anyone and his previous best friend could not believe the transformation. It didn't take long before Mikey was playing truant and then he started mixing with the wrong crowd. At first it was petty theft, then onto breaking and entry and ultimately to armed robbery. All of this was with the need to fund his ever-growing drink and drugs habit. The habit grew greater and Walter, besides being an evil bastard, was also his drugs provider, so Mikey became more and more of a pawn for his then step-father's whims. When his mother died, Mikey was so high on heroin he never even went to her funeral, instead robbing a gas station in the next state.

Ever since he dropped out of school Mikey had had run-ins with the law. The gas station robbery saw him get three years, but the drugs habit stopped him from coming out clean and able to make a fresh start. Miranda's mom had taken pity on him and he seemed to be getting his shit in order, at least for a while. They had eventually ended up getting married and Miranda was probably seven years old when the abuse had started back up and he had slumped back into the drink and drugs big time. Walter had died a year previously in a drugs deal that went badly wrong. He had tried one too many cons and he was taken out in an execution-style hit in Los Angeles. Mikey never went to claim the body; he was only interested in claiming the inheritance of his step-father's evil gains, a point for sure that would have helped fund his habit. When those funds ran dry he turned to pimping Miranda's mum.

Sheriff Reed turned off the main road onto the dirt track to the old barn. Dust was rising behind his patrol car and clouded his rear view. The barn looked deserted however, as a precaution he had radioed the sheriff's office to let them know where he was going. His boss had heard he was headed to the old barn and had radioed him on the way and told him not to do anything stupid, however he relaxed a little when Sheriff Reed had told him he was on a missing person hunt. The closer Sheriff Reed got to the barn the more deserted it looked. There were wheel tracks everywhere, a sure sign there had been recent activity, but having wound down his window, the only sounds he could here were those of the wheels running over the dirt road.

Leaving the car pointing back down the dirt track, in case he needed to make a quick exit, Sheriff Reed un-holstered his weapon. The Colt 5" barrel .38 special had been with him since he entered the service. He'd grown to live with it, but never felt comfortable with it in his hands. He put on a pair of light cotton gloves, with rough leather sewn into the palm and index finger, before getting out of his patrol car as the need to un-holster his weapon always made his hands clammy, and the gloves gave him more control that he might need one day.

He walked slowly to the door at the end of the barn and continued to listen. He kept looking from left to right and occasionally back towards his patrol car. Still no sounds or movements. Being so far out of town and away from the main road there were no man made sounds to be heard. The breeze had dropped and despite the low temperature Sheriff Reed felt himself sweating. He came to the door and it was slightly ajar. The barn was mainly in darkness as there were few windows that were not either boarded up of so dirty they had almost lost their translucence. He caught the faint smell of smoke that was coming from inside the barn but it was the smell generated by a brazier and not tobacco or weed. He pushed open the door slightly and could see little. He moved quickly inside and crouched down to make as small a target as possible, yet at the same time allowed his eyes to adjust to the darkness. A minute passed and then two. There were no sounds, no coughing, no telltale signs there was someone or some people in there. He pulled his flashlight from his belt and pointed the light down towards where the smell appeared to be coming from. The light picked up the brazier and a small shaft of smoke that was rising from it. He swung the light from left to right and then from the floor to the ceiling. The barn appeared to be deserted. Sheriff Reed briefly went back to the door and looked outside to make sure his vehicle was still there, it was. He was pretty sure he was there on this own. Staying cautious but a little more relaxed, or more likely relieved, he continued his search. There were no rooms off the barn and in one part it was pretty clear it had been used as a shit house, the smell had been well contained under a tarpaulin, at least until he pulled it back, and then almost vomited. Quickly dropping the tarpaulin he moved over to the brazier and looked inside. It had used to be an oil drum and the burning smell was the remnants of some logs that had been set alight to burn up the evidence, or at least some of it. There were still some deformed syringes with the needles attached, what looked like the remnants of a coke pipe and some, what he was sure would transpire to be, blood-soaked material, probably from when the user was too drunk to get the needle in properly for their fix.

He radioed back to the sheriff's office to report that the barn was empty, except for a pile of shit and the remnants of a big drink and drugs session. The number of Jack D bottles he saw would have cost a small fortune and he wondered which poor fucker had been robbed to cover this binge. He asked Sandra to let Brian, the farmer who owned the barn, know that he needed a major clean up and sat back wondering where Mikey could be. It looked like he was going to have to track down some of the scum and find out whether any of them had seen him, not that he believed any of them would tell him much.

He headed back down the dirt track and towards one of the less wealthy neighborhoods, a trailer park, to go visit Sam Sneed. Sam wasn't a user, or at least he did not believe he was, but he was a well-known alcoholic who liked to gamble. Sheriff Reed was sure he would have been at the game. He pulled up outside his trailer to the sound of dogs barking. Sam was slouched on a ripped sofa outside his trailer with a half empty bottle of BUD light in his hand.

"So, what do I owe this pleasure?" Sam said with the sarcasm dripping from his words. "Did I get done for jay walking…"

"Cut it, Sam. I want to ask you some questions about the crap game the other day."

"What crap game?"

"Stop playing Sam, you know what game and I know you were there."

"So what if I was there, I didn't do anything wrong."

"I'm not saying you did, I just want to ask you if you saw Mikey at the game."

"That worthless piece of shit was supposed to be there. He owes me money. The fucker must have chickened out. If he owes me he must owe most of the guys that were there."

"You saying he never showed up?"

"Clean your ears out, Reed, that's what I told you."

"How much does he own you?"

"Fifty bucks… plus interest. Guess I'm going to have me a free session with his missus to get even."

"Sam, don't even think about it. Your issue is with Mikey. If I hear you even touch her I'll bust your ass, and you won't get close to a drink for five years where you will end up. Understand?"

"Whatever, Reed. Just make sure when you see Mikey you let him know that me, Dave and Vince are all going to get our moneys back one way or another."

With that Sheriff Reed got back into his patrol car and headed back into town to one of the number of seedy bars that had sprung up over the recent years supporting the entertainment of the growing population that had moved in due to the mine that had opened five years before. He pulled up outside Jay's Place. It was a bar come strip joint come brothel. Jay, the owner, was American Chinese. He kind of stood out in the town as there weren't too many Chinese in the state, let alone the town, however he did well with his mix of cheap booze and cheap women, most of them were oriental and he seemed to have a steady influx of new talent. The type of clientele he had in there would never talk, but the rumor was he sold the oriental staff to clients and over the past three years there had been a dozen marriage ceremonies in the town involving Chinese women. Sheriff Reed had sent a dossier via his boss to the FBI on his suspicions of people trafficking but the FBI were too busy busting triad gangs in San Francisco and New York to care about a trickle of hookers ending up in "Hicksville". Jay was not one to show or spend his wealth and his most noticeable trait was his ugly halitosis. Sheriff Reed hoped he was not going to be behind the bar as he walked in and more importantly, that he could find Dave and Vince directly. The two were inseparable, but then they were dependent on each other for everything including their sexual desires. They were a pair of faggots and if it wasn't the drink or drugs that would kill them it would be a sexually transmitted disease. They knew they were on borrowed time and they didn't care about shit.

Sheriff Reed opened the bar door and spotted the two playing 8-Ball. Jonny Cash's "*I Walk the Line*" was playing over the speakers, drowning out any conversations he could hear from the handful of patrons. There was no sign of Jay behind the counter, but one of his newest imports was talking to a punter, well at least trying to communicate.

"Good day Dave, Vince."

"Well if it isn't old Sheriff BW," said Vince. "Unlike you to be in this type of a shithole. Sure this isn't a social call. So what have we done to upset you this time?"

"As far as I know nothing yet, unless there's something you want to tell me? Maybe you know something about the break in at the post office last week."

"Fuck you Sheriff, and stop bothering us."

"Trust me, boys, if I was bothering you, you'd be in the cells by now begging for help and giving me any information I wanted, so you could get your next fix. I actually want to ask you about Mikey."

"Same answer, fuck off and stop bothering us."

"I hear it on the grapevine he owes you money."

"So what if he does?"

"Well I just thought you might be interested in collecting, and the thing is, it seems he's gone missing. Now I am not going to put one and one together and make two, but Mikey goes missing and owes you money. Rumor has it, it was a few hundred dollars. That might be a pretty good incentive to make someone disappear. Now that's purely conjecture isn't it boys? Maybe now you might want to talk to me about Mikey?"

"We don't know nothing about Mikey disappearing. We were at a crap game for the past few days and there was no sign of him. I'd heard he was going to show up and he had our money, but the bastard didn't show. Not surprising with him. He's always late with his debts. He owed Sam also so I guess he couldn't pay up and did a runner."

"When was the last time you saw Mikey?"

"Was a week last Tuesday. I remember it clear, he'd come to get some stuff and told us he was going to pay us back everything at the crap game. Seriously, it was the last time we saw him."

"OK boys, well it seems that we have a missing person case, and you were the last people to see him. Just think about that and make sure you trawl back through those minds of yours and see if there is anything you might want to remember. When you do remember you'd better get down to the station and make a statement. You nice boys don't want to end up in those cells now do you? Just imagine what it would be like after twenty-four hours and not being able to shoot any shit into your arms. I know the message is getting through."

With that Sheriff Reed left Vince and Dave and headed back to the exit. As he got to the door Vince shouted across the bar.

"Hey Sheriff, you ain't got nothing on us, so stop fucking bothering us."

Sheriff Reed turned around, paused and said, "Maybe not and maybe, but you boys just better think about what I said otherwise next time it's the cells."

With that he walked through the door and back to his patrol vehicle.

As Sheriff Reed drove back to the station he was

thinking about the two separate meetings. From the pieces of information he had picked up it appeared that Mikey had not shown up at the crap game. Why would Sam, Vince and Dave make up a story about Mikey not being there? There was certainly no love lost between the three of them. They had different sources for their drugs, which was something he was going to crack before long, and they were unknown to be associated for any criminal activities. So if they had not seen Mikey, where was he hiding? As he pulled into the station he considered his options and concluded the only solution was to publish a missing persons notice. He knew the process well and considered giving it to one of his deputies to complete, but rejected the thought out of old time's sake.

Two hours later he had everything in place and the notice had been published, all that remained was to give Marlene an update. He could have done it by phone, but again, just in case Mikey had returned, he decided to drive round to her house on his way home.

"Hello, Ma'am. How are you doing?"

"Hello, Sheriff. We are doing well, thank you. Is there any news on Mikey?"

"Well I guess by you asking he hasn't returned home. I have nothing to report good or bad. I've published a missing person notice, and that has gone statewide, so we should start to hear back in the next twenty-four hours or so. I will keep you posted on any developments. Don't worry we will find him."

"Thank you, Sheriff and apologies for being such a nuisance."

"You are not being a nuisance, Ma'am. It's my job. Wish you a good evening and will be in contact soon."

"Thank you Sheriff. Just something for you, I will be going up to New York soon. I will be taking Miranda with me. Not sure for how long yet, but when I do leave town I will drop by the station and give you the address I will be staying at, just in case anything comes up."

"No worries, Ma'am. You and Miranda have a good

time and take care. New York is not my kind of place. Too busy and too many people."

With that Sheriff Reed left the house and headed home. On his way he got a call of a homicide on the far side of time, and hit the sirens and headed over. By the time he got to the scene three other squad cars had arrived and Sheriff Reed put Mikey out of his mind.

Wednesday, 15 October 1975

"Good morning, Ma'am, how are you?"

"Sheriff, Miranda and I are heading out today to New York. I just got the tickets last night and we will be leaving on the 11.05 am Stagecoach today to Charlotte. Our train leaves Charlotte at 1.46 am and we should get into New York tomorrow at 1.46 pm, so the schedule says. Here is the address we will be staying at. We should be away a couple of weeks over the mid term recess."

"No problems, Ma'am and thanks for the information. Will sure to keep you posted if anything else develops in relation to Mikey. I know it's tough, but so far there has been no new information."

"Thank you for the updates on the search for Mikey."

With that Marlene and Miranda left the station and walked the short distance over to the Sstagecoach station with an hour to wait for their bus to Charlotte. They walked through the parking lot and climbed the steps into the station and headed to the platform. There were only a few people milling around on the platform. There were a few more in the small café trying to stay warm. Fall was already turning to winter. The temperature had dropped significantly over the recent days. It was now only in the mid 40s and the wind had picked up. To make it even more depressing the rain was coming down constantly. Miranda thought how depressing everything looked when it rained, however inside she was smiling as she was moving further away from a place she never had any intention returning to.

The past two and a half weeks had been a real strain. Externally, she had come across as the concerned daughter worried about the fate of her father. Inside, she was dreading the Sheriff turning up saying they had found her father and that there was evidence he had been seen with Miranda. The more the days had passed the more she relaxed and now as she and her mom were on the platform the feeling was turning to a feeling of relief that she had really got away with it.

Marlene and Miranda headed into the small café and ordered coffee trying to stay warm. Every time the door to the café opened the bitter wind came through the place and stripped the heat that had briefly built up. Time passed and eventually the train pulled into the platform. Marlene and Miranda picked up their cases and headed to the second class carriage. Finding a couple of seats together they stored their luggage in the overhead rack and sat down. Five minutes later the carriage jerked as the engine got the train underway and without a look out of the window Miranda opened *The Liberal Imagination* by Lionel Mordechai Trilling. She had borrowed a copy from the school library and was sure it would not be missed as it was tough reading for most of her school friends, but immensely intriguing to Miranda.

The weather stayed with the train for the first six hours. It seemed that the whole country was getting drowned, but the farmers would tell you they needed the rain. As the train pulled into Quantico Station, Virginia the rain finally stopped. Street lights were just coming on in the distance as dusk had arrived. Miranda stepped off the train briefly to stretch her legs and to go and pick up a newspaper for her mom. It was cold, even colder than back at home. Miranda had heard about the winters in New York and hoped that they were just rumors and not reality. Yes, they had snow where she was from, but -20F was something she had never experienced, but surely it was too early for those types of temperatures. For sure, the wind was making it feel worse than it really was, but New York was still a good eleven hours away. Smoke was rising from factories from a close by industrial estate, and was being blown virtually at a right angle as it erupted from the chimneys. Wrapping her coat tighter around herself in an attempt, albeit futile, to stop the wind getting to her Miranda shivered and walked briskly to the news stand. There was little choice so Miranda did not take long to select The Free Lance Star and put $0.20 cents into a cup set aside for donations, before going into the small café to buy some hot coffee. With her meager purchases she got back onto the train and the carriage that was now deserted except for her mom.

"Thanks Miranda, the coffee will help put some warmth in us, it's real cold out there."

"Sure is Mom, sorry there was not much choice of papers."

"No worries sweetheart, this is just fine."

"So, Mom can we go over the plan? I heard you telling the sheriff that we were only going away for a couple of weeks, that's not true, is it?"

Marlene looked around the carriage to make sure they were alone.

"No, sweetheart it's not true. Sometime next week I'm going to contact Sheriff Reed and tell him we are going to be staying a bit longer. I'm going to tell him I've got a new job and will be enrolling you into a local school. I'm going to tell him with the stress of Mikey disappearing we need to be around my family, which isn't a total untruth. I've already managed to get an introduction to the 92nd Flying Street Dolphins swimming club and they had heard about you and want to meet you. They also said if you would be interested they have an opening for a part time swimming coach."

"Thanks Mom, I just don't think I can ever go back. I just want to forget about my father and start over. So when are you meeting up with Stan?"

"He asked me to call him as soon as I arrived in New York. I haven't told him about you yet, I don't want to scare him off in anyway, at least not before he signs that piece of paper. Once that's signed things will change significantly. Hopefully it will only be a few weeks before we can start planning our future, for the first time being in control of our own destiny."

"Mom, you are the best and I promise I won't let you down."

"I know sweetheart, you couldn't hurt anyone."

The train had pulled out of the station and darkness had set in. The gentle rocking motion of the train and the regular clicking of the wheels on the joins in the tracks soon cast a hypnotic trance onto both Marlene and Miranda and they fell asleep resting against each other as the train moved closer and closer to Penn Station, New York.

Thursday, 16 October 1975

06.45 am Miranda woke up. She ached and was still tired. The night had passed with her sleeping in patches. She still had the occasional flashback to the night she'd killed her father, but they were becoming less and less as the days passed. It was the uncomfortable position she'd fallen asleep in that had caused her the broken sleep and she started a routine of stretches to try and loosen up her muscles. Fifteen minutes later her mom woke up and, after a quick freshening up in the toilet, they made their way to the restaurant car to get a breakfast of porridge and coffee. There were only a few other weary travelers in at that time. The ones in first class were still asleep in their bunk beds, and would be having their meals delivered. You would not see the rich people mingling in the restaurant car, that would be way beneath them. The others were a mix of what looked like sales representatives heading to the Big Apple to make a sale for something or other and students heading back to one of the numerous universities.

Breakfast came and went and the next few hours were as monotonous as the previous ones.

Miranda checked her watch for the umpteen time, it showed 12.45 pm, and as the train neared New York she tried to remember the layout of the city from her school trip. She could remember the main attractions they had been taken to, but also could remember the seedy area she had met the dealer to buy the coke. On her school trip they had also arrived at Penn Station. 12.45 pm soon became 1.20 pm and then the train was entering into the station. Miranda had a real mix of emotions, but by far the most significant one was of relief, as if arriving at the station was closing a chapter in her life, and the station was the gate that could be closed behind her and almost as if she was starting life all over again.

The rain was back, not heavy, but a constant fine drizzle that would soon permeate through most clothing. The sky was overcast and, whilst it was only just after lunchtime, it felt much more like five or six pm. Before leaving the station Miranda and her mom took a quick lunch, both keen to get to their new digs for different reasons. Marlene wanted to make contact with Stan to let him know she was in town; she didn't want him destroying her plan by doing something stupid like finding another 'comfort blanket'. Miranda wanted to get to the digs and start to explore.

By the time they had finished lunch the drizzle had stopped, but the wind was biting and cut through their clothes and urged them on quicker to get to the subway station. The sound of the wind was soon replaced by the sound of the underground trains and the vibrations as they rushed through the tunnels. The sound, alien to Miranda and her upbringing, was yet another reason to make her smile. Even a simple noise like the underground trains made her feel more and more as though she was moving away from her past and into something that surely could only be better…

An hour and a quarter after entering the metro station, Miranda and Marlene arrived at their stop: Rockaway Avenue, Brooklyn. The area was a mix of predominately four story apartment blocks and fifteen to twenty story high risers. Green space was sparse and at this time of the year the trees were bare of any leaves leaving a depressed feel which was not helped by the sight of piled up garbage as the sanitation engineers had been on strike for three weeks. Finally they arrived at a nondescript tower block and Marlene rang the bell on number 16. Her cousin Anna answered the intercom and soon they were inside her apartment starting to thaw out.

Anna welcomed them in and started asking questions.

"So any news on Mikey?"

"No, nothing from Sheriff Reed. It's really strange for Mikey to go missing for so long, but I'm sure we will have some news soon. He always turns up like a bad penny."

"Yeah, I kinda never understood what you saw in him, but that's your issue. Let's get you guys sorted out. You are real lucky as "Granny" Emily from number eighteen passed away two weeks ago so I managed to get the apartment for you. Everything has been left in there… except Granny… so you won't need to buy much stuff."

Miranda asked, "So who was Granny Emily? Mom you never mentioned her."

Anna said, "She wasn't a relative, it's just she kinda acted as everyone's grandmother here so she became known as Granny. Just a piece of advice, stick clear of the landlord. He's a real creep. Rumor is he did time for messing with dead people and kids. I don't know if it's true, and honestly don't care. Just make sure your rent is paid on time every month and he shouldn't bother you. Come on I'll take you to the apartment."

With that Anna picked up a set of keys from the kitchen table and headed towards the door.

"The apartment is on the next floor up. The lift hasn't worked in the building for six months now, and the shit that owns the place has no intention of getting it fixed. The bins are supposed to be emptied every Tuesday, but since the union pulled the sanitation guys on strike they ain't been emptied for three weeks. At least with it being winter the smell ain't too bad, but when it happens in summer it stinks real bad. The local shops are OK for your basics but if there's other stuff you need you'll have to take the metro to downtown. As far as I know the phone line is still connected but you'll have to organize that yourself as I doubt the phone company knows Granny is dead."

They arrived outside number 18 and Anna opened the door from a key on the small bunch.

"There are two front door keys and two apartment door keys. The intercom switch is here, but make sure you know who is coming in before releasing the front door, there are a ton of winos and homeless people who ring the bells to get in and then doss down for the night in corridors."

With that Anna handed over the keys to Marlene and walked back through the door. As she headed to the stairs she said, "Let me know if you need anything."

And then she was gone.

Marlene and Miranda walked into the apartment and looked at the furniture and décor of a time period long since gone. It was clear that Granny had not done much, if anything, in decorating since 1940 something. Leaving their cases in the lounge Miranda and Marlene checked out the apartment and immediately came up with a list of things needed from bed linen to cleaning materials to basic foods. Within half an hour they had left the apartment, stopping at Anna's to get directions for the various shops they needed.

Saturday, 18 October 1975

"Good morning, Sheriff Reed."

"Good morning, Ma'am. Good to hear from you. I hope you arrived safe in New York?"

"Thank you, Sheriff. Miranda and I are both well, and yes we have arrived. I'm sorry for not calling sooner, but it took a day to get the phone connected. Can I give you this number?"

"Yes Ma'am, go ahead."

"It's New York, Brooklyn 633 9904. Is there any news about Mikey?"

"I'm afraid there's nothing to report at the moment. I've been back to his usual haunts on a regular basis and none of the scum he hung around has seen or heard of him. At first I just put it down to the scum not wanting to talk, but even they have started coming up with crackpot ideas about what happened to him. I'll let you know when something develops. Now you take care up in the Big Apple."

"OK, thank you, Sheriff, we will."

With that the receiver went dead and Marlene replaced it in the Bakelite cradle.

"No news then, Mom?"

"No, nothing sweetheart. I would have expected to have heard something by now. Never mind, I know Sheriff Reed will ring as soon as there is any news. Now let me call Stan and tell him I'm in New York."

Miranda went off to her bedroom to pack her swimming bag as she was going to the club for the first time. She was glad to be getting some normality into her life in New York and was even looking forward to the 5 mile swim she was planning on for training. Through the open door of her bedroom she could hear Marlene.

"Hey, Stan, it's Marlene, how's tricks?"

"Yeah, I'm in New York, got a place in Brooklyn."

"No problem, looking forwards to seeing you. Hope you is up for a fun time."

"See you later, handsome."

Marlene went into Miranda's room.

"Will you be OK tonight on your own? Seems as though Stan still has the hots for me and can't wait for me to go over to his place. The dirty old git will probably be half way to a heart attack already. Let's see if we can't speed it up."

"Sure thing Mom, no worries. You take care. I'm off to the new club now so catch up with you later."

With that Miranda slung her bag over her shoulder and headed down to the street and off to the Metro for the short trip to the swimming baths

Marlene went to her room and opened the rickety wardrobe door to choose the best costume to get Stan in the mood for signing off his will to her. With a smile on her face she picked the most revealing costume she had and then sat in front of her vanity mirror to make sure she looked the part for her liaison… It was business after all…

An hour later, Marlene was ready. She wrapped herself in a big fake fur coat and black arm length gloves. She had her stilettos in her bag, for when she got close to Stan's, and was wearing knee length boots. At least she should stay warm, considering what she was – or more importantly wasn't - wearing underneath. She headed out of the apartment and down to the metro station.

Thirty minutes later Marlene was pressing the apartment buzzer. Stan's place was in downtown. He had a top floor penthouse apartment overlooking the river. The buzzer was answered, not by Stan, but by the concierge who was well-paid to make sure only the right people were allowed into the building. Clearly, Marlene was expected. The concierge answered and immediately opened the outside door. He came round the front of the desk and welcomed Marlene letting her know that Mr. Aldridge was expecting her. He escorted her to the elevators and pressed the call button. Marlene was sure she was supposed to tip the concierge so pulled a $1.00 bill and handed it to him. He thanked her profusely and as the lift doors opened he reached inside and inserted a key and then pressed a button. Marlene entered the elevator and he said, "Just take the lift to the sixteenth and when the doors open you will be in Mr. Aldridge's apartment."

With that he withdrew his arm and the doors started to close.

Marlene reached into her bag and made the switch of shoes before she had reached the tenth floor. She was dressed to kill, and whilst that was not her current motive, she definitely wanted to progress the inevitable…

The elevator doors opened and Stan was standing there to greet her. He was dressed in an eclectic mix of clothes. Clearly, although he had never played the game, Stan was dressed in a set of tartan plus fours with matching golf shirt and tartan sleeveless jumper. He was clearly taking more than seriously the fact he owned a golf club! Marlene had the smile already on her face before the elevator doors had opened and this helped hide the comical sight of seeing this geriatric eccentric millionaire standing in front of her trying to look like a professional golfer just well past his prime.

Marlene walked into the apartment and Stan grasped her by the shoulders and kissed her fully on the lips. His hands started to wander and were soon inside her coat and his right hand covered her left breast. He massaged it until her nipple was erect.

Marlene allowed his hands to wander for a minute before reaching down to his trousers and feeling his erection.

"Stan, I guess you're pleased to see me," she said with a seductive voice. "I think I'd better take care of this before you explode."

All she got in return was a muted grunt. She deftly undid his belt and zipper and then pulled his plus fours and shorts down to just below his knees where his plus fours were tucked into his socks. Marlene kneeled down and then gently started to lick Stan's erection. For an old guy he was really hard, but she also knew he would not last long before he exploded. She stuck his erection into her mouth and licked around the end of his penis.

She could hear from the noises he was making he was getting towards ejaculating and withdrew his penis from her mouth. Marlene increased the tempo of stroking his erection and a minute later his load came out. It wasn't the shooting burst that would have potentially landed in her hair and on her face; it was more of a dribble that she ended up rubbing into his shaft as she continued to stroke him. Stan groaned with relief and pleasure and then his erection died down.

He sat down on a nearby chair and for a few minutes all Marlene could hear was heavy breathing and then the sound of Stan sucking oxygen. Clearly that little escapade had taken a lot out of him. *Shit*, Marlene thought, *I need to keep him going for a while yet*. Dying in the act was not an issue, provided the will was signed and in her name.

Two minutes later Stan was off the oxygen and the heavy breathing was almost back to normal. He was still sitting there with his trousers down so Marlene went over to him and stroked his cheek.

"How are you feeling handsome?" she said.

"Wonderful now, you truly are a godsend."

"No, I'm just here to make you happy."

"I'm sorry but at my age you have to take advantage when you get the urge…"

"That's OK handsome, that's what I'm here for to make sure you have a good time."

"Hey, are you hungry? I could sure do with dinner, all that exercise took its toll on me."

"Absolutely, I'd love to have dinner. We need to build your strength back up for desserts," Marlene said with a giggle in her voice.

Stan by now had stood up and re-dressed himself.

"OK, I'll call Jim to have my car sent around and we'll head over to my restaurant on 51st Street. I hope you like seafood, it's the best restaurant for seafood in this town and that's not just because I own it."

"That would be perfect, thank you. You are very kind."

"Marlene, at my time of life you tend to enjoy every day as if it's your last and what could be better than fine food in the company of a beautiful lady?"

"Stan, that's very sweet. How could anyone refuse such a challenge and a compliment?"

"Oh, I wish I'd met you twenty years ago when I could still party hard, we would have had a great time."

"Stan, we can and will still have a great time, maybe we just have to be a little select about the exercise and who does the work…"

"Don't keep talking like that or we won't get out the door, I am getting those feeling again."

"No worries handsome, you get the feelings and I'll manage them."

Stan called the concierge.

"Jim, send the car round. We're going to 51st Street."

"Good, tell him to be out the front in five minutes."

Stan put the receiver down and turned to Marlene.

"Are you ready? By the way you look stunning. All the heads will be turning when we walk into the restaurant and it won't be to look at me. It will be nice not to be the center of attention for once," he said with a forced smile, or what transpired for a smile.

Marlene could only believe that people took note of Stan because of his wealth, and his abrupt manner. Maybe in his youth he was a looker, but the best of his days were long behind him. He probably hadn't seen his penis in ten years judging by the size of his belly. His ridiculous dress sense only added to a picture of a sad, lonely person that was closing rapidly in on meeting his maker, and who simply had lost track of reality and was trying to remain noticed by his outlandish mannerisms. Marlene was very sure that no matter who saw them together they would immediately put one and one together. Sad old fucker with money, with a tart after his money. She didn't care as long as the money came. There was nothing physically appealing about Stan, all the time she had spent with him told her he was only really interested in one thing, himself. Marlene was not sure what the color of the sky was on his planet – probably purple by the décor of the apartment – but it was definitely a different color to the one in the world she lived, but this was business and a new future for Miranda and herself.

With the smile still in place on her face she submissively looked at Stan as he opened the door and walked out before her. Clearly along with his 'stunning' good looks, he had also 'stunningly' poor manners...

Marlene clung onto Stan's arm as they rode down the elevator to the reception area. Jim came from behind his desk and escorted them to the front door where Stan's chauffeur stood dressed in full uniform, as chauffeurs should – according to Stan – however, again his eccentricity showed as his chauffeur's uniform was deep purple down to his cap. The car matched the chauffeur, or was it the other way around. The rear door was open to a new Rolls-Royce Silver Shadow, in violet. Marlene wondered what it was with Stan and the color purple. Maybe she'd ask him one day.

Fifteen minutes later they pulled up outside SP. There were the usual bevvy of valet parking attendants lined up outside and as the car pulled up, Stan's door was promptly opened with a bow from the valet attendant, dressed in a purple uniform with a bellhop cap and a "Good evening Mr Aldridge, good to see you this evening."

Marlene's door was opened by another attendant similarly dressed and a "Good evening, Ma'am." With that they were escorted to the maître d' who was totally over the top with his welcome of Stan, making sure everyone in the restaurant knew that the most important guest had just arrived. Marlene, who was continuing with the ruse of being impressed with Stan's stature and importance, gushed compliments about the restaurant, staff, décor and atmosphere.

The maître d' was clearly not one for copulating with the ladies, his preference was clearly for the male variety and the exaggerated and effeminate mannerisms as he guided Stan and Marlene through the restaurant to Stan's personal table were worthy of an Oscar. Stan clearly appreciated his antics, maybe it made him feel masculine and macho surrounded by the faggot, either way the performance continued once they were seated and with the snap of the faggot's fingers, three waiters arrived. All of them young men, in their late teens or early twenties, who came to the table with lowered eyes almost not daring to look at Stan and Marlene. Their idiosyncrasies came across like the sex slaves of the maître d'. Either Stan had picked up on the changing face of society or he was taking advantage of the still developing social acceptance of homosexuality. There was still a profound stigma attached to homosexuality. The American Psychiatric Association had only removed homosexuality from its list of psychiatric disorders two years before and it was still a crime in New York to be a practicing homosexual. Marlene, with her line of profession, had to keep up to date with the law and concluded that Stan's reason was more to do with the power he wielded over his staff, than his desire to be considered a modern man…

Stan chose for both of them and barked out his orders to the subservient waiters. A bottle of Dom Pérignon Oenothèque, 1966 arrived and was handed to the maître d' and was sampled before Stan gave his nod of approval. Stan's glass was filled first and then Marlene's before a hasty retreat was made by the maître d'.

Stan faced Marlene and said, "To us."

"Yes, to us."

"So Marlene, now you are in New York I want to make sure you stay here."

Marlene kept her face in the same pose, but inside her heart was beating quicker sensing she was getting closer to the proposition she was planning on. Hoping her mannerisms were not giving away her interest or intent she said, "So exactly what are you wanting, Stan? I just want to make sure you're happy."

"Well, I don't want you working in any strip joints for a start. You're in my town now, and as you're my woman I don't want any scumbags getting close to you."

Not wanting to put Stan off by saying something that might interrupt him or make him change her mind Marlene just smiled and encouraged him with her silence to carry on.

"So, I want to make you a business proposal."

"What kind of proposal, Stan?"

Marlene wanted to make sure this stayed more on a basis where she could influence his will decision, but a regular income would be a pretty good start.

"OK, so I still have business to run and I can't be around all the time, but I want you to be available for me anytime I need you. I know you have your own place and that's fine, but I may need you at short notice for stuff. Dinners, parties and shit like that, and obviously for my private whims," he said with that smile.

He continued.

"So to keep you off the streets and out of trouble I'll put you on my payroll and give you $2,500 per month. So what do you say?"

Marlene reached under the table and stroked Stan's crotch.

"I'm not sure what to say, Stan."

Stan said, "OK, how about $3,000 per month."

Marlene continued to stroke his crotch and looked into his eyes. Inside, Marlene was trying not to show her excitement. $3,000 per month was huge. She had never eared that in a month before. OK, not what she was totally aiming for, but basically to be seen with the old fucker and jerk him off from time to time it was too good an opportunity to turn down.

"Stan, can I get a clothing allowance? You know I always want to look my best for you.

"Shit, you can have a company credit card, just don't go blowing it on shit. I'll be watching it."

"Stan, I promise it will only be to make sure you are

happy."

"Sounds like we have a deal."

"Yes, it does."

Marlene leaned over and gave Stan a brushing kiss on his cheek.

"I'll get one of my staff to contact you and get you on the payroll tomorrow. Now are you going to finish what you started whilst we were negotiating?"

"Sure, Stan," and Marlene deftly unzipped his pants and eased out his erect penis under the table and stroked him to ejaculation under the table cloth whilst the waiters came and went with their entrees.

Marlene said, "You must let me know if there are any specialties you would like."

Stan gradually replied, "You're doing just fine."

With that they focused on the food.

Friday, 21 November 1975

Scott was excited and was struggling to contain it. It was Cindy's eighteenth birthday today and he had a special date planned, with the single aim of ending up in bed with her. For the past month he had been planning the day and could not keep the picture out of his mind of Cindy naked on the bed with her legs wrapped around his shoulders as he ejaculated. Each night he had gone to bed mentally picturing the scene and each night he had ended up masturbating over the thought.

The body language from Cindy had all been heading in that direction. She had been saving herself until her eighteenth birthday. They had, for the past month, been getting more and more intimate. It had progressed from kissing and cuddling in the back of his pale blue Buick Riviera to bringing Cindy to orgasm at the drive through over the weekend by caressing her vagina through her panties and seeing her excitement through her erect nipples through the thin silk blouse. Cindy had moaned loudly as she came to orgasm and Scott was worried someone close by would hear and investigate, but fortunately whatever was on at the pictures had drowned out the moaning. She had returned the gesture by stroking his penis to orgasm, whilst he played with her firm breasts. Flushed after the acts Scott had tried to remove the stains off his leather seats without great success, but that didn't matter. Tonight they would be going all the way.

Scott had gone to a neighboring town to buy a pack of Trojans. Whilst his lust was driving him nearly insane, there was no way he was going to end up having a kid at the age of nineteen. Cindy was a real cute chick but there was no way he was going to get tied down.

Scott had considered checking into a motel, however he knew this would be impossible as word would get back to his and Cindy's parents. They could not stay away all night as Cindy had to be at cheerleader practice on Saturday and he had to be at his father's garage. Neither family approved of their relationship. Cindy's parents were well-off and she was going to Harvard in the fall. Nothing was to interrupt her education and then she would be married off to some investment banker or senior government type. Scott's family was from the other end of the spectrum. His dad's garage business paid the bills, but little more. Scott had a second job as a part time cook at Howard Johnson's. He'd managed to change shift for tonight with Billy, which meant he had to work a double shift over the weekend... but it was going to be worth it.

Scott had packed a rucksack with some gear to get Cindy in the mood. He'd gone down to the local convenience store earlier to pick up some fancy foods and had sneaked out from home a couple of glasses. Along with some Pepsi he'd also managed to get a 12fl oz bottle of Jack D. It had taken a month's wage packet to get, not because of the price in the shop, but the price guaranteed no questions. One of the creeps from Jay's Place had come up with the goods. Scott only hoped that as the cap was sealed that it was genuine, but it was too late now to worry about it. In the back of his car he had also shoved a blanket from his room and he had a small gas stove and camp light. Where they were going it would be cold and dark and whilst he was pretty sure it would heat up quickly as they were having sex, he wanted to make sure that Cindy was going to be, as best as possible, comfortable.

Driving to Cindy's cheerleader practice Scott felt excited, aroused and there was a hard lump at the front of his jeans. He pulled into the parking lot at the small stadium and could hear in the background the sound of the cheerleaders going through one of their routines. As he came from around the back of the small stand he caught sight of Cindy with her arms and legs spread out in the shape of a star, with her pompoms fluttering as she came back to land. Her short skirt revealing for a brief instant the blue gym pants. The sight only made the bulge in Scott's trousers even more significant and he stayed in the shade of the stand in case anyone spotted his erection.

42

Ten minutes later practice was finished and Cindy came running over and threw her arms around his neck and gave him a passionate kiss. She could feel the bulge between his legs and gyrated her hips that brought a low moan from Scott's lips.

"It's nice to know you missed me," Cindy giggled.

"Miss you? All I have thought about since I got up this morning is getting here to see you at practice. You were awesome. Oh, and happy birthday."

"Thank you. So where are we going?"

"I packed some gear in the car and wanted to take you somewhere we would not be disturbed," Scott said with a grin.

"Sounds interesting, let's go."

As they went back to Scott's car Cindy pulled on a fleece jacket and grabbed Scott's hand.

Scott had parked the car in a far corner of the lot and in the car Scott leaned over and gently kissed Cindy. Before long their tongues were in each other's mouths and Scott's hands began to wander. He gently caressed Cindy's left thigh before slowly creeping up to the edge of her panties. His fingers gently caressed the material and he felt moistness. He continued to caress for a few minutes and heard Cindy gently moaning. Scott eased his fingers inside her panties and felt her moistness. He plunged two fingers gently into her vagina and Cindy moaned louder as the dampness grew. He used his thumb to find her G spot and rubbed around the area where he hoped it was. He seemed to be close as Cindy started to gyrate her hips and thrust her tongue deeper into his mouth. The thrusting and gyrating continued until, with a moan of completion, Cindy came to orgasm. Scott gently withdrew his fingers, wet with her love juices, and wiped them on his jeans where Cindy could not see.

"Happy birthday, Cindy."

"Mmmmm, now that's what I call a present. Looks like you need a little bit of relief also," she giggled.

Unbuttoning his trousers, Scott's erection pushed out

43

over the top of his shorts, juices already running from his penis.

"I don't think this will take too long," Cindy said with a smile. Nine strokes was all it took for Scott to ejaculate his load. It seemed to go everywhere, but Scott was oblivious. The release and relief was enormous, but even after shooting his load his erection remained.

"I hope there's more where that came from," said Cindy.

"Oh God, yeah," said Scott. "I have been so pent-up all day just seeing you at practice and I almost came in my shorts."

Cindy giggled again and Scott knew that it was going to work out. His plan was already way beyond expectation and the hardest part was long since behind him. Pulling a towel from the back seat Cindy and he wiped up the remains of their love juices and, having straightened their clothes, Scott started the engine and headed out of the lot.

Scott headed out of town and towards their destination. Cindy leaning into him, holding his right arm. The journey passed with Cindy talking about her day at college and about her birthday presents. Soon they were turning off the main road onto a dirt track, and a mile further on they came to a deserted parking lot. They got out the car and Scott grabbed the gear from the back seat and they walked hand in hand up to the shelter.

Six months ago Scott had done some work at the shelter and had been given a key to one of the entrances. Before handing the key back he had made a Plasticine copy and from this at his dad's garage had formed a mold and created a brass replica. He was not sure why he had done it until his plan came together for Cindy's eighteenth birthday. With key in hand Scott and Cindy approached the deserted shelter. It was not yet dark outside and Scott spotted a side door that was slightly open. He knew it was normally closed with a padlock, saw it was missing, and hoped that there wano tramp living in there. He and Cindy slowed and quietly moved to the door. Scott listened at the door for a few seconds and heard nothing so opened it slowly and went inside.

Cindy said, "What's up Scott?"

"I'm not sure. This door should be locked with a padlock and its missing. Wait here while I take a quick look around."

"I'm not going to stand here waiting, let's go see together."

"OK but stay behind me, just in case."

Scott took out two flash lights from his pack, gave one to Cindy, and turned on his. The room was cold and little light came in from outside as all the shutters across the windows were closed. The old floorboards creaked as they walked, and the silence added to the eeriness. Scott entered a hallway with a number of doors of each side. The first room he entered was empty except for some racks. He knew from his short time there that this room was used for storage and came back out. Cindy had left his side and went to enter the room next door. Scott was walking towards the door that Cindy had entered when he heard a terrifying and terrified scream. He ran into the room to see Cindy with her flashlight pointing at the body of a decomposing figure. Cindy was still screaming and Scott caught up with her and wrapped his arms around her.

"OK, Cindy let's get you out of here. Come on. OK, yes it's a body. OK, come on let's get out of here."

Cindy was traumatized and Scott had to lead her out of the room and back out of the lodge. He got Cindy into his car and pulled the Jack D from his pack.

"OK, Cindy, drink this, it will help."

Cindy took a drink, coughed and spluttered and then downed the rest of the fiery fluid. She was in shock, and probably the only thing from stopping Scott going into the same shock was the fact he could focus on Cindy. He knew he needed to go to the sheriff, but how was he going to calm down Cindy, how was he going to explain to his and, more worryingly, to her parents why their daughter was traumatized? Any desires that had existed ten minutes before were now well and truly extinguished and with dreadful certainty of the shit he was in Scott drove off the parking lot and back to town to go and find the sheriff.

The journey back was a tense affair. The drive was only fifteen minutes, but Cindy was numb with shock. Scott was thinking of what he was going to say to the sheriff, but whatever story he came up with it all ended up with the same conclusion. Resigned to the fact he was in shit, he decided to stick to the facts, well as close as possible.

"Sheriff!"

"Good evening, Scott. How are you? What's up with Cindy?"

"Sheriff, there's a body at the shelter and Cindy found it. She's in shock and I didn't know where to go."

"Sheriff Dade, call the paramedics and then call Cindy's parents. Get them to meet you at the hospital. Scott, you and me are going to take a drive over to the shelter."

"Yes, sir."

Within five minutes the ambulance had arrived and Cindy was handed over to the paramedics who gave her a valium shot. Cindy was laid onto a stretcher and taken off. Scott looked over and thought it was probably the last time he would see Cindy. After this he would become public enemy number one with her parents and Cindy would not be allowed out unaccompanied. His dad would kill him. Sheriff Reed brought Scott out of his reminiscing.

"OK Scott, let's go."

"Yes, sir."

With that they went outside and past Scott's car to Sheriff Reed's cruiser and back down the road out of town heading to the shelter.

"So, what happened?"

"Well, sir, I was taking Cindy out from cheerleader practice for a birthday surprise. I'd got a little picnic and was going to give her a present. I wanted to go somewhere where we would not be disturbed…" Scott's voice trailed off and went quiet.

"Scott, I'm not interested in what plans you and Cindy had, you can deal with that later. What happened when you got to the shelter?"

"We got out of the car and were heading up to the shelter when I saw one of the side doors was slightly open and there was no padlock on it. That door was always locked with a padlock. I told Cindy to wait by the door whilst I took a look around. I kinda figured maybe a tramp was sleeping rough in there due to it being closed in winter. Cindy insisted on coming with me, so I gave her a flash light and told her to stay behind me. I checked out a couple of rooms before Cindy screamed and freaked out. The body is in the general living room downstairs."

"Did you touch anything besides the doors?"

"No sir, I just grabbed Cindy and came straight out, honestly."

"OK Scott, let's go see whose body we have in here."

With that Sheriff Reed switched on his flash light and entered the side door. He noticed there were no signs of a forced entry, but the padlock was missing. Could be someone had forgotten to attach, or that whoever was inside had removed the padlock. The floorboards again creaked and Sheriff Reed got on his radio.

"Dade, do you copy?"

"Yes, Sheriff."

"How's Cindy?"

"She's in the hospital and her parents have arrived. Shook up, but the valium has kicked in so she's resting."

"Good. Can you call Ted? Ask him to come over to the shelter. Tell him to come through the side door and not to touch anything. Also, get an ambulance over here and call the scene of crime team in. We will need the pathology team to do an autopsy and get us an ID. I have a feeling I know who we are going to find, but let's see."

With that, Sheriff Reed, with Scott at his side, went into the general living room. Lying next to a lounge chair was the remains of the corpse. Scott stood back as Sheriff Reed went closer to investigate. The corpse was showing advanced signs of decay and rooting back through his police training he remembered that it can take up to two months for a dead body to turn into pure skeletal remains. Looking at the remains Sheriff Reed could only estimate the corpse had been there for six to seven weeks. There were still remains of some hair and a few visible patches of skin. The clothing had not decayed and immediately Sheriff Reed recognized them. His hunch was right, he just needed the pathology team to confirm it. Shit, how had the stupid fuckwit ended up dead in the shelter?

Twenty minutes later, Ted called from the open side door.

"Sneed ,you in there?"

"Yeah, come on in. We're in the downstairs general living room, but don't touch anything."

"OK."

A minute later the beam of another flashlight came through the door.

"Jesus, what the fuck, who the fuck..." Ted did not continue.

"Ted, can you get the power on in here. We have an ambulance and a scene of crime team coming in. We don't want them working by flashlight."

"Sure thing, Reed."

With that Ted headed out of the room and down to the cellar and a few minutes later the exhaust of a generator could be heard. A few minutes later lights started to come on around the shelter. Finally, Tom came back into the living room and turned on the overhead lights. The sight was no less ghastly than under the flash light, however it clearly showed the pose of the body and it was not a natural one of someone just keeling over. Both hands were together parallel to the chest, almost like someone praying at church; however, Sheriff Reed knew this corpse would not even have known how to pray.

Another voice called from the side door.

"Sheriff Reed, it's Billy Turnbull. I've got the ambulance outside."

"OK Billy, wait there a minute, we're coming out."

A minute later Sheriff Reed, Scott and Tom all came out the side door.

"Here's the situation, Billy. We need to take a corpse to the morgue for a forensic examination. My guess is the corpse has been here for six to seven weeks. We need the crime scene team to do an investigation before we move the body but it looks like it is Mikey."

On cue, the crime scene team arrived and got to work. The corpse remained in situ whilst camera bulbs flashed and areas were dusted for prints.

"Sheriff Reed," Charlie, one of the crime scene team called.

"Yes, what you got?"

"Looks like some kind of chemical, cocaine or heroin, or compound of. There's a part used spliff that fell into the cracks between the floor boards. Can't say yet it's linked but it's in close proximity to the body and my guess is that Mikey was having a joint of whatever this shit was and it killed him."

"Thanks, Charlie. Let me know when you're finished and we can let Billy get the body out of here."

"OK, Sheriff. Won't be long now. We're pretty much done. There doesn't appear to be any signs of other persons being involved, certainly no struggles, nothing to suggest foul play. Will have a full report on your desk on Monday."

"Thanks, Charlie, much appreciated."

Sheriff Reed thought to himself at least that was a positive. Looked like a straightforward case of overdosing on some shit. Then Sheriff Reed considered how he was going to approach Marlene with the news. Well, he was going to do nothing until he got a positive ID from the pathology lab.

Fifteen minutes later Billy and his team had loaded the corpse remains onto a stretcher and into the ambulance and with its lights flashing headed out of the lot. The crime scene team left soon after having left up some tape and signs warning it was a crime scene and Ted turned off the power and secured the side door with a spare padlock. Sheriff Reed was in the last vehicle to leave with a shaken and quiet Scott. His drama was only just beginning.

Monday, 24 November 1975

The phone rang in Sheriff Reed's office.

"Hello, Reed here."

"Hi Sheriff, it's Doug at the pathology lab."

"Hey Doug, how's it going?"

"Well, better than the corpse you sent me over! I just completed the report and will have it over to you in the hour. You weren't too far off in your guess. Your corpse kicked the bucket somewhere between 20 September and 25 September. Death was caused by a concoction of chemicals IUPAC made up of exo, exo benzoyloxy methyl azabicyclo octane carboxylic acid methyl ester, didehydro epoxy methylmorphinan diol acetate and chloro-m-cresol tar acids alkyphenol fraction propan terpineol. In simple terms, it was a cocktail of heroin and cocaine with an industrial cleaning fluid. Either your corpse was planning on suicide or someone gave him some shit knowing it would kill him, or it is a new dealer who knows nothing about the shit they're dealing with."

"Shit, all I needed. Looked like a closed book of taking an overdose. Any chance of tracking where the shit came from?"

"Not exactly, but it's not the grade of shit we normally see in here. It looks like it's from out of state, but beyond that I can't be more specific."

"Thanks for that, Doug. Any joy on confirming the identity?"

"Yeah, you were spot on. It's Mikey alright. Hey, when you speak to Marlene pass on my commiserations. She put up with a lot with Mikey, but it still isn't the way to go."

"Will do and thanks again. Just a final question."

"Sure, go for it."

"You said the shit was not from inside the state. You any ideas who could give me a lead on where it might have come from?"

"You could try Dr Hernandez over in San Francisco; he is an expert in the drugs cartels and the supply chain and what ends up on the streets. If anyone could identify it, it would be him."

"Could I ask one favor then?"

"Sure, I'll send a sample over to him and let him know you'll be calling. Will take a week or so for him to get the sample."

"Thanks, Doug, appreciate it."

With that the conversation ended, Sheriff Reed set the receiver back in its cradle and sat back considering his next moves. He had to call Marlene. He would much prefer to talk to her face-to-face but she was up in New York. Maybe he should take a trip up there and tell her, but realistically that was not an option. He needed to pull in some of the shits from the crap game, he was sure one of them was not telling him something important. Maybe he could get the name of a new dealer that had moved into the area, or was passing through, that had sold Mikey the shit. Setting aside those thoughts he opened his drawer and found the number in New York and began to dial.

Tuesday, 25 November 1975

"Hello."

"Hello, Ma'am it's Sheriff Reed here."

"Hello Sheriff, how are you?"

"I'm doing fine Ma'am, but I wanted to talk to you. I have tried a few times, but I guess you've been busy. I would like to have done this face-to-face, unfortunately I just couldn't get up to New York."

"That's OK and very kind of you. I guess you have some news on Mikey."

"Yes, Ma'am, I do. There's no nice way to say this. Mikey is dead. He passed away from an overdose. I won't go into the details but he died some time ago. A couple of kids found him at the shelter outside town."

"Thank you, Sheriff, I was fearing something was badly wrong. Mikey had never been away for so long, it was not in his character."

"I'm really sorry to break the news to you like this. Is there anything I can do?"

"No... no thank you, Sheriff, you have been really helpful and I do appreciate you telling me. Do you need me to identify his remains?"

"No, Ma'am, that won't be necessary. I know Mikey was not perfect, but it would be better for you to remember him as you last saw him not like he currently is. The autopsy team has already got a positive result. They matched up a hair sample with samples we had on file. I guess the only positive out of the fact he's been behind bars is you don't need to go through the ordeal of identifying him."

"Sheriff, can I ask a favor?"

"Sure, Ma'am. No worries."

"Could you help me organize his funeral? I'll come back to town to get everything in order, but it's going to take me a few days before I can get back."

"Sure, Ma'am. I'll see Jason over at the undertakers, I'm sure he'll take care of everything. Again, I'm sorry,

Ma'am to give you such bad news. Are you sure you'll be OK?"

"Yes thank you, Sheriff, I've got my cousin close by and Miranda with me. I'll break the news to her shortly."

With that they said their goodbyes and hung up. Sheriff Reed sat back and considered all the reasons he joined up and remembered the one thing he hated doing was giving someone bad news. Marlene had had it tough with Mikey, and maybe today it was bad news, but sometime in the future she would see it as a blessing in disguise. He hoped at least that she would. With that he pulled over a file that had landed on his desk. Another bar brawl at Jay's Place resulted in Vince having a fractured skull and being in a medically induced coma. At least he would know where to find Dave if he needed to speak to him about the shit dealer...

Friday, 28 November 1975

"Hello Miranda, how was college?"

"It was great, Mom. The teachers are really pleased with my progress and they want to put me in for an economics exam next term."

"Wow, that's great. I'm really happy you've settled here. I've got some things to tell you so why don't you sit down."

"What's wrong, Mom? Are we having to go back to Roan Mountain? Has Mikey turned up?"

"Calm down, sweetheart. Firstly, we are not going to move back to Roan Mountain. New York is our new home. Yes, your dad has turned up. He's dead. He took an overdose."

Marlene carried on.

"I know your dad was cruel and evil and I should have done more to protect you before now, but he can't hurt you anymore. We can finally start our new life together and start to put the past behind us. I have to go back to Roan Mountain for a few days to settle our affairs. Sheriff Reed is helping me organize the funeral and I'll ask Nancy to help me with selling the house. I'll use some of what we get for the house to pay off Mikey's debts and ask Sheriff Reed to make sure the debts are paid."

"Why do that, Mom, you don't own those guys anything."

"I know sweetheart, but it puts closure on anything to do with our past. We won't need to be looking over our shoulders in case one of those creeps comes looking for us."

"You're right, Mom and thank you. I just can't believe we are finally free."

Marlene gave Miranda a big hug and a kiss and they both smiled at each other. Finally, they both had a great weight lifted from their shoulders. They were finally back in control of their lives. No longer fearing the terrifying mood swings, anger and brutality of being around Mikey they started to plan for the future. The only question raised was would they use this as a positive in their lives or to seek revenge on others...

Tuesday, 2 December 1975

"Hello, Sheriff."

"Hello, Ma'am. Nice to see you, and again my condolences."

"You're very kind, Sheriff. Thank you for sorting out the arrangements with Jason, the funeral is taking place later. I can't imagine anyone turning up, maybe only the people he owed money to. Could I ask for one final favor, that being when I sell the house can you make sure that Mikey's debts are paid off?"

"Are you sure, Ma'am? You don't owe anyone anything."

"I know, Sheriff, but it's just my way to make a total closure on Mikey and honestly I don't want to be thinking sometime in the future one of those creeps will track me down in New York and stalk me for the debt."

"I understand, Ma'am and for sure will sort out. I'll even get them to make signed statements making sure if they come anywhere near you they will spend the rest of their lives in jail."

"Thank you, Sheriff. You have been so kind."

"It's my pleasure, Ma'am. Do I take it from this you won't be coming back to live here?"

"No, Sheriff. Miranda is settled in New York, I've got a job that covers the rent and allows us to live and the memories will never leave us if we remain."

"I understand, Ma'am and can only wish you happiness for the future. I hope it all works out for you and Miranda, but don't forget there are people down here that will miss you and will welcome you guys back any time."

Sheriff Reed never mentioned to Marlene about the drug cocktail, he would follow that up to get closure. Marlene and Miranda didn't need to know about it. They needed closure, not the continuous thoughts hanging over them about whether Mikey had been murdered.

With that Marlene gave Sheriff Reed a hug and a kiss on the cheek and walked out of his office to go to the funeral.

Marlene was right. The church was virtually empty. Nancy was there and she and Marlene exchanged hugs. The only other people in the church were the priest, his alter staff and the organ player. The service did not take long and Marlene thanked the priest for the service and made a small donation. She said no they would not going to the burial plot and with Nancy they headed to the estate agent to make the arrangements to get her house on the market. She and Nancy spent the rest of the day sorting things out in the house and deciding what she was going to keep, what Nancy wanted and a few things that could be sold. Anything of Mikey's just went into the yard and a small fire was lit to burn his possessions; there was nothing of any value at least not to Nancy or Marlene. There was one small package that Marlene did pocket that Nancy didn't see. Marlene was pretty sure it was drugs that Mikey had hidden away, and they would have some value in New York.

Wednesday, 3 December 1975

Nancy dropped Marlene at the train station. They had sat up most of the night reminiscing and talking about the future. Nancy promised to come up to New York and visit as soon as she could. A small container would be leaving that afternoon with the items Marlene was taking back to New York and Nancy promised to keep her posted on developments with the house sale. With that, they hugged and Marlene disappeared through the entrance to the station.

As Marlene's train pulled out of the station she sat back in her seat taking a final look at a place she knew she would never return to. Any sadness she might have had was totally overwhelmed by the joy she felt at the final closure. A young couple walked into her carriage and wondered what the lady sitting on her own found either so funny or was so happy about. Marlene had a huge smile on her face.

Thursday, 4 December 1975

"Hello, is that Sheriff Reed?"

"Speaking."

"Hi, this is Dr Hernandez."

"Dr Hernandez, thanks for calling. I was going to give you a call early next week, so really appreciate you getting back to me."

"No worries. I got your package from Doug and wanted to give you my thoughts. The cocaine came from Peru. They are the biggest players in the market and seem to have the best logistics to get the shit into the USA. The heroin is from Afghanistan. Coke is pretty easy to come by across the States and there is no landing hub as such. Now, heroin on the other hand pretty much all gets channeled through New York."

"You seem pretty adamant about the sources."

"Yeah, I get samples sent to me all year round from law agencies from the producing countries and I keep a register of the grade and consistency of the production. I send the consolidated results to all the agencies that send me samples and they use the information in different ways. Some use it to track where the shit ends up and that helps them track the dealers and movers, others use it in homicide cases. The cocaine was from a batch eighteen months ago, the heroin was from a batch less than twelve months ago. The cleaning fluid was an unnecessary insurance policy."

"How do you mean?"

"Well whoever made this shit should have known the mix was lethal even without the cleaning fluid. The impact of the cleaning fluid would have been like an accelerator. I say should have known, rather than would have known because the market is growing quickly. There are hundreds, if not thousands of dealers out there who have no idea how to get the right mix. I came across a corpse three months ago where the individual had OD'd with an 80 percent pure heroin content. The average is 30% to

50%..."

"Is there any way of telling where this concoction came together?"

"Being honest with you, not in this case. Each dealer has their own style of how the cut and water down the cocaine or heroin before they move it on. In fifteen years of building up the register it's the first time I've come across this mix. It could be a special mix that someone came up with for a specific purpose, which would be my best guess, but like I say it could have been a rogue sample of a new dealer who didn't know what they were doing. Sorry I can't be more precise, but there are too many variables in this game and it's changing all the time."

"Hey, you've been more than helpful. If I were to ask you to take a guess at where you think it came from, what do you think is the most likely place?"

"I wouldn't admit this if I was ever asked officially, but my guess is this shit came from New York State. The logic behind that is heroin becomes less common the further you move from the State. The vast majority of it gets injected by bankers and other wealthy types. Across the rest of the States cocaine is more prevalent and with the mix of heroin to cocaine it's pointing in that direction."

"Thank you, Dr Hernandez, you have been a great help."

With that they said their goodbyes and hung up. Sheriff Reed sat looking through his office window and considered what Dr Hernandez had just told him. The case had been closed as death by an overdose, which it clearly was, but the fact that this concoction was going to kill was something he couldn't ignore. He decided to officially consider the case as closed, but kept the file in his desk drawer and would continue to do some digging and maybe when he had the chance go up and see Marlene and take the opportunity to hook up with an old friend of his that was working in Manhattan. There were no end of people he could consider would want Mikey out of the way, but he also didn't want to keep dragging up the past with

Marlene and Miranda, they had been through enough.

Wednesday, 24 December 1975

All the preparations were ready. A small artificial Christmas tree sat in the corner of the lounge, its branches adorned with silver and gold tinsel. Plastic cherries were dotted over the branches and a plastic angel sat atop. Under the tree there were a small pile of carefully wrapped gifts. Marlene had managed to put a few extra little things for Miranda under the tree. The payments from Stan had started to come in and just in time. The house had not sold yet and the bills had been starting to stack up, but the first couple of payments had eased the financial worries and as long as she kept her trick happy there was no reason why they shouldn't continue. *By this time next year...* she thought as she looked at the tree.

Miranda walked into the lounge and said, "What that look for, mum? You look pretty deep in thought?"

Marlene's look changed and with a smile on her face she said, "Nothing, sweetheart, I was just thinking about the future and what we might be doing this time next year. I'm sorry, I have to be over at Stan's place tonight, he has some plans or other, are you sure you'll be all right?"

"No worries Mom, I'm all set. A few more guys from the swimming club are meeting up at Angie's parent's house and were all having a sleep over. You need to see their place, they have this huge barn they have converted. It's really cool! I'll be fine."

"I know sweetheart but it's Christmas and we should spend it together..."

"Don't beat yourself up, Mom. Like you just said next year will be different and I'm sure we'll be spending it together."

With that Marlene reached over and gave Miranda a kiss and said, "What time are you heading over to Angie's?"

"Tom's picking me up around 5.30 pm."

"OK sweetheart, have fun, I've got to head over to Stan's now. See you tomorrow evening."

"See you Mom and Happy Christmas."

"And to you, sweetheart."

With that Marlene picked up her overnight bag and purse and headed out the door.

Wednesday, 31 December 1975

"Ten, Nine, Eight…"

Miranda, Marlene and a few of their new friends from the complex were in the lounge of the apartment. The New Year's Eve party had started at 8.00 pm and the drink had been flowing freely. Marlene had managed to escape from spending the night with Stan as he was struggling from his last session with her and had flaked out from excess vodka.

"Seven, Six, Five, Four…"

Miranda turned to her mom and they shared a knowing look. 1975 was ending and with it, they both knew was the closing of an ugly chapter in their lives. 1976 was going to be, could only be, better than the shit they had both endured.

"Three, Two, One… Happy New Year!" came the chorus from the room and immediately the sky started to light up outside with the launching of fireworks from all around the district.

Friday, 13 February 1976

"Miranda, that was a good session tonight."

"Thanks, Coach, it felt pretty good in there."

"Times were good, however we need to work out how we are going to get you that extra second off your time."

"Still not closed the gap?"

"No, and we're running out of time. The trials are only eleven weeks away now and we have to get that second off. We're going to have to do something dramatic if we are going to get you there. You're training hard and doing well, but we aren't going to make it without that improvement."

"Is there anything we can do, Coach? I really want to make it to the trails and if I can get there I know I can make the team."

"Look, Miranda, there is a way, but this conversation stays between us. OK?"

"Sure, Coach, I won't tell anyone."

"OK. There's this thing called Oxandrolone. It's also called Anavar or DHT. You know what anabolic steroids are? It's a pretty sure guarantee using it we can get you to the trials qualifying time and into a place on the team with DHT. For sure there is a catch as DHT is technically banned for use to enhance performance."

"OK, so does that mean it's not an option?"

"Hell no! Mark and Tom have been using them on and off for the past twelve months. Their times have come on in leaps and bounds. They have pulled close to 5 seconds off their PB's. You've seen their results in recent galas and State comps? They are pretty much guaranteed a place on the men's team."

"How come they have gotten away with it? Haven't they been tested?"

"Sure they have, but every time they come up clean."

"How's that Coach?"

"Well, and remember this is between us, the samples have been taken care of. You don't need to know how

66

that's done, but just to say at this level we can manage the situation. In the Olympics it may be we have a challenge, however if we do a short treatment session you should be clear by the time they start."

"OK Coach, if you believe it will get me over the line, I'm game."

"Excellent, I can see you in the team uniform already," Coach said with a smile. "Get changed then come to my office, there's no time like the present to get this going."

Thirty minutes later Miranda walked into the office. Coach was handing over a package in a brown paper bag to Tom. Their conversation finished and as Tom walked out of the office he gave Miranda a knowing wink.

"OK, Miranda, are you any good with needles?"

Miranda's mind wandered back to seeing her father injecting himself years ago and shuddered slightly.

"What's up, Miranda? Looks like you've seen a ghost?"

"Sorry, Coach. I was just having a flashback."

"One day you need to tell me about what happened, I am sure I can help."

"No worries Coach and for sure when I'm ready I will tell you all about it. Is there any other way of taking them?"

"Yeah, they can be taken orally, however it will delay the effect slightly."

"If that's OK, Coach, I'll take the oral version."

"Sure, no worries."

Coach got a key out of his desk drawer and went to a three drawer metal filing cabinet. Opening the cabinet he pulled out some swim tops and underneath was a locked metal box. With the key he opened the box and pulled out four strips of tablets.

"OK, so here's the deal. Take one tablet four times a day. Don't drink any alcohol and continue to train as normal. We should start to see the effects this time next week."

"Sure Coach, will do."

Miranda went to leave the office. As she did Coach said, "Miranda, whatever you do don't tell anyone, not even your mom. This has to stay between us."

"Sure, Coach, no worries. It's between us."

With that Miranda left the office and went to the changing rooms which, by now, were empty. She broke the seal holding in the first tablet and swallowed it with a swig from her energy drink. There was no taste to the tablet. With that done Miranda headed out of the club and back to the apartment.

Saturday 14 February 1976

"Marlene, this deal is important for me."

"Sure Stan, I understand. So what's the plan?"

"Well to ensure I get the bastard to sign I need to have some leverage."

"I guess this is where I come in… to act as the leverage?"

"Sure, Marlene. I don't want him getting his rocks off with you, but we need something that can be witnessed with maybe a photograph as evidence of his indiscretions."

"I can do that no problems, but how will I be able to let you know when to come into the room and catch him in the act?"

"That will be no issue. You need to get him into my office. I've had some modifications done here since I took over. I've had the club closed for the past three weeks and no members have been allowed anywhere near. The message given out was that we were making major renovations to the club in advance of the new opening, which is kind of true, however the members wouldn't be too happy with some of the modifications I've had installed."

Stan smiled that evil grin and continued. "So, parts of those modifications are to install security cameras hidden behind false walls and listening devices hanging from all the false ceilings. I got my team in from New York to make the 'modifications', so no one here knows any different. I have installed my own security team at the club to monitor the equipment. You now they say that all important business is done on the golf course, so these modifications will give me lots of inside information on what's going on in Detroit. In my office I can control the voice recordings myself. You know I don't want all my calls and private business deals being monitored, that just wouldn't be good. Both Riegle and Esch will be at the function along with their campaign teams. I have dirt on Riegle that he's cheated on his wife, which is not in the public knowledge, so it should be no problems to get him in a compromising situation. You need to get him close to this desk."

Marlene looked curiously around the office and said "Why close to this desk? Do you have a camera watching?"

"Nah. No cameras in this office, but I have had a panic button installed under the table, along with some other modifications." Again the evil grin came back. "Sit in my chair and feel under the table on the right."

Marlene sat down and felt under the table and felt the outline of a domed button

"OK, I can feel the button."

"So when you have him in a compromising situation you push the button and my security team comes busting in the door with me. Now move your hand to the left hand side of the table."

Marlene did and felt the cold outline of a gun grip. It was hanging from a holster at a height that would be easy to withdraw without drawing attention to someone sitting across the desk.

Stan saw from the expression on Marlene's face she had touched the gun

"It's a Smith and Wesson 357 magnum with a 3.5" barrel. Let's call it added insurance if the person across the table from me doesn't like my proposal… You won't need that. OK, let's go get ready for the party. Just to make sure the plan goes smoothly and makes him an easy conquest I'll have his drink spiked when he arrives."

"Stan, this deal must be real important to you."

"Yeah, for sure."

"Well you need to be relaxed for the meeting, so how about I make sure you are relaxed?"

With a smile on her face Marlene got up from the desk and went over to Stan and started to rub his crotch. It wasn't long before Stan had an erection. He said nothing as Marlene undid his zipper and pulled out his quivering tool.

"Now then, Stan, how about I have a suck of your lollipop?"

Kneeling down Marlene took his erection in her mouth and licked around the top of his penis. Stan started to moan and soon there was pre cum she was licking away. Caressing his shriveled scrotum she could feel his erection preparing to explode. She knew it was only a matter of seconds before he ejaculated. Pulling his penis out of her mouth she gave it ten vigorous strokes and he ejaculated onto the floor of the office. When Marlene was sure he had emptied himself she licked his now rapidly limping penis. Stan moaned and shuddered as the sensation of her licking sent jarring signals through his body and she stopped.

"Was that good for you?" Marlene said with a smile on her face. She knew what he would say, but it was important to keep up the performance. Her goal was not yet completed, but she knew he was going to sign sooner or later...

"Yeah, you are great. God, I wish I'd met you before." Zipping up his trousers he said, "We had better go get ready now."

With that Stan flicked on a switch next to his desk and they walked out of his office.

Fifty minutes later Marlene walked out of the shower in Stan's suite and saw Stan sitting in a large back chair sucking on his oxygen.

"Are you OK, Stan?"

In between a couple of rasping breaths from the tank Stan said, "Yeah, it just takes me a little longer to recover these days. You certainly know how to look after me. Just a shame I'm not a few years younger."

"Stan, you're doing just fine. So for this event how about I wear something sexy and revealing? I have brought a couple of outfits, do you want to choose or leave it to me?"

"You decide. I can't afford to get excited again just yet."

"No problems, Stan, you just relax and leave the rest to

me."

Marlene pulled an Yves Saint Laurent simple black number from the closet. Dropping her towel from around her naked body she pulled on a pair of silk panties and stepped into the dress. It had been tailored for her curves exactly and fitted like a silk glove. The split in the skirt ran up to the top of her thighs and only just covered the top of her panties. The top of the dress basically covered her 34 FF chest, with a plunging neck line that ended just above her navel. There was no back to it and it was held up by a simple press stud around the back of her neck

She slipped her feet into a pair of Valentino single rockstud leather pumps with 4" heels, in Jays Place back in Roan Mountain they were known as FMP's or fuck me pumps, and looked in the floor to ceiling mirror. The image that came back was of someone who was holding onto their looks, just. Her breasts were showing the first signs of sagging. Her legs were still shapely, however she was going to have to cut out the fancy dining if she was going to fit in this number for much longer. Her eyes still had a sparkle, but the lines were starting to appear on her face. Wearing the gear she was, she actually still looked like a high class hooker rather than the trash charging $5.00 for oral sex in a dingy alley. She looked at the outfit and smiled to herself. Six months ago there was no way she could have considered clothes like this. She was wearing an outfit that would have cost her three months' wages, and she had another ten evening outfits as expensive sitting in the Brooklyn apartment or at Stan's place. She smiled as she thought how easy it had become to spend Stan's money on that credit card.

She moved to the white antique vanity with etched beveled mirrors that she has persuaded Stan to have imported from France and got to work on her makeup. She had the art form down to a T and it took only ten minutes for the transformation to be completed. She finished off the performance with Penhaligon's Violetta Eau De Toilette that she knew would arouse most men... provided they weren't like the faggots in Stan's 51 Street restaurant.

The first guests started arriving at 6.30 pm. The important members of the club were there along with some celebrity golfers, the heads of GM, Chrysler and Ford and the politicians started arriving at 7.15 pm. All the invited guests were there by 7.45 pm in advance of the formal dinner. The event had been set up by Stan under the guise of how to develop Detroit, and to officially open the new Inglewood complex. With Stan there was always an ulterior motive, one that planned to make him even more money and power than he already had. This specific event had been set up so he could get a 21 acre plot near Lake Orion, along with planning permission, for a future development, but the price being asked for was not what he was prepared to pay and there were some awkward questions he did not want asking, so some leverage was required.

Marlene entered the function room set up for the formal dinner on Stan's arm. The reaction brought a smile to her face. She could sense some of the henpecked men undressing her with their eyes, trying not to let their ugly and, at best case, frumpy wives from noticing. The odd one of two were not quick enough and she could make out the under the breath verbal tirades they were getting.

They stopped every few feet to talk to the various dignitaries who had already arrived. After a half dozen of these Riegle walked in with his entourage. His wife was not with the party, which made the task even more straightforward for Marlene. With a discrete nod from Stan, Charles, his maître d' from SP, moved towards Stan and Marlene with three glasses of Dom Pérignon Oenothèque. Two glasses together and one on its own the other side of the silver tray. His arrival coincided with Riegle shaking hands with Stan and kissing the back of Marlene's hand.

"Ah perfect timing, Senator. A glass of Champagne to start the evening off I think."

The way Stan said it, it was a statement, not a question.

Not to offend his host Riegle took the flute and at the toast proposed by Stan he consumed half the glass.

Stan turned to Marlene with a sly grin as if to say, *over to you.*

Charles, with his assistants, marshaled the guests to their dining place and then with military precision directed the waiters as the courses were prepared and delivered along with more Dom Pérignon Oenothèque and sauvignon blanc from the Loire Valley for the ladies and Miller Lite for the men. Marlene had strategically been placed between Stan and Riegle and had been engaging in small talk with him and taking note that he had been unable to keep eye contact with her for long as his focus was regularly focused on her breasts. To ensure he was not disappointed, Marlene leaned forward every time he lost contact with her eyes to ensure he had the best view of her breasts. It was like the Pavlov's Dogs syndrome.

After the main course was cleared away Marlene leaned across and whispered in Riegle's ear, "You're looking a little pale, do you need some air?"

"That's an excellent idea," he slurred.

With brief eye contact with Stan, Marlene got up, along with Riegle, and headed to the door closest to Stan's office. Stan nodded to his Chief of Security at the back of the room, who exited to ensure that the electronic equipment was all still working.

Marlene hooked her arm in Riegle's, more to ensure he remained standing, as it was clear the spiked drink was having its effect. They stood out on the rear balcony for a few moments before Marlene asked, "Would you like to sit down for a while?"

Riegle agreed and she led him into Stan's office and shut the door. She guided him to the chair opposite the table and helped him sit down. At the angle of the chair to the table she made sure that the split in her skirt was in the right place as she bent over the table as if reaching for something. She had noticed as she had helped him into the chair that he had a significant bulge at the front of his pants, and was not surprised when, as she bent over the table, she heard and then felt him behind her. He put his hands on her waist and rubbed his harness up and down over her buttocks. He kissed her bare back and then gently went to his knees.

Marlene said, "Riegle, what are you doing... Someone might catch you... You must stop this... Please don't do this..."

She could tell he was not interested in conversation, and besides which it was only for the purpose of the recordings, as he threw the spare skirt material over her buttocks and it landed on the table and then he started to caress her vagina through her panties. Noticing Marlene's panties were wet he started to lick them, and at the same time inserted two fingers inside her vagina. With her moistness growing he rubbed his fourth finger around her anus before slowing inserting it.

Marlene leaned further over the table and felt the outline of the button and waited a few more seconds before pressing it as she was enjoying the tenderness of his tongue inside her vagina.

"You must stop this now... please..."

Marlene pushed the button, hoping that Stan and company might take a couple of minutes to get there so she could climax before the game was up.

As he was fingering her, he had managed to undo his pants and his erection was now free, ready to plunge deep into Marlene once he had brought her to orgasm with his tongue.

Ten seconds later the door to the study opened, and it took a few seconds for Riegle to notice other people had entered the room. As the door had opened Marlene said again, "Please stop... You mustn't do this..."

In rushed two of Stan's security officers, but not before a number of flashes had gone off.

The flashes were like a light going off in Riegle's head. He pulled his fingers out of Marlene and turned to look at the source of the light. There was a security officer holding a camera and, as he turned to face the cameraman, the flash went off again, catching Riegle in the kneeling position facing the camera with his pants around his ankles and erection in full view.

Marlene immediately ran out of the room and headed to the ladies restroom to finish off what Riegle had started.

Stan walked in behind the security team that was now holding Riegle by each arm.

"Seems we have a situation here, Riegle."

Riegle said nothing, he was still feeling the effects of the drug-laced Champagne and in fact, if it wasn't for the security guards he would not have been able to keep himself standing. His pants were still around his ankles, but his erection had subsided and, like him, was almost withering, wanting to end this current nightmare. He was not really fully able to grasp the situation, however he knew nothing good could come of it.

"Boys, help him back on with his pants and then get his Chief of Staff in here to organize him leaving our party by the back door. I am sure the good senator would not like to have any more of a scene than has already taken place."

Once he was dressed the security team sat him in a chair and stood either side waiting for Stan's next orders.

"OK boys, leave us alone and go and find his Chief of Staff."

When they had left the room, Stan turned to Riegle and said, "So we have a situation that I am sure you don't want getting out to your public and especially not back to Mrs Riegle….Screwing my partner is not something I take kindly to"

Riegle briefly shook his head, which Stan read as his agreement.

"So, here's what we are going to do. Monday I will have a package delivered to your offices. I strongly recommend only you open the package. When you decide, you let me know. Oh and if I don't hear back by Wednesday night another package will be delivered to Charlie Cain at the Detroit News. I'm sure you've heard of the kid…"

Riegle briefly nodded his head in understanding.

"OK, so we understand each other. Now where's that fucking Chief of Staff of yours?"

A minute later a concerned looking suit walked in the door and went over to Riegler. Before he could say or ask anything Stan said, "The senator is not feeling too well. My security team will show you the best way to leave the premises without anyone spotting you. Your car is being brought there now. Boys, please show the senator to his car."

Without any further words the senator and his Chief of Staff were escorted out of a side door from Stan's office and within a minute the noise of a Mercury Grand Marquis could be heard pulling away from the side entrance. With the senator safely out of the building and the paperwork as good as signed, Stan took a minute's worth of oxygen and went back to the dinner, the sly smile back on his face.

Marlene, having satisfied herself with an orgasm in a cubicle of the ladies locker room, went to the suite she shared with Stan and freshened up to make sure there were no telltale stains before rejoining in the dinner.

"You were magnificent, Marlene, it worked like a dream."

"It's lucky your team came as soon as it did, he was very overpowering and not gentle like you."

"Yeah I didn't like the way he was manhandling you, I have been thinking we need to make some changes to our relationship."

"What do you mean, Stan? Am I not keeping you happy and meeting your needs?"

"Oh hell yeah, just that sting tonight made me feel kind of jealous. I need to make our arrangement more permanent."

"Really, Stan? Is that a proposal?"

"It's about as close to one as I'll ever be able to get. So what do you think?"

Marlene's mind went into a spin. She could hardly

believe that she was literally a YES away from the inheritance of Stan's billions. She started picturing what she and Miranda would do with an untold wealth. She didn't even know how much a billion was, only it was a lot more than a hundred million and that was beyond her wildest dreams. She was snapped out of her dreaming with Stan saying, "Are you going to keep me waiting all night?"

"Oh no Stan and yes, for sure, absolutely, you can't believe how happy you have made me. Yes, yes, yes."

Stan grinned and then went off to make some more arrangements and greet more people. Marlene on the other hand wandered around almost in a daze. Six months ago she had been living a nightmare with a pimp for a husband who sexually abused their daughter, and now she was on the verge of becoming obscenely wealthy. The smile transfixed on her face was nothing to do with feelings for Stan; it had everything to do with her feelings for his money. The irony of it being 14 February came to Marlene. This was about as romantic as Stan could ever be, but then it worked both ways. Even being this close to the money she was not going to tell Miranda until the ink was dried on the paperwork and in a very secure place…

Wednesday, 21 April 1976

"Go, Miranda, go… keep pushing."

Miranda could just about make out the voice of her coach through the noise in the pool. She could see the expression more than hear it as she pushed the last 5 meters. Certainly she had noticed the change since taking the tablets. The session on Monday had seemed easier; she was hurting less as she had gotten out of the pool at the end of the session, almost as if she could have carried on for another ten lengths.

If this is what the tablets did then she wanted more…

"Keep pushing, Miranda,", her coach's voice was now clearly coming through. It seemed as though everyone else in the pool must have realized something serious was happening as the background noise had stopped. Miranda could sense, more than see, the wall was approaching. She hit the wall with her arm and whipped around to face her coach.

"OK, Miranda, get out and toweled down then come and see me in my office." With that, he turned around and headed away from the pool. Miranda trod water not sure what to make of her coach's words. Had she done something wrong? Was her stroke not good? She thought it had been as near a perfect time trial as she could have done, but still she didn't feel tired. Maybe she was not pushing hard enough and relying on the tablets too much…

The noise in the pool returned to its normal boisterous levels as she pulled herself out and grabbed her towel and swim bag. Into the changing rooms, and into a cubicle, to take her last tablet of the day.

Dried and wary she made her way to her coach's office. He was sitting there looking at lists of data on spreadsheets and Miranda wondered if that was hers or someone else's data.

"Sit down, Miranda, we need to have a chat."

"What's up, Coach?"

"Nothing, Miranda."

"I was a little worried at the end of the session, like I'd done something bad."

"Far from it, Miranda. I just didn't want to announce in the pool that you not just hit, but took 0.5 seconds off the Olympic qualifying time. Just."

"Seriously, Coach. I met the qualifying time… I don't know want to say…"

"Miranda, don't say anything, and don't tell anyone else. We don't want to draw attention to this. I knew you just needed a little help to get there. By the way, how is the 'medication' going?"

"I'm sticking to the regime, just like you said. No alcohol, no nothing and anyone who has seen me pop a tablet believes it's because I have a headache."

"Good girl. Now we need to keep a close eye on this and then decide when we will stop the 'medication'. Given the trails are in 8 weeks' time we need to stop them in 4 weeks."

"OK Coach, no worries. Just tell me when."

"Will do, Miranda. Now go finish your warm down routine and get yourself off home. Oh, and by the way, happy birthday for tomorrow."

"Thanks, Coach. You are the best."

With that Miranda left the office and suppressed the grin she was struggling to hold. She had the time to qualify for the Olympics and nothing could stop her. It had seemed an impossible dream, however here she was on the cusp of making the team. Finally, she thought, she could start to put her past behind her and focus on her future. The first step of her goal was only 8 weeks away…

Wednesday, 19 May 1976

The session was coming to an end. It had been the usual mix of endurance and sprints. The training group had got smaller and more focused the nearer the trials came. The noise level in this weekly session had dropped significantly as each of the five people remained focused on the objective of the trails and then the ultimate goal of a place on the Olympic team. The joking and banter had stopped a few weeks before and the coaches were almost brutal in their approach. Any minor mistake was accompanied by a tirade of abusive language and questioning if they actually wanted to make the trials... Even this, in Miranda's mind, was a small price to pay.

There were other prices Miranda was paying. At first she had ignored the signs however, the more she took the pills the more she noticed the changes. Her voice started to deepen and she had stopped singing at home as she had started to hate the sound of her own singing. It just didn't sound like her.

Her muscle tone had improved significantly, along with her body definition, however there were other visible signs of changes. Her hands were no longer small and lady-like. They had started to transform into what she could only describe as 'man hands', and then there was the Adam's apple. Miranda had first noticed this a few weeks ago, that she was starting to develop an Adam's apple. All the library research told her that both men and women have Adam's apples, however mainly it was only the male one that developed into the protrusion from their neck that she was starting to see. Her's was definitely more protruding than it had six months previously.

"Miranda... Miranda... out of the pool and in my office in ten minutes." The call back to reality had come from Coach. With a wave of her hand in acknowledgement, Miranda did a lazy kick stroke to glide her over to the side of the pool with the metal stairs to climb out. She still had a tablet to take and then get changed.

Exactly ten minutes later Miranda knocked on Coach's office door.

"Come in Miranda, take a seat."

"Thanks, Coach. How was it this evening?"

"Good as always, Miranda. Your times are good and consistent." There was a pause as Coach seemed to be searching for the right words to say. "OK, Miranda, the tablets need to stop. We have a month before the trials and we have not seen dramatic improvements for the past two weeks. In essence, the benefit is no longer coming from them. You have gained the maximum you are going to from them. Your condition is peaked at the right time so we need to stop them now and get the traces out of your system as best we can."

"OK, Coach, if you say so."

"I do, Miranda. It's essential now that we work with you clean so that we get you race prepared. The effects should give you the edge for both the trials and the Olympics themselves. Do you have any tablets left?"

Miranda looked directly at Coach and said, "No, I took the last of them today after the session."

It had come out so naturally that Coach took it at face value. The lie had come out so easily and Miranda was not sure why she had lied to him, but she had another strip of twenty tablets in her bag with her. She thought of them as her emergency backup in case she needed a top up. Being honest with herself, she had started to become dependent on them as they gave her a small buzz after taking them. What was clear in Miranda's mind was that she was going to need to find another source of the pills as twenty would not last her. OK, she was going to have to stay off them for a couple of months, but she needed them as a type of comfort blanket. They had made such a difference to her, not just physically but also in terms of her confidence. Once she popped one of those pills she felt an inner strength to the point she was almost indestructible. They had also helped control her mood swings. These had become more and more frequent and she had initially put these down to what she had escaped from. The physical abuse she had suffered from her father had stopped a long time ago, but she was, more and more, reliving the pain through nightmares. She never spoke to her mom about it not wanting to worry her and besides which the tablets helped...

Coach's voice again brought her out of her thoughts.

"Miranda, we need to do some tests to see what your levels of Oxandrolone are. Can you do me a sample in this tube?"

"Sure, Coach."

With that Miranda left his office and headed back to the changing rooms. She perched over the toilet bowl and, as carefully as possible without pissing on her hand, managed to get a sample in the tube. Finishing, she cleaned herself up and headed back to Coach's office with the sample in her sports bag. In his office she handed him the still warm sample wrapped in toilet tissue and said, "Here you go, Coach. So, what happens next?"

"I'll get this off to the test lab tomorrow and we should get the results in the next twenty-four hours. Come back tomorrow evening and we can discuss the results."

"OK Coach, see you tomorrow."

With that Miranda got up and left his office and headed into the mild 73 degree evening air. She experienced a real mix of emotions. The fact the DHT had done its job was not something she saw as cheating, it was just there as an aid to help her get to her potential more quickly. She had been sure she could have got there eventually, but it had done so to give her a shot at the team. She was nervous about how she would control her mood swings without her comfort blanket, but she did have her emergency supply and was sure by the time her pills ran out she could find another source, or maybe something better. She thought about how proud Marlene would be when she made the team, something she was convinced was going to happen now.

Miranda put on her headphones and plugged into her

Stereobelt, a gift from Marlene, who seemed to have the ability, via Stan, to get hold of technology not available anywhere else. She still got the unusual looks from people on her way home wondering why this kid was wearing some kind of earmuffs with a wire going to a box on her belt, especially in May with 73 degree temperatures…

Saturday, 12 June 1976

"OK, everyone let's get on the bus. We got a long way to go today and times to meet… and you all know about times…"

There was an outburst of laughing from the crowd assembled. The time was 4.30am; it was still very dark and the rain was still in the air, it was the fine type that seemed to float in the air but not actually make you wet. Marlene turned to Miranda and gave her a final hug and kisses and said, "See you in a few days."

"OK Mom. Have fun with Stan, and see you on Friday."

"Take care and stay out of trouble."

"Sure, Mom, you too."

With that Miranda climbed onto the first step of the chartered bus. It was going to take the team to JFK for the eight and a half hour flying time to California. Even at that time in the morning everybody was wide awake and excited about the next week. All of them had the belief they were going to make the Olympic team and this was just the next step of the journey. The months and years of training were now coming to the final phase. The nervous energy would keep them going, in some cases for the whole week, but many of them would pass out and sleep on the first flight to Salt Lake City after the initial burst of excitement. Adding to this only two people in the group of the twenty-one going on the trip had ever been on a plane before. All were wearing the club training suits that had been made especially for the event and each one had on the jacket and pants their names, the club name and logo and 'Olympic Trials, Long Beach California 12 to 18 June 1976'.

Miranda took a seat by the window so she could wave to Marlene as the bus pulled away and, once they were out of sight of the parents, relatives and friends that had come to wave them off, joined the banter with the rest of the team.

Nobody on the bus really noticed the scenery around them as they headed out of Brooklyn. The ride to the airport was only twenty-five minutes, and seemed to end as quickly as it started. As they pulled into the airport complex, Coach came on the bus tannoy.

"OK guys, when we pull up at the terminal I want the first eight off the bus to go and get trollies. The rest of you help unload the gear from the bus. When the trollies are loaded we are going to head to the TWA check-in desks."

The bus was soon unloaded and the group headed to the TWA check in area, and to the Group Check-In line.

"Right, I need everyone's ID please. Tom, you get the guys' and Miranda, get the girls'."

The check-in assistant greeted Coach with a trained smile and politely enquired about the team and what they were doing. She swiftly dealt with the verification of the ID's to the names listed on the tickets and then asked for each of the check-in bags to be loaded one at a time on the small weigh scale conveyor belt. Twenty minutes later everyone was checked in and heading to the security line. Even though it was early the airport was still busy with business people catching various red eye flights due to the number of missed flights as a result of another major power failure, also a testament to the fact it was the busiest airport in the US with 23,000,000+ passengers per year.

As they approached the security check, Miranda was less boisterous than the rest of her teammates. In her carry-on bag she had some essentials, including a strip of the pills. Trying not to show her nerves she approached the trayed conveyor system and placed her jacket and carry-on bag in a tray at the instruction of the security officer. With a final glance at her tray she walked through the metal detector, which remained quiet and to the end of the conveyor belt that had to pass through an X-ray machine under the scrutineering eye of another trainer officer. Miranda waited to see her tray come through the machine. She started to sweat under the arms as her tray had not appeared. Had the security officer seen her pills? Could he see her pills… she had no idea… and then her tray was spat out of the machine and she breathed a sigh of relief. Tom had seen the look on her face and came over.

"Miranda, are you alright?"

"Yes thanks, Tom, I just have a bit of a headache."

"OK, if you're sure. Is there anything I can get you? Some water maybe?"

"That would be great, if you wouldn't mind."

"Sure, no worries."

Tom headed off to a kiosk while Miranda put on her jacket and picked up her bag. Eventually, the rest of the team made it through, a few having extra bag checks and together they headed off to the shopping and food area. Many of the guys tucked into breakfasts but Miranda was not hungry. Her experience at the security check had destroyed her appetite.

Fifty minutes later the airport tannoy announced the departure of TWA flight to San Diego via Salt Lake City and the club team moved to the gate to start the boarding process. Miranda, clutching her boarding pass and ID, showed both to the TWA representative at the gate and followed Tom down the stairs to walk the short distance from the gate to the plane.

Tom turned to her and said, "How's the headache?"

"Better, thank you."

"So, where are you sitting?"

Miranda looked at her ticket for confirmation and said, "27F."

"I bet you have a window seat. That will be cool. You should be able to see Brooklyn as we take off."

"Where are you sitting, Tom?"

"I've got an aisle seat 21C. I asked for it so I can stretch my legs out and walk around. I don't like sitting still for long periods, it drives me mad. You ever been on a plane before, Miranda?"

"No, Tom. I guess you have?"

"Yeah, a few times with my dad. He's in the military and he seems to travel all the time. I'm sure his job sucks but he definitely gets to go to some nice places. Flying is kinda fun. Takeoff and landing are the cool bits. The flying stuff is like being on a train, only without the tracks."

With a smile he turned and walked up the plane stairs to a "Welcome" from the TWA stewardess.

"Ladies and gentlemen, welcome on board. My name is Captain Waddell and along with my crew I will be flying you to San Diego with an approximate forty minute stop in Salt Lake City. A special welcome to the 92nd Flying Street Dolphins swimming club from Brooklyn on their way to the Olympic trials in Long Beach."

There was an outbreak of applause and cheering from the passengers and then, with the safety demonstrated completed, the plane headed for the queue for takeoff.

Miranda found herself gripping the armrest of her window seat as the plane engines got up to full speed and then Captain Waddell let off the air brakes. The plane shot forwards and fifteen seconds later the plane took to the air. Miranda only released her grip on the armrest once the flight had leveled out. The fasten seatbelt lights soon went out and the stewardesses started pushing their trollies up and down the aisles offering drinks and snacks.

Tom came past and leaned over.

"Wasn't so bad was it?"

"No, you are right, it was pretty cool."

With that he headed to the back of the plane and into the restroom.

Miranda pulled out a book and started to re-read *The Liberal Imagination* by Lionel Mordechai Trilling. Engrossed in the book, Miranda barely noticed the flight and soon the fasten seat belt signs came on and the plane started its decent to Salt Lake City.

Ten minutes later the wheels hit the tarmac that sent puffs of smoke into the air as the stationary wheels hit the ground at 200mph. Captain Waddell hit the air brakes and reverse thrusters and the plane's speed dropped rapidly until the plane was moving at what seemed like walking pace towards the terminal building.

Captain Waddell came on the tannoy.

"Ladies and gentlemen, welcome to Salt Lake City. The local time is 10.30 am and the outside temperature is a pleasant 90 degrees Fahrenheit. Please remain seated with your seatbelts fastened until we have reached our parking stand and the fasten seatbelt signs have been switched off. For those of you going on to San Diego, please remain on the plane. TWA would like to thank you for travelling with us today and wish you a pleasant day in Salt Lake City."

Once the plane stopped and the passengers getting off at Salt Lake City had deplaned, Miranda headed to the restroom herself and felt the heat coming from the dessert through the open plane door.

Forty minutes later the plane doors were again closed and Captain Waddell came back on the tannoy to announce the flight details and advise that their expected arrival time in San Diego was 1.05 pm. Miranda relaxed in her seat now knowing what to expect and even being able to enjoy the experience.

Miranda must have fallen asleep as the next thing she remembered was a jolt as the wheels hit the tarmac at San Diego International Airport. Looking outside she thought she could just make out the Pacific Ocean.

"Ladies and gentlemen, welcome to San Diego International Airport. The local time is 1.09 pm and the temperature outside is a rather warm 105 degrees Fahrenheit. Hope you all remembered to bring sun screen and a hat… TWA would like to thank you for travelling with us today and wish you a pleasant day in San Diego."

As Miranda left the plane by the stairs the heat hit her. It was a dry heat that immediately brought moisture over her body. The training jackets of most of her teammates were already off and she followed suit. By the time she had made it to the air conditioned baggage claim area she was noticeably sweating and the contrast from outside made her shiver before her body reacclimatized.

"OK, guys," came Coach's voice, "grab your bags and

head out to the parking lot. We need to cross the road and you will see a bus with the club name on it."

Thirty minutes later the team had their gear and headed out into the heat of San Diego.

Sure enough, the bus was there and the process of loading the gear went smoothly and soon the team started the two hour road trip to Long Beach. The airport hugged the coast and climbing up the hills gave a wonderful view of the California coast.

Miranda thought San Diego was not a beautiful place, well, at least not where the airport was located, and as they joined Interstate 5 towards Los Angeles her impression didn't change with the brown and parched landscape.

The adrenaline was still keeping the team going. Now they were within hours of getting to the trials village and only a couple of days from their respective events, and the dream of a place on the team.

Coach seemed to be enjoying his time with tannoy systems.

"Guys, according to Miguel our driver we should be at the village between 4 pm and 4.30 pm, so we are going to pull over midway as there's a service area with some great views where we can get food and refreshments. So for those arty types amongst you, get your Kodak's ready. When we get to the village we will register and then you will get directions to your associated rooms. You all know who you are rooming with, and we will be doing random checks, to make sure you stick to those rooms... that's specifically for you Tom and Dave..."

The laughter died down and Coach went on...

"Dinner will be served at 7 pm tonight and we will have a team meeting at 9 pm to go through the agenda for the week. I will let you know at dinner where the team meeting will take place, so get in, unpacked and make yourselves at home. We all need to be on top form from the minute we arrive."

With that he switched off the tannoy the mood in the bus changed subtly from a holiday atmosphere to one of nervous anticipation and a focus on the potential rewards.

It was closer to 5 pm when the team bus arrived in the village. The registration process was pretty seamless and Miranda, with Julie and Trisha, headed to their digs. The rooms were functional but clean and they had soon unpacked and went off to explore the surroundings of the village. First stop was the pool area with its seating capacity of six hundred and fifty. The girls soaked in the surroundings for a good ten minutes trying to picture how the atmosphere would be with the galleries full of people screaming encouragement. Then it was off to explore the rest of the facilities and before they knew it they had to head to the restaurant where dinner was being served.

Conversation over dinner was made up of talk about the facilities and the associated accommodation they all had and then Coach stood up and guided the team to the conference room allocated for their team talk and inductions.

By 10.15 pm Miranda knew that the next few days were going to be intensive and there would be no time to go and enjoy the sights and sounds of Long Beach, so fatigued, along with Julie and Trisha, they headed off to their beds.

Monday, 21 June 1976

Miranda woke, as she had done for the past few days, early but refreshed. She got into her exercise gear and headed to the gym for her morning workout session. Today was the big day. She had made it through the heats and this evening was the final. The seventy-two entrants for her event had been reduced to the final eight and after this evening the two remaining would be getting their rewards of the trip to Montreal. It was going to be a long day as her final was not until 6.15 pm, but she got on with her work out and put the race out of her mind as best she could.

Breakfast was a muted affair as both Julie and Trisha, who had achieved PB's, had failed to make the team, since being knocked out had let their routines go, so the only people who showed up were the remaining four of the team who still had the opportunity to qualify.

After breakfast Miranda went to the library to carry on reading *Sincerity and Authenticity* and before she realized it she heard the clock chime for 12 pm and she packed up and headed back to the restaurant for lunch.

After lunch she headed back to the gym for stretching and a light workout with the weights and could feel the nerves starting to tingle with the anticipation. She knew tonight was going to be different. During the heats the pool had been packed but as the finals had come along the crowd seemed to get louder and louder, so tonight, with fifteen finals, was going to have a very special atmosphere.

At 4 pm Miranda left her digs with Trisha and Julie and headed over to the practice pool area to get prepared for the race. The balance was to push, but not to overexert and have nothing left for the race, and then it was time…

The first four swimmers had been announced and Miranda barely heard her name being called for her to make her entrance. She walked into a cacophony of sounds; people cheering, rattles being enthusiastically waved and even someone playing a trumpet. The noise died down briefly before the next contestant was announced and so the process was repeated until all eight swimmers were in the arena.

Miranda took a few seconds to look around before she stripped off to her swimming costume and then the starter called them onto their blocks.

"On your marks… get set…" and then the hooter sounded to set them off.

The eight swimmers left their blocks in the blink of an eye and then into their own rhythms and routines. Through the routine Miranda was vaguely aware of the noise. Breath… head down… head out… breath… head down.

The wall at the far end of the pool came into view and Miranda executed her turn and back in the other direction. Breath… head down… head out… breath… head down

The clock on the wall was showing 55 seconds, 56, 57, 58.

Miranda was close to the wall, it was going to be a matter of the touch. She could not tell how close the others were as she just kept looking straight ahead.

Fifty-nine, 1.00, 1.01, 1.02 and she touched the wall. It was going to be desperately close and she looked straight up at the electronic display that showed the results from the electronic pads build into the pool wall. Immediately, she saw her name and it showed she was in second place. The realization hit her immediately. She had made it.

"Congratulations, Miranda and good luck for Montreal." It was Wendy, her longtime rival and whom she had beaten into third place.

"Thank you, Wendy. I really appreciate it. I'm sorry you didn't make it."

That said, Wendy swam off leaving Miranda staring back up at the display. It was almost impossible to believe and she didn't want to leave the pool in case it wasn't real. Finally, she backstroked over to the steps and pulled herself out of the pool. She stared into the crowd and saw the beaming smile of Marlene and energetically waved to her, and then she had to leave the pool area as the next race was about to be called.

Leaving the pool Miranda went to the changing rooms and went about her business of changing back into her team wear before going to the officials.

"Congratulations, Miranda," said the official.

"Thank you, Ma'me" said Miranda.

"In order to complete the process and verify the result we will need you to provide a urine sample. It's part of our compulsory drug testing program. I'm sure you are aware of it."

"Yes, Ma'me."

"OK, please can you fill both sample bottles and bring them back to me as soon as you have filled them?"

With that Miranda went back to the ladies changing room and the toilet and locked herself in a cubicle. This was it, the final hurdle. She was confident nothing would go wrong, Coach had assured her it would be OK. Filling the two sample bottles she took them back to the official and headed off to the celebrations.

Wednesday, 23 June 1976

The team had returned home on Tuesday still buoyed with the fact three of the club had made it to the Olympic team. The journey back with the team had been a total high and having Marlene there was the icing on the cake. Miranda had thought the call from Coach to meet her at the club was just part of the follow up and went down to the baths with the smile that had not left her face since she had left the pool after the final.

"Miranda, sit down please."

"Yes, Coach, what's up?"

"There's no good way to say this, so I'll tell you straight. Both samples failed. Our contact was removed from the testing laboratory, and they are talking about pressing charges against him. You have been taken off the team and the times and results have been scrubbed. We both knew it was a risk and it didn't pay off. I'm sorry."

Miranda sat there stunned. There were no words to describe the feelings she had. One minute ago she had been ecstatic, on top of the world; the next she was heading into a bottomless pit of anger. She stood up and practically ran out of Coach's office and straight out of the pool not acknowledging her teammates, who clearly were not aware of her situation.

Leaving the club she walked and walked. The tears came and didn't stop for the next hour. She ended up in a small park and sat on a bench and then the tears were replaced by anger and hatred. Anger that she had been robbed of her dream and hatred at the fact she had been again used by a man. By the time the tears stopped and she was able to compose herself enough to walk home the burning desire to get even was beyond belief. She opened her sports bag and took out her spare strip of pills and popped three. She was going to need them to bring her down from where her mind was going...

"Miranda, what's up? You've been away so long I was starting to get worried."

"Sorry Mom, I just had real bad news. I've been taken off the team."

"What do you mean… That's not possible."

"It is, Mom,. My sample tests both came back positive."

"What do you mean came back positive… Positive for what?"

"For Oxandrolone. Coach put me on a course of it to get me to the qualifying time. It was supposed to be all OK as he had a contact on the inside that would fix the results. His contact got busted and the tests came back positive."

Miranda was talking like it was an out-of-body experience. She could see herself talking to her mom, but it was like someone else was talking. The pills had kicked in and taking three at a time was giving her a total out-of-body experience.

Marlene said nothing, what was there to say. Virtually at the same time they both broke down crying, hugging each other.

Sunday, 8 August 1976

It was 1.30 am when Marlene went into the bathroom. The evening before she and Stan had been to a dinner party where she had played the dutiful trophy wife role. 'Dressed to kill' was a phrase that Stan had used and had brought a wry smile to her face. If only Stan had realized that's exactly what was on her agenda.

Marlene had ensured the wedding certificate was hidden in a safety deposit box in one of the downtown banks, along with a copy of his final will and testament leaving all his assets to his new wife. Marlene had had a difficult task to work out. How long after the charade wedding would be long enough to not arouse suspicion when Stan passed away, how to make it look like Stan had passed away naturally – which, considering his state of health probably wouldn't be difficult to convince anyone – how to get Stan to sign over his business empire to her as the sole recipient. So many different considerations, but at last everything was in place, and it was time to act.

Marlene felt no remorse about what she was about to do. It was, after all, her inheritance and she wanted to get her hands on it as soon as possible. She had for some time been having an affair she had kept from Stan, which was not difficult, but also from Miranda. She was not interested in making anything permanent but it had been a great source of excitement and release to have a real life sex toy. He knew nothing of Marlene and asked no questions. Once per week they would meet up at a hotel out of town and fuck for a few hours before going their own ways.

In the bathroom Marlene quietly got dressed. It was important that when Stan was found she was away and with an alibi and had agreed to meet with her dress designer early that morning. She had widely published the event and was deliberately taking a scheduled flight to Chicago where her dress designer was preparing an exhibition of his latest creations. Stan's – soon to be Marlene's – personal chauffeur would be waiting at the lobby in thirty minutes, so she had time. She wanted to leave the apartment as close to Stan's demise as possible.

Marlene had put on a pair of medical latex gloves for the suffocation. In his sleep, Stan's breathing made him even more vulnerable. A few times in the past few weeks he had woken up in the night struggling for breath and frantically reaching for his oxygen mask. Marlene, as the caring wife, had immediately gone to his aid each time this had happened. She had been letting a few of the staff know of Stan's deterioration, building up more of the illusion of the caring wife so there would be no consideration it was anything but natural causes when Stan died. Marlene was only speeding up the inevitable, but she had some important decisions to make and deals to be signed and for those she needed the financial resources that the inheritance would provide.

Five minutes before she was due in the lobby, Marlene walked over towards Stan who was lying on his back snoring. His breathing was uneven and he stirred slightly as she approached his side of the bed. She didn't hesitate and clamped her right hand over his mouth and pinched his nostrils together at the same time. For a couple of seconds Stan's brain processed there was an issue and then he tried moving and found he could not. He tried to open his eyes but his sleep had been so deep he felt as if he was at the bottom of a well trying to look up and only seeing darkness. His energy was draining fast, as was his life. The pressure was building up inside his chest and his right arm feebly tried to move towards where he thought he had last left his oxygen mask. Tighter and tighter was the feeling in his chest. Still he was unable to move or see through his eyes. His last thought before he expired was that of wondering where Marlene was. Surely she must have seen his struggle…

Marlene waited another sixty seconds after she saw his chest stop moving and felt the last of his feeble efforts to move before removing her hands from his nose and mouth. She removed the blindfold he had fallen asleep wearing and noticed with satisfaction that his eyes were closed and not open or showing an expression of shock. She had persuaded him the previous evening to wear the blindfold as part of their sex and told him to keep it on so they could carry on after he had recovered from his first ejaculation, knowing full well he would not be capable of another session. Straightening the sheets around where he lay, she quickly moved his arm out of the bed and to a position where the oxygen mask was close by and then re-connected the oxygen supply. No small detail had been missed in the preparation and it was essential no clue was left to point at anything other than natural causes.

She stripped off the latex gloves and put them in her handbag along with the blindfold. She pulled on another pair and, picking up her travel bag, walked to the bedroom door. Taking one final look from the bedroom door she closed it behind her and then opened and closed the apartment door behind her. Only after she got into the elevator did she strip off the other set of latex gloves and stuck those in her handbag as well.

The elevator reached the ground floor and Jim was waiting by the door to escort her to the car.

"Good morning, Mrs. Aldridge."

"Good morning, Jim. How are you this morning?"

"Very fine thank you, Mrs. Aldridge and yourself?"

"Very fine also, thank you, Jim."

"Do you know if Mr. Aldridge will be needing his car this morning?"

Marlene kept a straight face.

"I am not sure, Jim. He's been having another restless night and I didn't really want to leave him, but he was insistent before we went to bed that I should go. So who am I to ignore his demands?"

They both smiled that knowing smile of understanding that Stan was a complete bastard and no one went against his wishes.

Marlene carried on.

"I would have the car brought back just in case, but

based on his sleep pattern I don't think he will be too energetic today."

"Understand and appreciate, Mrs. Aldridge."

With that he opened the door to the Rolls and Marlene stepped in. Shutting the door behind her, the car immediately pulled away heading for JFK and the early bird flight.

Friday, 29 July 1977

Miranda waited expectantly to go up on stage and collect her graduation certificate. She had finished her finals in the top 1% of the year and was now set on taking her place at Harvard. So much had happened since her disqualification from the Olympic team, it seemed as though that had been more than a year ago.

She had gone through a tough summer after her disqualification. She had gone into a nose dive of depression and a deepening hatred of men that had become an obsession. She had used up the last of her Oxandrolone soon after returning from the trials and it wasn't long before she sought out dealers in stronger drugs. The Oxandrolone would help for a while but it was not providing enough relief. She found a dealer who was able to provide a huge range of uppers and downers, and had tried pretty much all that was on offer on the 'menu'. She was taking the drugs in the apartment only when Marlene was away with Stan, which had been quite frequently, and had been pretty good at clearing up the evidence. If Marlene knew she was taking drugs, she had not been showing it. Miranda thought she must have known, she had been living with a drug addict in her father, but didn't want to raise the topic and let Miranda go through the phase and try and get over the Olympic disappointment her own way.

Miranda had done everything in her power to not watch the Olympics and especially had not read anything in the papers relating to the swimming and results. The only news she heard was that Wendy Boglioli had come third in a time that Miranda had bettered and knew she could have improved on. The anger she had felt at Coach was so intense she had not since set foot in the swimming baths and had completely shut out all the people associated to swimming.

It had been three months after the news from Coach that Marlene had told Miranda about her getting married to

Stan and that he had died in his sleep some months later having signed his empire over. That news had helped significantly in Miranda getting some semblance of perspective back in her life and was probably the reason Marlene had mentioned it. They had gone from being destitute to immensely rich in such a short period of time that Miranda no longer needed to worry about where the next meal, or more importantly at that time the next cash, was coming from for her drugs. Her dealer had been arrested some months ago and Miranda had found a way to wean herself off the concoctions she had been taking to focus on something else. Probably the arrest of her dealer had at least prolonged her life, if not saved it.

Marlene and Miranda had moved out of the apartment and into a penthouse suite on West 56th Street. Marlene had pretty much liquidated Stan's assets and moved the cash into various offshore accounts to ensure it could not be reclaimed by the government, and had invested in a number of properties in different countries. One thing had become clear to Marlene was the value of investing in "bricks and mortar". She had used a large chunk of Stan's money to make investments in land and building projects and had bought out a number of both real estate and construction companies sitting as the private partner, allowing the companies to continuing running them. She had hired the best lawyers in New York to build her web of secrecy and hidden activities so she remained invisible to the markets around the world. The last thing she wanted was interest being shown in how she had come into the money in the first place.

Miranda had never asked about Stan's death, just taking Marlene's word that he had died in his sleep. She had seen the coroner's report showing he had died of massive organ failure due to the fact he had stopped breathing. There was nothing in there to believe there was any other reason for his death.

Miranda and Marlene initially were very close after the Olympic ordeal, but the relationship had changed subtly since Marlene had focused on building herself a new life. They were close, but had grown apart, emotionally. Miranda had witnessed a few of the men that had passed through Marlene's life since Stan's demise and recognized them for what they were, toys for Marlene's whims. When Marlene did socialize she was never seen with the same man on her arm twice and had, in certain circles, become a must-have conquest for both available and married men alike. None however got close and nor would they. Marlene's hidden past was going to remain just that, as was Miranda's. As part of the new life she had also changed hers and Miranda's surnames with the aid of her highly paid lawyers. Miranda's surname change had come into effect from Saturday 30 July 1975, and her graduation certificate was already in her new name.

Miranda was called up to the stage, and took a few seconds to look around the school hall for a final time. She was not going to miss it. It was going to be consigned to the trash can as soon as she had her certificate. She had not been a loner at school, but she had pretty much kept herself to herself, not getting close to anyone, especially boys, which had given her an image of being frigid.

There was muted applause as she walked onto the stage and after shaking various dignitaries' hands she walked off the other side into the next chapter of her life.

Wednesday, 22 July 1981

The celebration preparations were complete. Graduation day had arrived and the 3,000 plus students passing out today were getting up after the graduation ball the previous evening. The vast majority having consumed a little bit too much alcohol and a few trying to remember who and where they were.

The bunting was fluttering in the summer breeze and the band was practicing on the elevated bandstand close to the main stage.

Miranda was dressed in the compulsory cap and gown and chatting to a small group from her class. It had seemed such a long way off when she had entered the campus for the first time in October 1977; however the last four years had soon gone by. Miranda had buried herself in her studies. Her aim had been to suck up as much knowledge and information about good and bad business deals with a specific goal to understanding the complexities of the profit and loss accounts. Understanding the links between these and therefore the reasons why companies succeeded or failed. Her tutors had been impressed with her as a freshman; she seemed to be able to take on board pretty much any scenario they could lay in front of her and her innovation for finding solutions to the challenges they posed had them talking about her as a potential business leader of the future.

Miranda had flown through the first year examinations, however this had come at a price. She had become more alienated since her arrival at Harvard. She had developed an almost superior attitude to her peers and she was not particularly popular with them. This bothered Miranda not at all, if fact, it appealed to her as she didn't need to pretend to have relationships with either boys or girls.

She did not stay on the campus with the rest of the freshmen. Marlene had brought a serviced apartment on Huron Avenue and Miranda, who had passed her driving test a couple of years before, drove to Harvard each day in

her Porsche 911 Carrera G-Modell, specially customized and imported from Germany; another gift from her mother. It was Miranda's first experience of living away from home and she found it suited her. She had not found too much difficulty in finding a local dealer and was able to indulge her spare time in getting high on coke. She still suffered with the phobia of needles so her drugs had to be smoked or snorted and she didn't like the fact that the smoke used to cling to everything, which invariable cost her another $20.00 for the Philippino maid to make sure it disappeared.

The only person Miranda was even remotely close to was Professor Andrea Laird. She was young for Harvard lecturers, in her early thirties. She was insanely intelligent and with a Mensa IQ of 159, she was seen by many as a complete eccentric. She was also sexually confused. Genetically, she had been born a woman, however in all her mannerisms she dressed and acted like a man. She would do pretty much anything to hide her female genetics. She wore no makeup. She always wore Savile Row suits tailored and cut just how a man's suit would be and it was rumored that she even had a plastic prosthetic penis sewn into her trousers to enforce the message that she hung to the left. Under the suits would be a high neck buttoned shirt and college tie. She had short black hair, which would either be gelled into place or would have a military crew cut. Outside of class she was also considered a recluse and nothing was known about her private life, or even where she lived. There were plenty of rumors about her S&M fetish, but these were just rumors made up by students who had frequented such places, consumed way too much Jack D, and believed they had seen someone of the same height and build dressed in dominatrix leather spanking or whipping one of their friends.

Professor Laird had picked up on Miranda's business talent soon after she arrived. Miranda had been one of only a few students since she had been teaching at Harvard who actually understood the message and techniques she was giving. At first she had looked on to see how Miranda would cope, but the more she saw of her the more she started to take her under her wing and help to develop and hone the talent.

Miranda thought back to how her relationship with Professor Laird had developed, and wondered what had become of her since she had left Harvard under a cloud of suspicion over the suicide of one of her pupils at the end of Miranda's third year.

It had been the first term of the second semester when things had developed between the two of them. A Friday afternoon they were ensconced in Professor Laird's office. They had been digging deep in to a particular business scenario relating to a Goldman Sachs investment. Time had passed and before they realized it the office clock in the office chimed 6 pm. Wanting to carry on the investigation and analysis, Miranda had suggested they get dinner. Professor Laird had agreed and they had headed in Miranda's car to a quiet Italian restaurant near her apartment. Miranda had explained that her ambition was to get into the food business, mainly due to the 100% mark ups and operating income potential as opposed to any particular desire to be recognized as a cuisine guru.

"Professor, when you consider the McDonalds business model it is simplistically brilliant. It has combined standardization with a perceived need for their product. Basically, they are minimizing their costs by the standardization of their stores and menus they offer. There is none of the changing of ingredients on a daily or weekly basis as most other restaurants have to offer. The potential to keep their costs down are being maximized, and they are providing a product that will be consumed in a matter of minutes, as opposed to the challenge of a typical restaurant where your revenue stream is driven by the time and speed you can effectively get a table of guests though a three or four course meal."

Professor Laird was watching Miranda with interest as Miranda continued.

"At the same time the need is generated as kids are the best weapon to get adults to part with cash. Brainwashing kids into a need, generates an emotional guilt in parents. This need then transitions from the kid to the adults as it subconsciously becomes not a luxury of eating out to a part of daily life. *Why bother to prepare dinner at home when I cannot only buy a cheap meal out, but can also do so without even getting out of my car?* This then becomes a lifestyle change. Again, the menu has changed little since it was started. The basis is around fried food and a taste that subconsciously appeals to many people. The more restaurants that are opened the broader the market becomes, and then the potential to export the brand can create limitless opportunities. The brand can be taken to many other places. Imagine the Government subcontracting its catering services or even allowing, for a fee, the restaurant chain to set up on armed service bases. Consider there could be 10,000 young service personnel who would be willing to spend hard-earned money in there as opposed to cooking for themselves. The Government would be getting money from the restaurants in the fees and taxes paid by the service personnel and the restaurant themselves. Take the same model into schools, hospitals, cinemas and sports stadia for example. Captive audiences with a vast majority of them becoming subconsciously addicted to their products…"

Miranda continued on with her analysis and assessment and outlined her idea for a food business venture. Professor Laird joined in with basically what was a business plan in the making giving pointers and suggestions. The conversation continued through the starter and main course. Both were drinking Merlot and by the time the double espresso's arrived there were three dead bottles of wine.

Both of them seemed to have reached a state of relaxed excitement by the thought of pushing this business venture forwards. The adrenaline from the confidence of success of how this business opportunity would take off, combined with the effects of the Merlot seemed to pass through the barrier of teacher and student. Before Professor Laird could say anything Miranda had sent the waiter away with the bill, paid in cash with a generous tip. The suggestion from Miranda that they continue at her apartment around the corner was met with agreement from Professor Laird, who had some time ago realized she was going to have to get a taxi home at some point, so why not from Miranda's apartment, besides which she thought Miranda was very cute as well as intelligent.

They left the restaurant arm in arm, partly to help each other walk in a straight line and partly because Professor Laird wanted to be in physical contact with Miranda. To other people walking down the street past the shops and restaurants they just looked like a couple enjoying a Friday night out in Boston.

Arriving at the apartment complex, Miranda extracted a set of keys from her purse and let them into the foyer. They walked over to the elevators and both were giggling at a shared joke as they waited for the elevator to arrive. They entered the empty elevator and headed to the top floor and Miranda's penthouse apartment. As they approached the apartment front door Miranda stumbled and Professor Laird caught her arm to stop her from falling. As Miranda steadied herself she found herself face-to-face, lips inches apart. Both felt a magnetism from within and their mouths came together that developed into a long and passionate kiss. Professor Laird pulled Miranda closer to her and soon their tongues were exploring the other's mouths. Both were very aroused but Miranda briefly pulled away to get the key in the lock so they could explore this situation in privacy.

As they entered the apartment they came back together and the kissing started again. This time their hands started to explore each other's curves. Miranda felt Professor Laird's hands caressing her buttocks and then gently squeezing them. Miranda had her arms over Professor Laird's shoulders and was caressing her neck and the back of her head. Professor Laird removed her left hand off Miranda's buttock and slowly and sensually moved it up her side until she came to the large mound of Miranda's right breast. Professor Laird caressed Miranda with her hand moving from the middle of her back to the base of her breast, almost as if she was teasing Miranda. Then with great sensitivity she moved her hand upwards and followed the curvature of Miranda's breast until she came across the erect nipple that was sticking proud under Miranda's blouse. Her hand stopped there and she felt the erect nipple with her thumb and forefinger. Initially gently rubbing it and then lightly squeezing it and then intermingling this with harder tweaking. Miranda started to moan with pleasure and soon Professor Laird removed her right hand to repeat the process on Miranda's left breast. Miranda could feel herself getting very wet between her legs and moved her right hand down over Professor Laird's back and caressed her buttock before moving her hand around the front and then starting to stroke between her legs. Miranda's moans were soon joined by those of Professor Laird. Miranda's stroking became more forceful and deeper, and with each movement felt her fingers penetrating slightly further into Professor Laird's vagina through her trousers.

Professor Laird was gently thrusting her vagina against Miranda's stroking fingers, yet at the same time she started to unbutton Miranda's blouse. With the final button undone, Miranda was temporarily forced to remove her hand from the very wet patch that had developed on Professor Laird's trousers, to allow her to take her arm out of the sleeve of her blouse. With her blouse off, Miranda felt the gently movement of Professor Laird's tongue running from the top of her neck to between her breasts. This continued until Professor Laird pulled her mouth away and gently kissed Miranda's right nipple before covering her breast with her mouth and licking her erect nipple with her tongue. Miranda quivered slightly. She had orgasmed and could feel her juices running down the inside of her left thigh.

Miranda undid the buckle on Professor Laird's trousers and soon the zipper was down and her trousers fell to the floor. Miranda didn't wait to hear them land on the floor. Her hand was immediately exploring inside Professor Laird's panties. What Miranda felt was smooth, hairless skin and wetness. Finding the top of Professor Laird's vagina she gently pushed her first two fingers directly down and traced the outside of her vagina lips. As her fingers approached the bottom of her vagina she curved her fingers and gently inserted them inside her vagina. The juices were warm and sticky and Professor Laird let out a pleasured moan. Miranda then gently pulled her fingers out before pushing them back in again. She repeated the motion again and again. Professor Laird joined in by thrusting her pelvis forwards and backwards in an opposite movement that meant when Miranda's fingers were entering her vagina they were going deeper and deeper. A few minutes later Professor Laird let out a small scream and Miranda felt even more juice flowing over her fingers.

She withdrew her fingers and with the briefest of pauses guided Professor Laird to her bedroom so they could undress each other and explore all their perversions.

Miranda lay on the bed her legs apart and Professor Laird let her tongue run around the outside of her vagina. The caressing of her tongue made Miranda tense up and then Professor Laird inserted her tongue and started licking inside. She found her clitoris with her tongue and then started to suck at it. At the same time with the juices running over her anus Professor Laird inserted her middle finger on her left hand into Miranda's anus. Again, Miranda could feel herself building up for an orgasm. Professor Laird could sense this and withdrew both her tongue and finger. She lay on the bed besides Miranda and they kissed passionately again, and then it was Miranda's turn to explore Professor Laird's vagina. She licked around the outside before inserting her tongue and then let her tongue withdraw before licking her anus and then pushing

110

it inside.

Miranda climbed over Professor Laird until they were in the sixty-nine position and then they were both eating each other out and inserting fingers up each other's anuses.

The sex went on for the best part of an hour, as each one could feel the sensation of orgasms coming before the other one stopped. It was a sense of teasing, yet at the same time both were able to express themselves in different ways.

Miranda could feel the tension leaving her body and Professor Laird again brought her to the point of orgasm, only this time the teasing stopped and she was heading beyond the point of control. She could sense that the sex was coming to its climax and redoubled her energies to ensure Professor Laird came at the same time. In a final intense moment of sexual pleasuring they both came to the boil and orgasmed within seconds of each other.

They lay in the same position for twenty seconds whilst they allowed the full impact of the orgasms to surge through their bodies before Professor Laird rolled off Miranda and lay by her side. The last recollection Miranda had before waking up was the warm breath of Professor Laird on the back of her neck.

When Miranda woke up the following morning, Professor Laird had gone, but wafting from the kitchen was the smell of fresh brewed coffee. Naked and feeling remarkably relaxed and comfortable Miranda walked to the kitchen and poured herself a cup. By the percolator was a handwritten note from Professor Laird, saying if she needed any help to call her day or night with a number Miranda guessed must have been her home one. With a smile on her face she took her coffee back to the bedroom and headed for the en-suite to wash away the external signs of the passion from the previous night.

During the four years that Miranda was at Harvard her relationship with Marlene grew more and more strained. Miranda was happy to be independent, as long as you called having a paid housekeeper as being independent.

She spent less time back in New York and had, for the time, being decided that her home was Cambridge, Massachusetts. Marlene had provided Miranda an allowance that allowed for her to indulge in pretty much what she wanted and it had been squandered on three major outgoings: clothes, jewelry and drugs.

As Miranda waited for the ceremonies to start she thought that her life was finally getting back on track and, with the help of the coke, had pretty much been able to bury the ugly experiences from her past. If she was being honest, Miranda knew she was kidding herself, but she kind of convinced herself if she ignored her past it hadn't happened. With the exception of Marlene there were only a handful of lawyers who really knew who she was. Everyone at Harvard knew her as the name on the certificate from her high school. She had no plans ever to return to the shit hole where she had come from and as for Brooklyn... well, it would come in handy one day for telling everyone about her rags to riches story...

Another couple of developments were also just around the corner and Miranda was looking forward to her inheritance that had been promised on graduation with the right grades. Marlene had not been more elaborate, but Miranda was pretty sure she would be set up for life with the inheritance. Once the ceremony was over Miranda would be heading over to the office of one of the lawyers Marlene used and in there, when she showed the head partner of the firm her certificate, he would provide her with the letter and associated documents for her inheritance.

With so many students passing out the ceremony took most of the day. Miranda's pass out was due around 12.30 pm and when her turn came she sauntered towards the stage to a polite round of applause from the seated spectators. After the number of students that had already been introduced the fact there was any applause at all surprised Miranda, but she didn't care. The fact Marlene had not even managed to make it irked Miranda, but again, she thought about what was coming next. The fact Marlene was not there had also given Miranda some concerning thoughts. Was she not there for a reason? Maybe Marlene knew the inheritance would not be seen as enough and so she had stayed away. What was not enough? That was a thought Miranda had had for some time. She had never fully found out how much Stan had been worth. What Marlene had done with his assets had been kept away from her and the few times she had asked some questions the lawyers had clamped up tighter than a duck's ass.

She had the impression he must have been very rich to have afforded the private jet that Miranda had been on a couple of times, but since his death the plane had either been sold or exclusively used by Marlene. The apartment they had moved into was the only visible signs of the wealth, even the Rolls-Royce had disappeared. Miranda had tried to do some research on Stan's old companies, but they seemed to have been sold off to various private companies for seemingly a lot less than the market value. Miranda was not sure if this was because Marlene wanted her hands on the cash for something else, or if she was overawed with the numbers being offered, considering where she had come from. Either way, it was a concern that Miranda could be disappointed.

By 12.50 pm Miranda's section was completed and, after the compulsory Class Of '81 photographs had been taken and the final '… stay in touch…' conversations had been done, Miranda got into her car after first removing her cap and gown which she threw on the back seat and headed over to the lawyer's office.

"Good afternoon, Ma'am" the receptionish said as Miranda walked in.

"Good afternoon, I have an appointment with Mr. Watson."

"Yes Ma'am, he's expecting you. Could you take a seat for a moment whilst I let him know you're here? Would you care for a drink? Tea, coffee, maybe something a little stronger?"

"Coffee would be fine."

"OK, I'll be back shortly."

With that the receptionist stood up from her desk and headed down the corridor behind her desk and stopped at the end and knocked twice on the door. She entered Mr. Watson's office and once he put down the phone notified him Miranda was there to see him. Mr. Watson asked her to bring Miranda along, and soon she was back and, with a smile, asked Miranda to follow her.

The receptionist stood aside as she opened the door and announced Miranda as she entered the office. Mr. Watson stood up and strode over towards the door to formally shake Miranda's hand and guided her to a set of relaxed chairs with matching table for more relaxed meetings.

Miranda took in the details of the office. It was large, almost split into three separate areas. There was the work desk Mr. Watson had come from, which was pretty much free from clutter. The center of the desk was taken up with a computer monitor. There were the usual framed photographs of the family, taken on some holiday trip, and separate ones of the kids doing some sporting activity. The other side of the desk was taken up by three different telephones, each a different color. Miranda was sure there was a meaning for each color. Behind the desk was the company name and logo embossed on a clear glass sheet some 6' wide by 3' tall. Either side of that were the compulsory certificates showing the company registration documents and also the accreditations associated to Mr. Watson. Clearly he had either spent a lot of time studying in his spare time, or had not started practicing before he had hit 30... or, wondered Miranda, maybe some of the certificates were just for show and unreal. She made a mental note to check our Mr. Watson and see how genuine he was, or maybe he was just milking his clients, including Marlene...

A separate part of the office had a formal board room with a George Nakashima walnut trestle table. The table was surrounded by sixteen antique Victorian boardroom chairs with green leather bases and backs.

The final section of the office was taken up with a four seater Aspen sofa and three Aspen chairs by Terence Conran, surrounding a glass topped coffee table.

Miranda may not have appreciated all the designer names, but was sure this office alone had cost more than a small fortune to kit out.

"Please sit down, Miranda. How was the graduation ceremony?"

"Thank you Mr. Watson. It was OK, if a little tedious. Waiting around for a timeslot to get the certificate is not really exciting."

"Yes quite." Mr. Watson made a quick evaluation of Miranda.

Sitting in front of him was a young lady who clearly was used to getting her way. The way she held her head, almost looking down her nose at him, stated she was not interested in small talk and was here for one purpose and one purpose alone. Mr. Watson had never met her mother. The few phone calls had been concise and to the point and he could see where Miranda had picked up the trait of being direct and to the point. In his eyes she was attractive, but definitely not beautiful. Her Adam's apple protruded and he noticed her hands were not small and delicate as he would have expected of someone with her frame and size and she was definitely not proportioned well when admiring her breasts. They seemed to be a few sizes too big for the frame that carried them. She was dressed casually in tight-fitting jeans and a loose cotton sweater, but it was the shoes that he noticed. Six inch heels that strongly suggested here was someone who was aware of their lack of height and wanted to make up for it with accessorizing her footwear.

Mr. Watson was letting his mind wander and was picturing Miranda standing in front of him naked except the shoes... He had a thing for high heels... He could show this feisty spoilt bitch a lesson or two however was snapped out of his lustful thoughts by his secretary knocking on the door bringing the coffee.

After his secretary left the office he said, "So Miranda, I guess you are here to collect your inheritance."

"Very perceptive, Mr. Watson," Miranda said with a tight smile. "It would be helpful if we can complete this transaction at the earliest opportunity as I have some other meetings I have to go to."

Mr. Watson hid his feelings well and smiled.

"Absolutely, Miranda, I will just go and get the documents, but if I could take a copy of your certificate. I hope you understand I will need to take a photocopy for the records for auditing purposes."

"As you like, Mr. Watson," she said reaching into her shoulder bag and pulling out the scroll she had just been handed.

"I won't keep you a few moments," and with that he left the office to get his secretary to make the copy whilst he went to his safe in the strong room to get the inheritance details.

Miranda took the opportunity when he left the room to take a closer look at the room, furniture and specifically the certificates. She made some brief notes of a number of Mr. Watson's certificates and was sitting back on the sofa when he walked back into the office after five minutes.

He walked back in holding a number of documents: Miranda's original certificate which he gave back to her, the photocopy of the certificate which he showed to her and a large manila envelope that was anything but well padded.

He ripped the seal off the envelope and initially pulled out a sheet of papers, which turned out to be the legal documents concerning the inheritance. He passed the two copies over to Miranda so she could read them and see they were identical in all aspects. He explained that one signed copy was for her and the other signed copy for him... for the records for auditing purposes.

Mr. Watson then went back into the envelope and

pulled out a letter, which was from Marlene and he started to read it aloud.

"Miranda, as you are hearing this letter being read, it means that you have successfully got the grades and have now passed out of Harvard. Congratulations and I never doubted you would. You have always had a determination and resilience to succeed no matter what the odds. You, like I am, should be very proud of what you have achieved, especially considering the challenges before we moved to Brooklyn."

Mr. Watson looked up at this point and saw no change in Miranda's features. It almost was as if she was not listening, just waiting to hear the punch line and what it meant. He started to feel Miranda was more than just a selfish bitch, he got the impression in that brief glimpse that there was no emotion in this person only a drive and passion for something that no man would ever conquer. He carried on.

"It is now time for you to stand on your own two feet. You have been well cared for over the past four years at Harvard and the apartment and car are effectively in your name. Along with this I am transferring the ownership of the restaurant on 51st Street. It will be interesting to see how you develop that after your Harvard training, and if you want to get rid of the faggots I have another opportunity where I could use them."

Mr. Watson again briefly stopped reading and looked up at Miranda. Whatever private message this was, was unclear to him, however he knew what a faggot was and didn't want to know what sordid business was involved with faggots and a top end restaurant in New York.

"Finally, I am also transferring the sum of $1,000,000 to your bank account. This should be used by you as you see fit to see you through your life. When I pass away there may or may not be another inheritance. I promise you only one thing and that is I will not leave debts for you to pay off on my death. Make sure you come back to New York when you can. Love, Marlene."

With that Mr. Watson put down the letter on the coffee table and lightly pushed it across to Miranda. He looked at her and she sat staring at him. The look he gave her was very strange. As he sat there he could almost see the cogs going around in her mind. Was she happy or upset? He had no idea. She signed both copies of the legal document, and picked up the letter putting both into her shoulder bad. It was only when she spoke that a chill went down his spine.

"Well, Mr. Watson, I guess if the money has transferred our business is complete."

With that she stood up and said, "No need to show me out, I know the way."

She walked across his office, out of the door, down the corridor and out of the building without even acknowledging the receptionist

Mr. Watson sat there for a full five minutes as he pictured the almost feral look in her eyes and the unemotional way she had spoken to him. It was almost psychotic. His previous image of her bending over his board room table naked except her shoes was expunged from his mind and he was glad she had left his office and the building. He hoped beyond all hopes that he would never have to meet her again.

Miranda sat in the Porsche and stared through the window for a full five minutes. Her mind was a fury of thoughts. One million dollars was nothing, she was convinced, compared to what Marlene must have got when Stan died. How could she survive on $1,000,000? To the normal person this was more money than they could ever have imagined. To Miranda, with the lifestyle change witnessed in the past five years, it was nothing. Her apartment alone had to be worth that. It was inconceivable that she only got $1,000,000. Was this a test from Marlene? What should she do next? The restaurant in New York was not part of the business model she had been thinking about. Keep it or sell it? Maybe she should sell it so that Marlene could not get her hands on the faggots. Miranda assumed that Marlene wanted them for some type of brothel, maybe an up market escort service… with extras. Either way she was not going to let Marlene have them. As for that creep Mr. Watson. She'd seen the leery way he had started at her. She knew in his mind he had been undressing her and she was determined to get the dirt on him. Marlene had once said to her it was always a good thing to have a pet lawyer, and she was determined to make Mr. Watson her pet…

Almost without conscious thought she started the car and drove back to her apartment. As she pulled into the parking garage she had no recollection of the drive back from Mr. Watson's offices, but already building up in her mind was the basis of a plan, which was more about getting even.

She entered her apartment and slammed the door behind her. She kicked off her shoes and pulled out her special box. She laid out a line of coke and was soon snorting herself into a mellower place. Forty minutes later and with a glazed look in her eyes she sat on the sofa with a notepad and started scribbling notations and doodles that signified something relevant to her. Five hours later and with the best part of a liter and a half of Merlot inside her Miranda stretched whilst sitting and looked at a twelve page business plan. This, she decided, was how she was going to make herself a role model for women across the States, and show those fuckers that thought with their cocks who really was in charge. The combination of the coke, the wine and the adrenaline leaving her veins had a combined impact and she passed out on the sofa with a wicked smile on her face

Monday, 31 August 1981

"Good morning, Mr. Watson, I hope you had a good weekend?" his secretary asked as he walked into her office having just arrived for work.

"Yes thank you, Rochelle, and yourself?"

"Yes thank you, Mr. Watson, I visited my mom in Hartford."

"Excellent and how is she doing?"

"As well as can be expected, Mr. Watson. The home says she has early stages of Alzheimer's, but they take great care of her and we had lunch out on Saturday with the family."

Mr. Watson said with a pleasant smile, "Good, please let me know if there is anything we can do to make her more comfortable. You know, a happy employee makes a productive employee."

"Yes, Mr. Watson and I know. It's really appreciated you pulling some strings to get her into that home. We just wouldn't have been able to afford to send her there if it wasn't for your contacts. Oh, there's been a change to your calendar today. Mr. White, who you were supposed to be seeing at 4.30 pm has had to cancel as he has gone out of state for a few days for work reasons. He said he will re-arrange one he gets back."

Mr. Watson was quietly pleased. Mr. White was one of those customers who brought a regular cash flow into the business, but was also pretty high maintenance. He basically would not see any of the other partners and his visits normally lasted a couple of hours with him telling Mr. Watson how good he was and never actually asking for anything. Mr. Watson would love to have him taken care of by one of the junior partners, but knew it would never happen. He was already planning to make a call to Kirk to get in nine holes before his evening appointment. His plans were interrupted when Rochelle carried on.

"I have had a late replacement request and the lady was very insistent on seeing you late this afternoon. I tried to

120

put her off, but she would not be persuaded. She said she had some important information and needed some help."

"Really?" said Mr. Watson, "and who is this lady?"

"Well, she wouldn't give me her surname, only her Christian name. She's called Miranda."

The color drained from his face and Rochelle picked up on it immediately.

"Mr. Watson, are you OK? You look very pale, like you have just seen a ghost."

"Errrrr yes Rochelle, just a little bug I picked up over the weekend, I'll just get some water and take a seat and I'll be fine."

With that he stumbled into his office and shut the door. He sat down on the sofa and tried to calm himself. His mind was full of W's. Why did she want to see him? What was her motive? What had she uncovered about him? Who had she been talking to? The picture filling his mind was not a pretty set of thoughts. He thought he'd done a pretty good job of hiding his past. There was no way Miranda could know anything about him. He was sure he was overreacting... or was he?

The day passed pretty much as normal and by early afternoon he had fairly well regained his composure to the extent that Rochelle commented.

"You certainly look a lot better now, Mr. Watson. I can try and cancel your 4.30 pm appointment if you would prefer so you can take off early. It's not good to see a client if you are not 100%."

"Yes, you are correct, but I'm fine now, thank you. Probably a bug that has been going around the church."

Inside, his stomach turned slightly and he thought he'd better use the john to empty his bowels before Miranda arrived. He excused himself and shut the office door locking it, before heading to his personal closet.

At 4.28 pm there was a knock at Mr. Watson's office door. The door opened and Rochelle stood aside as Miranda strutted in. As she passed Rochelle she said, "Coffee black, and bring a flask. No creamer, no sugar and then I suggest you leave. Mr. Watson and I have confidential business to deal with and it will be late before we finish."

Without looking over her shoulder she strode over to the boardroom table and sat down putting her bulging shoulder bag on the table.

As she headed to the boardroom table Rochelle looked at Mr. Watson with a quizzical look. He just nodded slightly as if to say *just do as she said* and she left the office, quite upset by the brief encounter. She wondered if Mr. Watson's illness in the morning had anything to do with the visit that had just started. She was a protective person of her employer and for mainly selfish reasons took care to make sure he was not upset. He was, after all, the reason why her mom was in the highest rated retirement home in the state.

Ten minutes later she knocked on the door and, at Mr. Watson's answering, entered the room and headed to the boardroom table with the coffee pot and a fine bone china cup and saucer. The complexion on Mr. Watson's face was similar to that she had seen that morning and clearly she was right in her assessment that Miranda, whoever she was, was the cause of his unease.

"Mr. Watson, it was good of you to meet with me at such short notice," Miranda said.

Those feral eyes were staring at him and he felt like a rabbit caught in the headlights of a fast-moving vehicle.

"Miranda, it's a pleasure to meet with you again. I was wondering how I can be of assistance to you. Is there anything unclear about the inheritance?"

"No, Mr. Watson there is nothing unclear about the inheritance. There is a lot wrong with it, but that is a matter I will take up directly with my mother and is of no relevance to you. I am here to discuss other, let's say, opportunities."

The color had started to drain from his face and the cold shiver down his spine came back as it had the last time they met. His fears started to come back and haunt him, and he found that his hands were shaking slightly, so he put them under his legs hoping that it would not be visible to Miranda.

"Well, I'm glad you came to me to discuss your opportunities," he said trying to show an external calm.

"I am not so sure you will be happy to hear what I have to say to you, but there might be a solution."

Mr. Watson's thoughts had gone into meltdown. How much did she know about him and why? What had he done to her to warrant such investigation? He didn't know but was sure he was going to find out.

The knock at the door allowed him the briefest of respites as Rochelle brought in the coffee. He could see by the look on her face that he was in fact showing the signs of stress as he had done in her office first thing that morning. *Shit*, he thought, *I'm in real shit and I'm showing it…*

After Rochelle left, she did as Miranda had said. She thought about staying behind, but she didn't want to get any more upset by the woman. A woman who would have been around the same age as her daughter. She could never imagine a lady of that age emitting such an aura of… She thought for a few seconds and tried to formulate what it was that Miranda was emitting. Was it anger? Was it rage? Was it hatred? Was it power? The only thing she could associate it to was evil. It was almost as if the devil had walked in the room. She silently crossed herself and rapidly got her coat and purse and, as quickly as she could, left the building.

"I really don't know what you mean, Miranda. I know nothing about you, and, besides some brief dealings with your mother, know nothing about your or her business activities."

"And that is how it will stay Mr. Watson, or should I call you Mr. Whiting. I assure you, you will only know what I want you to know and do what I want you to do."

The revelation that she knew who he actually was came as a bolt of lightning and his worst fears came boiling back to the surface. How the hell had she found out who he was?

"I suggest, Mr. Whiting, that you go and use the bathroom before you shit yourself in front of me. You look like shit and you need to be very attentive to what I am going to tell you."

Mr. Whiting almost ran across his office to his closet and barely made it in and closed the door before he threw up. He had to pull his pants down at the same time before the diarrhea arrived. His closet smelt ugly and he sat there shaking for five minutes before he stood up. He flushed the john immediately without looking at the mixed contents of vomit and shit, and it took another two flushes to finally get rid of the remnants before he washed his hands and face. His color was now a darkish grey and the bags under his eyes were very pronounced. He put his jacket back on to hide the sweat stains that has appeared in multiple places on his shirt and under his arms and walked back to where Miranda was sitting.

"Ah, Mr. Whiting, you are looking so much better." It was almost as if Miranda had changed personality. The feral look was gone and replaced with a genuine looking smile as if interested in his wellbeing. Mr. Whiting was convinced now she was psychotic. The personality change was dramatic and instantaneous. When she spoke again her eyes were more giving a look of danger and warning than of pure evil.

"So, shall we go through the elements of your background you have tried to hide so well, or do you want to fill me in so I can remind you of your past? Well, let's put it like this. I know the picture, so I will be able to very quickly understand if you are just a lying piece of lowlife, or if you are actually smart enough to know how to survive. The choice is yours. Oh, and by the way, I have no plans for this evening, unlike you who has a dinner appointment with your slut of a receptionist at the Langham Hotel. And that room you have reserved will give you a great view of the city whilst you are, or more likely she is, screwing your brains out. I am sure your wife would be very interested in your planned business trip."

Mr. Whiting sat very still. Stunned by how much information she knew about his plans, yet knowing nothing about this person the other side of the table. Two things were for certain, his lustful evening had just turned into a washout and he was pretty sure by the time this conversation was over he would be sure he knew who was going to be pulling his strings from now on...

Miranda left Mr. Whiting's office at 8.15 pm and headed back to her apartment. She smiled to herself at her first success. Mr. Whiting was now a quivering wreck, putty in her hands. He had blabbed for a good hour about all his misdemeanors and her dossier on him was now very complete. She had made a mental note to complete the evidence file on him and locked away the information she had already got in her filing cabinet in her study at the apartment. She was sure he would not be causing any issues.

As well as completing the blackmail folder she had given him the task of setting up a number of daughter companies with untraceable links to a parent company. The parent company name she had chosen for herself was Matriarg Vennote and was to be registered in a tax haven to be determined by Mr. Watson.

In one session she had achieved two major steps forward. Firstly, she had identified and hooked her pet lawyer and secondly, she had started the process of creating, what she believed, was going to be the most powerful business in North America. Extremely satisfied with herself she headed over to the Langham Hotel to enjoy an expensive meal and that exclusive room that Mr. Whiting was not going to be taking advantage of, yet was going to pay for. She, after all, only had $1,000,000 in the bank and that just wasn't enough.

Thursday, 10 September 1981

"Miranda."

"Yes."

"It's Mr. Watson speaking."

"I take it that you are calling me from a place where others can hear you."

"Unfortunately yes, I just wanted to let you know that the companies are established, and I'll call you as soon as I get back to my office."

"Thank you, Mr. Watson. I look forward to your call."

With that the line went dead and Mr. Whiting put down the receiver. He was relieved. He had worked hard to create the environment Miranda had specified. He had made some minor modifications to her request but was happy with the result. He was confident it would meet her needs. He had briefly considered sending her a bill for his services. The thought passed quickly and decided he needed to find a way to clear this through his company, or just write it off as hours he was not going to be paid for. The cost of setting up the new companies would be written off as miscellaneous expenses. If Miranda wanted the activity hidden he was going to comply.

Miranda sat back in her apartment and contemplated the call. She was now in business. Next step was to establish bank accounts once she had the company details and these would be set up with cash transfers. She called her bank to have cash prepared for her to collect when she needed it and decided that $50,000 in each of three different bank accounts would be a suitable starting point. The cash wouldn't gain interest, however she needed to have assets available at any time an opportunity arose. Having set the wheels in motion she focused on the other calls she needed to make.

Monday, 4 January 1982

Miranda walked into the reception and went up to the reception desk. It was manned by two middle-aged ladies dressed in identical business suits with the logo of the financial advisors institution emblazoned on the breast pocket.

"Good morning, how can I help you?" the receptionist asked Miranda politely.

"Good morning, I have an appointment with Mrs. Chippendale."

"Thank you, can I have your name please?"

With the registration details completed, Miranda was guided to a seating area in the lobby where she waited.

Ten minutes later Mrs. Chippendale walked into the reception and across to Miranda. Shaking hands she said, "Welcome, Miranda, it's great to see you and we are very excited for you to be joining us. We have a formal induction program for you. I will explain it to you when we are in my office."

With that they walked to the bank of elevators behind the reception area and headed to the fifth floor.

The elevator doors opened into a large open plan office surrounded on three walls by glass fronted and door offices. The offices with outside window views were clearly allocated to the more senior people and each had a name plaque and function attached to the outside. Mrs. Chippendale led Miranda to a conference room, without an outside window. She offered her coffee and then sat at a laptop that was open and connected to an overhead projector.

"OK, Miranda. Like I said, welcome. We will go through your induction timing and most of today will be given over to HR activities."

Miranda sat up straight and took in the information. First she was given her badge come clocking in card. She was told about her working hours, breaks and lunch. She was given the information about how to book a holiday, what to do if she was ill. The induction was thorough if, as Miranda found it, boring. It was, after all, just a necessary evil as part of the bigger picture. The pay check would help, but what was more important was the information she would gain from the brokers and analysts she would be working alongside, and maybe the opportunity to make some additional monies…

Mid-afternoon and the induction programme was into the section in the manual of sexual harassment. Miranda's interest was piqued at this topic.

"So we have a zero tolerance policy to any form of sexual harassment. We are very proud of the fact we have no reported cased of sexual harassment and we do not expect this to change. It is one of our key performance indicators. Sexual harassment comes into a number of different categories from the physical, to the verbal to the psychological. Each employee is inducted – as you are currently being – in the policy and on a six monthly basis are tested for their understanding of the policy. I am sure you will never experience such a situation however if you do, this is how you report the harassment."

Mrs. Campolong then detailed the associated process that Miranda memorized instantaneously. Smiling internally she thought this would come in useful in the future. She also thought, as she looked at Mrs. Campolong, it was highly unlikely she would ever be subject to sexual harassment. She looked like a sumo wrestler, who was actually a frustrated wannabe teacher. Definitely one that would be able to recite the procedure down to the page and subsection in the manual.

By the time the HR team members had been through the conference room, it was 5 pm and Miranda had a pretty good understanding of the way this business was supposed to run. She had already picked up some areas that could be exploited and this knowledge was tucked away for a later date. At 5.10 pm Mrs. Chippendale came back in the room.

"OK, Miranda, that's enough for Day One. So how was

it for you?"

"Very helpful, Mrs. Chippendale. The training information is very thorough and insightful. Everyone has been very helpful and supportive. Thank you."

Miranda thought it better to come across as the conforming, ass kissing newbie…

"Thank you, Miranda. So see you tomorrow at 9am and I'll take you to your manager for the next step of your induction."

With that Miranda got up and with Mrs. Chippendale left the conference room and headed to the elevators. She exited the elevator at the ground level making sure on the way to clock out and headed to the car park and the drive back to her apartment, and to carry on with her studies. She was planning to get her Master of Business Administration by the end of the year. OK, so it was another qualification, but there was also a bonus payment of $20,000 associated with getting it, which was significantly more important.

Tuesday, 17 May 1983

Miranda had been the model employee. The after work study had taken up most of her spare time, however in mid-December she had walked off with her MBA and had very carefully secured her bonus payment. She had worked long hours and got through her three month trial period appraisal with a glowing report and was on the fast track to management and success.

During this time she had come into regular contact with the Divisional President. He was a guy in his early sixties who was widely connected in Boston social circles and from time to time Miranda had been asked to accompany him on corporate events and speaking appointments. He was a sharp businessman and Miranda had picked up a lot of tricks and techniques from him in the way he dealt with people, situations and the subject matter. He was also the ideal candidate for the next step of her grand plan.

"Miranda, don't forget the engagement this evening, we need to be there at 6 pm."

"Yes Mr. Gregory, no problems. I'll meet you in the foyer."

"Thank you Miranda, this one is kind of important to me. I'm collecting an industry award for some reason, but I have a side meeting with the senator. He wants to talk to me about running for office in his place, as he's decided not to go for re-election next January when the Senate election is due. I am going to need to tap into his election funds."

"Wow that's very exciting, Mr. Gregory. I am sure you will make a great senator."

"That's very kind, Miranda. I know you are not so interested in politics, but you never know if I get in you might want to change your mind."

"Thank you, Mr. Gregory. I will give it a lot of thought when that happens."

With that Miranda left Mr. Gregory's office and headed back to her cubicle. Tonight would be the perfect time to put her plan into effect. She needed to ensure she was dressed correctly for the occasion and decided that it was worth leaving the office at lunchtime to get properly prepared. Once back at her desk she called one of her contacts at the Boston Globe.

"Fanny, I have a tip for you."

"What's that Miranda?"

"Just trust me on this one you need to be at the Hilton tonight at 6.30 pm. Mr. Gregory has a meeting with the senator and I think there will be an opportunity to get some interesting information about Mr. Gregory's political aspirations."

"OK, this sounds like a good scoop. Are you going to be there?"

"For sure."

"OK, will see you then."

"Yes, but don't acknowledge that you know me as this is just for you. I need to remain anonymous."

"For sure, Miranda, do you want the cash in the same account?"

"Yeah, but don't transfer for two weeks. I don't want to create any kind of link in case anyone does any digging."

"Sure no worries, will take care of it."

With that Miranda hung up the phone and headed to the parking lot to head back to her apartment via the hairdressers. She thought an afternoon of pampering was in order to be at her best for Mr. Gregory.

At 5.45 pm Miranda arrived in the Hilton foyer. She had been greeted by the host receptionists and had been furnished with the compulsory glass of Dom Pérignon Champaign. Miranda stood there quietly studying the guests who were arriving. The gentlemen were dressed in evening attire and the ladies in a variety of outfits from cocktail dresses to ballroom gowns. There had been a real flurry of activity when the senator had arrived with his entourage and his trophy wife, who was probably only three or four years older than Miranda, and less than half the age of the senator. She had visions of her mother on

131

the arm of Stan. At 5.58 pm Mr. Gregory arrived in formal evening wear and walked straight over to Miranda.

"Miranda, good evening. You look stunning."

"Well thank you, Mr. Gregory. Like you said, this is an important event, so I had to make a big effort to not let you down."

"Most kind and greatly appreciated." The way Mr. Gregory's eyes took in Miranda told her that her plan was on track for success. He seemed to be talking to her chest and struggled to drag his eyes away. Miranda took the opportunity to shift her posture to push her breasts further forwards and she could almost see Mr. Gregory's eyes light up. She could smell the Jack D on his breath as he spoke and she was sure he had consumed a significant amount before he had left for the event. He had a reputation of enjoying a drink and this was going to help play into her plan. Miranda had checked the hotel out prior to the function and had had established the best place for her plan to be successful. It was important that Mr. Gregory had his meeting with the senator and then, after what she believed would be a successful meeting, and Mr. Gregory lolling in his success and planning for his next and first political step, she would strike. Miranda had also been pleased that Mr. Gregory had not brought his wife along as that would have just complicated matters. For the time being it was important to just ensure Mr. Gregory had his glass refilled at every opportunity

In the background Miranda spotted that Fanny had walked into the lobby carrying a case with her equipment and had gone over to the event receptin desk asking where she could set up to do interviews and photo shoots. She had been given a PRESS badge and walked into the ballroom that was being converted for the evening to host the dinner and function.

Miranda turned her focus back on to Mr. Gregory who was clearly more interested in her assets at this moment. She interrupted his leaching.

"So, Mr. Gregory, when is your meeting with the

senator?"

"Yes the meeting," Mr. Gregory said, reluctantly changing his focus trying not to make it too obvious of his interests in Miranda's breasts. "I will meet him at 7.15 pm in a suite that has been reserved for his meetings on the eighth floor. I also have a suite booked on the tenth floor, maybe after my meeting you would join me there to go over the details of the meeting. Unfortunately, the meeting with the senator is purely a one on one."

"Absolutely, I understand and would be happy to discuss the meeting afterwards."

Miranda had kept a straight face, but could not believe her luck. Things were playing into her hands perfectly she just needed to let Fanny know the arrangements.

With that they walked into the ballroom and every few feet Mr. Gregory was stopped, or stopped to say hello to some personality or other. Miranda dutifully followed him around and made a mental note of the people he was associating with; a clear benefit of a photographic memory. By the end of the night she would have the names and highlights of the meetings with the people Mr. Gregory met with and would soon have them archived in order of potential opportunity to exploit in the future.

At 7.12 pm Mr. Gregory excused himself from Miranda and headed to the bank of elevators. He soon disappeared from sight and Miranda was approached by a guy slightly older than her, who clearly was taken in by her physical attributes. She found out he was the son of the owner of one of the well-known private banks and immediately she plugged him as the typical young spoilt kid that thought with his cock and almost certainly the brain matter possessed by his father had bypassed his generation. She was sure he was used to getting conquests by using the family name as part of his chat up routine, and so he tried on Miranda. *Fucking idiot* Miranda thought, but decided he was worth knowing as you never knew when you might need to get back a favor from a rich banker's son with no brains.

Thirty minutes later Miranda spotted Mr. Gregory entering back into the ballroom. He seemed to be in a good mood and Miranda judged the meeting had gone well with the senator and that he had got the keys to the election fund kitty. He strode over to Miranda and whispered in her ear.

"Excellent meeting, will tell you about it later. Just need to get through dinner and the speeches."

He grabbed a glass of Champagne from a tray being held by a drinks waiter wearing white gloves who was walking by and suggested to Miranda they headed to their table.

Miranda was not hungry but forced herself to eat some of each of the courses placed in front of her. The adrenaline was kicking in as the moment approached. She excused herself as she saw Fanny heading to the ladies' restroom and followed her. She caught up with her as she opened the restroom door.

"Hey Miranda, how are you making out with Mr. Gregory? He's up for a big award tonight."

"Yeah, he told me earlier."

Fanny looked around the restroom and saw all the cubicles were empty and she and Miranda were the only ones in there before continuing.

"So, what news of our future, Senator?"

"So far all I have is his meeting went well with him. He intimated that the purpose of the meeting was to ensure he would get the keys to the money chest to support his campaign. I can only guess until I meet him later in his suite that he was successful."

"Did I hear you correctly???"

"Yep."

"So, where and what time?"

His suite is on the tenth floor, room number 1001. I am sure you can get in there and set up your recording equipment in plenty of time. Give me twenty minutes from when we leave before making an entry and make sure your camera is ready..."

With that Miranda headed to the restroom door, whilst Fanny headed to a cubicle.

Miranda made it back to the table just as the host for the evening called everyone to quiet and opened the floor to the first speaker. The speakers were all senior figures in Boston society and clearly were trying to outscore themselves ass kissing the senator. An hour later, speeches completed and the meal remnants having been cleared away, the host stood back up to announce the awards were just about to start.

Mr. Gregory turned to Miranda and slurring his words slightly asked her, "So, how do I look?"

"You look good, Mr. Gregory and congratulations in advance."

"Thank you Miranda. Could I ask a favor?"

"Yes, Mr. Gregory."

"Could you find a waiter and get me a Jack D and Coke?"

"Absolutely, Mr. Gregory."

Miranda spied a waiter and caught his attention. He discreetly came over and Miranda gave him the order, ordering herself a sparkling water at the same time. As he walked away Mr. Gregory was called to the stage. To generous round of applause he walked to the stage and started on a speech before he was to be presented his award.

As he was talking the drinks arrived. Miranda thanked the waiter and then, taking a look around the ballroom ensuring everyone's attention was on Mr. Gregory, carefully removed a small screw capped tube from her purse. Checking to ensure Mr. Gregory was not looking in her direction she poured the contents into the Jack D and Coke. *Sweet dreams* she thought as the Flunitrazepam, or as it was better known Rohypnol, was the 100% guarantee her plan was going to work.

Ten minutes later Miranda saw Fanny standing by the entrance to the ballroom, camera in hand taking photographs of the speech and presentation ceremony.

Five minutes later Mr. Gregory came back to the table with his certificate plaque and picked up his drink and drank a good two fingers worth before Miranda said, "That was an excellent speech, Mr. Gregory. Very inspirational."

"Thank you, Miranda. I thought it went well. Let's give the formal dinner another ten to fifteen minutes and we can go to my suite so I can tell you about my meeting with the senator."

He gently placed his hand on Miranda's exposed thigh and she just smiled back. In her mind his mannerisms were exactly what she thought of all men, they only had one-track minds. They couldn't think beyond the next time they were going to have sex; they really were just so simplistic and primitive animals. Miranda was convinced the only reason they were seen as the dominant species was because of them being naturally physically stronger than women, but she was going to challenge that dynamic once and for all.

Ten minutes was as long as Mr. Gregory could wait and he and Miranda excused themselves and headed to the bank of elevators. The doors opened on the tenth floor and, turning right out of the lift, they walked to the end of the corridor where the suite was located. Taking his keycard slightly hesitantly from his pocket he opened to door. It was clear to Miranda that the effects of the drug were kicking in. Shutting the door behind Miranda he offered her a drink as he poured himself another Jack D and Coke. Miranda sat on the sofa in the lounge of the suite and ensured her legs were not crossed so Mr. Watson could see more of her thighs, maybe even her panties.

The provocation was all that Mr. Gregory needed to take his state from control to a lack of control. He staggered across the room unsure why everything felt like it was happening in slow motion and it felt like an out-of-body experience. He had never had the feeling before with drink and was not sure of exactly what he was doing or going to do. He seemed to have lost control of his limbs; they seemed to be working without the signals from his

136

brain. One thing he was sure about was a throbbing feeling coming from his groin, and his body was going to do something about it.

Miranda saw him staggering over and noticed the erection that had grown in his trousers. She started talking but Mr. Watson seemed to be in a trance.

"Mr. Watson, are you all right? Mr. Watson, what are you doing? Mr. Watson, please don't touch me like that. Mr. Watson, please stop doing that. Mr. Watson, please take your hands off me," and on she went for the purpose of the recording device, wherever it was hidden.

Mr. Watson had managed to get his trousers down and was trying to force himself on Miranda. She could control what he was doing as he had lost complete control of his limbs by now. Miranda allowed him to take his shorts down so his erection was fully on display and pretty much in her face. It was then that she heard a double knock on the suite door. It was the signal from Fanny, a one minute warning.

Miranda took the opportunity to rip open her dress at the front, pull her panties around her ankles and ensure her the skirt on her dress was above her waist before the door opened and Fanny strode in camera first and clicking every few seconds.

Mr. Watson clearly had no idea what was going on and with the blood rush to create his erection he was now struggling to even stand up and seconds later fell to the floor in a crumpled heap out cold.

Fanny said, "Miranda, are you OK? What the hell happened?"

"I don't know Fanny, he asked me to come to his suite and wanted to talk about his meeting with the senator and the next thing I know he's trying to force himself on me. Hands everywhere, it's lucky you came when you did. You see what he was about to do. If you hadn't managed to get the door opened I am sure we would have been raping me now. I am so grateful. I need to get out of here. I am petrified of what he might do to me. I don't know what

137

happened to him, he just collapsed as you came in the room."

Fanny went over to Mr. Watson and felt his neck.

"There's still a pulse. I'll call 911, not that he deserves it."

"Can I go somewhere else? I don't feel safe in here."

"OK, Miranda, no worries. You lock yourself in the master bedroom and I'll sort this out. You know the police will want to be involved."

"Do we have to involve them? I am sure I will lose my job over this and I didn't do anything wrong."

"Don't you worry, I have all the evidence we need to show you are innocent. Stay in the room until I get you."

"Thank you, Fanny. I really appreciate it."

With that Miranda went to the master bedroom and Fanny heard the door lock turn before she called reception and asked them to call 911. Whilst she waited for the hotel staff to arrive she went to the cabinet where she had hidden the recording device and packed it away. It would make interesting listening later.

Ten minutes later the sirens from the paramedics EMS could be heard arriving at the hotel and the two paramedics were ushered directly into an elevator that had been held to ensure they got to the suite soon enough. Mr. Gregory was now lying in the recovery position with a blanket covering him from the chest down. It covered the fact that his pants and shorts were still around his ankles. He was breathing relatively evenly but they found his pulse was weak, and could smell the effects of the Jack D every time he breathed. Initial summation, until they pulled back the blanket, was Mr. Gregory had consumed too much alcohol. Pulling the blanket back they both looked at each other with a knowing glance. The dirty old man had consumed too much alcohol and was trying to get his rocks off, and clearly was not up to both activities. They wondered how to explain this to their superiors. The lady who had called them for their help could not explain what had been going on and she had been passing and the door hadn't been closed properly when she heard the sound of someone falling and went to investigate and found him on the floor. They didn't really believe her, but she showed them a PRESS card and one of them recognized her from her articles in the Globe, so maybe it was true. The question still sat in their minds, why would a prominent local figure be passed out in his hotel suite with his pants and shorts around his ankles nowhere near the bathroom and the john?

Without further word they went about getting a mask on Mr. Gregory's face so they could get him breathing oxygen of the portable tank and organizing the portable trolley to get him into the ambulance and down to A&E. The hotel night manager had made an appearance and Fanny explained the same story to him as to the paramedics and the second time she had it sounding much more convincing. He had, in fact, enquired after where Miranda was as he had last seen Mr. Gregory and her heading to the elevators earlier. Fanny had explained there was no sign of Miranda as she happened to be passing and hoped the night manager would not be checking the other rooms in the suite. He also seemed satisfied and, more importantly, didn't see any potential risk of bad publicity from this incident. It would not do the hotel any favors if one of its senior 'celebrities' had been taken ill at his hotel for a reason than natural causes. He quickly left to assure a few of the guests there was nothing to worry about and one of the guests had had a suspected heart attack in their room, but his fast acting and professional staff had gone to the guest's aid. *Might as well turn it into some positive publicity* he thought…

Miranda had been in the master bedroom the whole time. She had listened to the conversations with the paramedics and the hotel manager and her smile broadened as Fanny weaved the story. To the outside world this was simply going to be a simple case of Mr. Gregory being taken ill at a function, so it would be up to Mr. Gregory how he wanted to handle this. Miranda felt confident that both she and Fanny would be significantly better off in a few days' time.

The ambulance with its lights and siren blazing made it to the A&E entrance inside ten minutes. The paramedics had decided on discretion being the better part of valor and had pulled up Mr. Gregory's shorts and pants before loading him on the trolley, so at least when he was taken off the ambulance there would be no embarrassing questions to be answered. The emergency room staff went to work on Mr. Gregory immediately and decided not to take blood samples due to the fact that they knew he had been drinking. They needed to flush the alcohol out of his system first and then understand if there were any other complications. They sedated him and hooked him up to all the monitors necessary and stuck a plasma drip into his arm. Thirty minutes later, with the vital signs on the monitors stable, Mr. Gregory was wheeled into a private room. It would be another twelve hours before any of his family, friends or colleagues would be allowed to visit him; doctor's orders. It would also be another twelve hours before he would have blood taken and by which time with the plasma going through the drug that Miranda had put in his drink would be diluted to the extent that it would be hardly recognizable unless it was specifically being looked for. Unknown to Miranda it was also playing into her hands.

Miranda waited for a good thirty minutes for all sounds to stop before letting herself out of the master bedroom. She had tidied herself up and put on her coat and walked to the entrance door of the suite listening at the door for a few minutes. A couple returning to their room was the only sound she heard and she waited for them to get to their room before opening the door of the suite wearing a pair of silk gloves. She didn't want to leave any traces, just in case. Letting herself out she quietly shut the door behind her and then walked to the emergency exit. It was the staircase by the side of the elevators that guests would have to use in an emergency and the elevators were out of action. She carefully walked down the ten flights of stairs that would take her to the reception level and then went down another flight that would bring her out at the underground car park level. She wanted to avoid being seen exiting the hotel to avoid any questions. It was not an easy task in the stilettos and her feet ached by the time she was at the underground car park, but the pain was easy to put aside as she calculated in her head how much this evening was going to make her, even considering Fanny's cut. Miranda needed to avoid the valet guys and made her exit from the underground car park from a service door and headed away from the hotel to where she had parked her car a couple of blocks away. She had parked in another hotel car park and went to the reception to validate her car park ticket before getting into her Porsche and heading back to her apartment.

An hour later she called Fanny.

"Fanny, how's things?"

"Very good thanks, Miranda. I think we are both going to be happy with the results. So I didn't get the scoop on the political ambitions of Mr. Gregory, but this information should help us both significantly."

"Absolutely, Fanny. So, how about 10% of whatever we get out of Mr. Gregory?"

"Sounds good to me, Miranda. How do you want to play it?"

"First thing is can we get a copy of the audio tape and a spare set of the photographs?"

"For sure, that's easy. I'll do both myself."

"Excellent. The fewer people that know about this the better. Once you have the copies can we meet up and let's see what our next steps are. I would imagine they will be keeping Mr. Gregory in hospital over the weekend, so we have time to agree the approach."

"Sounds like a plan, give me twenty-four hours to get the copies done. I will need to do the photographs when the dark room is not being used. Normally there is no one in there over the graveyard shift, so I'll do it tomorrow

141

night. I will tell you that the evidence should be extremely interesting for Mr. Gregory to see. I would imagine his political ambitions are in the balance and that has to be worth something."

"For sure, Fanny. I checked out he has a personal fortune in the tens of millions, so I'm sure he won't miss a million or so."

With that both Fanny and Miranda started laughing and then said their goodbyes.

Wednesday, 18 May 1983

Miranda had taken the day off, having rung into HR to report she was feeling unwell and needed to see a doctor. It was simply a ruse as she needed to meet with Fanny and work out the exact next steps once she had the evidence in her hands.

Mrs. Chippendale had wished Miranda a speedy recovery and hung up. Miranda did not have long to wait before her phone rang and Fanny said, "Miranda."

"Yes, Fanny."

"When can we meet?"

"Any time. I've rung in sick so am clear for the day."

"OK, how about 1.30 pm near your place. We can do lunch at the same time."

"Perfect."

Miranda gave Fanny the name and address of a quiet bistro close to her place and then they hung up. The excitement in Fanny's voice had been clear. It seemed to suggest that the evidence she had was going to add serious value to the claim.

At 1.30 pm they met up at Trattoria Pulcinella on Huron Avenue.

"Hey Fanny."

"Hey Miranda, this looks a neat place."

"Yea it's not too well-known but the food is good and the owner has a history and is keeping his head down."

"You never cease to amaze me with your catalogue of dirt on people. I hate to think what you know about me," she said with a smile.

"Fanny, you know what I'm planning, so I'm sure you can appreciate the need to always be at least one step ahead of your enemies."

"Sure, Miranda, so let's see if your guy can find us a quiet place to see and hear what I've got in my bag."

With that they headed into the bistro and were shown to a booth at the far end of the bistro, and Antonio was given the clear warning from Miranda not to let anyone interrupt them. Fanny and Miranda waited until the Merlot had been uncorked and poured by Antonio before Fanny went into her bag and pulled out a portable tape recorded. In a socket on the side she plugged in a wire and handed Miranda an earpiece.

"OK, Miranda, this is the taping of the time you were in the room with Mr. Gregory. Put the earpiece in and I'll play the tape from where it picked up the conversation, if that's what you can call it."

Miranda put the earpiece in and then Fanny pushed down the play button. At first there was just a static hissing sound, but then voices started and whilst slightly muffled Miranda could clearly recognize her voice and what was being said

"… Mr. Gregory, are you all right?… Mr. Gregory what are you doing?... Mr. Gregory please don't touch me like that... Mr. Gregory please stop doing that... Mr. Gregory please take your hands off me... Mr. Gregory please don't rape me"

Miranda was pleased with the recording as she had hoped that it would capture her becoming more and more desperate and it was almost as though the poor recording added to the reality of the situation. The recording stopped and Miranda took out the earpiece. She looked up at Fanny and smiled.

"That came out better than expected."

"Yes, and I have the perfect alibi for the recording also. You see, I was booked into the room next door to the suite and I just happened to be testing the recording equipment and had been getting ready to go back to the event and run some interviews when it started to pick up the struggle from the room next door. As it turned out I recognized the voice as yours and left the equipment running in my room as I headed to the suite and then came in. It would also explain why I had my camera with me as it was hanging around my neck to make sure it was with me before going to do the interviews and get some shots for the Globe."

"I like it Fanny, it hangs together well."

"Oh yes I had plenty of time to think about it over the graveyard shift last night as I was pulling off these."

She went back into her briefcase and pulled out a brown envelope and passed it over the table. Miranda opened the lip and saw twelve to fifteen large prints. Making sure there was no one in the vicinity, Miranda pulled the prints out and the smile on her face widened. The photos may not have shown Miranda in her most magnificent poses, but they clearly painted a picture of Mr. Gregory trying to rape her. Mr. Gregory was clearly oblivious of his photograph being taken, as at no point did he even look like he was going to turn around. It looked like his animal instincts were focused on Miranda's exposed breasts and vagina. The added bonus as far as Miranda could tell was that the expression on her face seemed to show genuine shock.

"These are great, Fanny. You should take up fashion photography I think you'd be a natural."

"Thanks, Miranda, but there's too much corruption and male supremacy in Boston to divert my attention to female submission to male whims. These models are just soft porn fantasies for the dirty perverse bastards that run society today."

"Amen to that sister, but there's serious money to be made, and that's an even better way to get back at the bastards."

"Yeah I understand your view, Miranda and we are fighting the same battle, just from different bases. I am sure this won't be the last time we are able to strike together in this cause."

"I'm sure you're right, so what's the next step? Do you want me to go to Mr. Gregory with the evidence or are you going to approach him?"

"No, I'm going to reach out to his attorney tomorrow morning first thing and suggest he and I meet together for lunch. Mr. Gregory is still in hospital and I've heard he will be kept in until Sunday. I've got a doctor friend that works in A&E. She told me that the first twenty-four hours is been taken up with trying to get some blood in his alcohol!. She said he's not in danger of croaking it, but they are being very careful not to do anything until they can get the alcohol out. He's having no visitors until tomorrow, not even his wife. The message being put out is he may have had a minor stroke. No mention of the alcohol and absolutely no mention of you. I am pretty sure his attorney has been heavily involved in keeping the booze out of the news. He knows Mr. Gregory's intention to run for the Senate, and he was at the event and saw him pushing back the Jack D's. He's even stated that the slight mumbling in Mr. Gregory's speech was the first signs of the stroke hitting. This is being buried by everyone and it directly plays into our hands."

"Excellent, so you should have more news mid-afternoon tomorrow?"

"Yes, I will play it by ear during the meeting on when and how to get the 'fee' agreed. We go in for $1,500,000. I reckon for this we should be able to settle for around $1,000,000. I'll get it transferred into one of the Globe's 'hidden' accounts held for shall we say covering unusual expenses and into that account you gave me. That way the trace will be cold before it gets to your account, and then you can transfer $100,000 to my retirement fund account. Nice and clean. We have some real whiz kids when it comes to washing the cash."

"It's a deal."

"This tape and the photographs are your copies. I've got the originals and the camera film ready to hand over once the monies are transferred over."

"Do you think there's any risk the attorney will bring in the police?"

"Are you being serious? He and Gregory will want this burying deeper than Watergate. This is going to be easier than taking candy off a baby."

With that Miranda put the brown envelope in her bag and they ordered lunch. Miranda could not stop smiling through lunch. Fanny asked her, "So what are you finding so funny?"

"I thought $900,000 would weigh a lot more."

They both laughed and finished up the meal. Fanny paid for dinner as she was expensing it and they parted ways outside.

Thursday, 19 May 1983

"Hello, Mr Burke, this is Fanny from the Boston Globe."

"Hello, Fanny," answered Mr. Burke with a pensive tone. "It's a long time since we last spoke."

"Yes it is. So how's Mr. Gregory doing?"

"I'm not going to answer any questions relating to the personal health matters of Mr. Gregory, and especially not to a journalist. If you want to know developments you can get them from the press releases being published by his employer."

"Yes, I know but they don't really seem to be saying anything."

"And?"

"Well, I was just wondering if his employer or others might be interested to know exactly what did happen the other night."

"Fanny, what the hell are you talking about? What lowlife have you been talking to and what bullshit have they been telling you? Trust me, you publish anything and we will sue the ass of the Globe and destroy your reputation."

"Really, Mr. Burke, I thought you might be interested in a sensible conversation about how to protect Mr. Gregory, however if you want an exposé to blow up whilst he's in hospital, recovering from a non-event of a heart attack, go ahead and continue to insult me. It will make awesome reading and yet again highlight the pieces of shit you suits really are. So again, it's up to you."

"You ain't got anything." However there was a slight hesitation in his voice and Fanny picked up on it immediately.

"Your choice, Mr. Burke, however I'll be at Seventh Inn on Newbury Street at 1.30 pm. If you aren't there by 1.45 pm I'll enjoy my lunch and then take the photographs and recoding to the print room and we will be on the evening edition. I'm sure after the night time news bulletins come out on CNN and Fox, Mr. Gregory will be

148

a real celebrity for all the wrong reasons."

With that, Fanny hung up the phone, sat back at her office desk and smiled. Mr. Burke would be there, that she was sure of.

At 1.30 pm Fanny walked into the Seventh Inn and picked a discrete table, but also one where she could see the entrance door from. She had just been served an iced tea when the short, fat and balding figure of Mr. Burke waddled into the restaurant and started to look around, trying to spot Fanny. She didn't immediately move, she took a couple of slurps from her iced tea before standing up and gesturing to a pensive Mr. Burke. He ignored the hostess that was looking to direct him to a table and waddled with the most assertiveness he could muster over to Fanny.

"It's very good of you to come over and see me, Mr. Burke."

"Cut the crap, Fanny, what is all this bullshit about?"

"Mr. Burke, I suggest you sit down and, for your own interests, I really suggest you cut the volume and the attitude. If I was you, I wouldn't utter another word, besides ordering a drink - and as a recommendation, make it a very strong one – before I have finished explaining the world of shit you and your client are in. Like I said, if you want to try and take this male moral high ground bullshit, you are going to have a really, really nasty experience. Even if you were the best attorney in the US, you wouldn't have a chance, oh and that would be if you were the best."

Fanny left the insult hanging there and she could see that Mr. Burke was still in two minds.

"OK, so I will give you a flavor of what is coming."

With that she pulled out a photograph of Mr. Gregory lying on the hospital trolley in the suite at the Hilton. The photograph was taken before the paramedics had pulled Mr. Gregory's shorts and pants back up.

"Where the hell did you get this from, what kind of sick photograph is this?"

"Sit down, Mr. Burke and you will find out what kind

149

of sick photograph this is. Don't sit down and you and especially Mr. Gregory will be looking at a minimum of ten to twenty years in a federal prison with no chance of parole. I highly doubt you would want to defend your client and tarnish the reputation of your law firm. So stop fucking me around and sit down."

It was almost as if a switch had clicked on in Mr. Burke's head. He sat down at the table opposite Fanny not taking his eyes off the now turned over photograph.

"Call the waitress over and order a drink, poison of your choice, especially as you will be paying for dinner today."

Mr. Burke went to say something but decided to keep his mouth shut for the time being. He waved over to the waitress and ordered a Bloody Mary. He had the feeling that the photograph Fanny had shown him was not the only bit of bad news he was going to get in the next hour or so.

"Very good, Mr. Burke, now I hope I have your attention."

Fanny said nothing else as Mr. Burke's Bloody Mary was delivered. She politely asked the waitress not to disturb them and said she would be ordering lunch later, once her guest had left. With that, she turned her attention back to Mr. Burke. Despite the air conditioning in the restaurant Mr. Burke had started to sweat.

"So here's the real story about Mr. Gregory. He attends the awards ceremony and it happens that I have a room next to his suite. Unfortunate for him maybe, but fortunate for me and for uncovering the type of person he really is. So I am in my room preparing to go back to the ballroom to carry out some interviews with my tape recorder and camera. I have my tape recorder running in the background and am just preparing to do some test recordings to make sure everything is working, when I pick up through the wall of my hotel room the following."

At this Fanny handed over to Mr. Burke the same ear piece that Miranda had listened to the recording on. She had pulled the portable tape recorder from her bag whilst she had been talking to Mr. Burke.

Mr. Burke looked at the ear piece and had a quizzical pensive look on his face. Fanny said, "Just put it in your ear, preferably one you can hear with."

Mr. Burke grabbed the ear piece and inserted it. A second later Fanny pressed the play button and looked at Mr. Burke's facial expressions.

"… Mr. Gregory, are you all right?… Mr. Gregory what are you doing?... Mr. Gregory please don't touch me like that… Mr. Gregory please stop doing that…Mr. Gregory please take your hands off me… Mr. Gregory please don't rape me"

Fanny could tell what Mr. Burke was listening to, as she could see the color rapidly draining from his face. He could barely believe what he was listening to. He tried to convince himself that this was just a con. It could have been recorded at anytime, anywhere. At the same time he had seen the photograph Fanny had shown him of Mr. Gregory naked from the waist down on the paramedic's trolley. Surely this couldn't be true… could it?

Mr. Burke pulled the ear piece from his ear and looked at the tape recorder as if staring at it would make it evaporate. He turned his attention back to Fanny. He looked as white as a ghost and Fanny was not about to give him a break.

"So do I have your attention now, Mr. Burke?"

Mr. Burke slightly nodded. He was struck dumb by what he had just listened to and the sight of Fanny pulling out a dozen large-sized photographs from a brown envelope did nothing to help. He grabbed his Bloody Mary and downed half of it in one gulp.

Fanny carried on.

"So shall we take these one at a time, so you can see the gory details of Mr. Gregory and the animal he really is?"

Fanny was thoroughly enjoying the situation. Mr. Burke epitomized what she hated about men and was exactly where she wanted him. His initial arrogance and self-assuredness was gone. In its place was a frightened creature trying to work out how to get the shit he was being handed on a plate fixed, with damage limitation his primary thought. Reluctantly, he took the photographs off Fanny and looked at them slowly one at a time. He had already lost the color from his face from the tape recording, and Fanny noticed that he had developed shaking hands and that a vein was pushing noticeable in the side of his neck.

Mr. Burke went from photograph to photograph, clearly seeing the evidence, but finding it impossible to believe. He had known Mr. Gregory for twenty-three years. He had always been a real gentleman, so he thought, and had never had the slightest indication he was anything other than committed to his wife and kids. This was, he thought, so far out of character, that he was struggling to comprehend what he was seeing. Could these photographs be forgeries? Was the technology available to doctor photographs… would a journalist have access to the technology if it was possible? Questions were flooding through his mind. It was almost as if Fanny could read his thoughts.

"Before you come out with the crap that these are forgeries, I will now fill you in on the rest of the details."

Mr. Burke returned the photographs to the envelope and Fanny took it back.

"As mentioned, I heard the scared shouts from Mr. Gregory's suite and immediately left my room and went to bang on the door of the suite. For some reason, when Mr. Gregory had gone into the suite he had not shut the door properly. Maybe his mind was already focused on raping that young lady, who knows, but he clearly was distracted by something and my guess it would be on what he was planning. That would make it pre-meditated rape. I told you I was preparing for the interviews and had my camera around my neck. Compulsively, I reached for it as I headed for the room, knowing if there was something

152

wrong going on the only way to prove it would be photographic evidence. As you well know, Mr. Burke, in this city women don't have an equal standing with men, so it would otherwise have been the word of a young woman against that of a supposed pillar of Boston society. Clearly, again the odds would have been in favor of the pillar of the society. No doubts you would have organized the judge to be a friend of Mr. Gregory, or as minimum, someone who owed him a favor. This time, unfortunately for you, Mr. Burke, the evidence is there in black and white... well, actually color and documented on the tape. You can try and think these are forgeries. I have already tracked down the paramedics and they have a sworn statement locked in a safe at the Boston Globe confirming what they saw when they entered the suite. Now you tell me Mr. Burke, about the 'bullshit' reason for coming over here. I really don't care if you believe it or not, however you have exactly three hours before I go to print. If I haven't heard from you by 5pm today, it will be interesting to see which photographs make the front page. I have enough photographs to keep publishing for a week. This will not go anywhere and I am sure you will agree will destroy the reputation of Mr. Gregory and anyone associated with him."

The message from Fanny was very clear and Mr. Burke was already thinking about what it would cost to keep this out of the papers and bury it forever.

"Now, Mr. Burke I suggest you finish your drink and get your ass out of my sight. You will be able to get me at the office. I'm going to have an enjoyable lunch first and I guess I will be back there around 3.30pm."

Mr. Burke took this as the end of the meeting and struggled to un-wedge himself from the booth and waddled over to the door and out without looking back. Fanny smiled to herself and called the waitress over to order another Merlot and a very tasty lunch.

Fanny finished her extended lunch and went back to the office. She placed the envelope in her bottom drawer and locked it, pocketing the key. She headed to her 4pm staff meeting and was working on the front page for the early edition when a colleague entered and told her there was a Mr. Burke holding on her office line. She walked back to her desk and picked up the phone.

"Good afternoon, Mr. Burke."

"OK, so how much is it going to cost?"

"As we are keeping pleasantries out of this, $1,500,000 into an account that I will provide you later."

"What the hell are you talking about?"

"I think you heard me very clearly, Mr. Burke. This is not a discussion topic. Either you get the monies transferred by tomorrow 5 pm or we have ourselves a wonderful weekend exposé. The choice is yours."

"OK Fanny, you've made your point. I can't get that money together by tomorrow evening."

"Really, Mr Burke, so how much can you get together by tomorrow evening?"

"Look, I can get $1,150,000 max. I'm going to have to pull this from a number of different places that you don't need to know about."

"Quite honestly, Mr. Burke, I don't care where you get the monies from. Let's just agree that once I have confirmation the monies has been transferred into the account a courier will be delivering the envelope with the evidence to you at your offices. I will take care of ensuring the lady in question forgets this situation has ever happened and your Mr. Gregory can continue with his political career unquestioned. Do we understand each other, Mr. Burke?"

Mr. Burke muttered something down the line.

"Sorry, Mr. Burke, I can't hear you. Do we have a deal?"

"Yes for fuck's sake."

"Good, Mr. Burke, now get to work. Like you said, you have to get this together from a number of different locations and I'd hate for you to be late. You will have the account number in the morning delivered to your offices.

Oh, and before you go, and just in case you consider trying to track the account or even doing something stupid like calling the cops, just remember what is at stake here."

The message was clear and Mr. Burke understood it. He was sure Mr. Gregory would want this hidden, and he was in two minds to even discuss it with him, unless he raised the subject, when he did get out of hospital. Whilst he had been considering his next move the phone line had gone dead and it took him a few seconds to realize it. He placed the receiver down and then went to his rolodex to start making the necessary calls. This was going to take some time and he was going to have to work pretty late to make sure everything was in place for the transfer.

He didn't have time to think about it now, but one day he was going to get even with that bitch…

Fanny left the office at 5.30pm and headed back to her condo. She pulled up on the drive and parked her Buick next to the side door. She went into the condo and headed to the telephone. She dialed the number from memory and it was answered on the first ring.

"Hey, Fanny."

"Hello, Miranda. How long have you been sitting by the phone?"

"Since 4.30pm, I was getting worried. How did it go?"

"The money is being transferred tomorrow afternoon."

"Seriously. As simple as that?"

"Well what choices did Mr. Burke really have? The evidence could not have been more damming. He would have tried to talk me down, but I didn't give him the opportunity. One lesson I've learnt dealing with them bastards is never, ever give them a chance. They worm out of anything if given even the smallest of chances."

"That's great news, Fanny, so what happens next?"

"I'll send over the account details in the morning and by 5pm tomorrow you will be $900,000 better off."

Fanny was not going to tell Miranda that she had sealed the deal for higher than the $1,000,000 they had discussed. Miranda was going to get what she had been told and

155

Fanny was going to make a little more. Well she had done all the hard work, so she justified to herself that she should get a bigger cut.

"I'll be in touch tomorrow when I have more information."

"Thanks, Fanny, appreciate it."

With that they both hung up. Fanny considering that long overdue vacation she could take and Miranda thinking about the fact she was on the verge of doubling her bank balance in the next twenty-four hours. Her plan was moving along.

Friday, 20 May 1983

Fanny arrived in the office early and organized for a courier to collect an envelope from her office at 09:30. Inside the envelope was a simple message and instructions for Mr. Burke, along with the account details. She was sure it would be an account Mr. Burke would recognize, she was convinced that this would not be the first or last time Mr. Burke would be doing this activity. If this was a person not knowing how to pull the strings there would be no way the cash would have been available for transfer today.

The courier came at the allocated time and the envelope headed to the offices of Mr. Burke. All Fanny could do now was sit back and wait. She was soon caught up in the breaking news of the day. Two local stories were developing one relating to the imminent launch of the Challenger space shuttle along with the first US woman astronaut, Sally J Ride. The second related to the imminent opening of the Brooklyn Bridge linking Brooklyn and Manhattan. The major international news was of a devastating car bomb in South Africa being blamed on the outlawed Africa National Congress.

Miranda was nervously wandering around her apartment. She had decided to call in sick again, for show and besides which she didn't need to send in a doctor's sick note according to the procedures until the fourth day of any individual sickness period. She was actually wondering if she would even have to go back there and considered if there was anything in her cubicle that was worth going back to collect. She deliberately had not taken any personal trinkets to the office and she had no photographs on the walls like the others along with paintings or drawings their kids aged three or four had done for them. The only thing she considered was the financial data she had pulled on various businesses she was looking into acquiring with her newfound wealth. It might be wise to go in to remove any evidence in case when her cubicle was being cleaned out for her replacement they came across the data and decided to investigate as it would probably be seen as suspicious as it was not the type of company they would be investigating. Additionally, when Mr. Gregory finally realized what had happened and what it had cost him, she was pretty sure he would do some digging...

Miranda decided to go there after normal working hours to minimize the chance of bumping into anyone she knew or worked with. Most of her colleagues left at 3pm on Fridays, so if she arrived after 6.30pm her office area should be empty and only the security guards would be around. In fact, the entrance she would be using would not be viewed by the security guards as it was a rear entrance only used by workers. The only issue would be that if she used her badge to open the door it would be recorded so she may have to wait around until one of the cleaners went out for a cigarette and then she could make a play of using her badge but actually not register it. Additionally, by then she should have had the news from Fanny that the monies had been transferred and it would look even more suspicious to anyone checking. She continued to pace around the apartment almost counting the seconds.

The phone on Fanny's desk rang at 3.47pm.

"It's me."

"Hello, Mr. Burke. I presume you are ringing to tell me the money has been transferred."

"Yes, where's the courier with the file?"

"Waiting for me to call them."

"Well, call them."

"Once I have verified the money is in I will."

Fanny hung up the phone without another word and headed out of the office. She went over to the Finance section and into a small office where Katrice was talking to someone on the phone. A few minutes later Katrice hung up.

"Hey, Fanny, how's it going?"

"Well, that all depends."

"OK, you had word about the transfer?"

"Yeah, can you confirm?"

"Sure, give me a minute."

With that Katrice's fingers flew over her keyboard to check SWIFT transactions that had been registered that day. She came across the one that Fanny had been expecting and enacted three immediate SWIFT requests to different accounts. The money had been in the slush account less than 2 hours before it was sliced, diced and split. Katrice was $5,000 better off. Fanny was $245,000 better off and Miranda would soon be getting the good news of her $900,000 bonus.

"Done, now all I need to do is wipe the data disk and no one will be the wiser."

"Thanks Katrice, have a great weekend."

"Sure you too, don't blow it all at once."

With that Fanny left the office and headed back to her desk to give Miranda the good news. First though she would call the courier to tell him to head over to Mr. Burke's office with the envelope. She would call him, after she had spoken to Miranda.

"Hello, Miranda."

"Hey, Fanny, everything OK?"

"Everything is perfect."

"Really, the money got transferred?"

"Absolutely."

"Wow, thank you."

"It was my pleasure."

"So what happens now?"

"Well, the courier is on his way over to Burke's office with the originals. I'm going to call him after we hang up and tell him that and also that as part of closing the situation you will submit your resignation letter, with immediate effect, and it will be posted tomorrow to that lady that heads up Human Resources. The letter will be real simple around saying something like:

Dear whoever you need to send it to,

Unfortunately I have to advise you of my decision to

resign with immediate effect. I have some very personal reasons for my decision, however want to take this opportunity to thank you for your support and help during my time with the company. Whilst I do not want to disclose my personal reasons, I can assure you I am not going to be taking up a new assignment with a competitor and have yet to decide my next opportunity.

Many thanks… love and kisses…Miranda

That should do it. If you get a chance take a photocopy of it for your own reference. You probably won't need a copy ever, but, like my mentor once told me, it's better to be safe than sorry. I'd better give shit for brains a call now."

"OK, Fanny and thank you again."

"No worries, Miranda. Stay in touch and let me know how things work out for you."

"Hopefully, if things work out you will see the results in a few years' time."

"Good luck."

With that Fanny and Miranda hung up and Fanny then immediately called Mr. Burke. The phone was answered almost before it rang in Fanny's ear.

"What kept you? Where the fuck is that courier?"

"Well, Mr. Burke it seems that your manners still haven't improved so I'll keep it nice and short, mainly as I don't want to waste any more of my precious weekend time talking with scum. The courier will be with you in five minutes, and the reason for the delay was checking to ensure there were no traces on the money. The employee in question is in the process of sending her with immediate effect resignation letter and will not be going back to the company. Oh and finally I do hope Mr. Gregory is feeling better and maybe he will stop using his cock to think for him in future, otherwise God help this country if he does make it into politics and government."

Without waiting for a reply Fanny hung up the phone, tidied up her desk and headed out of the office. She was going to the theatre this evening with some girlfriends and didn't want to be late.

Mr. Burke waited for closer on ten minutes before the courier arrived. He personally signed for the envelope and almost pushed the courier out of the building before heading back to his office to check the contents. He didn't want to play the tape as he didn't have headphones and would have to listen to it on the machine speaker. That he would do when he was sure everyone else had left the building. He found the roll of film and the prints. He did think that Mr. Gregory had some style. The tart in the picture was pretty hot stuff and he might just keep the pictures for his own amusement. Despite this, he locked the evidence in his office safe except the tape which he would play before he left for the evening. He had actually wanted to head down to the local dealership as he had his eyes on, and now the cash for, the new Pontiac Trans Am. He thought the sacrifice worthwhile to ensure he had the recording; he could always go to the dealership tomorrow.

The nerves seemed to have left Miranda after the phone call. She had stopped pacing around the lounge and decided to get dressed to go to the office. She put on a pair of jeans and sneakers and a long-sleeved jumper. She wanted to be as invisible as possible when she went to the office. With that she picked up her shoulder bag and car keys and headed out of the apartment.

At 8.25pm Miranda pulled up into a parking lot close by the office. She looked around the company parking lot and couldn't see any cars she was familiar with. Looking up at the building the lights were off on her floor and she walked down the street between where she was parked and the company parking lot. Walking to the end of the block she turned right and approached the back of the office building. The rear door was closed and there was no sign of anyone. Miranda stayed in the shadows watching and waiting. Ten minutes later there was a shadow cast through the door and she took the opportunity to walk towards the door with the hope that whoever was heading to the door would actually open it and head out to the car park. Her luck held out and as she was approaching the door one of the sub-contract cleaning staff was opening the door to head out for a smoke. The janitor held the door open for Miranda. She flashed her badge at him as she walked passed and exchanged pleasantries. The janitor let the door go and went about his business of lighting up. Miranda, in his mind, was soon forgotten; he was thinking about the game tomorrow and how he was going to get a bet on without his wife finding out.

Miranda walked down the dimly lit corridor and headed to the emergency exit staircase. She needed to go up eight flights of steps, and regretted she couldn't use the elevators. By the time she had climbed three flights she was out of breath. It took another twenty minutes to make it up the remaining flights of steps and by the time she was at the level of her office she was sweating freely. The emergency stairs had no air con, and it took her another ten minutes to regain her breathing. *The positive*, she thought, *is on the way out it's all down*. She also thought she needed to get back to the gym but at no point did she consider giving up the coke…

She opened up the emergency door a fraction and looked into the office corridor. The lights were off with the exception of one of the offices on the far side of the floor. She tried working out whose office it was and, considering the options, was amazed that either of the names that sprung to mind would be working this late on a Friday. She opened the door further and crept into the corridor. She walked slowly and quietly to the end of the cubicles and waited to hear if there was any movement from the area of the light source. Not hearing anything she peered around the end of the cubicle and spotted the office with the lights on. The office was empty which would mean John had left the office for the day, or he was elsewhere in the building and could be coming back any time. If he was somewhere else why were none of the lights on?

Miranda stopped still as she heard the sound of an office filing drawer shut. The noise came from Mr.

Gregory's office and then she saw the thin beam of light that looked like a torch move up and down. Then she heard the sound of another cabinet drawer being opened. Someone else was doing a bit of extracurricular activity. She backtracked and headed to her cubicle. She knew where all the information she wanted to collect was and carefully pulled open the second drawer down on her desk side drawers. She recovered the paperwork and was putting it into her shoulder bag when she heard the drawer in Mr. Gregory's office slam shut. Whoever it was didn't seem too happy and this was followed by the sound of steps walking over the wooden floor in hard leather soled shoes. Miranda carefully closed the drawer and got onto all fours and crawled under her table, pulling her desk chair in front of her. Unless the other visitor was going to look directly under her desk she would be invisible to them. The footsteps continued until at Miranda's desk and then stopped. Miranda tried not to panic, thinking she would be uncovered any second. She peeked from her hiding place and recognized the outline of John. He stood where he was for five seconds then turned around and went back to his office. Miranda waited under the desk and heard muffled noises coming from John's office. A minute later the light went out and only the emergency lighting filled the room. John again walked passed Miranda's cubicle, not stopping this time and headed for the elevators. Thirty seconds later the ping of the elevator arriving rang through the silent office. The doors opened shedding light into the room and then a shadow was cast as John entered. The doors shut and the elevator headed to the ground floor.

Miranda pushed away her chair and crawled from under the table. She stood up and stretched a little to uncramp some of her muscles from the combination of walking up the stairs and then crouching under the desk. She turned and looked at her table and realized the reason John had stayed there for so long. Sitting on top of her desk was her purse. In the rush to put the papers in her shoulder bag she had forgotten she had removed her purse. John was probably just being considerate and thinking about should he look after it for her, and probably decided against it as it might raise questions as to what he was doing in the office after hours. This however left Miranda with a real dilemma. If she took the purse, John would wonder when she didn't go in on Monday where had her purse gone. It may be a small risk, but she was sure the shit was going to hit the fan and that could be taken as the smallest of clues that she had been into the office. Alternatively, she could leave the purse there, which she hated the thought of as it was a genuine Louis Vuitton, not one of the cheap Chinese fakes that had started to appear. Eventually, Miranda decided to empty the contents of the purse of her cards and essential information, ensuring there was no personal information in there and just leaving it, as she had found it, with $15.00 in small demonization notes and quarters. To the inquisitive eye it should at least suggest that Miranda had not been in the office.

Checking her bag to ensure the remaining contents of her purse were safely stored and the documents she had come to collect were also still there, she walked along the corridor away from her cubicle and towards the emergency exit door. Opening it slowly she listened for a few seconds, before hesitating and shutting it again. In the back of her mind she was curious as to what John had been searching for. She reached back into her bag and pulled out a pair of hospital latex gloves and a pocket torch. She slipped the gloves on and went to Mr. Gregory's office and searched the same filing cabinets that John had been rifling through. She didn't know what to look for specifically, however when she came to the bottom drawer of the cabinet she found a folder with each of the department personnel names on. Out of curiosity she pulled her own file and found herself looking at her resumé and some photographs of her that she had no idea had been taken. Additionally, there were accounts of her activities and also a list of pros and cons on her performance and as she scanned further down there was a line stating conquest capability with a rating next to it of three. Miranda was not startled with the finding but, putting it together with the photos, her surprise turned to anger and then amusement as she realized she had had the last laugh. Putting her file back she checked the files of other female colleagues from the office and they were a similar format with an associated conquest capability score. The others were much higher, which she took to mean Mr. Gregory thought them to be an easier conquest than Miranda. *Fucking pervert,* she thought as she put the last of the files back in the cabinet. Maybe she would send discrete notes to her other colleagues telling them of the files and wondering what the HR Police would make of the files, especially thinking about the conversation from her induction.

"I am sure you will never experience such a situation however if you do, this is how you report the harassment."

How many of her other colleagues had been conquered by Mr. Gregory? Her beliefs of all men just thinking with their third legs was only supported by seeing the information. She did, for the briefest of instances, consider photocopying the files to share, but pushed away the thought for two reasons. Firstly, it would question how Miranda had got hold of the information and secondly, it was tough shit on her colleagues. She had to look after number one... herself. She was sure none of them would look out for her.

Feeling justified in her thinking she decided to pull John's file. The same base database was there and the score card system excluded the conquest capability. At least Mr. Gregory didn't appear to be bisexual. On the last page Miranda looked at it stated that John was identified as being the 'casualty of war' of a business acquisition that had gone wrong. There had been lots of talk about that transaction and in reality, John was following an order from Mr. Gregory. The transaction had cost the company $25,000,000 and it seemed Mr. Gregory had found his scapegoat. John was to be terminated in exactly two weeks' time. She then saw another side of the perverse and sick nature of Mr. Gregory coming out. John was to be fired on April Fool's Day!

Miranda put the folder back in the filing cabinet and shut it. Switching off her torch and putting it back in her shoulder bag she headed back to the emergency exit and repeated the exercise of opening it slightly to listen for sound. Hearing nothing, she opened the door enough to get into the stairwell and took the steps down to the ground floor where she made her exit from the building by the same door she had entered. Once outside the building she peeled off the latex gloves and stuffed them into her bag. She would dispose of them somewhere else on the way home. The last thing she needed to do was to prepare her resignation letter, so on the way home she pulled into a novel café that had opened recently where artists and writers were encouraged to work and at the same time part with their money. The café had artist's easels around the outside walls. They were spaced evenly between floor to ceiling glass windows to allow the artists to get their inspiration and natural light. Around a small table with four chairs were a mix of three typewriters and a modern new word processing machine. Miranda ordered a cappuccino and sat at the word processor. She quickly typed a letter to Mrs. Chippendale and printed two copies out, courtesy of the printer sitting at the end of the bar that looked something like a large plastic filing cabinet. She paid the waiter for the coffee, the use of the machine and the prints. Finishing her coffee she left the café and headed home. She would post the letter tomorrow, and, provided there were no strikes over the weekend, the letter would be in Mrs. Chippendale's hands on Monday morning.

Monday, 23 May 1983

Mrs Chippendale arrived in the office at 8.45 am and went to the coffee dispenser to fill her Disney World mug. It was her part of her daily routine for the past twelve years, Monday to Friday. She'd had a good weekend and was looking forward to this week as her boss from New York was coming over and he had told her that he was coming over with good news. She had images that the promotion she had been thinking about for a couple of years was finally going to happen, and so when she got back to her office she was smiling.

At 10 am the internal post arrived and Mrs. Chippendale was handed a bunch of envelopes. She flicked through the pack and came across a handwritten addressed letter *FAO Mrs. Chippendale*. It wasn't unusual for her to get a letter like this. Normally it was someone tendering their resignation, so she thought she might as well get the bad news out the way. She opened the letter and read the contents. She was very surprised. Miranda had resigned with immediate effect. It seemed totally out of character and she was only talking to her last week and she seemed so focused on her job and seemed to be enjoying what she was doing. With a sigh she got up and decided to go and see if Mr. Gregory had returned to work. It was probably the last thing he needed to hear after his suspected stroke, but she had a duty to inform him as the director of the office and ultimately, Miranda worked for him.

Mrs. Chippendale picked up the letter and made a photocopy for her files and then took the original up to the eighth floor and went directly to Mr. Gregory's office. Mr. Gregory was in. His door was shut, but she could tell he was very angry at something or someone as his voice was coming clearly through from behind the closed door as he spoke to someone on the phone.

Mrs. Chippendale was just about to turn around and go back later, as clearly now was not a good time, but Mr. Gregory had spotted her and gestured her to come into his office. As she opened the door she heard the phone click onto the receiver. As she walked in his whole demeanor had changed. He smiled and stood up to shake her hand.

"Good morning, Mrs. Chippendale. How are you this morning? Did you have a good weekend?"

"Good morning, Mr. Gregory. Thank you I am fine and the weekend was great. I was worried about you. How are you and I hope as you are back you have had the all clear?"

"Thank you, Mrs. Chippendale. I am not exactly sure what it was, and the doctors are not sure either. They say all my vital signs are OK and for my age they say I am physically like a person ten years younger. All the more strange as to what happened and the doctors have no clue as to why I blacked out. Either way, I am back and I assure you I wouldn't run the risk of crossing HR's path by coming back before I was fit to do so," he said with a smile.

"OK and great to hear. Unfortunately I do have a little bit of bad news for you, but it can wait till later if you would prefer?"

"No, that's absolutely fine. I take it someone has resigned in the team?" he said with another smile.

Mrs. Chippendale smiled also and said, "Unfortunately I seem to be the bearer of bad news whenever I go and see people. You are correct and I was rather surprised to get this letter."

As she handed over the letter she continued, "It's from Miranda. She has resigned with immediate effect citing personal reasons. She asks in the letter for me to pass her thanks on to everyone at the company and specifically you for your mentorship and support."

Mr. Gregory could barely contain his emotions. His face went red and he didn't say anything for a few seconds whilst he collected his thoughts. Finally he said, "Really, that's very kind of her and it's a huge shame."

With that it seemed the conversation was over and Mrs. Chippendale, feeling awkward, turned and exited the office. She hoped she had not insulted or upset Mr. Gregory however she definitely had seen him change completely as soon as she had mentioned Miranda's name. *Interesting*, she thought, however she was not about to ruin her opportunity of a promotion by launching an investigation on a hunch with her boss due in town in a couple of hours and decided to park the experience in her mental trash can. After all, it was just another employee that had left.

Mr. Gregory sat in the office staring at the letter. He had not yet seen the evidence but Mr. Burke had vividly described the photographs and the tape recording. He had no recollection of the events, or even ending up in hospital. Waking up there had been a complete shock and he had not been able to piece together anything from walking into the hotel suite to waking up in the hospital. It was like his memory had been erased. Whilst he had housed ambitions of conquering Miranda, he struggled to accept he had lost control of himself and was sure there was more to it, but nothing made sense. The doctor at the hospital could not explain, and could only suggest it had been stress related. The doctor had stated it took some time to stabilize his condition due to the level of alcohol in his system, but he had not drunk more than at any other social event for as long as he could remember. The fact that Mr. Burke had buried the situation was a positive, but there were potential loose ends out there. He again read the letter and wondered how much Miranda had got from the fortune it had cost him to bury the story. He was mad at the fact that something he could not remember had cost him so much money and that is what bothered him the most. It was his money and he didn't want anyone else to have it. Maybe he would have to get some form of revenge by firing John immediately. He wanted to wait until the first of April, however he had a burning need to take revenge. Putting his personal predicament to one side he opened the door and called John into his office…

Sunday, 16 October 1983

Miranda walked into the small cramped office at the back of the restaurant. Seated at the desk was a man in his late sixties or early seventies. His face painted a multitude of pictures. It was the worn face of someone who had been working long hours over many years, not taking care of himself and was showing age had caught up on that lifestyle. The eyes were still burning with intensity but the once bright blue eyes had lost the shine. 'MD' as he was known to everyone stood up as swiftly as he could from his desk and shook Miranda's hand.

"It's a pleasure to meet with you, Miss Miranda."

"Good morning, MD."

"Can I get you a drink?"

"Black coffee, please."

Miranda was relaxed and smiling. She was dressed in another of her revealing outfits, chosen deliberately to smooth the deal that was going to take place. She had researched MD. He was known as a shrewd businessman who had set up his first outlet in 1956 and was now sitting with a total of 267 outlets around the United States. His particular ingredients had appealed to the masses of kids out there craving a sugar rush and the long-term obesity issues that were coming. His outlets combined the traditional seating area with a drive thru for those too lazy to get out of their vehicles and a merchandising store where you could get a multitude of different apparel, pins, Zippo lighters, jewelry and photographs.

For Miranda, the deal was another step forwards. Her business empire, to this point, had been on a state by state basis, but here was an opportunity to have a pan-America business, and as important, if what she had been able to uncover was correct, control of a $90,000,000 business with room to expand. One of the things that had immediately struck Miranda was the huge potential to create a market for the merchandise by having it personalized by location and state. There were always

170

going to be those kids that just had to have a bigger collection than their friends… It was a self-generating cash opportunity. Miranda had already figured out that all the products needed to be made and distributed from a central location – which would improve the costs significantly, and would far outweigh the costs of transport – and then have them personalized at the end of the process before they were dispatched. She was sure she could find a cheap way to do the personalization.

Miranda switched tracks back onto MD. Whilst she wanted to close the deal and get her ideas underway she had to keep a clear focus… one thing at a time. She had yet to meet anyone yet who was operating at her intellect or speed. MD was on his fourth marriage currently; a sign of two things. Firstly, his first love was his business and secondly, he had a reputation for playing the field; probably trapping his victims by the fact he was a self-made multi-millionaire. He was also due for a triple by-pass operation next month. He was a large guy, weighing in at 300lbs who clearly had been eating his share of the profits and it just added to the fact that his appeal to women had been financial, rather than looks and athleticism. The way Miranda saw it was that this operation was a last chance for him to get a few more years, but the reality was he wouldn't make it through the operation.

MD came back into the office carrying two coffees and a bag of donuts. He fell, more than sat, back into his reinforced chair and offered the bag to Miranda. She smiled and politely declined the offer.

"So, MD, tell me about the revenue stream."

"That's what I like about you, Miss Miranda, straight to business. You get so many people who want to talk around the subject."

"Well time is money, MD, so about the revenue stream."

"Yeah. It falls into three categories. Firstly, you have the food side. This tends to be highest from lunchtime onwards until closing at 9pm. Food represents just over 50% of the total sales and makes around 60% of the profit. Then you have beverages. These are about 30% of the sales and add another 30% to the profits. The final element, which is something I am considering dropping is the merchandise. I started it as a bit of a gimmick and it brings a contribution. Sales are 18% but only brings 10% of the profits."

"Is this picture the same state by state or are there differences?"

"It tends to be the same. What you see differing state by state are the product mixes. We offer set menus but in California, Arizona, Florida and Texas I've seen that more cold drinks are sold than hot drinks, whereas when you look at Michigan, New York and Alaska it's the other way around."

"Are the menu prices the same state by state?"

"Generally yes, but there are different local taxes so what the customers pay is different. There's not a lot we can do about that."

"So, what are your plans for expanding the business? Are you going to expand the menu? Are you going to launch any new stores?"

"I have plans to open up another fifteen stores next year. Those plans have been put on hold until I have my surgery. I like to make sure I get to as many of the stores as I can before they open, you know, to make sure they are as they should be. Saying that, the company that manages and builds the restaurants has had enough experience to do it without me. I am not planning any major menu changes. We are going to add some new beverages that have started to become popular with the kids, but that's about it."

"How does the management company work? Do you pay them on a fixed contract basis? Are the contracts fixed prices and are there penalties included for, say, delays?"

"Well, I will be honest, it's an area I am not comfortable with. I have seen in the past three years the costs from opening new restaurants growing and I need to address it. You see, Don who owns the company, is a personal friend of mine, and it's kinda difficult for me to get around to this."

"I am sure it is, MD, but no worries I can definitely deal with those opportunities," Miranda said, smiling and letting her jacket fall open a little more revealing more of the plunging V-neck dress.

MD was trying to keep his eyes in his head and was having a major issue talking to Miranda's face.

"I am sure you can, Miss Miranda. So, what's your proposal?"

"Well, MD, before I give you my proposal I wanted to get some facts in front of you. Last year you had sales of $89,724,355 and you showed a profit of $6,101,256 or a profit margin of 6.8%. Sales have been showing a reduction for the past three years, but you have opened forty-seven new stores. In other words, your margins are being eroded by two things. The first one is the seemingly out of control costs running the business like those of your management partner. The second one has to be the growth in competition. In this business area you should be looking at significantly higher profit margins. Your competitors are working smarter and have tapped into more automisation in the preparation of the menu."

"Yes, Miss Miranda, I am sure they have," interrupted MD, "but my goal is to give the customer the personal touch."

"MD, that's a noble cause but it is one, on the current track, that will put you out of business inside the next three years. Based on your profit margins today you will barely break even next year and by the end of 1985 you will be recording losses. You might survive into 1986, but my estimate is you would be closing in time for Christmas '85."

"Miss Miranda, I am sure you are right, but I'm not in the best of health to tackle the issue."

"That's no issue, MD and that's where I come in. Basically, I'm going to offer you the opportunity to keep

173

running the business and be involved for as long as you want. In return I will ensure the fortunes of the business get turned around."

"So what does that mean?"

"To start with, I will buy your company for $5,000,000, which, based on the current profit forecasts for the next three years, is actually way over the price it is actually worth. As you are the solitary share holder the money will go directly to you. You will get a 2.5% share of the profits annually for the financial year once submitted, audited and signed off. You will continue with the menu, food and beverage developments. I know nothing about the preparation and cooking side of the business and honestly, am not interested. On the other hand, I will take control of the company overall and will focus on the new stores and improving the margins. My company, Matriarg Vennote, will be the new owner. Your chief finance officer will report to me on a monthly basis a set of key performance indicators that I will give to him once the deal is agreed."

"Miss Miranda, you are basically asking me to hand over my company to you?"

"No, MD, I'm going to give you a lot of money to help you to continue to realize your dream. I'm going to ensure the 3,916 people working for you across this country have job security. I'm going to make sure the core aspects of why your business has been successful previously come back to the fore. By your own admission you are not up to the task."

MD looked across the table. He knew Miranda was right but didn't want to admit it. Miranda had been like an ice cold bucket of water being thrown over him. The reality of the situation hit him and for the first time in many years the cheerful smile left his face. He knew he was going to have to accept the deal. Most of his backroom staff had been with him since the start. He owed it to them to ensure there was stability in their jobs. They had mortgages and bills to pay. Healthcare prices had rocketed in recent years and his policy of offering private healthcare to all his workers was now a considerable cost driver.

MD thought back to the first phone call out of the blue when Miranda had seemed to be the light at the end of the tunnel. He had known something had had to change but was not equipped to deal with it, and certainly hadn't been prepared for the meeting they were having now. MD was a people person, not a hard-faced business person and now coming face-to-face with one he realized why he couldn't keep the business running as it had been. He knew the writing had been on the wall. He considered taking what Miranda was offering him for the business and splitting the cash with all his employees; it was the least he could do for selling them down the river. That's how it felt to him. The talk of him continuing after the sale was unrealistic. He knew that after all this time working for someone else just wouldn't work. His organization ran like clockwork because everything had been done the same way for years. He couldn't bear to see everything he had built up changed and deep down he knew Miranda knew that also. His options were non-existent. He had to take the money and hope that Miranda didn't destroy everything he had spent his life building up.

When he spoke his voice was low and calm belying his emotions.

"Miss Miranda, we both know what you are proposing and what the implications are. You know it won't work with me working for you, it's not because of you, and it's simply that after all these years of being my own boss it would be impossible to work for someone else. All I ask is that you do what you can to take care of the people. They are like family to me."

"MD, I understand what you are saying and I can't promise something that I can't necessarily keep. You know as well as me the costs of this business are killing it and what I can commit to is turning around the fortunes. There will be casualties along the way, that's just a sad fact of life, but I am sure the vast majority of your people will see prosperity from the changes. So, do I take it we have a deal?"

It was more of a statement than a question. This was it, MD was painted into a corner. The likelihood of another investor coming along any time soon was remote. He needed to get things sorted out before he went in for the surgery. His next words would seal his and the fate of all 'his people'.

"OK, Miss Miranda, you have a deal."

"Good, MD, I'm glad you can see the wisdom of the decision."

"Just one thing please, let me tell my people first."

"Sure, however, if you are planning a general communication to the workforce I want to vet it first."

"Yeah, no worries. I want to talk to my backroom staff and explain what is going to happen."

"OK with that but we need to get the deal signed first."

"Sure, I will keep quiet until the ink is dried on the contract."

With that Miranda stood up and without shaking MD's hand turned and headed to the door. As she reached the door she turned and said, "I'll have the contract with you in the morning, so expect to have the signed agreement back by the close of business on Tuesday. I can't wait until after that as I have another deal that depends on this one to complete."

"OK, Miss Miranda, I'll have it back to you by then."

With that Miranda let herself out of the office with a smile on her face that MD couldn't see. She realized it would be the last time she would see him and in fact, had already worked out how she was going to get the business without paying the $5,000,000 sale price. It was all going to work out perfectly.

Tuesday, 18 October 1983

MD sat in his office staring at the brown paper envelope. He had refused to open the bulky document. He hated paperwork and this one brought his phobias to the surface. The package had been received yesterday morning and he had just left it on his desk, delaying the inevitable until the last possible minute. He was now at that time. His people had seen a difference in him in the past forty-eight hours. The ever-present smile was missing and he had avoided, as much as possible, all his friends and colleagues. MD kept going over in his mind if it was the right thing to do or not, and every time coming up with the same answer. Surely it was the only way to protect his people… surely.

MD was interrupted with a knock on his door and Roger, his CFO and oldest friend, walked in. He shut the door behind him and sat in the chair Miranda had been sitting in on Sunday.

"OK, MD, what's going on? You have been acting and looking like you've been given the news you have the Big C. Don't tell me you are worried over this operation you're having? You know you have the best doctor looking after you and you'll be back in no time."

"Hey, Roger. You're right, I'm not worried about the operation."

"Is it to do with that woman that was here Sunday?"

"How do you know about that?"

"MD, your movements are known about in every corner of the company. You can't take a shit in your closet here without someone in the Orlando restaurant knowing how many sheets of paper you used to wipe your ass with."

MD smiled for the first time in the past two days.

"You know, Roger, you have always found a way to get my good side to come out no matter how difficult things have been, and we have been through many over the years. You're a great guy and a truly great friend."

"OK, MD, I'm all welled up and will start crying in a

minute... so what the fuck is bothering you? In case you hadn't noticed, everyone is talking about the fact your fifteenth wife has run off and left you for a sanitation engineer in Dallas, or you have been considering giving everyone a raise... Seriously, the team here is worried about you."

"Thanks, Roger, and I have to apologize, and I know this will stay between us, but that envelope is the reason for my transition. Yeah it has to do with the lady that was here on Sunday. Basically, she buys poorly performing companies and turns them around. She wants to buy me out, and I have until exactly forty minutes time to sign the contract in that envelope and then a courier will take it away."

"Holy shit, MD, you are selling up?"

"Roger, you know better than me that if we don't change something soon there won't be anything left to change. That woman had all the information at her fingertips. I have no idea where she got it from but she could tell me to the month when we would be going out of business, and unless she has got access to your personal files she is one smart cookie."

"Yea but, MD, we can get more money pumped in, we just need to call in a few favors."

"True, Roger, but it is still just masking the issue we both know we have. Our costs are killing us and we both believed that opening more restaurants would be the answer as we would just increase the sales to cover our costs. The issue is the more stores we open the bigger the overhead cost becomes and it's unsustainable. I haven't got the heart to start closing shops, it basically means I failed."

"Don't be silly, MD, you are anything but a failure."

"Well it sure feels like I am one at this moment in time."

"So how much is she offering?"

"$5,000,000."

"$5,000,000 for the business? Is she serious? You can't

be serious... can you? You're going to sign aren't you?"

"Roger, I don't have any choice. This is the one and only offer we're going to get and the timing is right. I need things fixing in case anything goes wrong with the operation and also, we're getting too old to still be in this game. Business has changed and we're dinosaurs on the verge of becoming extinct."

"MD, I understand and sorry. I don't want to be hard on you. I understand the logic and I know you want to do the right thing for everyone. Are you going to read the contract before you sign it? That envelope hasn't been opened yet."

"Yeah I need to, I have just been putting it off. You know we are from the old school where we did things by word of mouth. Nowadays, everything is formal and I hate all that bullshit that is written down. It's like lawyers have their own language. Bottom line for me is she hands over $5,000,000 and I sign over the company. I asked her to take care of the staff, but I guess I'm just pissing in the wind if I believe she is going to keep things the way they were. I probably won't recognize the place in six months, but at least with the cash I get I will be able to make a little gesture to the team. I'm going to split the cash with the staff. Kind of an exit by me bonus."

"That's a great gesture, MD, and I know everyone will appreciate it, but is it the right thing to do?"

"Yeah, Roger, it is the right thing for me to do."

"OK, MD, you're the boss."

"Not for much longer, Roger."

"Whatever, you'll still be the boss in my eyes. So, when is this deal going through?"

"I sign now and basically the deal becomes live as of first thing tomorrow. Do me a favor and don't say anything until I can announce to the staff that this deal has gone through."

"Sure thing, MD."

With that, Roger got up and left the office. MD turned his attention to the envelope and ripped it open. He briefly read the first page that in legal terms said he was selling, Matriarg Vennote was buying the company and he would be paid $5,000,000 for the privilege. MD then ignored all the rest of the document until he found the sheet that he had to sign. He picked up his Mont Blanc fountain pen, a gift from his friends for the company's fiftieth anniversary and signed the document. With that, he returned the document to the envelope and waited for the courier to arrive, not giving it another thought. He had to turn to another task. Clearing his office and preparing for the upcoming operation.

Wednesday, 19 October 1983

Miranda sat in her office and looked at the contract that the courier had brought over the previous night. She was smiling at how easy the deal had been and how little resistance she had had from MD. Maybe she had been lucky, but that wasn't it. She had carefully checked out the key elements. Here was a business in desperate need of someone coming in and shaking it up. The profit potential was enormous and just needed some vision and strategy. The owner of the business didn't recognize the significance of the opportunity and was not in good health and was old. No, Miranda thought, she had chosen well and the result was what should have happened. Her business empire had just jumped from a $45,000,000 to $135,000,000 turnover. As the only shareholder in Matriarg Vennote she was going to pull in minimum 5% of the turnover into her private bank accounts or in real terms, $6,750,000 annual salary. Not bad for a start.

She could not believe her good fortune. In fact, it was clear MD had not read the contract properly, or had not got a lawyer to read it, or maybe even understood the contract It was almost like he had just picked up the signature page. Buried deep in the 'blurb' were all kind of conditions relating to the sale. The most significant for MD would be the fact that the $5,000,000 would be put in a trust fund redeemable by MD twelve months after the sale date to protect from the limited due diligence process possible to do on the company in the timescale for the deal to go through. In essence, if any issues arose in the first twelve months of ownership there would be a fund set aside to cover those costs. These could include things like unpaid tax bills, unpaid debtors or if any costs or assets needed to be written off. This, per se, was not unreasonable; what should have been questioned by MD was the fact that after the twelve months was up, if MD did not formally claim the monies, it would default back to Matriarg Vennote.

Miranda sat back and thought it was pretty much

guaranteed that she would get the company without actually paying a dime for it. She could only picture the face of MD when he realized he was going to have to wait twelve months for his money, and twelve months was a long time for someone seriously overweight, facing a triple bypass having just realized he has given his business away and there was nothing he could do about it. The only question in Miranda's mind was whether he would actually make it to the operating table.

Playing the odds that she felt were stacked in her favor she reached for the phone to close the other deal she had mentioned to MD using the $5,000,000 she was not going to spend...

"Jeff, get your ass in here!" Miranda shouted from inside her office.

"Yes, Miranda," Jeff said, walking into her office.

"I need a press release on the purchase of Master Donuts. You know what it needs to say."

"Yes, Miranda. Something along the lines of Matriarg Vennote is pleased to announce the acquisition of Master Donuts. Master Donuts is the latest acquisition of Matriarg Vennote a company whole owned by you with the purpose of supporting jobs in the United States and building a strong foundation for security in the communities it operates in. With immediate effect you will take over as CEO. Master Donuts is a $90,000,000 turnover company employing 4,000 employees across 40 States. This announcement further shows the diversification of Matriarg Vennote and the vision of its owner to promote the development of women in business."

"You know, Jeff, with a bit more training you might actually work out."

"Yes, Miranda, I am sure with your guidance and wisdom I will."

"OK, now get your ass over to MD's place and get working on the changes. Once the press release is prepared get it out to Fanny at the Boston Globe first.

Sunday, 8 May 1984

Miranda was sitting in her office checking a monthly report submitted by the new CFO at Master Donuts. Things had been progressing well since the take over seven months previously. Jeff, at least, seemed to be able to follow her instructions.

The expansion plans MD had were immediately put on hold and the focus moved to increasing sales with the current outlets. It had taken three months to get a supplier and the logistics set up, however now each of the states and the stores in those states had personalized merchandise. It had been an instant hit. Miranda had instructed Jeff to make sure that when merchandise was sold the zip code and name of the purchaser was taken. It proved to be a simple way of allowing Miranda to see how her idea could be measured. Within weeks there were the first purchases made by the same people in different states. Now, four months after the launch, she sat back with a smile; as if she needed verification her idea would be successful, the report was telling her she had been right.

Despite the fact it was 7.15 am on Sunday, Miranda picked up her desk phone and dialed Jeff. Miranda had long forgotten about any social taboos or even the principle of what constituted a working week, or the laws governing them. She owned her own business and no one was going to tell her what she could or could not do.

"Jeff."

"Good morning, Miss Miranda." Jeff's voice was surprisingly awake considering the time, however he had, over the past months, got used to the Sunday morning call. He had figured out Miranda's call pattern. It was clear she didn't sleep much, and he knew of her drug-taking which seemed to allow her to work pretty much twenty-four hours a day. Sunday mornings had become a specialty for Miranda. Jeff was sure she didn't go to bed on a Saturday night and had linked this with one of her drug-taking sessions. It seemed she used that time to come up with a multitude of new ideas and strategies. He thought the hours may be shit but the pay was good and if he had to be a kiss ass employee the pay and benefits were too good to ignore.

"So, what's happening?"

"Well, you've seen the latest financials from Master Donuts. Your idea on the merchandise has been well-founded. We are starting to see multi-state purchases and the impact to sales and profitability has started to come through. Sales are up 6.5% over the past three months and profitability is up 11.25% for the same period."

"Yeah, it's nice to be proven right, so here's what we are going to do now. I want advertisements in all the state newspapers promoting the merchandise. Let's give it a little publicity now we can see there is a market there and I want to come up with some new merchandise. We need to expand into other areas of collector interest. I want to see small teddy bears wearing a shirt with the name and location of the store on. We need to go after the soppy teenager market, you know first 'love', emotional teenage girls. I also want to see handbags and material briefcases with the logo and outlet details on. These will be produced by my company Bags For All. I will send you the designs today, provided I can find a courier working on a Sunday. I need to set up my own courier business but I will get to that business later. So, what else is happening?"

"Well, the new management team here seems to be working out. It's still early days but they are showing the improvements you were demanding. They are starting to be given a little more license to move the business forwards themselves. As well as the merchandising improvements there has been a 14% reduction in overhead cost by changing the work practices. They are also building a case to develop and manage their own expansion activities. On that point we have held back the only open installment on the company owned by Don, $724,990.00, and have prepared and submitted the case to sue them for fraud. It got to them on Thursday last week, so I am expecting a first response early next week. Based on the evidence we have got it should be a pretty straightforward case. We are suing them for $2,750,000. If you agree we should settle at $2,000,000 out of court. I am sure we could get the full amount but you know how long that will take to get settled."

"Yeah, I agree, if you can get it settled in the next three weeks. If there is a risk their going beyond that then make sure Mr. Watson is ready and primed to go for the jugular. That bastard Don is going to pay."

"Sure, Miss Miranda, I've already given him the papers and he prepared the submission."

"OK, what else?"

"We are already working on the healthcare plan. There were some challenges with making the change that the healthcare plan was restricted to management positions only. We lost a number of employees in the outlets, but that immediately benefited us with the overhead reduction. We just didn't replace the ones that left and were able to implement the new operating processes. We gave all the outlet staff that signed new contracts a 6% pay rise. Even with this we have seen the net 14% reduction in overhead cost. The full impact of the healthcare package reductions will be in place by the end of August due to the timing of the policies. The vast majority of MD's back room staff have either left or have submitted their resignations. I will say this did cause us some challenges over the first few months as they were very loyal to MD and also very anti-change. It was difficult to understand all their particular ways of working, Roger, the CFO, was a prime example of this. 'His record keeping made me question whether he had ever studied finance or financial reporting. I am sure he only got the job as he and MD went back so far. He's been put on garden leave and will finish at the end of October. We need to keep him for a bit longer as we have to close out the financial statement for 1983. We had to apply for an extension of the deadline due to the mess we came into. The local government team is working with us on this so I am not expecting any fines as a result. Roger is playing ball with us as he is personally liable for any issues that could come out."

"Can we find some, get him to pay, and still be clean with the tax people?"

"I am looking into it, but he is more incompetent than corrupt. Will keep that in mind as the investigation continues. How much are you looking for?"

"Well, let's say I'll share the findings with you Fifty-fifty as a bonus, so there's the incentive for you, wouldn't you agree?"

"For sure, Miss Miranda. I will ensure we can find something."

"Good. Make sure it's off the record and you get the payment made to that offshore account."

"Will do. On another subject, I am not sure if you heard but MD's health has been deteriorating rapidly. His surgery went well, according to the specialist, however he didn't react well to the fact the money for the sale of the company was tied up for twelve months after the sale. When he found out he almost had another heart attack. It really sent him into a tail spin and he ended up in hospital for two months."

"Shit happens, Jeff, should we send him flowers…" Miranda's voice was cold and sarcastic.

"Well, maybe we should, he passed away last night."

"Well that is sad news, isn't it?" Miranda's tone didn't change. "I think we should make sure his funeral arrangements are taken care of, to show how we care. Take care of it, Jeff, and also make sure Watson gets the deposit back."

"I will be in touch with him tomorrow to start the process. We need to be a little bit sensitive on timing. We don't want the authorities digging into the deal. I would suggest waiting until the twelve months are up and allow for the situation to die down and then just enact the contract. It's only another four months to go and then it will be enacted. I know you want to get the money back immediately but this would stop any potential questions."

"Let me think about it, but make sure you get a copy of the death certificate over to Watson."

"Will do, Miss Miranda."

"Anything else?"

"Nothing else to report so far today, Miss Miranda."

"OK, well keep an eye out for that courier."

Without a further word Miranda hung up the phone. Jeff hung up his handset and sat back in this chair. For sure he had never met such a cold person in his life. He knew that he was only an asset to Miranda as long as he was implementing her will and that could not last forever. It was clear to him she trusted no one and he was sure there were other people she had on her payroll to check up on what others were doing. He made a mental note to follow up on that discrepancy he had seen in the finances reported by Roger. Jeff realized he needed to make the most of this opportunity that Miranda had offered. He also made a mental note to check the personal wealth of Roger to understand how much this little opportunity might be worth to him.

Tuesday, 24 December 1985

Everything had gone according to plan. The conversion work in the apartment had been completed on time, despite, Miranda thought, the incompetence of the contractor who had been engaged to complete the task. The nursery was ready as was the live-in au pair suite which was adjoining the nursery. It was a self-contained area and had been made possible by Miranda purchasing the adjoining apartment so her residence now covered the complete top floor of the apartment block.

Miranda had made extensive searches, or at least had had others do so, to find her the correct au pair to raise her child. Miranda would technically be the child's mother, but this was going to be a relationship of convenience and necessity. The au pair would be the child's surrogate mother, and she was being well-paid to take care of the child. The bond, in essence, had been secured by Miranda having the au pair carry her child using her eggs and a male donor she had 'persuaded'. The persuasion had come from the evidence she had found in Marlene's apartment. The donor was an MIT graduate with doctorates in Engineering Mechanics and Business Administration, a highly regarded member of the Senate with a multi-billion dollar business empire, and a former football star. A pre-requisite for Miranda's designer child was going to be a combination of intelligence and sporting ruthlessness. She had specified to the doctors that the child must be a girl.

Miranda had always seen the need to have an heir to carry on her mantle and her focus was to ensure the child had a structured and focused upbringing. When Miranda retired to her dream island she would hand over the running of the empire to her and then enjoy her retirement away from those evil bastards of the opposite sex... There was no way Miranda was going to go through the aggravation and pain of having the child herself, besides which, it would distract her from her goal to become the richest business woman in the world.

Today was the due date for the birth, so Miranda thought it was only right to go and see the au pair in the private clinic and make sure everything was on plan. Arriving at the clinic, the senior matron greeted her at the front door.

"Good afternoon, Miss Miranda."

"Hi, how are they doing?"

"Just fine. The waters have broken and we should see the baby coming in the next few hours."

"OK, is there an office I can use? I have some calls to make."

The senior matron was used to Miranda's mannerisms and certainly could not understand why she was having a child. She almost felt sorry for the unborn child. She supposed the only positive was that Miranda clearly had money and that was also always good news for the clinic. Putting aside her personal feelings, the matron escorted Miranda to a small conference room she knew was not being used. As she was leaving the office Miranda called over.

"Can you get some coffee sent in?

The matron was in two minds about telling Miranda what she thought and simply nodded in recognition. Why is it, she thought as she walked into the corridor, rich people are so arrogant? Definitely with Miranda there was this sense that she saw herself as more important than anyone else and it was clear she had no manners. Maybe rich people believed that manners were only applicable to everyone else and they were above them. Either way, she would be glad when the payments had been received and Miranda and her entourage had left the premises.

The matron went to the canteen and gave the request to a member of the catering team to have coffee taken to the conference room and couldn't help herself.

"When you go up there, do so on the premise that you are walking on egg shells. If it wasn't for her age I would have said that woman is going through the change!"

Her colleague gave her a quizzical look. She had never

heard the matron talk bad of anyone before and it was totally out of character. If Miranda had the matron spooked, then she would sure be following her advice and proverbially walking on egg shells.

3.59pm. Miranda had been called ten minutes earlier and told that the au pair was in the final stages of labor. As Miranda had arrived in the delivery room the au pair was sweating profusely, despite the air conditioning and looked drained. Miranda thought how wise she had been not to go through the process herself, besides which, giving up the drugs for nine months or so had not been an option. The baby girl came out crying too much, a sign, Miranda had been told, was a good thing as it ensured the lungs were working and the baby was breathing. Miranda could not see any visible deficiencies. The baby had its arms, legs, feet, toes, hands and everything looked to be where it should be. She turned to the matron.

"OK, the baby's name is Imogen. Make sure the associated paperwork is brought to my room for signing. Don't be long with the paperwork, and get some fresh coffee brought up."

Having seen baby Imogen for a matter of seconds, Miranda walked out to the delivery room and back to the conference room to pick up the call she had ended.

The matron only hoped that no one else in the delivery room had heard Miranda. It seemed as though the conversation had not carried as the midwives and the au pair were totally focused on baby Imogen. She was grateful for small mercies. She would talk with the midwives as soon as she had organized the coffee to see how quickly they could get this lot out of the clinic. She had originally planned for them to stay in the clinic for two days after the birth, however the matron could not bear to think that Miranda would be back, and it was only $10,000 they would lose, a small price to pay. She had never met such a cold woman in all her twenty-six years at the clinic. In her eyes, Miranda shouldn't have been allowed to have a child. It was clear to her there was no biological reason why Miranda had not conceived herself. She had had to undergo the same tests to ensure her eggs could be used for the conception and could only fathom that Miranda had an ultimate goal, which she wanted to know nothing about.

Miranda sat in the conference room and was ranting.

"What the fuck do you mean? How could you screw up the deal so badly? I gave you very simple instructions? Are you too dumb to follow them? Get off the phone, I'll deal with this myself. I'll decide later what I'm going to do with you."

With that, she slammed down the phone. The canteen lady had been standing outside the conference door and was about to enter when she heard Miranda's verbal tirade. It had frightened her just listening at the door. She felt sorry for the poor person at the other end of the phone and now clearly understood what the matron had said. She waited a few more seconds to make it seem as though she had just arrived before gently knocking on the door.

"Yes," came the voice from behind the door.

Tentatively, she opened the door and saw Miranda was sitting at the table frantically writing things on sheets of paper. There was no sign of the aggression she had heard through the door. As Miranda saw the pot of coffee in her hands she actually smiled and thanked her. Smiling in return she quietly exited the room without sharing another word. She was very glad to get out of the conference room. She had to go and find the matron and tell her about her experience. It had really bothered her, and actually not bothered, more accurately, had frightened her. She sped up her walk to get as far away from the conference room as quickly as possible.

Miranda was seething with rage. The simple deal that should have cost her $1,500,000 was currently sitting at $1,800,000 due to the fucking incompetence of that stupid CEO. He would pay, that's for sure. First thing was to make sure he recouped the money. She didn't care if it was on the current deal or another one, but for certain he would have to get it back and she would double-check his

191

accounts to make sure he didn't try and claim it back in some backhanded financial transaction. That was the trouble with hiring people, it was a necessary evil. Miranda wanted to do everything herself and if there were enough hours in the day, she would. She had experienced enough times, and men were the worst, that when people worked for someone else they just didn't care about money. The only time they cared about a result was if there was a bonus to be had for them. They were great at spending someone else's money on fancy meals, expensive wines, hotels and entertaining clients. Well this fucker would find out the painful way what it meant to screw up.

Miranda moved her thoughts away from the fucked up deal to if and when she would tell Marlene about the new addition to the family. Her thoughts were interrupted by the operator at the clinic calling.

"Miss Miranda, there's an outside call for you."

"Who is it?"

"A gentleman called Mr. Watson"

"OK, put it through."

With that Miranda put the thought out of her mind of calling Marlene with the news about Imogen. That could wait, this call could be important.

Sunday, 15 June 1986

It was a bright, warm day in New York. Temperatures were in the high 90s and there was more than a touch of humidity in the air. Marlene had decided to walk to the restaurant for lunch. It was too nice outside to ride in the car. She had given the chauffeur the afternoon off, and was looking forward to her latest liaison. Her latest conquest to be was a young entrepreneur who had moved into the neighborhood and she had met initially in Starbucks. He would be different to the norm. This guy was intelligent, witty and clearly smart. He was only a few years older than Miranda so certainly should be able to last for a few hours…

With a smile on her face, Marlene left the penthouse suite and, having exited the elevator, walked out of the lobby onto the pavement. She turned left and started walking. She was thinking about the dramatic change in her life in the past ten years. It had been a remarkable transformation. She had gone from being pimped out to make ends meet, to having a life of luxury where money was no longer a concern. Admittedly, she had been very loose with her newfound wealth and needed to address the slide. She had invested a lot of money in different businesses and ventures that had not worked out. She didn't possess the business acumen to make the right decisions, and was down 90% on her initial 'inheritance' from Stan's untimely death. Even then, just 10% of what she had started with was enough to live on more than comfortably.

She smiled as she thought of how shit her life had been until that geriatric had come along and how easy it had been initially to con him and then kill him. She still believed that she had just helped him along and he was a terminal case just hanging on by a thread. There was never any feeling of remorse or guilt, it was just a timing issue and the timing had been right, for her anyway.

Marlene changed her thoughts to Miranda. She was

surprised how much they had grown apart. They were now down to a call every so often. It wasn't even a weekly scheduled thing. The split had started with the Olympic trials fiasco and finding out that Miranda had been doing the drugs. She couldn't understand, after all Miranda had been through as a kid, why she would take them after that shit. She had always been so against it. Marlene was sure that Miranda hated all men and was not sure if she was queer or just asexual. Miranda never spoke to her about personal stuff anymore, and Marlene had stopped trying to find out. She had done what she needed to, to get her on her feet. The $1,000,000 in the bank, the house, the car were more than generous to give her the right start, and provided Marlene managed to stop the cash flow rot, there would be more to come. It was clear to Marlene that Miranda had been expecting more of an inheritance however she had to earn her own living. No, she thought to herself, she had done what she had needed to do and felt no remorse or concern about how her life had turned out.

As she reached the crosswalk the light for pedestrians turned to red. Marlene, engrossed in her thoughts did not notice it and started to cross the road. In her peripheral vision was sure she had seen people crossing the road in front of her. The reality was the people crossing in front were at the far side of the road. At the same instant she felt and heard the vibration and beeping of her pager she had in her bag. She had taken half a dozen steps across the road, when a fire truck with sirens and lights blazing came around the corner from the opposite direction. There was a squeal of wheels and brakes as the driver saw this woman standing in the road with her attention focused on her shoulder bag.

No matter how far he turned the steering wheel, the momentum of the 40 ton truck took over and the vehicle started to skid towards the woman. To the driver and the horrified passersby it was as if a horror scene from a film was being recorded in front of their eyes. It was only a matter of seconds, but to the fire truck driver and the firemen in the truck it seemed that time had slowed down. The driver screamed at the woman, a futile exercise if she hadn't noticed the fire truck in the first place. He had been driving fire trucks for seventeen years and had come across most situations you could imagine and his only thought was maybe this woman was deaf... she had to be... everyone knew the sound of a fire truck. In milliseconds he considered how to avoid the woman. Could he try and drive behind her? No, there were too many people standing at the cross walk. He had no options but to hope he could get the truck to pass in front of her. Surely the woman would notice the enormous vehicle bearing down on her, but she just seemed to be transfixed on her bag, only looking up in the second before the truck smashed into her body.

The driver's skill had stopped a head-on impact with the woman, but he and the rest of the firemen heard the thud as the passenger side front door area came into contact with her. After the thud came a sickening sight as one of the woman's arm lifted into the air and appeared through the side window. Even more sickening, a few seconds later the driver and crew felt the rear of the truck judder slightly as the rear wheels ran over the body. If the woman wasn't dead with the impact, she was certainly dead from having the weight of the fire truck run her over. The professionalism and training of the driver kicked in and he brought the vehicle to a controlled stop down the road before, ashen-faced, turning to his colleagues. There was a stunned silence where none of them could quite comprehend what had happened. Bob, the senior fireman, in the truck broke the silence.

"Tad, get on the radio to central and tell them the situation. They need to send another unit to our job. Bill, get down to the intersection and help the cops when they get there if they are not there already. See if there is anything that can be done."

Turning to the driver he said, "Brian, let's get some air, OK?"

He helped Brian down from the truck and kept the truck between him and the crushed figure of Marlene.

"I know this is of little help at this moment in time, Brian, but this was not your fault. You are not to blame for this, and we all saw what you did to try and avoid whoever it was."

"Bob, I just killed someone…"

"Hey Brian, I know someone died, but you didn't kill them. It was their own stupidity that killed them. Trust me, Brian, there was nothing you could have done. There is nothing anyone could have done."

Bob knew the shock had kicked in big time and it was something he had dealt with many times, and experienced himself, in dealing with fires where a building's occupant had died and the shock and guilt had come. He sat Brian on the front fender of the truck and spoke into his radio to talk to central to get a support vehicle down to their location. He had to get Brian to the shrinks at the earliest opportunity to make sure the guilt didn't mind fuck him for good.

"Brian, I've got some guys on their way that will take care of you. Trust me they are really good. Now take this and have a drink."

He handed Brian a plastic bottle of water and a valium tablet to help relax him.

Bill knew what to expect but the sight almost made him gag. Like most firemen he had seen many dead bodies, some horrifically burnt and so badly burnt you couldn't actually tell they had been human. It was clear that whoever this was wasn't a tramp. Just seeing the clothes they had been wearing he could tell it was someone with style and money. Could well be a local from the area. Definitely not dressed like a tourist. The dress had a very neat set of tire tracks running over it. The torso was crushed flat. The head was still attached, just, and looked grossly out of proportion to the rest of the body. There was blood and guts running from the body for 50 feet from the body as if the impact of the truck had basically made the body explode like running over a balloon filled with water. The sight conjured up a picture of a cartoon. A number of the passersby were crying and screaming hysterically. At the same time Bill got there a squad car arrived to join the solitary officer who had witnessed the accident. Traffic had come to a standstill and soon the junction had become a mess of vehicles who could not see there had been an incident. Hooting their horns as they figured it was just another New York traffic snarl up.

Bill jogged back to the fire truck and grabbed a fire blanket and then back to the accident and covered the woman with the blanket. The officers were talking together when he got back and made their introductions.

"Hi, I'm Officer Miller."

"Hi, Firefighter Hillman, please call me Bill."

"Thanks Bill, so what happened?"

"We were reporting to a 911. Lights and sirens as standard practice in a built-up area. We were coming to the intersection behind us. Lights were green for us and the traffic in front getting to the intersection had pulled over, same the other side of the intersection. We were doing 35 mph to 40 mph as we came around the corner and then in the middle of the road appeared a female pedestrian. She was standing still and reaching inside her bag. Brian, sorry Driver White, tried swerving to avoid her. Unfortunately the momentum of going around the corner and making a tighter turn caused the vehicle to skid slightly. Driver White had the vehicle under control at all times, but just couldn't make the turn tight enough to miss the pedestrian. The vehicle hit the pedestrian at roughly the front passenger door and then, as the rear of the truck's momentum continued, the rear wheels ran the victim over. I would say the victim died with the impact of the truck, it was a horrible thudding impact. I hope for their sake they were."

"Thanks, Bill. I spoke to the officer at the scene who witnessed the accident and he gave the same account. It seems as though we have a case of a jay walker who, for whatever reason, decided to stop in the middle of a busy road. We need to get to know who the victim is and maybe there will be more clues. Looks like the victim could have been distracted by something to do with her bag. The victim could have been deaf. I don't think, looking at the evidence, the victim was visually impaired. The other reason might have been suicide; however, who the hell has the guts to walk in front of a fully laden fire truck? That would have to be one sick person, with real serious issues! I know this city is crazy but that would be a first for me, and I've been on these streets more than twenty-five years. We will need a formal statement from all your guys, but it can be done over at your station later, I'll get someone over to take them later. I'm sure as hell wouldn't want to be in your driver's shoes. That is some nasty shit to have to carry around with you. The self-imposed belief you killed someone can be a real mind fucker."

"Yeah, Brian is a great guy. Married with two kids. It will be tough, no doubts, but our squad has a great shrink. If anyone can fix Brian, it will be the shrink. If it's OK I'll get back to the engine. Do you need anything else from us? Any photographs?"

"No thanks Bill, you and the guys are free to go. The refrigerator boys will be here any time, and then we can get the road sweepers in and then go about getting this shit traffic freed up. No doubts we will make headlines again tonight with someone bitching about the volume of traffic in the city and what are the cops doing about it…"

"Good luck with that, officer."

With that, Bill walked back to the fire truck. Brian had already been collected by the shrink and was being whisked off to some place to get to work on him away from the station. Bill caught up with Bob and gave him the low down on the conversation with the cops. There was nothing else for them to do, so the crew mounted up and with Bill at the wheel, the truck headed back to base.

Ten minutes later the wail of a siren slowly making its way through the blocked streets could be heard and Officer

Miller was hopeful it was the refrigerator boys. He had been notified they were stuck in the traffic, but finally they came into view and pulled up by the still covered remains of Marlene. The driver got out and came over to Officer Miller.

"Sorry we're late, Chief."

"No worries Tom, glad you made it at all. It's not a pretty picture under the canvas."

"I'm not sure any RTA is ever a pretty sight, you just get more immune to them the longer you do this job. So, let's take a look then."

Tom pulled back the canvas so he could assess the victim. He immediately came back with, "This reminds me of a Daffy Duck cartoon."

He carried on with his inspection, working out how best to get the remains up and keep as much of them intact as was possible. There still had to be a postmortem, no matter how obvious the cause of death was. It was hardly a secret how this person had died, but there would be clues potentially as to why. His partner was by his side and they discussed different strategies to lift the remains. Finally they had their plan made up and they pulled from the back of their refrigeration van what looked like two wide handheld snow plows. With the aid of one of the police officers, who held the canvas to cover as much of the sight from the spectators that were still gawking, the snow plows were gently eased under the remains until they were confident they had the best opportunity to lift the corpse without any other significant damage. They pulled a collapsing trolley from the unit and then carefully lifted the plows to align the remains on the trolley before pulling the plows away and using the canvas as a cover again, loaded the stiff into the unit.

Five minutes later Tom bade farewell to Officer Miller and headed with sirens blazing to the local morgue. The sirens weren't actually necessary as the body wouldn't be going anywhere, but Bob wanted to get back. He was heading to the game tonight and didn't want to be late.

199

A further forty minutes later, the road sweepers had been and cleared up as much of the blood stains as was possible and finally, with a huge sigh of relief, Officer Miller was able to open the road again.

Miranda had hung up the phone having left a message for Marlene. She had finally got around to calling Marlene about Imogen. She had tried the apartment and it had gone to some type of voicemail. She thought, having left the message, it's up to Marlene to return the call and find out the news.

Tuesday, 17 June 1986

"Date: Tuesday 17 June 1986. Time: 9.37 am. The corpse is a white female aged approximately forty-five to fifty-five years old. No significant features are visible, except she is unnaturally thin. OK, turn the tape off and start again… I couldn't resist." The cheerful voice of Andrew O'Leary, Head of Pathology, said turning to his assistant. Ingrid smiled back. She had, over the years, warmed to Andrew's morbid sense of humor.

"OK," said Andrew, "let's start again."

Ingrid went back to the tape recorder, rewound the tape and pressed play and record at the same time.

"Date: Tuesday 17 June 1986. Time: 9.37 am. The corpse is a white female aged approximately forty-five to fifty-five years old. No significant features are visible. Multiple organ destruction caused by a major impact…"

The autopsy continued for another forty minutes with no signs as to why a perfectly healthy middle-aged woman would walk in front of a fire truck. From a pure pathology perspective it was an open and shut case, nothing suspicious. There were no signs of drug use, the woman had no hearing or visual impairments and his suspicions moved more to mental health issues. Having switched the tape recorder off he and Ingrid moved to a different table where the lady's shoulder bag was sitting. The contents that had spilled out had been placed back inside and there were clear signs as to what had killed the woman. There was a well imprinted tread mark of one of the rear tires that had continued over the bag and over the body. The contents had identified who the victim was, hence the reason Andrew had to perform the autopsy himself. There were high-ranking people in the city asking questions as to why one of their wealthy types was lying in a morgue and they didn't want any surprises to come out.

As Andrew was going through the contents of the bag he came across a damaged pager in a partly zipped inside pocket. He had considered investing in one himself, but the hospital was in the process of organizing them for key staff so had held off. They certainly were not cheap and he was not sure being able to be contacted any time of the day, or more importantly night, was such a good idea. He pulled the pager out and noticed the display was still showing with an out of state number. He wondered if the police had spotted this and made a note to check this with Officer Miller. Making a note of the number he managed to get to another screen that gave a time and date. Making a note of them also he headed to his desk, asking Ingrid if she could call the canteen to get some coffee sent down. Back at this desk he picked up the phone and called Officer Miller.

"Hey Brian, Andrew speaking."

"Andrew, good to hear from you. What's going on in your place? Probably not a lot surrounded by all those stiffs, and if there is, I don't want to investigate."

They both laughed at the in joke and Andrew continued.

"Say Brian, you know the very thin rich lady you sent me a couple of days ago, did you record that she had a pager?"

"Hang on a minute, I'll just go and check the file."

"OK."

A minute later Brian came back on the phone.

"Andrew, there is no record of that in the report. Where did you find it?"

"It was in an inside pocket which was partly unzipped."

"Must have been missed. Probably with the contents having been spread across the road and having identified who the victim was the guys figured there was no reason to investigate further. You find anything interesting?"

"Well, I can probably help you solve your mystery."

"Really and how's that?"

"Well, I can tell you probably to the second when she got killed and why."

"Seriously, because of the pager?"

"Yep. A call came in at exactly the same time the fire

truck must have been coming around the corner. I can only surmise exactly what happened, but try this for size. Marlene, that's her name, is approaching the crossing. Light is still green to cross or starting to flash. Plenty of time in her eyes. She's local and knows the light timing and system. As she steps into the road her pager starts beeping and her focus is drawn to it. Rather than ignoring it, she stops and tries to get the pager out of her bag. She was trying to unzip the pocket with the pager, but the zip was sticking. I saw that there was material caught up in the zipper itself. She may not even have looked up and seen the fire truck before the impact. Bottom line is, the pager going off seems to be the reason she was oblivious to the noise and activity around her."

"Jesus, that would fit perfectly, and would also explain why someone well-known and highly visible with no known health issues would end up under the wheels of a fire truck. Can you get this into your report as a logical conclusion? It would add weight to the closure on the case and head office wants it closing yesterday."

"Seriously, Brian I can't see any other reason as to why this would have happened. Sure, will write up the case and hopefully it will then be closed. By the way do you recognize this number?"

Andrew read out the number he had taken off the pager screen.

"Hang on a minute, will just check the file again."

Three minutes later Brian was back on the phone.

"You ain't gonna believe this Andrew. Yeah we have this number on file."

"OK, so whose number is it? The governor, the mayor… the senator… I give up."

"No it's her fucking daughter's number."

"Holly shit, good luck in explaining that."

"Andrew, do me a favor and don't mention you were able to recover the number. Better still, can you destroy the pager now and say that after your inspection it stopped working?"

"Sure Brian, no worries. Will have the report on your desk by late afternoon."

With that they said their goodbyes and hung up. Andrew took a drink from his cold cup of coffee and hoped the hot new one would be there soon and, putting the pager down on his table, went back to see who was next on his long list of stiffs to dissect.

Wednesday, 25 June 1986

Miranda arrived at the church ten minutes before the service started. She was wearing a black thigh length dress with full face veil, black jacket and six inch black stilettos. Since the news had reached her about Marlene's death she had been frantically trying to find out about her inheritance. The news that Marlene had died had been greeted with the same feeling as if her hair dresser had left town. It was more of an annoyance. Their relationship had not improved and Miranda was only focused on one thing and that was herself.

As she entered the church she spotted a few people she knew from the papers and TV. It seemed that Marlene had been quite the opposite of Miranda. The church started to resemble a who's who of New York's social scene and it disturbed her as her inheritance was paying for this event.

As she was ushered down the aisle of the church to her front row pew heads turned in her direction. She caught the looks of the women eying her up with prejudged resentment and the men eying her up as a sexual fantasy. *Fuck the lot of them* was the only thought going through her mind. She was only at the service as it was a precursor to the official reading of the will and she couldn't just turn up for that... although it had been a serious consideration.

Sitting in her pew, she crossed her legs and her skirt rode up even further. She was sure the old guy sitting directly opposite was going to have a heart attack and a sinister smile crossed her face under the veil. *Typical fucking pervert*, she thought, *he wouldn't last five minutes with me*.

Miranda kept her eyes staring straight ahead and soon the hymn music started and the paid choristers sparked up with the priest walking in from the vestry. Miranda wasn't sure he was singing, it looked like he was miming. He arrived at the altar and as soon as the hymn ended he addressed the congregation.

"We gather here today to celebrate the life of Marlene,

who has now returned to her home with Our God, The Father..."

Miranda was not sure when Marlene had converted to or become a Catholic, quite ironic considering her previous profession, and switched off as her mind wandered onto more important things... how much was her inheritance...

The service was the necessary length and soon enough the priest was disappearing back in the vestry for a tipple of the special altar wine and to check on the revenue stream from the funeral. He still had to go to the graveyard for the burial – extra revenue, but there was always time for the altar nectar...

Miranda waited until the congregation had left before standing up and making her move. She calculated that it would be seen in a much better light that she didn't rush out; not that she cared about them but you never know when you might need some favors in the future. She opened a small vanity mirror and carefully smeared some of her eye liner makeup to gave the impression she had been crying and at the same time checked the church was empty. Checking she was going to be the last one out she stood up and walked briskly to the large oak doors which were open and streaming in the mid-afternoon July sunshine.

Miranda walked with some little difficulty over the cobbled path, and then onto the grass, with her heels immediately slicing into the earth like a hot knife through butter. Balancing on her toes she managed to make the remaining distance to the graveside and, with the rest of the congregation, waited for the priest to arrive to say some more passing words before the coffin was gently lowered into the grave. Again, Miranda waited by the grave willing the rest of the congregating to go so she could get on with the important part of the day. She had spotted Marlene's lawyer discretely standing away from the grave and when the congregation had left she turned and walked over to him.

"Good afternoon, Miranda, my deepest condolences."

"Good afternoon, Mr. Magruder, I presume you have the information I am looking for?"

If Mr. Magruder had been surprised at Miranda's directness he hid it well.

"Actually, we need to talk, so maybe I could escort you over to my office."

"I have my own car I'll see you there in twenty minutes."

"OK, Miranda I'll see you shortly."

Miranda was concerned with Mr. Magruder's comment. She was frustrated that he had not just said yes, however getting into an argument in the graveyard was not going to get the answers she wanted. Without saying another word to Mr. Magruder she turned around and headed back to the car park, again struggling over the grass and path, before getting to the tarmacked roadway.

Seventeen minutes later Miranda arrived at the offices of Mr. Magruder. The building was typical of such a lawyer. It was in a well-to-do suburb and took up the four stories of the mid terrace property. Outside, on the wall were the obligatory plaques identifying the names and qualifications of the lawyers housed within. As Miranda walked up the steps the door was opened by Mr. Magruder himself. Clearly he either knew a short cut or had not kept to the speed limits to be there before her.

"Thank you for coming over, Miranda."

Mr. Magruder still appeared unfazed by the initial conversation with Miranda at the church. Miranda didn't respond. Mr. Magruder continued.

"If you will come this way to my office we can go through the details."

With that, he led Miranda up two flights of steps to his office which was significant in size and decorated in a modern art deco style. It didn't fit in well with the rest of the building which had seemed to be stuck in the 1970s. Dark wooden paneled walls, wooden floor tiles with the occasional rug and lots of wall lights pointing upwards at old photographs of how the building and area used to look at the turn of the century.

In his office Mr. Magruder showed Miranda to a chair at a small conference table and picked up a file from his desk.

"Can I get you a coffee, Miranda?"

"Black, no sugar."

"OK."

With that he pressed an intercom on his desk.

"Mrs. Alexander, could you bring coffee for two please."

"Certainly Mr. Magruder," came back the answer.

Before the coffee arrived Mr. Magruder decided not to talk about the will itself focusing on small talk instead.

"So, Miranda how are things in Boston these days?"

"Things are going well, Mr. Magruder. I have been diversifying my business activities in a number of different fields. It is important to have a balance and make sure not all your eggs are in one basket."

"A wise policy if I may say so, Miranda. I see too many business people so focused in one particular area and they end up strangling themselves as they do not have the vision to see and act outside the box."

"I see that a lot and its good news, for me at least, as those companies are easy to acquire and then to maximize the profit from them."

The coffee arrived and, after pouring Miranda a cup, Mr. Magruder started.

"Miranda, the reason I wanted to discuss your mother's estate with you in my office is that there is an issue. Marlene did not have a will in place before her untimely death. I had been trying to get her to address this subject for the past year, however she didn't see it as a priority. She was more focused on enjoying the sights and sounds of New York. Putting it simply, trying to get the will resolved will take a significant amount of time. It is clear that you are naturally the only direct family member involved in the claim, however her business activities were, shall we say, well-hidden and will unfortunately take a long time to unravel, if we ever fully unravel them."

"Are you telling me that there may never be any inheritance?"

"That is a possibility, Miranda. Marlene had made it very clear that she didn't want your name associated to any of the businesses she owned. It was, as she told me, for your own protection in case any of the businesses got into difficulty and you were then legally accountable for them. She was doing it for your benefit. Unfortunately there is a downside with this."

"So you are saying that there is no inheritance? What am I supposed to do sit back and wait whilst you sort it out?"

"Unfortunately yes, Miranda, I cannot give you any more of a precise answer than that currently."

"Who owns the apartment and everything inside?"

"That's a little clearer. That was in Marlene's own name and I have been working as a priority to ensure those assets are transferred to you. It will take me another week or so to complete the transaction, but I should have that completed by the end of the month."

"I want three evaluations carried out on the apartment, and, at the earliest opportunity, the apartment to be put on the market. I want you to deal with it personally and also I want an evaluation on all the contents, excluding personal artifacts. I want at least one of those evaluations to be completed by an out of state evaluator. I need a key to the apartment and also the code to Marlene's safe."

"Miranda, I understand and will carry out your request. I cannot give you access to the apartment at this time, you must appreciate the situation."

"Mr. Magruder, you can stick the situation up your ass. Give me the keys. I expect the apartment to be sold by the end of July and I will tell you what I will accept for it once I have seen the valuations. Is that clear?"

The feral look was back in her eyes and Mr. Magruder could see a dangerous situation rising. He considered digging in his heels, however the look in Miranda's eyes told him enough. The difference between Marlene and Miranda was stark. Marlene had been very laid back and very liberal in her dealings. Miranda on the other hand was cold and direct. There was no emotion or feeling just a burning personal drive. For what? He didn't know or want to know. For sure her reputation from word of mouth was accurate. Definitely someone who you didn't want to get on the wrong side of.

Switching subjects, Mr. Magruder said, "As a separate point, can you let me know how you would like to cover the costs of dealing with Marlene's estate?"

"That's simple, Mr. Magruder. It is entirely in your hands how much you get paid. You will get 1% of the assets made available to me. I will see every invoice, transaction and document associated with the dealing. I am sure you understand that it is in all our interests to maximize the potential of this situation."

Mr. Magruder could barely believe the cold and callous nature of Miranda, however it was clear that she knew what she wanted and he could see a good potential out of the deal. This transaction, if the stories about Marlene were true, could represent a good personal pay day. The standard fee his company charged would go through the books the balance would certainly help his lavish lifestyle.

With no further conversation Mr. Magruder went to his floor safe and opened it, keeping his body between the safe and Miranda so she couldn't see the combination. It was an old habit. Having relocked the safe, he returned to the conference table a minute later having pulled out a set of keys.

"Here are the keys to the apartment. Can you return them tomorrow so that they can be available for the valuators and potential clients? Unfortunately, Marlene's other set of keys are still with the police until the pathology investigation is closed."

"Mr. Magruder, if I get the necessary support at the apartment the keys will be with the concierge today. It

210

won't take long to do a final inspection. Oh, before I forget, I expect to see a catalogue of all the assets that are going to be sold, photographs and valuators' estimated pricing. I would hate to consider there is an opportunity for someone to take advantage of this situation."

Mr. Magruder was clear this statement was aimed at him, seeing as he was directly responsible for all the transactions.

"Miranda, that is very clear and I will ensure everything is clearly documented."

With that, Miranda stood up and headed to the door. As she reached the door, she turned around and said to Mr. Magruder, "Remember, I expect the valuations and catalogues next Monday. As an incentive, if you don't meet the deadline your commission will reduce to 0.75%."

With that, Miranda let herself out the office and walked out of the building.

Mr. Magruder sat at the conference table for a few minutes mulling over the meeting with Miranda. As she had walked out of the room the only thing he could think of was Miranda was a human version of a black widow spider... Sighing he walked over to his desk and picked up the phone to start getting the apartment and estate closed down.

Miranda walked over to her car and headed to Marlene's apartment. She arrived twenty-two minutes later and pulled up into one of the spaces reserved for Marlene's apartment. She entered the lobby from the underground parking via the elevator and walked over to the head concierge.

"George, I need cardboard boxes, bubble wrap and tape sent up to the apartment. I need the boxes making up, and when I call down will need the porters to take the boxes and have them sent to this address."

As she spoke she handed a business card with her Boston address on.

"Yes, Miss Miranda. I will have the boxes sent up immediately, and my deepest condolences, Miss."

"Thank you, George. I appreciate your concern."

"Miss Marlene was a lovely lady and it's a huge shame. She seemed to have settled so well here. It may not be the place to say, miss, but some of her visitors were pure scoundrels I believe more interested in her money."

"Thank you, George and it's not out of place. Unfortunately, I believe they might have already taken advantage. I don't suppose you would know who these individuals were would you?"

"Actually, Miss Miranda I do and will ensure a list of the names and other details I have on them is sent up to your mother's apartment shortly."

"Thank you, George. Can you add your contact details on there as well? I may be looking for your services soon. I am probably going to be heading to New York from Boston."

"Thank you, Miss Miranda. It would be a pleasure to serve you."

With that, Miranda headed for the elevator and up to Marlene's apartment. The elevator doors opened and Miranda unlocked the front door and walked inside. The lobby, as with all the rooms, was immaculately clean and it was clear that either the cleaners hadn't heard the news or figured they needed to keep working until told otherwise. Miranda made a note to tell George to tell the cleaners to keep coming, until the apartment was sold.

Miranda went into Marlene's study and found the wall safe behind the painting. Taking the painting off the wall and opening the safe using the piece of paper with the combination written on, Marlene started to empty the contents. Miranda had, on one of her brief visits, seen Marlene open the safe and had been close enough to make a note of the combination. *Payback*, she thought to herself. Just then the doorbell to the apartment rang. Closing the study door behind her she opened the door and in came three porters all carrying cardboard boxes, bubble wrap and tape. Putting the packing materials in the foyer of the apartment the porters left and Miranda headed back to the study.

Miranda collected the jewelry first. She wrapped it in the bubble wrap and packed it in the first cardboard box. Included were a wide selection of diamond encrusted bracelets, necklaces, earrings and rings. It seemed Marlene had favored diamonds over gold. All were designer jewelry pieces and would get a good price. Maybe, she thought, she might keep some of the more selective pieces for herself. Next came the shoes. Marlene had the same shoe size as Miranda and this was one of the few areas they had had in common. The collection would rival that of Imelda Marcos and it took Miranda the best part of two hours to sift through the shoes she was going to keep and the others would be part of an auction.

By the time Miranda had selected the wardrobe she wanted for herself the cardboard boxes were full. She had taped them up and called down to George to have them taken away and carried by a courier to her Boston address. That done Miranda went back to the study to go through all the other materials she could find that might have some relevance to her inheritance and for her business activities. She came across a file with Polaroid photographs that looked like incriminating evidence and planned on linking the photographs up with the list from George later. Nothing else of significance turned up so Miranda turned to Marlene's bedroom. Another hour later and it was clear to Miranda that Marlene had nothing of relevance stashed away in the apartment. She was frustrated by the lack of information and documentation and it just endorsed the feeling that Miranda had that her mother had been liberal with her newfound wealth and it was going to make things more challenging to recover the assets she believed she should be entitled to. Surely there must be more than just a couple of bank accounts, the apartment and the Rolls-Royce she had seen in the car park.

Locking the apartment door behind her Miranda took the elevator back to the lobby and walked over to George.

"George, here are the keys to the apartment. A guy

called Mr. Magruder will be in contact shortly as he is charged with organizing viewings and the sale."

"Yes, Miss Miranda. It's a shame you won't be moving in."

"No, George, it's not my style. I'm going to get a place on 7 East 76 Street. That's the reason I need your details so you can take care of me over there."

"Very good, Miss Miranda. Please call whenever is convenient and I'll make sure all arrangements are taken care of. Do you have an idea of when you are likely to be moving?"

"Not yet but will give you a month's notice and I will be increasing whatever Marlene was paying. Let me know what you need and I'll get it organized."

"Thank you, Miss Miranda, you are very considerate."

"Yes, George that's true, but good help is hard to find."

With that, Miranda headed back to the elevators and went down to the garage for the drive back to Boston. She had left the veil in the car and when she got back in she threw the veil out of the car. She had no intention of going to any other funerals, and she wouldn't need it for her own.

Wednesday, 31 December 1987

Miranda was surprisingly looking forward to the party this evening. She had been working for herself continuously now for the past five years and the sixth anniversary of Matriarg Vennote had passed a couple of months ago. Miranda felt she needed to chill and let herself go. Tonight was a select group of likeminded women, most of whom Miranda had met over the past couple of years in various ventures which had proven to be beneficial for them all. The age range of the women was from twenty-eight to forty-nine, all having a burning ambition to prove to the opposite sex that women were better in business. It had become almost a cult with Tracy as the unelected leader. All the women at the party were wealthy to the point they didn't need to work, but for them work was their life and outside their quarterly gatherings very few of them had any form of a social life to talk of. None were married. A few had partners but their relationships were, at best, opportunities for them to have inhibited sex, to those that partook, the only benefit men offered. The others who had partners only had sex with other women. They were the dominant ones their partners just sex slaves to their whims, but well-rewarded.

Miranda had been pretty much celibate over the past five years. She had never found the time and had settled for self-pleasuring when the urge arose. She had a range of sex toys to support that need, but what had got her excited about the party tonight was that Professor Andrea Laird had called her a couple of days before to see how she was doing and seeing if Miranda wanted to meet up as she was stopping over in Boston before heading back out to Australia where she was now working. As soon as she heard Professor Laird's voice her mind shot back to that night and without hesitation said yes and told her they were going to a party.

At 5.30pm the doorbell at Miranda's apartment rang and she opened the door. Professor Laird stood there with that cute and sexy smile she remembered and Miranda threw her arms around her neck and they enjoyed a passionate embrace. Miranda could feel her nipples becoming very erect, which had a lot also to do with the fact that Professor Laird had slipped her hand up Miranda's jumper as they were kissing.

Miranda pulled away briefly and holding Professor Laird's hand pulled her into the apartment. Shutting the door she said, "It's great to see you again."

"You too, I often wondered how you would make out and, looking at this place, you did alright for yourself."

"It's been tough, but we can talk about that later. We have two hours before we have to be at the party and I hope you are not thinking of staying anywhere else tonight. We have some catching up to do."

With that, she led Professor Laird into her bedroom and unbuttoned her suit jacket. Slowly and carefully she let her hands wander over the curves stopping at her breasts to feel the mounds and then very gently rubbing her fingertips over Professor Laird's nipple until they were protruding through her blouse. She then slowly, whilst they kissed again, unbuttoned her blouse exposing more and more of Professor Laird's bare skin until her blouse was undone completely and pulled out from her trousers.

Miranda stopped kissing Professor Laird and let her hands gently pull apart the openings of the blouse until her breasts were fully exposed. Miranda bent down and started to lick Professor Laird between the breasts whilst caressing her mounds and nipples. Professor Laird moaned gently. She could feel herself getting very wet between her legs. Professor Laird was sure Miranda must have been able to read her mind as she moved her hands from her breasts and her tongue took over licking and teasing her nipples whilst her hands slipped down to her waist and unbuckled her belt and undid the button holding her trousers up. Within seconds Professor Laird's trousers were around her ankles and Miranda had got her left hand inside her panties feeling her very wet vagina. Miranda plunged her index and middle finger on her left hand inside Professor Laird, and Professor Laird moaned more loudly and tried to open her legs further to give Miranda more access. Unfortunately her trousers stopped her movement.

Professor Laird caressed Miranda's neck and kissed the top of her head. Miranda stopped licking Professor Laird's nipples and their mouths came together again and soon their tongues were exploring each other's mouths in an ever-growing passionate way. It was clear they were both deeply aroused by the situation and both had pent-up sexual frustrations that wanted and needing releasing.

Professor Laird, not wanting Miranda's fingers to stop exploring her vagina, managed to kick off her right shoe so she could step out of her trousers. Her panties were still trapped, but on the third attempt managed to get her right foot out of them. Now she could spread her legs wide and Miranda kneeled in front of her and with her fingers inside started to lick the front of Professor Laird's vagina.

Miranda could taste Professor Laird's juices. They were flowing freely and copiously. Miranda plunger her fingers in deeper and the moaning from Professor Laird intensified. Ten minutes later Professor Laird felt she was going to explode. Miranda had pushed her onto the bed and her legs were spread as far wide as she could ever imagine possible. Miranda was switching between sucking on her clitoris and plunging her tongue inside her. She had taken her fingers from inside her vagina and, with Professor Laird's own juices, used it as a lubricant to insert her fingers up Professor Laird's ass. Professor Laird being finger and tongue fucked to orgasm. She could not remember the last time she had been so far out of control of a situation. Her moaning had become a scream of pure ecstatic pleasure growing and growing to the point where she had lost control of her bodily functions and had actually pissed all over the bed covers, but it seemed only to make Miranda more and more frantic in her actions. Professor Laird was convinced she was going to pass out when she finally orgasmed. She screamed with pleasure and relief and her whole body shook as the orgasm took over. Even then Miranda did not stop. She kept up the fingering and sucking and drank down Professor Laird's orgasm juices. Professor Laird twitched a few more times before Miranda finally stopped and withdrew her fingers from her ass.

"My God, Miranda you were fucking wonderful. Now it's my turn."

With that, Professor Laird struggled off the bed and stripped off her blouse and pulled her other leg out of her trousers before pulling Miranda's jumper over her head exposing her large breasts and erect nipples. Miranda clearly had enjoyed giving Professor Laird an orgasm and had probably had been pleasuring herself at the same time. Professor Laird licked Miranda's nipples to ensure they stayed erect and put her right hand under Miranda's skirt and felt her naked underneath, but there were juices running down her thighs. Miranda's vagina was completely shaved and smooth.

Professor Laird gently bit each of Miranda's nipples and then moved her tongue down to Miranda's belly button, something Miranda liked with an intake of breath.

Professor Laird knelt down and looked up at Miranda. Her hands were working their way up Miranda's legs, one heading for her ass the other for her vagina. She said, "You know I really like a shaved pussy. Let's see if we can make this pussy purr."

Without saying another word Professor Laird's head disappeared under Miranda's skirt and then the gently licking and kissing around Miranda's vaginal lips started. Professor Laird didn't penetrate her vagina for a long time, but Miranda could feel herself becoming more and more aroused. She hadn't realized how sensitive her pussy lips were and the more and more Professor Laird didn't penetrate them, the more and more Miranda got aroused and could feel herself thrusting against Professor Laird's lips and tongue. She so desperately wanted to be penetrated and Professor Laird knew it and continued to tease her. Professor Laird was riding with the movements like a small boat in choppy seas. Miranda was holding Professor Laird's head and was trying to almost push her head into her vagina, but Professor Laird continually managed to stop the penetration.

Miranda was moaning and it was getting louder. She could feel herself coming to orgasm without any penetration, something she never realized was possible and then, when she least expected it, Professor Laird entered her with her middle finger on her right hand up her ass, her left index in her vagina and her tongue penetrating her vagina at the same. The result was like Miranda had received an electric shock. The orgasm was like being hit by a tidal wave. It was instantaneous and all-encompassing. Miranda had no idea how, but when she came down from the orgasm she was lying flat on her back on the bed and Professor Laird was eating out her pussy. Miranda wrapped her legs around Professor Laird's neck and within minutes was orgasming again. Within fifteen minutes she had achieved four orgasms and felt all the tensions and pent-up sexual needs being released.

They lay exhausted on the bed Professor Laird gently caressing Miranda's neck. Miranda looked over at the bedside clock and turned back to Professor Laird.

"We're going to have to get ready for the party, you coming for a shower with me?"

Professor Laird needed no further encouragement and, like giggling teenage girls, they chased each other into the bathroom and continued to explore each other's bodies like a new couple exploring sexual boundaries together for the first time. They gently and sensually washed each other's bodies, with Professor Laird sexually teasing Miranda at every opportunity. Miranda had stopped trying to resist the urge and let Professor Laird bring her to another orgasm. *Fuck the party*, she was thinking, but she had to go, and besides which she was going to have fun tonight. There would be more sex later.

Almost reluctantly they both got out of the shower and went about their routines for the party.

"Miranda, do you have a pair of panties I can borrow?"

"Sure, Professor Laird, but I was thinking it would be kind of more fun if we both went out without underwear."

"Now that's a really cool idea, easy access and all."

"Absolutely, you never know when the opportunity might arise and we don't want to be hampered with additional challenges."

"You are right, Miranda, so what are you going to wear? I think it would be awesome you going out in one of your mini dresses with your pussy on display, however one of your party guests may want to take advantage, and I'm not sure that's on the agenda... unless you want a manage a trois?"

They continued to get ready and Miranda pulled one of her Christina Stambolian evening dresses from the closet. She liked the dresses, but mainly for the fact that Christina Stambolian was designing and making dresses for Princess Diana. She added a pair of Gucci 5" black studded leather pumps and finished off her outfit with a faux mink coat by Jean Muir, and a string of pearls around her throat.

Professor Laird re-dressed in the clothes she had arrived and wandered back into the lounge. Miranda followed her out and pressed an intercom button.

"Maria, can you bring two Bloody Mary's."

"Yes, Miss Miranda," the au pair's voice came back over the speaker.

Professor Laird gave Miranda a quizzical look. Miranda explained.

"Maria is my au pair."

"OK ,so I deduce from that fact you have a kid?"

"You deduce right."

"So where is the father?"

"No idea, he was a willing donor, and before you ask no, I didn't have the kid myself. There was no way I was going to distract myself going through that crap of childbirth. Maria was the host and is responsible for all aspects of the kids life and upbringing."

Professor Laird was not shocked by what Miranda was telling her. She knew Miranda was different and if she wanted to have a kid and raise them this way, who was she to have an opinion?

"So, what's the kid's name?"

"Imogen and she's two years old."

"Cool, so where's the party and what time does it start?"

"The party is five blocks away so we'll grab a cab, and we need to leave after our drinks."

"Sounds good."

Maria walked in with a silver tray with two Bloody Mary's on, gave the drinks and without saying a word walked out of the lounge. Professor Laird's eyes followed the cute and well-formed ass of Maria as she walked out of the room. Miranda caught it and said, "Forget it, I don't allow it with the paid help. There are better options where we are going."

They toasted each other with their glasses and Miranda went into the bedroom to pack her purse for the night out. She was going to let her hair down tonight and decided she would be up for anything, so packed some coke into her purse to help the 'anything'.

At 7.20pm the cab was waiting outside and Miranda and Professor Laird, leaving a trail of expensive perfume, got in and continued to tell each other of their experiences since they last met at Harvard. Five minutes later they arrived at the elegant residence of Rose. She was the host for the evening and the front door was opened by their host before they had even the opportunity to ring the doorbell. Rose kissed both Miranda and Professor Laird on each cheek and Miranda made the introductions. Rose was in her early sixties but looked considerably younger. She had made her money in oil and had spent, by looking at her, a considerable amount of her wealth on cosmetic surgery. There were no wrinkle lines on her face and her breasts clearly had been worked on as they were as pert as would

221

be expected of someone in their twenties. Rose clearly wanted to show off her surgeries as her outfit was as revealing as it could be without her being totally naked.

Miranda and Professor Laird were escorted into the reception room where the rest of the group were chatting and enjoying a four-piece lady string group playing a mix of modern and classical pieces. Soon, Miranda and Professor Laird were engrossed in conversations in the group; the rest of the group wanting to know more about the mysterious friend Miranda had brought along.

At 8.30pm the group were notified that dinner was being served and they all moved into the dining room where the maître d' was guiding them to their seating places. There was one large circular table they all sat around. They were served with a 1980 Pinot Grigio as an aperitif and then the food started to arrive.

Professor Laird was sitting on Miranda's right hand side and engrossed in a conversation on the ethics of genetically modified food with Paula, the thirty-five year old owner of a string of gymnasiums across the State. The alcohol had started to kick in for Miranda and she let her right hand rest on the left thigh of Professor Laird. Professor Laird, without stopping her conversation, let her left hand wander across Miranda's right thigh and towards her vagina. Miranda opened her legs and allowed Professor Laird's fingers to caress her naked pussy. Miranda pulled her chair closer to the table which allowed her dress to ride up slightly, giving Professor Laird easier access and, unlike before in the bedroom, Professor Laird allowed her fingers to penetrate Miranda. Miranda hid her moaning by taking swigs of her wine. She was excited by the actions of Professor Laird and also that she was being pleasured in public. She was pretending to be focused on her drink so she would not be disturbed by Angela who was sitting on her left. Miranda was excited by the fact that only a small amount of the table cloth was hiding her being pleasured from Angela and all the waiters who kept wandering past filling glasses and collecting plates. She could feel the juices running from her vagina and when she did orgasm she was sure she was going to be caught as she shuddered. Angela had seen the shudder and asked, "Miranda, are you all right?"

"Yes thank you, Angela. I just had a strange sensation."

Professor Laird had withdrawn her fingers and was drying them on the napkin. She turned from her conversation with Paula and gave Miranda a knowing smile before excusing herself and heading to the toilet to clean up. Miranda sat there glowing with the alcohol and the after effects of the orgasm. Shortly after Professor Laird came back, Miranda made her excuses and headed to the toilet. She sat on the john and emptied a small tin out of her purse. Pulling out a piece of cardboard, she laid it on her legs and straightened out a piece of aluminum foil before tipping an amount of white powder onto the foil. Pulling a credit card from her purse she segregated the powder into even amounts and straightened the powder into five evenish lines. Satisfied with the results, and having put her special box back in her purse, she lifted the cardboard towards her nose and then, holding the cardboard in one hand, she blocked one nostril and snorted the first line off the foil. She waited about thirty seconds before snorting the second and then the third and fourth lines.

Miranda could feel the effects of the heroin kicking in as she stood up. The buzz was coming and when it arrived it hit her like a speeding train. She stumbled back onto the toilet and let the sensation kick in. She hadn't managed to snort the fifth line and a portion of it fell on the floor. The out-of-body sensation had been pretty much instantaneous after she took the fourth line. She was seriously hallucinating and was actually looking down on herself and from her vantage point and was sure she could see the heroin she had spilled on the floor. *Fuck it*, she thought, as she fell off the toilet putting her hands out to try and cushion the fall. She positioned her head as close to the powder as she could and started snorting again. *No point in wasting this shit, it's expensive,* she thought.

Her vision was starting to be impacted and she couldn't make out if all the powder had gone. She felt across the tiled floor and came across something slightly gritty and assumed it must have been some of the powder left over. She tried looking at her fingers but there were too many of them, and they had changed into some form of fucking donuts... She pointed them in the general direction of her mouth. She licked her fingers but something was not right. Miranda was sensing a burning from deep inside. This was not supposed to happen. She was used to this shit. Admittedly, she normally only had two lines but then she had never mixed the heroin with alcohol, it was one or the other. The sensation was getting worse. The pain became excruciating. She started sweating profusely and gasping for breath. It felt like someone had a hot knife and was sticking it in her heart. The last thing she vaguely remembered before passing out was the sensation of her bowels emptying themselves.

Professor Laird had not immediately noticed Miranda was missing. She assumed that she had been caught up talking to someone outside the dining room. She had been engrossed in the conversation with Paula. That was not the only thing that had been stimulating Professor Laird as Paula had been caressing her inner thigh for the past ten minutes, a movement that ended with her fingers undoing the zipper on her trousers and initially gently caressing her vagina. The caressing had become more intense until her fingers actually penetrated her and found her clitoris. The conversation had continued, although Professor Laird had found it more and more difficult to concentrate on the subject in question as she was getting highly aroused and could feel her juices running over Paula's fingers. She was at a point where she wanted to climax and held Paula's wrist and tried to subtly thrust her pelvis to and fro without attracting attention from around the table. Professor Laird only let go of Paula's wrist once she had climaxed. Paula gave her a knowing smile and was diverted in another conversation. Professor Laird thought there could be an interesting night in store if things didn't work out with Miranda.

Professor Laird again excused herself to use the toilet. This time to clean up herself. She could feel her trousers clinging to her inner thighs and the juices, whilst they had been hot coming out of her, were now cold and uncomfortable. She was very relieved her suit was black as if it had been a light colored one the stain would have been visible to everyone watching her leave the room.

She walked out of the dining room and headed to the toilets. She could not see Miranda and actually wondered if she had left the party. Maybe she had spied Paula fingering her, but she was pretty sure Miranda hadn't seen and also would not care. She had not come across as jealous. Vengeful yes, jealous no. Professor Laird was under no illusion that sex to Miranda was just that. It was something Miranda needed from time to time and today it just happened to be Professor Laird that had been supplying the sex.

There were two toilets next to each other which was a slight understatement. They were more than just a john. Besides the mandatory basin there was a vanity table with full a wall width and height mirror. The rooms had hairdryers, a bidet and two comfortable chairs. They were large enough to hold a small orgy. The toilet door on the left was open slightly and Professor Laird went to go in but stopped short and went to the other door. She tapped on the door and called Miranda's name. There was no answer. She tried turning the door handle but it was locked from the inside. Professor Laird banged a little harder on the door and called Miranda's name again. Still no reply. Then Professor Laird caught the smell of shit. It was a nasty putrid smell and was coming from underneath the toilet door. There was someone in there and Professor Laird was pretty sure it was Miranda. She walked back into the dining room and walked over to where Rose was sitting.

225

"Rose, excuse me for interrupting, could I have a word with you in private please?"

"Excuse me Nancy, I won't be long I can't wait to hear how your case went."

Rose got up and followed Professor Laird out of the room.

"Professor Laird, what's up?"

"Rose, I'm sorry to bother you but I think Miranda may be in trouble. I was just going to the toilet and noticed she hadn't been at the table for some time. One of the toilets is locked from the inside and there is an ugly smell coming from there. I banged on the door a few times and called her name, but there has been no answer."

"Right."

Looking around Rose saw William, her English butler.

"William, get some tools to get the toilet door open, we may have an issue with one of our guests. Can you also call 911, we may well be needing them."

"Yes, Miss Rose, right away. I will make the call and have you inside there in a couple of minutes."

"Very good, William."

Inside three minutes William had called the emergency services and requested paramedic support for a potential unconscious person locked in a closet and had removed the door handle. From his back trouser pocket he pulled a plastic card, and slid the card slowly down the gap between the door frame and the door above the door catch mechanism. Within a second he had released the sprung bolt and the door was open. Keeping the card in place until he could get his fingertips into the gap he slowly opened the door and smell of diarrhea hit everyone. Miranda was on the floor and not moving. She had lost all her color and was a dark shade of grey. William moved inside and put two fingers to the side of her neck.

"There is a pulse, Miss Rose, but very weak. The best I can do until the paramedics arrive is the keep her warm."

He stood up and gathered five towels from a pile on one of the shelves and covered Miranda from her neck down.

"Could one of you stay here and keep an eye on her so I can get some cleaning materials?"

"Absolutely William, go ahead, I'll keep an eye out for Miranda and also for the paramedics."

"Thank you, Miss Rose, I won't be long."

Professor Laird was silent and shaken. Only a few hours ago she and Miranda had been enjoying each other and now she was unconscious on the floor, looking like death and seemingly very close to it. She could only imagine the cause and didn't know whether to share it with Rose. To Professor Laird, Rose came over as cold and uncaring. Not surprising that Miranda was an 'associate' or 'friend'. They seemed to share a similar sense of self-preservation at others' cost and Rose was looking at Miranda lying on the floor more as a concern as if there was any damage to the fixtures and fittings, and to get rid of the smell, than for any concern over the wellbeing of Miranda.

A couple of minutes later the sound of sirens could be heard as the paramedics closed in on the house. The door was already open when the two paramedics walked up to it. They were escorted to the toilet by William. Rose had gone back to the dining room to tell the other guests that Miranda needed attention and shut the door to the dining room as if to block out the drama that was taking place only feet away from the party.

The paramedics walked into the toilet and one bent down to address Miranda and her vital signs. He looked up at his colleague with a grave look on his face.

"Pulse weak, dilated eyes."

Without another word he got to work on Miranda, fixing an oxygen mask and finding a vein he set up an IV lock before attaching a saline bag. He then prepared a shot of adrenaline, used mainly for people suffering from an anaphylactic shock. At this point in time it was essential to get something into the body to counter whatever was in there. These two steps should hopefully at least stabilize

227

the body's systems.

Without looking up he addressed Professor Laird.

"Miss, any idea what we are looking at here?"

"I'm really not sure. She was fine when we arrived here."

"OK, that doesn't help much. Do you know if she has a history of illness, any known medical issues?"

"I'm sorry I don't know her that well. I used to be her professor at university."

"OK miss, thanks."

"The only thing I can tell you is that she had a few Bloody Mary's, along with wine and Champagne during the evening. I wouldn't say enough to cause this situation, but…"

"But what, miss?"

"Well, I have a hunch she may have taken some drugs."

"What type of drugs?"

"I'm not sure, I don't do drugs, but as we were getting ready earlier I saw in her purse a small box. I was intrigued so took a look inside and there was some white powder in there. Honestly, I have no idea what it is."

"OK thanks, miss. Frank, can you search the lady's purse? Check and see if that piece of cardboard and foil has anything to do with this. We need to find out what shit she may have got inside her. Then radio control and tell them what we are dealing with."

"OK, Ben."

Frank quickly came onto the small box Professor Laird had been referring to. He opened the lid and saw the sealed bag with the remaining powder inside. Opening the bag carefully he put the index finger of his right hand in and let a small quantity of the powder attach to it before withdrawing it. He looked at it closely and then tested a small amount on his tongue.

"Ben, tastes like heroin."

"Shit. That's just what we need. Drink and drugs, a real classy combination. How much of that shit did she take in? I can see residue of the heroin around her nose. We need to

228

get her to A&E urgently. We don't have the equipment to deal with this properly."

Frank got on the radio whilst Ben fitted the IV saline drip and as he was talking to the control room headed out of the house to the ambulance to get the trolley. Within minutes he was back and they had Miranda on the trolley and heading back to the ambulance.

"Miss, are you going to come to the hospital with the lady?"

"Err no. I don't know her that well and there's nothing I can do or tell you beyond what you know."

Professor Laird didn't want to get involved, she was out on a flight in the morning and the party was just a way of spending the evening before the flight the next day.

"OK, miss, no worries. We'll take the best care of her we can. Do you know if she has any relatives we can contact? We need to get her insurance information."

"All I can tell you is where she lives and there is an au pair who lives there. Her name is Maria."

With that, Professor Laird wrote the details of Miranda's address and contact number in a small notepad Bob had with him. The paramedics left and soon the sound of the sirens faded away as they headed to the A&E unit.

William had stepped into the toilet and was cleaning up. He had subtly lit a number of scented candles and within fifteen minutes it was pretty much like there had been no drama. The evidence had all gone and the party was continuing unabated.

Professor Laird stood around, unsure what to do. Rose was back being the host and the atmosphere in the dining room was very relaxed. Paula came up to Professor Lard and put her arm inside hers and pulled her back into the party.

"Forget about Miranda. She's in capable hands. Now where were we?"

With that Professor Laird was escorted back into the party. Paula was clearly interested in exploring more of Professor Laird and soon, even Professor Laird was able to

229

forget about the earlier experience and even about the state of Miranda. She had more interesting things to consider before her flight in the morning.

Thursday, 1 January 1988

The only sound heard in the intensive care room was that of the monitor measuring heartbeat, pulse and breathing patterns. The beep sound was not regular. It was reflecting the battle that was going on between the medical professionals and the shit that was charging through the body of its victim. The medical professionals were trying to fight the equivalent of a division of heavily armed tanks with hand guns. They had at least found out what the poison was inside Miranda. The laboratory technicians had pulled out all the stops through the night and the analysis had identified the heroin as being cut to potentially catastrophic levels. It was a real nasty cocktail of heroin and Dexedrine, and the medical professionals were pretty convinced either they were looking at a suicide attempt or a victim of an ugly drug deal. Whatever the reason for the shit being inside Miranda they were running out of options and time.

"Blood pressure is dropping again. Shit, I am not sure how much more it can drop before we can switch off the monitors" Dr Fata said to his assistant Pedro

"The way things are it might be best if we just turn them off now. Who knows what this is doing to her brain. If she wakes up she could be a cabbage, notwithstanding the damage it's doing to the heart."

"Yeah a distinct possibility, Pedro. We need to get a breakthrough soon or there won't be anything to wake up. I shouldn't say this but if those paramedics had been five minutes later we wouldn't even be here, she'd just be another drug statistic in the morgue. There's nothing else we can do but wait and see if the antibiotics create any form of a protection. The only positive is there is no apparent swelling on the brain, and the fact she's in a coma. I'd like to say it's a medically induced one… but I'm not sure we have had any influence on it!"

"I guess all we can do now is keep an eye on her. Keep pumping in the adrenaline and saline and do something I

231

have not done in a long time, and that's pray."

"Wow, pretty scary stuff for a respected doctor to say."

"Yes, true but honestly, in thirty years of medical practice I've not seen anyone in this state pull through."

With that they settled down to a routine of checking Miranda on a regular basis, registering vital signs and checking on the drips and speed of feed. Every hour a set of intensive care nurses would come in and give Dr Fata and Pedro a ten minute break. They didn't go far in case the alarms went off.

The routine carried on through the night until Dr Fata and Pedro were replaced by Dr Parry and his assistant, Jimmy.

The routine continued day and night over the next five days. Miranda was kept in a medically induced coma the whole time. In reality, no one would know what the result would be when she was brought out of it however there was an agreement between Dr Fata and Dr Parry that she would be brought out of the coma on Wednesday 7 January…

Wednesday, 7 January 1988

"OK, Pedro. The moment of truth, heads or tails? Heads, she wakes up as if nothing has ever happened. Tails, she's a cash cow to the hospital until someone turns off the machine… or she runs out of cash."

Dr Fata had pulled a dime out of his pocket and flipped it end over end into the air. As it came down into the palm of his hand he covered the coin with his other hand.

"Tails."

"Well, let's see what the greatest medical brains in Boston can determine is the output of the last five days' treatment."

He opened his hands and saw the coin pointing heads up.

"OK, so we have a split decision," he said with a smile. "Let's go and find the real medical answer."

Dr Fata and Pedro headed down to the intensive care suite and called the duty staff into a small conference room.

"Good morning everyone. As you all know we are going to wake this lady up out of her coma. We are going to bring her out gradually so be ready to react to any change as it comes up. We'll start the process at 09:30, and plan to have her operating under her own steam by 11.30. Any questions?"

There were none from the duty staff and they all headed out to the intensive care suite to carry on with their duties until 09:30.

"So how are things looking, Pedro?" Dr Fata asked for the tenth time in the past thirty minutes.

"Situation is the same as last time. All monitors are reporting normal. It seems as though our patient is behaving herself"

"Good. We should know more in the next thirty minutes."

The tension was increasing with every minute that was passing. They had gone beyond the point of taking the patient back into a coma safely. Any slip up now and they would surely have, as minimum, severe brain damage and almost certainly a heart attack to deal with. The decibel level of the equipment pinging seemed to have risen, however the concentration of all the staff seemed to have blocked out all other sounds.

The final cocktail of drugs was now being induced. Dr Fata's eyes were systematically going through the different report points. Still, everything was showing all was going well. Maybe, just maybe, there was a chance this one may pull through.

An alarm went off when the drug bag was empty. This was swiftly replaced with an insulin drip.

"Pedro, check the patient's pupils."

"Dilated, as you would expect to see, Dr Fata."

"Good news, now we wait. Let's see when this sleeping beauty wants to wake up."

Miranda could feel a brutal headache. It was like someone had got her head in a vice and was squeezing it. She tried opening her eyes but struggled. They felt like lumps of lead. The pain in her head was ugly. She tried moving her left arm but, like her eyes, it felt like a lump of lead. As she tried to open her eyes again she was vaguely aware of a noise in the background. She tried to concentrate. If only the fucking pain in her head would go away.

"Dr Fata, the patient is conscious."

"Excellent."

"She has tried to open her eyes a couple of times and there was definitely a twitch of the left arm."

"I bet she has the mother of all headaches. Administer some morphine to try and deaden the pain."

"OK, Dr Fata," one of the nurses said.

Gradually the pain subsided enough for Miranda to try opening her eyes again. This time she was successful and started to make out shapes that materialized into people's faces. If only the ringing in her ears would stop, and then she passed out again.

"She's unconscious again," said Pedro.

"That's OK, Pedro she's now operating on her own. Good job team, we have our patient back from the dead. We'll wait for nature to take its course. Let me know when she wakes up fully. I guess in approximately twelve hours. Keep the drips going and fingers crossed."

With that, Dr Fata left the intensive care suite and headed back to his office to find out his next challenge. A road traffic accident where the patient had been cut out of the vehicle. The vehicle apparently had flipped after hitting a patch of ice and landed on its roof. Multiple traumas to the head, bleeding on the brain and the driver, a nineteen year old male, had a blood alcohol content of 0.091 when he had arrived. Tails was a sure fire answer on this one… but the parents of the patient had money…

Friday, 1 April 1988

"George, can you help Maria with the luggage please?"

"Sure Miss Miranda, I'll go right now."

Miranda was sat on a chaise longue overlooking the East River. The five bedroom apartment was suitable she felt for someone in her rising status. She strongly believed in turning her gains into meaningful visible assets and besides, her competitive nature had reduced $900,000 off the $16,500,000 price tag. Also it allowed her to cleanse some of the cash that had arrived from her expanding business network. Her accountants had been working overtime to find the solutions to those specific challenges and what she had seen and been told suggested the transactions were watertight from an IRS perspective… The apartment was on Leonard Street, a few blocks from where her new headquarters were going to be based. She had rented a 21,000 sq feet office building and with her charming skills had negotiated an agreement allowing sub-tenant rental and also the option to purchase the complete property outright at a time she chose, for a preset price built into the contract. She had agreed a $15.00 per square foot price which was reasonable, she felt, with the evidence she had shown the landlord of his discretions with a number of male prostitutes. The landlord came from a strong orthodox Jewish family his father being a well-known and respected Rabbi. She could probably have got it for $10.00 per square foot, but that may have well raised questions she didn't want to be asked and besides which, the landlord was getting money for nothing as her company was taking over the maintenance arrangements on the building, which also allowed for Miranda to install certain modifications in all the offices that none of her employees or sub-tenants would be aware of. Well, the landlord would be getting money for nothing once she moved in. The final nail in the deal was that she would not pay any rent until she moved her headquarters in, even if her sub-tenants moved in before her…

Her investment in Exemplar Systems the previous year was proving to be most advantageous. They had a small team who had become her personal security experts, assessing risk and implementing solutions to meet Miranda's requirements. Miranda had taken the recently introduced Computer Securities Act and decided she would develop a Matriarg Vennote Security Act that ensured every company she invested in had hidden cameras and microphones installed, all operated remotely and serviced by Exemplar Systems. The synergy benefit of this would be that all her companies were contributing to the profitability of another of her businesses…

Her new headquarters were being housed on the top two floors of the five story building. With the refurbishment of the building and the shared reception, postal and other services the $35.00 per square foot being charged would result with an annual net profit after paying off her headquarter fixed costs. She already had tenants lined up and they were all due to move in within the next month.

Miranda's main concern currently was whether it would be a Chardonnay or a Pino Grigio.

"George, before you go, I'll have a Chardonnay."

"For sure, Miss Miranda. Will you be dining in or out this evening?"

"I have a dinner appointment at 7pm so just take care of the others."

"For sure, Miss Miranda and have a successful evening."

"Thank you George, I expect this evening will prove to be very fruitful."

At that point Maria walked into the apartment pushing Imogen in a buggy. She was asleep clutching a stuffed toy dog she called Moreland, well it was the name on the tag when it had been brought. Miranda briefly thought how very cute Imogen looked as Maria pushed her past into the nursery. Another couple of years and she would be off to boarding school with Maria moving close by. It was going to be the best education money could buy. No thought would ever be put into the emotional side of raising Imogen; that was Maria's responsibility.

As Miranda appreciated the Chardonnay she thought about the timing of her move. It had kind of become important to put behind her the whole fiasco from the party. She knew from a business and social standing perspective her reputation was badly tarnished and she needed as quickly as possible to re-establish herself in a new territory. She also recognized that none of the people from the party had even tried to contact her since to check on her welfare, reinforcing her belief that her life would never be troubled by having friends, only acquaintances. She had considered California but felt her real power would come by moving to the Big Apple. It's where business was really done and to succeed there would naturally bring her success elsewhere. Tonight was the start of that reinvention.

Wednesday, 26 September 1990

Sheriff Reed had been having mixed emotions about this day for months. The inevitability of retirement was something he was kind of looking forward to, but he knew he was going to miss it the minute he stepped out of his office for the last time as a serving officer. For sure, times had changed. Criminals were getting more and more sophisticated in their activities, but that had only created more satisfaction for him personally when another villain ended up behind bars.

With a sigh he started the task he didn't want to do, emptying his drawers. At that moment Sheriff Blink stepped into his office.

"Good morning Frank, how you doing this morning?"

"Mixed emotions. I was just about to start to clear out my desk, but I'm glad you came by, it helps me put off the inevitable for a while longer…"

"Yeah, that I can understand, but you got exciting plans coming up. It won't take five minutes before you forget about us guys."

Both men knew that wasn't true, Sheriff Reed had been tied to his job for so long it was seen as his partner and his wife had been his mistress.

Sheriff Reed said, "Anything interesting going on out there today?"

"Usual stuff. A homicide overnight, two aggravated burglaries and an RTA death. Nothing for you to worry about or to stop the party later."

With that he left the office and Sheriff Reed to start the cleaning his desk. Sheriff Reed knew what was in his desk drawers, so he decided to start with the three drawer filing cabinet and see if there was anything he'd lost or forgotten.

It wasn't until he opened the bottom drawer of the cabinet that he came across the file of Mikey. After five years he had completely forgotten he had put the file in his cabinet and not back in the records office. He picked up the file, sat at his desk and opened it. He read through the front sheet summary and the facts started to flood back. He wondered what had become of Marlene and her kid Miranda; she would be a young woman now. He had meant to catch up with them when they had moved to New York and felt a small pang of guilt for not keeping his promise to stay in touch. Marlene was a good lady who had endured a real shit life with Mikey. The case itself had been closed, but as he read through the reports he felt there was still something that didn't quite fit together. Why would Mikey have killed himself with such a concoction? He had been a druggie a long time and knew the different shit he was taking. Who in their right mind would go up to a deserted place, break in, sit down and smoke a joint that would kill them? Mikey would have had to have known that there was cleaning fluid in there, unless... Sheriff Reed sat there and thought there had to be a logical explanation, but the only thing that came to his mind was that Mikey had been given the drugs by someone he knew and clearly trusted... or thought he trusted.

He got out of his chair and with the file in hand went to the records room. He was about to put the file in the correct storage box when he saw the Xerox and decided he would take a copy of the file and, when he had some spare time, would follow up on his hunches. If nothing else, it would help keep his mind active; he certainly didn't intend to end up on the morgue slab in five years time. A number of his colleagues who after a lifetime of working and being active had deteriorated to vegetables and morgue meat because they had switched off completely the day they retired...

With the original back in the storage box and the copy in the briefcase in his office he carried on with the task of emptying the drawers. He had never kept much there so his briefcase was hardly bulging and he certainly wouldn't be needing any cardboard boxes to carry away.

By 3pm he had done the rounds and spoken to everybody at the station. The conversations had been very repetitive as, with the exception of a few of the older sheriffs, the majority of the younger guys there had had very little interaction with him. He had been after all the boss, and his people skills had never been his strong point. He stood up from his desk, picked up his briefcase and headed out. As he pulled the door behind him he switched the lights off, taking a final look around and a shudder went through him. This was it. In twenty-reight paces' time he would be outside the station heading to his pickup and retirement. His routine was about to be changed forever and it didn't sit well with him.

He counted the paces and stopped at twenty as he bid his farewells to the reception team and then he was outside feeling the afternoon sun reflecting off the tarmac paved parking lot. Without looking back he walked over to his parking spot and SUV.

He pulled up on his drive to see bunting up decorating the outside of his house and thirty or so people on and around his drive. His wife had sprung a surprise retirement party and there was a gathering of neighbors, friends and a couple of his colleagues from the station who had been out on patrol whilst he had been at the station. It was going to be a long day and night as there was a formal dinner being held for him down at the town hall later being hosted by the mayor. Getting out of his SUV he took a Bud Light handed to him by his wife looking forwards to an afternoon and evening of drink and reminissing about the old times.

Wednesday, 20 September 1995

Fanny was enjoying her early retirement. She had left Boston six years ago and used a significant amount of her newfound wealth to find a more peaceful and simple life. She had brought a small cottage by the sea in the Caribbean and become a little bit of a hermit. She had given up the glamour and hustle of modern day living for a much more basic existence and to live out her life doing what she wanted to do. Time had no meaning to her life now. Simply, one day followed another. She got up when it was light and went to bed when it was dark. She had no television and her only modernism was to have to have an internet connection that allowed her to catch up with things in the world as and when she wanted. She had installed a library with over a thousand books and her computer, via the internet, allowed her to publish her writings under various aliases. Once or twice a month she would walk into the small village to have a leisurely lunch and chat with some friends Reggie and his wife, Aiida. They had been very kind and helpful to her when she had arrived and made sure she was left alone to get on with her life.

Hurricane Lewis had wrecked significant parts of the Caribbean less than three weeks ago but life had started to return to normal as Fanny made her way to The Lobster Pot restaurant. She always enjoyed the 5km walk through the tropical surroundings and the temperature was a pleasant 83 degrees Fahrenheit with only a slight breeze. By the time Fanny arrived at the restaurant she was ready for her usual and, as was her custom, walked in by the staff entrance to spend some time with Aiida who would be slaving away over the cooking whilst Reggie spent the time socializing with the customers.

"Hey Aiida, how are you?"

"Well it's great to see you, Fanny. We are doing just fine now that evil storm has gone."

"Yea, I stayed holed in whilst it came through. It was a

pretty rough one. Did you have any damage?"

"Well, it didn't blow the cobwebs from between Reggie's ears, but it did take some of the roof off so we had to close for a week to get the place back in order."

"I'm sorry to hear that."

"Could have been a lot worse for us, twenty minutes down the road they lost fifteen houses and old Aretha was killed by falling debris."

"Oh, that's terrible."

"Yea but at least she had a good stint she was ninety-two."

"I'm sure the long life here is sown to the excellent food and chefs," Fanny said with a smile.

"You know woman, you are right about that. Just think what the life expectancy would be if Reggie was cooking…" They both laughed.

The general conversation carried on for a few minutes before Aiida stopped cooking and looked at Fanny.

"Fanny, I don't want to concern you but someone was asking about you last week."

"Really! Who?"

"It was a serious looking redbone lady. I would say in her forties, not from around here. She had an accent similar to the one you had when you first moved here. She showed me a photograph and asked if I knew of you. For sure I said no. She enquired using your old name and a photograph from the Boston Globe, so I'm pretty sure she has no knowledge of you changing names. She said her name was Miss Smith and she was a friend of your auntie who's been really sick recently."

"Thanks, Aiida. I have no idea who that would be or even how anyone could track me to here. You know how careful I have been to hide my tracks. What is more is that I'm pretty sure it's someone I don't want to meet."

"Why's that, Fanny?"

"I have no living relatives…"

"So what are you going to do?"

"Keep a good watch out for anything suspicious and lie

low. Don't worry if you don't hear from me for a while, I am going to stay out of sight. If nothing suspicious happens I'll be back for lunch at the end of October. If you hear or see anything more of her just send an email to that account I gave you."

"OK but you've got that gun, yeah?"

"Sure but I won't need it. It's probably just someone looking for an angle on me from the past. I used to be famous once. Besides which, if it was bad news who ever has heard of a middle-aged female assassin?"

They both laughed, as much to release the tension, as they walked through to the restaurant tabled area.

Miss Smith was feeling very pleased with herself. Her appearance had changed dramatically and she no longer looked like the middle-aged woman who had been talking to Aiida. Her skills in makeup and appearance had transformed her into a rotund elderly American tourist. The fact that on this trip to the Lobster Pot she was accompanied by a man of similar looking age, both of them acting like typical American tourists overseas, had been camouflage enough. Neither of them was given a glance by the other diners. Miss Smith had done her homework well and knew that this restaurant was a popular stop off by tourists doing sightseeing tours with the holiday companies. This disguise also allowed her to conceal more of the listening devices she had left on her first trip to the restaurant. She had already replaced the two devices she had hidden last time as the batteries were due to run out shortly and she was convinced the cook knew more about Fanny than she was letting on. In her trade you quickly learnt the signs for someone who was not telling the truth. Her source in the Caribbean Police Force had only been able to give her an approximate area to go on and she had spent three weeks prior to finding The Lobster Pot searching and checking out other popular restaurants. She still had an hour before the bus would come past and pick up the tourists enjoying lunch. She and her partner had ordered lunch when the cook and a well-tanned lady walked into the restaurant from the kitchen. The reason Miss Smith was feeling well pleased was because walking into the dining room was the person she had been looking for, albeit she looked considerably different from the passport photograph she carried around with her.

Keeping up her appearance of being the loud tourist she told her partner she was heading for the ladies and bumped into various people and tables to get to the toilet corridor. She excused herself as she pushed past Aiida and Fanny who looked at her with the knowing look of 'well there's another American tourist...'

As Miss Smith headed to the ladies she looked over her shoulder she saw Aiida and Fanny heading around the corner to the patio section. In a matter of seconds she dived into the kitchen and recovered the recording device from a dusty shelf and pocketed it. She marveled at the technology available, as the device was sound activated, so it didn't run constantly and it was super silent when it was running. She was back at her table before Aiida returned from the patio area. She had one more thing to do and before she sat down and instructed her partner......to all around she was clearly the boss between them.....to come with her and take some photographs. The harassed partner was the focal point for the diners on the patio and Fanny was no exception. She didn't notice when Miss Smith expertly dropped a small transponder the size of a dime into her bag. It was highly unlikely that Fanny would notice it even if she saw it as it was to the untrained eye was an East Caribbean dollar. This special coin would help Miss Smith find exactly where Fanny lived as long as she kept within 250 yards.

The only question now was whether the bus would arrive before or after Fanny finished lunch. The bus pulled up on the opposite side of the street and Miss Smith and her partner walked around the far side of the bus. Her partner got on and mingled with another group of American tourists who had been lunching further down the road. Miss Smith disappeared into public toilets and came out five minutes later, after the bus had left. She had changed into a pair of jeans and a T-tee-shirt with a long black wig covering her hair. The padding she had worn and her clothes had been stuffed into a bin in the ladies toilets and the bag she had been carrying was turned inside out which had now become a different color and pattern. She had a pair of white headphones stuffed in her ears like she was listening to an MP3 player, with a pair of locally sourced cheap sunglasses covering her eyes and she loitered by the bus stop as if she was waiting for a particular bus. The only thing she hadn't changed was the trainers, but she doubted anyone would notice. The transformation was spectacular. She now looked more like the thirty-five year old woman she really was.

Fanny left the restaurant at 3.25pm. She looked around to see if there was anything suspicious going on. Realizing she would not know what looked suspicious or not – she was not trained for that – she decided to take a short detour before heading home. Ten minutes after leaving The Lobster Pot she arrived back at the front door and had to admit she had not seen anyone following her and tried to put aside her neurosis about someone following her.

Fanny definitely walked back more quickly than she had to get to the restaurant and when she saw her cottage she started to relax. She felt safe and at ease, as it would have been impossible for her to not have seen someone following her, especially through the meadow as it was an open space and no one could hide in the open. Despite this she let herself into the cottage and bolted the front and back doors. Despite the air conditioning that was buzzing in the background she found she was sweating. She sat on the sofa in the lounge and thought about why someone would be looking for her. No matter how long she thought about it she could not think of anyone, unless… surely not…

Fanny had taken some pills to help her relax and she

fell into a sleep and woke around 9pm. The cottage had become stuffy and she decided to take a short walk down to the stream. By 9.45pm she was walking back to the cottage, feeling refreshed and more at ease. She was going to have an early night and then tomorrow make decisions as to what she might do.

She let herself back into the cottage, bolted it and put the latch on the front door. As she finished putting the latch on the door a voice said,

"Good evening, Fanny. I've been waiting for you."

Fanny swung around to see a lady sitting on a dining room chair pointing a gun at her. She froze.

"Why don't you take a seat before you fall down?"

To Fanny everything was happening in slow motion. Questions were flashing though her mind… who, what, why, how…

The lady continued.

"You are asking yourself all kinds of questions and wondering how I found your cottage and how I got in and probably, most importantly, why."

Her voice softened considerably.

"Why don't you come and sit down and have a drink. I took the liberty to make a pot of tea." She picked up a cup with tea already in. "The tea will help with the shock and then we can have a little chat and get things cleared up."

Fanny was confused, scared and yet at the same time seemed only too willing to do something to take her mind off what was going on. She stumbled over to the table, sat down and picked up the black tea that the lady had poured taking a sip of the warm fluid. She downed the contents and started to feel a little better, at least briefly.

She started to have blurred and double vision. She felt as though she was having an out-of-body experience. She could see herself sitting at the table opposite the lady who had laid the gun on the table in a relaxed position.

"So, Fanny we're going to have a little chat. Well, to be precise, I'm going to ask you some questions and you are going to answer them. You see you have just swallowed a good dose of Midazolam. You may not be familiar with it but it is also known as a truth drug. Just in case you think you can counter this, I will share with you I am a highly trained interrogator and I will find out what I need to know. Your cooperation depends on the outcome of this session. Let's say you have some influence on the outcome. Do I make myself clear?"

The soft tone had been replaced with an aggressive tone that left Fanny under no illusion she needed to cooperate to have any chance of getting through this.

"Yes."

"Good, so let's start with your real name."

The questions came quickly one after another seemingly innocent in their request and the answers seemed to confirm to Miss Smith that Fanny was cooperating.

Thirty minutes later the questions stopped and Miss Smith said, "OK, you have told me all I need to know, so all you need to do now is sign this piece of paper and the ordeal will end."

"What's on the paper?" asked Fanny.

"Fanny, you don't get to ask questions. You do as I say, remember?"

"Yes."

Fanny could barely see the paper, let alone read it and she took the pen Miss Smith handed to her and attempted to sign. Doing the best job she could she dropped the pen on the table. Miss Smith picked up the pen and the signed paper and put it in her bag.

"So here's the deal. That drug you took was mixed with Temazepam. The Temazepam will kick in in the next five minutes and you will fall asleep. I will be off the island before you wake up and you will never be able, but don't even try, to find me. I wouldn't head back to the US for a very long time. Oh and by the way Mr. Gregory sends his regards…"

Fanny was more shocked. Mr. Gregory had tracked her down and before she passed out she briefly realized that what she had signed must have been some form of confession to his set up all those years before. It was her last thought as she collapsed off the chair onto the floor.

Miss Smith got up from the table and prodded Fanny with her trainer to check she was out and then unbolted and unlatched the front door before heading out to the small shed by the cottage where she had seen a wheelbarrow. She found a small can of WD40 and sprayed the wheel bearings to make sure it was noiseless before moving it outside the front door. She went in and carried out Fanny and dumped her in the wheelbarrow and headed off down the path to the stream; a point she had spotted earlier whilst Fanny had been asleep before her walk. Tipping Fanny out, she took the wheelbarrow and collected a full load or rocks of various shapes and sizes and dumped them next to Fanny. She repeated the exercise three times before transferring the mound of rocks into the stream by the side of a rocky overhang. She then went back and picked up Fanny and dumped her in the water before carefully stacking the rocks on top of her. After the first ten rocks were positioned Miss Smith didn't need to weigh down Fanny, the rocks were ensuring she didn't rise to the surface. Stopping for a moment she pulled out a small camera and took a number of photographs of Fanny submerged and held down by the rocks. Putting away the camera she continued piling up the other rocks which took another twenty-five minutes. By the time she had finished there were no signs of Fanny and it looked to the casual observer that the rocks had fallen as part of erosion by the stream. She again pulled out the camera and took shots from a number of angles.

Fanny never woke up from her sleep; she drowned before the effect of the drugs wore off.

Having listened to the recording from the restaurant Miss Smith knew she would not be disturbed, so rather than rushing to get away she went back to the cabin, putting the wheelbarrow back in its place and then stripping off and showering, hanging her wet clothes on the washing line to dry out overnight she went to sleep in Fanny's bed. She was asleep in minutes; after all, it was just a job. Her nonexistent conscience was clear…

Miss Smith knew she had plenty of time before Fanny was reported missing, but she wanted to collect the remaining half of the payment that was due after the job was completed at the earliest opportunity. Having slept very well, considering the physical energies used the previous night, she got up, did stretching exercises, showered again and, having helped herself to a breakfast of fruit and coffee, she prepared to leave the cottage. Once dressed, she pulled on a pair of rubber washing up gloves and cleaned everything she had touched. The bed linen and towels went into the washing machine which she switched on. By the time the washing cycle had been completed her DNA would be wiped clean. It took the best part of three hours for her to be confident she had left no traces in the cottage. Her final act in the cottage was to retrieve the transponder from Fanny's bag and, keeping the rubber gloves on, she pulled the front door closed before pocketing the keys for disposal at a later time, in a different country.

Leaving the cottage she followed the path past the point where Fanny was entombed, taking one last look at her handiwork and smiling to herself she carried on for the 10 km walk to the nearest village where she could catch a bus back to civilization.

Sunday, 24 September 1995

Miss Smith was not in a good mood; in fact she was really pissed. Despite having returned to Boston two days previously she had still not been able to contact Mr. Gregory on the cell number he had provided. They had agreed at their meeting not to discuss anything on the phone but to use it just to set a meeting point and time. She was getting the feeling Mr. Gregory's vengeance might have waned during her absence, hence him not getting back to her. She decided that more direct action was required to re-engage Mr. Gregory's attention.

When taking on the assignment, she had done some background checks on her client. She had no interest in why Mr. Gregory wanted some woman found, a confession signing and then ensuring the bitch remained out of circulation. Miss Smith, rightly or wrongly, took that as being taken out; in her eyes, dead people didn't and couldn't talk. What she found was her client had been a pretty successful businessman until he dropped out of society circles some twelve years ago and had basically since then been living in a remote part of Massachusetts outside of Millers Falls off Montague Road on a ranch on the edge of Wendell State Forest.

As she turned into the ranch entrance there were grazing cattle in the field to her right. The field went for approximately 500 yards up to the line of trees that probably marked the start of the forest. To her left was just an open expanse until in the far distance was another forested area. From her research the ranch was classed as a 50 acre estate and the sweeping drive was half a mile long. She approached the house, which was a large three story building with outhouses, garages and surprisingly, ten cars parked outside.

Miss Smith was immediately wary. She was unsure if she should continue, however if any observer was watching from the house it would look very strange to see a car drive a half mile off the road, turn around and leave.

She decided to take the risk and challenge Mr. Gregory, no matter who was in the house.

She parked next to a Cadillac Eldorado Touring Coupe, making sure her car was pointed towards the drive in case she had to make a quick exit. She got out of the car. Miss Smith had only the ignition key in her hand and left the doors unlocked, again a trick she had learnt some years before on how to reduce the time it would take to get in the car and get away. She remembered it as someone telling her about the KISS principle – Keep It Simple Stupid.

She was carrying her purse which had inside two manila envelopes, one white and one brown. The white envelope contained an abbreviated report; the brown the full report, signed statement and the photographs she had printed herself. What happened next would depend on which envelope Mr. Gregory received.

She walked up the steps to the front door and found it to be open and could hear multiple voices coming from inside.

"I don't agree. There has to be something wrong." A man's voice could be heard in an agitated tone.

"What do you mean?" Answered another man.

"He's saying that he had an agreement with the old man on this farm." This came from a lady.

"What agreement?"

"That the ranch would be handed over as a complete entity and not split between the families."

"Well, the will doesn't say that, does it?"

Miss Smith stopped outside the door to what was a large lounge where the conversation was taking place and continued to listen.

"Unless you have it in writing and signed by the old man it's not an agreement, it's just his ramblings."

"Like hell it is. He promised me the farm and I'm having it."

"OK, gentlemen and ladies." This from a new voice and one Miss Smith took as likely being a lawyer. "It is clear there is some disagreement in terms of the will, but legally, the will is binding. You for sure have the right to pursue legal actions against each other, however as the executor of the will can I give you some advice."

The room was silent as the executor paused for breath.

"My advice is very simple: do not take the legal route. Take a step back from your positions and consider the overall picture. You are looking at proceeds from this will in the region of $20,000,000. This has to be shared equally between the three children of the late Mr. Gregory and one tenth of the proceeds are to go to the people I named before. Should you chose to go the legal route I would envisage somewhere in the region of $4,000,000 will be wiped off the proceeds just in legal fees, and none of you would get access to those proceeds until the case has been closed in court, and then you might not get the share you believe you are entitled to. Add to this that, from experience, such court cases do not take any precedence and I would estimate the process to take an additional eighteen to twenty-four months, and that's if there are no complications. If I may be so bold as to suggest you all get off your egos, recognize this is something you didn't have before, and come up with a mature proposal amongst yourselves. I can come up with suggestions if you cannot get a final agreement, but consider what this is about."

The room fell silent and Miss Smith could imagine what was going through the different people's minds. She thought now was as good time as any to make her entrance. She now well understood why Mr. Gregory had not been answering her calls, and she considered her luck at turning up when the executor of the will was there, as trying to get her monies from one of the squabbling siblings would prove to be very challenging.

As she walked through the door nine pairs of eyes turned to her.

"Good afternoon," she said.

"Who the hell are you, and what are you doing on this ranch?" It was from the man she heard saying he had an agreement for the ranch.

"My name is Miss Smith and I am a business partner of Mr. Gregory."

"Well you have made a wasted journey, he died two weeks ago."

"I'm sorry to hear that Mr.?"

"I'm Mr. Gregory Junior."

Miss Smith went on.

"My condolences to you and all the whole family. I presume my business is now to be dealt with by the executor?"

"You are correct, Miss Smith. That would be me. My name is Jim Beardshall."

Miss Smith went up to Mr Beardshall and shook his hand.

"I appreciate this may not be the best timing for you, however would it be possible to have a few minutes of your time in private?"

"For sure, Miss Smith, we have just come to a point where the family is going to do some thinking so I guess I will have an hour or so."

Mr. Beardshall turned to the gathered family members and said,

"So, you have an hour to come up with your decision. If you find an agreement I will support it. If you don't find an agreement the will goes back with me and you will find me at my practice and let me know who will be representing who in court. I will be discussing Miss Smith's business opportunity in the kitchen and would appreciate for us not to be disturbed."

With that, he walked out the door Miss Smith came in and she followed him across the vast reception area to the kitchen where he shut the door behind her.

"So, Miss Smith, can I get you a coffee?"

"That would be most kind, Mr. Beardshall."

He went over to the stove top kettle, ensured there was water inside and turned on the gas. Once he did this he turned to Miss Smith.

"I'm very glad you came over and I am sure it is pure

luck I was here reading Mr. Gregory's will. I knew Mr. Gregory for the past ten years and he often asked me questions or sought advice over different subjects. We became friends through the process and he told me about you."

Miss Smith's face showed a trace of concern that was picked up immediately by Mr. Beardshall.

"OK," he said, "let me rephrase that. He told me that a lady called Miss Smith was working on a project for him in relation to his time at one of the finance institutions in Boston. He told me you were pulling together information that was going help him in a court case he was planning against one of his ex-employees that had cost him personally a lot of money and also a career in politics."

"I can confirm the project, but his reasons were not important for me. I was asked to track down a key witness and get information that could be used in the court case."

"I presume by the fact you have arrived you were planning to give Mr. Gregory an update or have completed the project?"

"Yes, I tried calling Mr. Gregory a number of times in the past week but now I understand why he didn't answer his cell."

"Can I ask you what number you were calling?"

Miss Smith reeled off the number from memory.

"Interesting," Mr. Beardshall said. "I have no register of that number. I wonder what else Mr. Gregory was hiding. So, Miss Smith the only way I can verify you are who you are is by asking you how much of the fee is still owed. You can appreciate the predicament I am in. Mr. Gregory told me a couple of days before he died about this 'project' and a Miss Smith – which I take is not your real name – would turn up and in exchange for a report would be coming to collect…"

"$25,000, Mr. Beardshall."

"Well it's either a very good guess or you are the person I was expecting to show up at some time," he said with a smile. "So, do you have the report? I might as well have a copy as at least it can be used as traceability for the accounts."

Miss Smith was glad she had prepared the two copies. Mr. Beardshall didn't need the full version. He just needed a version for the records. The file would go nowhere but a dusty filing cabinet and that would be the end of the story. She pulled out the white envelope and handed it to Mr. Beardshall. This version of the file didn't detail where Fanny had been located, nor did it have the photographs or a full account of what had happened since she had taken the job on.

Opening her purse so Mr. Beardshall could not see inside she pulled out the white envelope and handed it over.

Mr Beardshall asked, "I presume this is the only copy of the report?"

"That was the agreement."

"Do you mind if I scan the report before making the payment? Mr. Gregory did make a strong point that this had to be a cash transaction. I will keep my thoughts to myself on that subject and will have to find a way of ensuring it passes audit traceability."

"I appreciate that, Mr. Beardshall and I am sure Mr. Gregory had his reasons for doing this discretely."

She did not mention that it was the only way she would take the contract on. His choices had been cash in used bills or gold. Miss Smith had no intention of leaving an electronic trace of her movements. All her bills were paid in cash and if she ever used a credit card it was one that was untraceable a lot like travel service providers had access to.

Mr. Beardshall opened the envelope and started reading the file. Midway through he looked at Miss Smith and said, "I know you are not interested in the case but didn't it at all pique your interests?"

"Honestly, Mr. Beardshall, corruption, blackmail, scams happen every day. I make a living by providing information to those that want to pay for it. What they do with that information is their business. Honestly no, I have no interest."

Saying that, Miss Smith was getting more intrigued with the situation, clearly Mr. Beardshall thought there was something of relevance, albeit she had to this point not been interested to look more than collecting the outstanding payment.

"OK, Mr. Beardshall just to humor you, why do you think this is interesting?"

"Well, from what Mr. Gregory told me the blackmailers, and by the way this signed confession is from one of them, took a very large amount of cash from him. He mentioned a sum in excess of $1,000,000."

Miss Smith didn't show any external sign, but internally she thought there might be another potential payoff if she chased down the other blackmailer. Clearly, Fanny had been the minor benefactor in this case from the information she had been able to extract and it appeared Mr. Gregory didn't know or wasn't sure who the other blackmailer was otherwise he would have instructed Miss Smith to go after them. Or had he assigned that to someone else?

"So, he wanted to get his money back or what?

"It was two things: clearly he wanted to get his money back with interest but he also wanted to destroy this person the same way his career had been destroyed. It seems that despite Mr. Gregory's personal wealth his political ambitions were also very important. He was, at the time of the scandal, planning to run for State Governor. I guess his desire for revenge never left him."

"Well, I guess this is where it ends. If it's OK with you, Mr. Beardshall I have to get back to Boston. I have another appointment later tonight."

"For sure, Miss Smith."

Mr. Beardshall pulled a large envelope out of his briefcase and handed it to her.

"Please check it. I have a couple of times."

"Thank you, Mr. Beardshall. I will."

Miss Smith opened the envelope and counted out 2,500 one hundred dollar bills. All were used and the quick sample check she did showed they were not consecutive bills. Putting the envelope into her purse hiding the brown envelope she said, "Well thank you, Mr. Gregory. I'll be on my way and good luck with the warring family."

"Yes, I just hope they have taken their heads from up their arse's and see things sensibly, but I am not highly confident."

They shook hands and Miss Smith let herself out of the kitchen as Mr. Beardshall made some notes in a ledger he had pulled from his briefcase. *At least one point of closure in the will*, he thought and then turned his attention back to the families in the lounge.

As he walked into the lounge he said, "OK so have we seen sense…?"

Miss Smith left the ranch, got into the car and sat there for a minute working out her plan. She did have another meeting that evening and it could turn out to be a lucrative job. It was a tailing job where she was getting $2,000 per day to build up a case on a husband that was cheating his wife. It was kind of her bread and butter business as there were a lot of rich women looking for a female private detective, which was her registered trade and she was on the verge of expanding and taking on board a couple of staff. It was relatively easy money charging $2,000 per day and paying the staff $1,000 per day, but only paying when they were working. It was still significantly higher than anyone else was paying, but her belief was that if you paid well you brought secrecy, especially when it would be 75% in cash…

She wondered if the file she had would be worth following up. It depended on who had been the beneficiary of the blackmail. Probably, she thought, someone who had ended up marrying some person of influence and living off their purse strings. She decided that she would do some digging in a few days' time as she had promised herself to take some days off and get some sun in Miami.

Putting it to the back of her mind she started the car and headed back down the drive.

Monday, 11 June 2001

Frank walked slowly down the airplane steps at Newark. There was no direct flight and it had been really neat seeing the mountains from the propeller plane. He'd managed to get some photographs as the skies were clear and the view was as far as the eye could see. As he had walked out the door he'd said a final goodbye the stewardess who had taken real good care of him on the flight. She was a local from New York and had given him tips on where to go and what to see whilst he was in town.

Frank had been planning this trip for some time and had timed it around when his wife and a group of her friends had decided to take in the sun in Florida for ten days. Secretly they were all looking for retirement homes and were planning to spring the news on their better halves when they returned.

Retirement had been good to Frank but now was the time to mix pleasure with some old unfinished business. He walked over to the arrivals terminal and waited for his luggage. Twenty minutes later he had his luggage and headed to the line of yellow cabs New York was famous for.

"Good morning, sir. How's it going?"

"Exceptionally well thank you and you?"

"Mighty fine thank you, sir and where are we going this morning?"

"I'm staying at the Hilton Time Square, but was hoping you could give me a tour of the city so I can get my bearings."

"You're the boss, no problems. My name's Sammy."

"Pleased to meet you, Sammy, I'm Frank."

"So, Mr. Frank is it your first time in the Big Apple?"

"I've been once before but it was over twenty years ago so I'm guessing a lot has changed since then."

"For sure, sit back and enjoy the ride. You want to sit up front? It's a better view."

"Thanks, Sammy. Sounds like a plan."

With that Sammy pulled out of the taxi rank and joined the throng of traffic heading into the city.

"We'll start off in Brooklyn, then onto Queens before getting to Manhattan."

"Thank you, Sammy. So how long have you been a cabbie?"

"Twenty-five years now, Mr. Frank. Another three years and I'll be retiring and heading over to Florida to get away from winter… and all the traffic."

They both laughed as they sat in the first of many traffic jams of the journey. Three hours later, having seen the major highlights of the city, Sammy pulled up outside the Hilton.

"Thank you, Sammy. That was great."

"No worries, Mr. Frank. Seeing you are in town for a while have one of my business cards. Give me call if you need me, I work days so if you need me just call. I will make some excuse to my boss."

"You got yourself a deal there, Sammy."

Frank paid the bill and collected his luggage off Sammy. Shaking hands, Frank walked into the lobby of the Hilton and headed for the check-in.

"Good morning, sir. Can I help you?"

"Yes, miss. I'm checking in. The name is Reed, Frank Reed."

"Yes, Mr. Reed, welcome to the Hilton. I have a junior suite for you on the tenth floor. It has views over Times Square. I hope you will like it."

"Thank you, that will be perfect."

With a few pieces of paper signed Frank was handed his room key and, as he picked up his bags, the receptionist said, "I hope you enjoy your stay with us, and have a nice day."

"Thank you and you too."

Frank headed to the bank of elevators and up to his room. The first consideration after unpacking was to get a late lunch and then do some sightseeing. The taxi ride had given him a good taster, but he was going to take the open top bus tour tomorrow. It was a perfect way to explore the city. This evening he was going to wander around Times Square and see which show he was going to take in whilst he was in town.

Wednesday, 13 June 2001

Frank left the Hilton at 9am. He had enjoyed a light breakfast and decided he was going to walk the three miles to his destination. He had to be there at 11 am.

Walking through the bustle of Manhattan, Frank stopped midway to his direction at a Starbucks and enjoyed a wet skinny decaf cappuccino. He had been advised by his doctor to cut out the caffeine and calories to help his cholesterol levels, and his recent addiction to Starbucks cappuccinos was, in Frank's mind, his little naughty of the day.

Frank arrived at One Police Plaza at 10.45 am. As he walked up to the building he had taken in the enormous size of the building at thirteen stories tall. In comparison, his old headquarters in Roan Mountain were miniscule. The building itself was ugly, unlike the old headquarters on Center Street which was a beautiful building. This place painted a very different picture. To Frank it said 'don't fuck with us'

With a smile on his face he walked into the main lobby. It was a huge place with five different reception desks. He walked up to one and behind it sat a very serious-faced middle-aged man.

"Good morning, sir. How can I help you?"

"Good morning," said Frank. "I have an appointment with Dr. Hernandez."

"Yes sir, if you would just sign in here, I'll let Dr. Hernandez know."

"Thank you."

With that, Frank filled in the obligatory form stating name, occupation, who he was visiting and signing to accept all the associated terms of visiting the facility. That done the receptionist folded the paper into a plastic wallet with a material necklace so as to define he was a visitor and then went to one of the chairs facing the reception desk to wait for Dr. Hernandez.

Frank had set up the appointment a month previously.

He had done some checking and found that Dr. Hernandez had moved from San Francisco some years ago as they had set up a new laboratory with state of the art equipment and staffed to meet the growing needs of international policing forces to deal with drugs and drug trafficking. In the building Frank had just entered there were over 1,000 employees in this function alone and Dr Hernandez was now the boss. Frank had spoken to Dr. Hernandez after tracking him down in New York and, after a brief conversation, Dr. Hernandez had been only willing to meet with Frank and discuss the case he had been investigating sixteen years earlier. Like Frank, he hated it when a case wasn't closed...

Frank was brought out of his thoughts.

"Frank?"

"Yes, Dr. Hernandez?"

"At your service."

"It's great to finally meet you after all these years."

"You too Frank, let's head to my office and I'll show you around my little enterprise on the way."

"Great, thank you. It will be great to understand what I've been missing out on over the past decade."

"You might be surprised with some of the developments, especially in forensics and for sure, in drugs trafficking."

"I sure hope the developments are giving us an edge. There should be compulsory death sentences for the scum who traffic that stuff."

"I understand the sentiment. The criminals are getting more and more devious, both in the drugs and how they are transporting them. I heard the other day that one of the cartels in Mexico brought an old Soviet sub and have been using it to get inside US territorial waters to deliver. Can you believe it?"

"A sub to carry drugs. Wow, that's ingenious, I understand what you mean about being devious."

"Seriously, that's just the start of it. The amount of money involved and the reality of the riches that come with this industry – and it is an industry albeit a criminal one – then the cartels are turning more and more to business solutions. It's estimated to be a four billion dollar annual revenue. It's been growing exponentially by between 200% and 300% per year for the past fifteen years."

"Those are some serious numbers, is there nothing that can be done to stop the growth?"

"Sure, there are some high-profile cases that come up where fields of poppies are destroyed, however many of the fields are days away from civilization and combine that with family threats and people disappearing, to set examples, there's a kind of dictatorial loyalty that lives in the poppy growing areas. The cartels have taken some of the nastiest people who've walked the planet and made them into the personal protection units for the drug lords. There are some ex-workers who have made it to the US and the stories they have told about the abuses and punishments these monsters hand out make even the most hardened officer feel sick."

"So why don't we just send in the Special Forces to take them out?"

"Well there's another issue, called US foreign policy. The trouble is, it's like the wind, it keeps changing direction. On day we are all about kicking the asses of the drugs lords. Next day we don't like whose leading the country and we end up sending arms to these assholes and even training them so we can create a revolution from the inside. It's pretty fucked up. The sad reality is that more and more drugs are ending up on the streets of the US every year and there is clearly a market for it. If no one did drugs there would not be a market. Again, this is where the cartels have become very business savvy. They bring out a new drug and flood the market for a few months, then they have a shortage to drive up prices and the addicts out there will do anything to get their fixes, as you know. Part of the solution is stop it at source, the other part is education. The youth of today want everything now and don't believe they

265

need to work for it; even easier if you can point a gun in someone's face and take it."

"You make some good points. I had my fair share of those assholes to deal with, just sounds like it's a growing number."

"Unfortunately it is. So here we are the first and last line of defense against the drug lords."

Dr. Hernandez opened a door by typing in a four digit code on the pad on the side of the door. The door hissed as it opened. It was a good 6 inches thick and had rubber seals all around it. Before Frank could ask, the quizzical look on his face had clearly been seen. Dr. Hernandez said, "Before you ask, this is the outer door of a temperature controlled laboratory. We keep the temperature and air pressure constant in order to ensure the samples we receive are not contaminated."

Dr Hernandez continued.

"We keep all the samples we get. As we go through the next door on the left hand side are the archive rooms."

Dr Hernandez waited for the outer door to seal fully before entering in another code and the next door started to open automatically.

Frank asked, "Do we need any of those forensic gowns to be in here?"

"No, Frank. The important element is to control the atmosphere, although we do normally insist that the guys working here wear proper shoes... but that's in case they drop anything on their feet..."

They both laughed.

Dr. Hernandez and Frank walked into the laboratory. It was an enormous space split up into rooms full of benches and equipment with people working at every station. Frank noticed immediately the laboratory was anything but quiet. Music was blazing out from different areas and multiple different styles all seeming to compete with each other. Dr. Hernandez smiled at the look on Frank's face and said, "Just because we are the last line of defense doesn't mean we can't have a happy work place. When we first set up it was a very serious environment. All the guys were so focused that they were on a mission they believed the only way to win was to be in a sterile environment. We learnt the lesson. Back to the athletics analogy, we are in a marathon not a 100 meter race. The first couple of years were challenging. We lost a couple of guys to burn out, and then we figured out we needed to pace ourselves. We changed the way we worked. Drugs don't work on a 9 to 5 environment so we adjusted to operate 24/7 and allowed the guys to come up with ways of making the workplace a fun place to be. Every month we have a trip where different shift teams go away for chill out time and to have fun – Vegas, Key West, Colorado amongst others. Every year the complete team goes away at least twice."

"Great ideas and I'm sure your team appreciates it."

"Well, our employee turnover rate is the lowest in the state and there is a waiting list to join, so I think we are doing something right." Dr. Hernandez pointed to the left. "On the left are the archives. Like I said, we hold samples of all the shit we receive in there. It is tagged and bagged and we have a state of the art filing system so we can find anything from anywhere in a matter of minutes. We log everything from the source, the dealers, the place it was found, how much was found, who found it and a list as long as your arm. Basically, we start to build up a picture and then we let the technology help by building up maps and routes of where, how and changes in drugs and movement. This information is shared with all the law enforcement agencies around the States which they use in their predictions of when drugs will arrive at certain times and who to be looking for. Every year our strike rates are improving and the federal government love the results. We are able to get additional funding when we need it, but everyone knows the task is not getting smaller."

They continued walking and Dr. Hernandez continued the commentary on each of the different laboratories and their specialties. It took the best part of thirty minutes to walk from the entrance across to Dr. Hernandez's office.

As they walked into the outer office a lady with graying hair, Frank assessed in her mid fifties, wearing a floral patterned dress seeming to be very formal considering the environment, stood up.

Dr Hernandez said, "Let me introduce you to Rosie. Rosie, this is Frank, the guy I was telling you about. Frank, Rosie has been putting up with me for the best part of twenty-five years now."

Rosie walked over and, with a genuine smile, said,

"Welcome to the doorway to hell. It's good to finally meet you, Frank. Could I get you a coffee? Actually, Dr. Hernandez, it's twenty-four years, nine months and sixteen days, to be precise."

Frank replied,

"Thank you, Rosie and yes please… black no sugar. By the way, is the reference to the doorway to hell the one as you enter the laboratory… or this one here?" Frank pointed at the door that was the entrance to Dr. Hernandez's office. All three laughed and Dr. Hernandez escorted Frank to his office.

Dr. Hernandez's office was a corner suite that overlooked City Hall Park. Having taken in the view Dr. Hernandez showed Frank to a set of couches close to the office entrance and sat down. A couple of minutes later Rosie came in with two cups of coffee set them down and left, shutting the door.

"So," Dr. Hernandez started, "what do you think of the place?"

"Very impressive. It's great to see the detail. Just that comment from Rosie shows the meticulous details your team clearly has."

"Yes, Rosie is a godsend. She has been a complete rock, not just for me but for the whole team. She's a lot like a surrogate mother to so many of the team here. We hit it off from Day one. Fortunately, she and my wife are good friends, otherwise I reckon I would have been divorced by now. I've certainly seen more of Rosie in the past twenty-five years than my wife."

Dr. Hernandez continued.

"So, let's get down to business."

Frank picked up his bag and pulled out the old photocopy of the report on Mikey. Frank said,

"You know, I have read this report so many times I could probably recite it word for word. The stuff that killed Mickey, the more I look at it, was not an accident. Every time I read it, it looks more and more like it was a concoction designed to make sure it killed."

"You could well be right, Frank. We've been able to pull together a lot of information from what you gave me originally. I'm pretty sure I can tell you where the base shit came from and also who sold it."

"Really?"

"Yes, and potentially even who they sold it to."

"How?"

"Well, it goes back to our archive system. We started searching our database and came up with seventeen potential sources. With the dates you gave us from the death we did a search to three months prior to that and then expanded the search to six months. That's when we hit the information in this folder."

Dr. Hernandez put a file on the table and the two of them swapped folders. Before Frank picked up the folder Dr. Hernandez said,

"Take your time to read the file and digest what's in there. If you need anything just ask Rosie, I just need to go to a meeting and will be back soonest."

"Thank you and appreciate it."

With that, Dr. Hernandez got up and left his office with Frank staring at the folder.

Frank picked up the folder, curious about its contents, excited and a little nervous. It was the same feeling he used to have with every case he dealt with when the trail had gone cold and he'd managed to find a nugget of information; a hunch that had turned out to be the decisive point in being able to nail the criminal. He opened the folder and started reading.

An hour and a half later Dr. Hernandez walked back into his office to see Frank standing by the window. Frank had not heard him enter the room, still lost in his thoughts and trying to make sense of what he had read.

Frank had read the file from cover to cover and had specifically focused on the diary from the dealer. The pusher was a guy named Tyrone – according to the diary. He was an addict himself and died from severe complications from his addictions. It was simply only a matter of time and which of the organs failed first. His autopsy was a classic of what happens with the excess of heroin addiction…

The deceased identified as Tyrone. Full name not known at time of production of this autopsy, however subsequent information suggests the deceased to be one Mark Hancox of no fixed abode.

The report went on:

… include collapsed veins in both arms, bacterial infections of the blood vessels and heart valves. Abscesses (boils), and other soft-tissue infections were witnessed on his neck and upper torso.

It continued:

… Significant damage was recorded in the lungs, liver, kidneys and brain. Hepatitis B and HIV were also identified in the deceased.

In the summary the coroner had written the following:

… besides the organ damage it was highly likely that the deceased had significant mental health issues, including depression and antisocial personality disorder. With the level of tissue damage seen it was highly likely that the deceased experienced sexual dysfunction and psychosis…

To Frank it was like reading something from a nightmare. Tyrone or Mark, whatever his name, had probably welcomed death as a relief from the pain he must have been living day in, day out. How he had sunk to such levels Frank did not want to know but he could guess it had been the same way many had succumbed. His

270

thoughts went back to Mikey and he probably would have ended the same way, if he hadn't been fast-tracked to the grave....

Frank wondered why Tyrone would keep a diary, grateful that he had, but maybe another police officer would be doing the same with Tyrone as he was doing with Mikey, trying to unearth the facts so the case could be closed.

Frank went back to the diary and read the part that had been highlighted by Dr. Hernandez:

16 March 1973

12:30 – Open for business. Jim is in for his regular hit. The guy is like clockwork. Need to settle his tab. He's past due by two weeks. He's got to find $100.00 before he gets his fix. Let him know no dough no smack. He was shaking like a rabid dog. He will be back in a couple of hours. Some poor bastard is going to get done over, but shit happens.

12:48 – Sherry "Legs" is in for a party batch. Some rich kids are in town looking for a good time. Make some cakes with aspirin and charge a premium. The rich kids can afford it. Should make it easier for Legs to empty their wallets...

13:07 – Shit Face looks like he's ready to explode. He's a fucking animal. If he wasn't such a good source of income I'd mix him some shit he'd never remember. Have to keep one hand under the table just in case I have to put a bullet in the fucker. He fucking shoots a complete load into his vein in the stall and then collapses on the floor. Fortunately he's back around in ten minutes and leaves with no drama. See you tomorrow Shit Face...

13:24 – Fucking assholes arrive to collect the rent... Always as three. One on the door stopping anyone getting in. One behind, he's an evil piece of shit. I seen him snap some dealer's spine with his bare hands for not showing the complete inventory. Poor fucker died a real slow death watching his intestines pouring out of his stomach once he was paralyzed he cut him and emptied him like he was a

271

fucking chicken. Mr. Evil sees all is OK, takes his cut and leaves... Sick thing is he doesn't even do drugs just lives off the fear of the sick psychos he has as muscle. At least my next delivery is going to happen...

13:41 – Jail bait! No idea of her real age, looks a lot older than she really is. The mannerisms give her away. She's nervous, not sure what to ask for. Trying to pretend to be the real deal. She's after something special. She's pretty fucked up over something, but no room for sympathy here. Let's see how much she wants this shit...

14:05 – Fuck me, that was worth it. She was real tight. First time I've managed to shoot my load in months. The hookers are like fucking a bucket, but she had a tight pussy and ass. Doubt she will be back, but won't forget that in a hurry.

14:19 – Well what a fucking surprise... Jim's back and looks like he had a good time. He's got blood on him and hands over $120.00...

It went on.

Frank re-read the diary entry. His mind going into overdrive, with his natural instincts pulling him back...facts, facts, facts. This guy had a huge number of people getting their shit from him, so why should this one be so significant? He was trying to put facts around a guy claiming to have sex with a juvenile. For sure, the word of a dead junkie would never stand up in a court, but it was another lead that he was going to follow up on when he got home.

"So Frank," said Dr. Hernandez. "What do you make of it?"

Frank snapped out of his thoughts and turned around to face Dr. Hernandez.

"How much trust would you put in the ramblings of a junkie?"

"Good question and normally I would say very little. Reason being is that most junkies don't document their activities."

"Yeah that was my thinking also. So, back to the

272

question how much faith would you put in the diary?"

"There had to be some reason behind keeping it, so if you think it through what would be the purpose?"

"To try and keep track of his clients in case he needed an alibi at some point?"

"Could be."

"Maybe he got some weird kick out of having records on his 'clients' like it was some kind of verbal porn?"

"Yeah, I could see some connection there, but maybe there is something more in the background of the junkie."

"What we know about the guy is limited. He was not a resident of the city. The information pieced together on him was that he moved in about five years before he died. At the time, investigators spoke to some of his users and the only thing that came across with some form of consistency was that he was good at math."

"So, do we know anything about the potential of this guy being this Mark character?"

"Again, it's circumstantial but a guy called Mark Hancox disappeared from Pontiac, Detroit around the time Tyrone turns up in our back yard. Trouble is, Mark had no record in Pontiac that could be traced."

Frank looked quizzically at Dr. Hernandez.

"I know, real strange especially if you know anything about Pontiac. There was a missing persons person alert for him, but no record. All we had to go on was a vague description from a geriatric neighbor giving a description that could be Tyrone, but honestly, could be any black African American male under 180 pounds. She could only describe him as a quiet guy kept himself to himself, no lady friends. She did say she once went into his apartment and said it was neat and tidy, but saw lots of books on the kitchen table, like school books that kids write in."

Frank said, "OK, let's go out on a limb. Tyrone is Mark. Mark was a teacher in Pontiac. Mark leaves Pontiac pretty quickly and ends up a pusher in New York. So why would a teacher leave a place overnight?"

"Well," Dr. Hernandez said, "because some serious shit

is coming his way. Some kind of kid abuse and the parents are seeking immediate retribution? Maybe he got caught with his fingers in a till?"

"Yeah could be. Maybe that was the name he was using and actually his real name is something else. It could be someone cottoned on to who he was and found out he was living under that alias."

"That's possible, but where's this going, Frank?"

"How about I paint a picture for you? Sixteen years ago a young girl is getting badly abused by her druggie father. The abuse is that bad she plans to stop it permanently. She goes on a school trip to New York and comes across Tyrone. He sells her the base shit. She takes the shit back home and finds a way to get him alone in a log cabin that was not used in winter. She mixed the shit with some other chemicals to make sure it does the job it's supposed to. Her father obliges and takes the shit and OD's. With me so far?"

"Yes."

"Now, what if I tell you that young girl disappeared with her mother in the late seventies after they moved to New York. They had to change names and take new identities. I searched all records for the pair from when they left Roan Valley. The trail just disappeared in June '77. I wanted to catch up with them for old time's sake and to see how they had got on in their new life in the New York."

"They could have moved on again, it's really not that difficult to disappear if you want to."

"I know, but the only trade Marlene knew was prostitution. She could have taken a blue collar job, but that would leave a trace and why would you change your identity? They were trying to hide the past and I think Marlene hooked up with a wealthy client and liked living the high life with him. I guess, if you have money and the background those two did you would justifiably want to hide the past. Being a prostitute in Roan Mountain was never going to make you rich."

274

"Or they died."

"Sure, that's a possibility also, but again, there would be records either of death or missing people. Nothing I could find. It was like they just vanished into thin air."

"It is very strange, so what's your theory then, and who are you referring to?"

"You ever heard of a company called Matriarg Vennote?"

"No, should I?"

"Well it's a parent company for a lot of different businesses from food to manufacturing to fashion and so on. The company started up in 1981 and from what I could find out has one 'employee'. A lady who in 1973 would have been sixteen years old, with a very difficult history to trace… No matter what digging I did I could not find out anything other than some corporate bios. I've always prided myself in working with data, facts and figures, but in this case I am going fill in some of the gaps with theories.

In late '75 the two move to New York. The reason for the move is to get away from the past, but also due to the fact the mother has a wealthy benefactor living in the area who has the hots for her. I don't think she would have told the benefactor about her daughter in order not to complicate the situation. She finds some way to get her hands on his money, must have been via a will, as wealthy benefactors in New York would have some serious connections and knowing Marlene, she would not have done anything to put Miranda in harm's way. With the benefactor out the way… they start up the new lives."

"Well it sure fits together, but you know only too well that you need evidence to back that theory."

"I know and a big part of me doesn't want to believe it either. Marlene was a nice lady forced into a bad profession by a guy she loved. Basically, she married the wrong guy. The daughter, Miranda was a nice kid also, never in trouble except what her father dished out."

"So what's your plan?"

275

"That's a good question, Dr. Hernandez. I don't have the resource or access I used to have as a serving officer. Probably I'll end up handing over to the Department of Justice and see if anyone there is interested in following it up."

"Well good luck, Frank however you go with it. I just hope I have been able to help."

"More than you realize, Dr. Hernandez. The more I think about my theory the more I can see it is how it happened."

"Just don't fall into the trap. You know only too well to test the truths and the theories."

"For sure, but this case does need closure, and thanks again."

With that Frank shook hands with Dr. Hernandez and then in the outer office with Rosie before heading out of the building to carry on with his sightseeing.

Monday, 9 December 2002

Miss Smith was pretty tired. She had been working long hours for the past two weeks. The job had been more complicated than she thought originally and needed some of her special skills to get the evidence required. Each night she had gone to the office block and hid in the ladies room once the cleaners had been in and waited until the office emptied and then set to work. The filing systems were easy enough to get into but the pure amount of data she was going through was enormous. Tonight's task was to focus on the electronic files as she had come up with nothing in the paper records. Whilst computer hacking was still in its infancy so was computer security and made even easier as one of her employees had managed to get the passwords to bypass what security the company had. The honey trap with a spiked gin and tonic thrown in was the key to the key, so to speak.

Miss Smith had left the ladies at 10.30 pm, having heard the last worker leaving forty-five minutes before with the audible click of the office door shutting. There had been no noise or movement since and she knew that the office would not be inspected again until the morning. She was glad to leave the toilets. Whoever cleaned them really OD'd on the bleach and the smell was something that remained with her for a good hour after she left them every night. Hopefully, she thought to herself, tonight would be the last one on this job. She only had a few remaining files to check on a couple of different machines.

Making her job a little easier was the fact that in this office it seemed there was a policy to leave the computers on at night. She hadn't figured why but it was helping her as the bluish green haze coming from the monitors would cause no suspicions if there were any patrolling security guards.

Carefully putting a plastic sheet over the office chair she sat down at the director's desk and, with her latex medical gloves on, she started tapping on the keyboard entering the associated passwords. Within minutes she was in the files and smiling broadly. Pay dirt! Downloading all the files could take some time so she inserted the first USB stick. It took ten minutes to fill the first USB stick and the process continued for nearly three hours, by which time Miss Smith had eight loaded USB sticks. She had simply written on the outside of each one with a permanent ink marker pen the numbers one to eight so she could transfer them in order later.

It was 2am by the time Miss Smith was finished and she decided, rather than wait until the office opened in another five and a half hours, to leave by the fire exit. She was tired and wanted to get home as soon as possible, besides which there was nothing else she needed to close the job, except hand over the files and get paid…

Leaving the office after picking and relocking the office door she headed to the fire escape stairs. The interior security plans weren't there to stop intruders, once inside the building, She decided to put that thought away for later as another business opportunity. The door she opened was not alarmed. The one which exited at ground level would be but she had the tools to deal with that. The stairwell was only dimly lit with emergency lighting. It was cold and musty as she walked down the thirteen flights of steps. The stairwell was not heated and the outside 12 degree Fahrenheit temperature could be felt permeating through the walls. Miss Smith could see her own breath as she walked down the stairs.

The ground floor exit had a simple magnetic catch circuit that, when broken, would send a signal to the security desk warning the door had been opened. It was easy to bypass with a wire loop. To cover up her exit for as long as possible after inserting the wire loop she disconnected the magnetic catch attached to the door itself and used an adhesive to attach it to the magnet attached to the wall. She figured the next time anyone would look at that door would be during an annual maintenance schedule, which was due next June, and unless it was someone taking their job very seriously it would likely be a lot longer before the issue was discovered. For sure, no one in the office would realize they had been hacked.

As she opened the fire door the cold air hit her with vengeance. Not only was it stupidly cold but the wind that was blowing was making the temperature feel more like -10 Fahrenheit. Miss Smith checked again to make sure her thermal fleece was closed up to her neck and walked away from the building following the same path she had done every during the job to avoid the security cameras.

Ten minutes later Miss Smith arrived at her car, got in and turned the engine on. She turned the heater up to maximum and got out again to start scraping the windows that had all iced over. She didn't have a can of de-icer with her, but that would probably have had little effect at these temperatures. Having scraped enough to see where she was going, but by no means a total clear view, she climbed back in and moved away from the curb. She felt the tires struggling for grip on the asphalt and crept forwards towards the turning and the main road.

There was little traffic around and once onto the main road she relaxed a little as it appeared the gritters had been out. Pulling into the left lane to turn left towards the Interstate she hit a patch of black ice. Doing what was natural to the majority of people in that situation she stamped on the brakes and turned the steering wheel in the opposite direction. This only aggravated the slide and with the road going downhill the car started to pick up speed.

Joe was standing behind the snow plow checking what was blocking the grit bin. He had noticed the grit spray through his rear view mirrors had stopped a few hundred yards back. With the hazard lights flashing and a sign up three hundred yards back down the road he was pretty sure, even in this weather, he would be seen and be safe. He had just put his hand into the outlet pipe to clear a large clump of grit that was stopping the flow when his truck was hit. It wasn't a rear impact, it was a frontal impact. It was hit hard enough to push the snow plow back. The force of the impact snapped Joe's arm at the wrist like it was made of balsawood. At the same time he slipped under the grit dispensing mechanism. Attached to the plow by his broken wrist, Joe's issues were not finished. The initial impact had moved the truck enough to dislodge the balance between the tires and friction that normally would have held it in place had it not been for the black ice, and also for the fact the grit had not been dispensed for the previous 200 yards. The truck started to gather pace as it headed back down the road. Joe was screaming with agony from his broken wrist and the fact his back and legs were being ripped by the ice and uneven surface of the road.

The truck continued until the slope gave way and the tires regained the battle over friction. Joe had not fared well. He was unconscious, bleeding heavily and had also sustained a serious head injury. He had moments to live as, in that temperature, the cold would finish him off before any paramedics would arrive on the scene.

Miss Smith had fared little better. Her car had hit the snow plow at 55mph. The momentum from the skid had made it into a lethal weapon and one she was unable to control. Cursing for not having changed to winter tires she braced herself for the impact with the front of the snow plow. Just prior to impact her car hit a small pothole that caused it to turn by 90 degrees and change the impact point to the driver side door. At that speed the car was almost sliced in half just forward of the central pillar. The impact of the two and a half ton vehicle happened with the screech of metal and a brief and despairing scream from its driver.

Miss Smith died instantly. She, like the car, had been cut in two. There was virtually nothing left of her upper body; her lower body was still in the seat in the same place with her legs in the seating position and her feet on the pedals.

When the joined vehicles came to a stop there was an eerie silence for more than ten minutes before the sirens of the emergency response vehicles could be heard.

Amazingly, Miss Smith's car's fuel tank didn't rupture and resultantly neither vehicle caught fire.

First on the scene was Officer Paul Bayfield, followed a few minutes later by the paramedics. Officer Bayfield had checked the passenger car for any signs of life and was checking the snow plow when the paramedics pulled up.

"Good evening, officer."

"Good evening guys. Shit night and it's just got worse. Seems we have two deceased; one a street engineer who was dragged under the plow for some distance from what I can make out so far. The other, who was the driver of the passenger car, well I'll let you guess on the sex. There isn't a lot to go on."

"Great, well look at the positives we won't have to freeze our butts off trying to carry out first aid in this weather."

"Yep, I guess that is a positive. Not so lucky for me, I have a shit load of work to do now and I only had forty minutes of my shift left."

"Shit, that sucks."

"Yep, I'd better call in the reinforcements and then call the civil works department and give them the good news they have a man down and one of their plows is out of action."

"Well just go and do a check to back up your findings and then we can log it for your report."

With that, the paramedics got out of their ambulance and Officer Bayfield climbed into his car to make the necessary calls.

It took a good four hours before Officer Bayfield was able to leave the scene. A shit day had got even worse with his wife screaming down the phone at him about him missing his kid's school play and how he didn't love her or his kid. He knew marrying a Mexican immigrant would bring some challenges, but he was seriously thinking about ditching her and having her shipped back across the border, but then he'd never see his kid again.

Putting his domestic woes behind him he headed back

281

to the pound where the two vehicles, after they had been separated, had been taken for forensic examination. As he pulled into the pound the hearse containing both bodies, or at least the remnants of them, was just preparing to leave. Pulling into a parking lot as close to the warehouse door as possible he got out and headed to the relative warmth and a cup of coffee before looking for more information and evidence.

The pound team had already done a provisional look over the vehicles. The only paperwork in the plow was the vehicle license documentation and a rather worn version of *Penthouse*. The license documentation seemed to tie up to the vehicle and the civil works department had already sent out a tow truck to collect the stricken vehicle. They needed it back gritting at the earliest opportunity.

The contents of the car had been laid of the same table. There was the normal junk associated with a car, most of it really should have been trashed but left as the car owner clearly didn't see it as necessary to dispose of it. What caught Officer Bayfield's attention was a plastic carrier bag holding a large brown envelope and by the side of that twelve USB memory sticks. At first he thought they were cigarette lighters but when he got closer he recognized them for what they were. A few of the secretaries in the office walked around with them when they were taking information between people. It seemed to him that a small bit of plastic and metal had replaced paper. He was not a technophobe, he just didn't understand it and honestly, if he didn't need it for his job then leave well alone...

Leaving the memory stick to one side he picked up the envelope and opened it. The first thing he saw were the pictures of a dead woman and what appeared to be a rock pile in a river. Putting the pictures down he pulled down a twenty-five page report which took him fifteen minutes to read and was a step by step account of the locating, extraction of a signed confession and murder of an ex-journalist. The report advised him of who had completed the report, to whom it was for, and the name and address of the victim. Checking back to the date of the report it was from seven years previously.

"Great, my shit day has got even worse," he said out loud to no one.

Putting the file into the envelope with the photos and putting them with the memory sticks in the plastic bag he logged out with the pound manager and got back in his car to head back to the station to complete what was for sure going to be a complex report back to his boss.

Tuesday, 21 July 2003

New York was encountering its warmest, and most continuous period without rain, since records began. The temperature had not dropped below 89 degrees Fahrenheit in ten days and it was forecast to get even hotter tomorrow. In comparison to other parts of the States it was far from extreme but for New Yorkers used to the mid 70s at this time of the year, it was just another excuse for the complaints that regularly filled the coffee and deli shops through the city. Imogen, however, had other thoughts on her mind. She had woken at 7.15 am knowing it was a big day, but the fact she had not gone to bed until 4am didn't help when the alarm clock went off. Opening her eyes her vision was blurred and she hoped it would wear off with a shower. She reached over to where she thought the table was and missed hitting the alarm clock. Struggling to make things out she managed to work out she was actually lying with her head at the foot of the bed and groaned as she made the effort to turn round and find the alarm that was increasingly getting louder and louder. Finally she felt the off button and stopped the noise that probably coincidentally seemed to set off the realization she had a pounding headache.

"Get your lazy ass off the bed," she said out loud to herself, as if that would make it happen. She lay there for a few more seconds as some more vision came back but still pretty blurred and she briefly wondered a few things:

- Had she drunk something last night that had fucked up her eyesight?
- Was the dope doped?
- What actually had happened last night?
- How had she ended up in her own apartment and in her own bed?
- Why did she have a pain coming from her ass?

Rolling over she thought she could answer at least some of those questions as lying the correct way on the bed was her current partner, Amanda. She looked so cute and sexy with her long hair covering most of her face as she quietly slept through the alarm. Imogen was pretty jealous that Amanda had booked a day off work today knowing they were going to Imogen's graduation party. In fairness, Imogen was very happy despite the aches and pains from last nights excess , that she had found Amanda. She was very caring; very sexy and not after her money. An added benefit was she liked to party and was an incredible partner for sex and the pain from her ass must have been from the Kinx penetrator strap on.

Imogen couldn't lie there any longer and tried to quietly walk to the bathroom, her head pounding with every step and hoping that a cold shower would help to at least allow her to get through the day without passing out or throwing up. Turning the shower on to the lowest temperature she gasped out loud as the freezing water hit her skin. It was so cold her nipples were on end but it started to have the desired effect of throwing off the smog filling her head and her vision slowly started to come back. Five minutes was the maximum she could stand at that temperature and she then had to switch to hot water. She showered thoroughly deciding she would fix the headache with some aspirin in her coffee followed up with a couple of cans of Red Bull. She would skip food until tomorrow and definitely no vodka or weed for the next forty-eight hours...

By 8.15 she almost felt human, if only the aspirin would kick in. Adding a new pack in her purse she headed out the apartment door after giving Amanda a kiss on her still sleeping head. Imogen would normally have taken the Metro for the forty minute commute to Marymount School but this morning, dressed for her graduation and in her current fragile state, she was taking a taxi. Adding to that her real mother was going to be there today, well she had threatened to be there, so she wanted to be as much on her game as possible.

Having given the address of the school she sat back in the taxi and put in her earphones and turned on the Red

Hot Chili Peppers *Californication* album she had downloaded on her iPod to avoid any possibility of having to talk to, or more likely having to listen to, the taxi driver and she mentally prepared for the day ahead…

Imogen sat in the back seat of the taxi with her eyes closed and her thoughts turned to the meeting with her mother. She could not complain about her life, at least not for the materialistic sides. Growing up she had only to ask and she got. Whereas the rest of the kids would have a Bic pen, Imogen would have a Mont Blanc; the rest of the kids were dressed by Macy's, Imogen was dressed by Gucci and so on it went. Even at the private school she had gone to at $45,000 per year tuition fees, she was seen as the fashion leader and person to materialistically aspire to. Her friends had been more like groupies and for many years Imogen had mistaken what friends actually were and it was something she had gradually painfully learnt and grudgingly understood. She hadn't understood at first her desire to be liked but over the recent years she had kind of figured out that she was jealous of the groupies as they had parents who showed care and love. That could not have been further away from Imogen's life. What she had thought was a normal upbringing was seen as being freaky and weird by her peers and the gifts she showered had been her way to fit in and be seen as normal but the back talking never went away. Maria was as close to a mother as Imogen had, but even there it was not a loving relationship, it was a business one. Simply put, Maria was paid to bring up Imogen and, whilst she did the right things, there was not the emotional bonding that mother and daughter would have.

Imogen saw her mother normally a couple of times per month and the odd weekend when she was not doing something with her growing empire. She had been to the cinema once with her and even then she had walked out of *Toy Story* to receive an important call. Imogen was never told who her father was and had never pushed the subject with her mother. Without the real parental role models in place Imogen had had to figure out who she was, what she was and what she was looking for. She was highly intelligent and had strolled through the early years of her schooling and was now graduating as the top student, not just of the year but the school had ever produced. Her results had been as close to flawless as deemed possible, but six months before she had met Amanda and her personal life had dramatically transformed. Finally there was someone showing care and attention, someone who was fun to be with and who lived a little on the edge. Imogen had come of age in a very short period of time and was loving it.

Maria was still around and living in the apartment Miranda had brought to allow Imogen some freedom a couple of years before, but her role had had moved from au-pair, to mentor to today, where it was more of housekeeper. Imogen would still take her laundry to Maria and rely on her to get her stuff she needed from the shops but for the past six months she had, in effect, moved in with Amanda and her one bedroom apartment in Greenpoint.

Imogen was sure Maria had not told her mother she was no longer living in the apartment with her, it would only lead to an end in employment and Imogen was sure Maria was being well-paid. Imogen herself had no intention of telling her mother of what was going on and Amanda was not interested in Imogen's family or background. She felt it was best to keep her life segregated.

Whilst she had massively enjoyed the last six months she was not particularly looking forward to Fall as all the discussions, if they could have been called that, to this point had been that Imogen would follow her mother and attend Harvard. That didn't sit well with her current arrangements and Amanda.

Putting that thought aside for the time being, the focus of today was to ensure she made it through the day and the for sure guaranteed press frenzy that would be at the graduation. Not because it warranted it, but because Imogen was sure that one of her mother's marketing guru's would have leaked to the press that she would be attending Imogen's graduation and clearly that would be an excellent photo opportunity for her mother...

"Hello, Imogen."

"Hello, Miranda."

There was a rule, in private she could call her mum, in public she had to call her Miranda. It was really screwy, but as Miranda was surrounded by people Imogen didn't recognize Miranda was clearly the right call. Miranda was being overly friendly.

"So, how's my princess?"

"I'm really well thanks, really looking forward to graduating and making you proud."

"You always make me proud," came back the reply.

Imogen was internally wincing, hoping she was not coming across as false as Miranda was. She felt this Must be what it would be like to be an actor in a film.

"Let me introduce you to..."

The list of dignitaries she was surrounded by was impressive and some of the names she knew from the major TV networks. The introductions seemed to go on forever and Imogen was glad when the announcement came over for all students to take their places. Imogen politely made her excuse to leave Miranda talking to Barbara Walters from ABC News.

The pomp and ceremony lasted a couple of hours and of course there was a reference to their distinguished guests, the only one named being Miranda who smoothly stood up and accepted the applause. As the students started to leave with their friends and relatives Imogen walked over to where Miranda was sitting. Miranda waved at her whilst her cell was in her other hand up by her right ear. Imogen sat patiently until the call was finished to see what was next.

"Let's go eat," said Miranda.

"OK." Inwardly Imogen was wincing, not food, please not food…

The two headed out of the school theater towards the main entrance where Miranda had her car and driver waiting. The chauffeur held open the door for Miranda; Imogen opened her own and they both sat in the rear in silence until the chauffeur had them on the road away from the school and the glass divide window was up.

"So," said Miranda, "what's your plan?"

"Well, I was thinking of taking a gap year and getting a job in the city."

"Might be a good idea, you're not thinking of skipping Harvard are you?"

"No Mom, just wanted a break before starting."

"You kids these days just want it easy. A break, you've just finished school and you need a break! OK, so say you take this year out what are you going to do?"

"Well I was thinking of getting a job in a finance house to get experience and work out what I want to specialize in."

"Makes sense, but you won't learn what you need to know from one of those companies. Here's the deal, either you go to Harvard this Fall or you come over and work for me."

Imogen was inwardly happyish. There had to be a catch, but at least she could see a way to continue with Amanda.

"I'll take the job with you please."

"Good girl. You need to learn the family business, I don't want to be in this game for the rest of my life and you need to be ready to take over. Take two weeks off and then come see me."

Changing subject Miranda asked, "You happy with Maria and the apartment?"

"Yes Mom, she takes good care of me."

"Good. You let me know when that situation changes."

"For sure I will."

The rest of the journey passed with Miranda answering

289

or making calls and Imogen staring through the window as they headed to whatever the restaurant of choice would be. Imogen couldn't believe her luck. There had to be a catch, but up to this point it hadn't come. Two weeks' vacation… staying in New York… not having to go to Harvard in the Fall… wow… Her thoughts turned to Amanda and coming up with a special treat for them to celebrate.

Wednesday, 1 June 2005

"Welcome to Rheinlander Aircraft, Miss Miranda."

"Yeah whatever, have you got the updated business plan ready?"

This was not going to be a good day and Jeff knew it from the first exchanges. The silky-like bullshit he had fallen for at the time Miranda had been courting the business acquisition was gone. Like many others in the past, and for sure in the future, Jeff saw the two sides of Miranda and they could not have been starker. He had fallen for the persuasive charms and vision Miranda shared. The big picture about bringing jobs back to the US, putting Rheinlander back on its feet, making it a major name in pleasure aircraft manufacturing had soon been forgotten as the reality of the new owner came home. The only thing Miranda cared about was herself and her own wealth. By the time the reality had set in the only thing Jeff could do was play along and hope to God the visits didn't happen on a regular basis. Up until now the visits had been on a monthly basis and only for a day at a time. Flying in on the Rheinlander company plane, so all the costs were picked up by Rheinlander, it had become a day to avoid on the company calendar. Just a day trip from her was costing him $20,000. At first the senior staff were keen to be seen in her presence. Over the past six months it had taken all Jeff's skills to make sure his CFO and COO were actually in the building when she arrived.

Miranda had brought the company in 2003 with a lot of pomp and ceremony. Governor Jim Doyle had been the proud guest of honor at the inauguration ceremony and had shown his support by granting a ten year token corporate income tax rate to help Rheinlander get back on its feet. What had looked, to Jeff, like a gift from the gods when Miranda had come in to rescue the turnaround progran looked more and more like a trap he had naively walked his company into…

The headache that he had had for the past week was

now a full-blown migraine and it was not going to get any better any time soon.

Chuck, the regular pilot, had been off sick the past week and Tyler who was standing in didn't have the same 'exposure' to Miranda's whims, or the same diplomatic skills. It wasn't Tyler's fault, but by the time the plane had touched down on the runway outside the factory Miranda had already got a good head of steam up. Tyler had taken a good hour of abuse from her before the plane finally landed and he could hand her over to the waiting Jeff. To add to the mood her current PA, Clarence, had puked up in the cabin and the smell of the vomit stayed in the plane for the last forty-five minutes of the flight.

Jeff called over his HR Manager to take care of Clarence and escorted Miranda to a waiting golf buggy for the short drive to the company entrance.

"So, do we see the business plan first or the new executive pleasure craft?"

The pain in Jeff's head was getting worse. Neither the business plan nor the new craft were ready. The team had worked through the night for past four days to get the executive craft ready but had come across a number of time-consuming challenges, mainly driven by the fact his team was exhausted working eighteen hour shifts. As long as Miranda didn't ask to see a test flight he felt sure he could cover the plane's readiness, at least he hoped he could…

For the business plan, no matter how he had tried – and he had been running the company on a shoe string for a long time – he just could not get the numbers to stack up. They needed more sales and also they had to get the customers to pay up front to foot the component costs as his credit lines had run dry.

"Let's take a look at the plane first as we are outside already," said Jeff.

"OK. Did you make the changes to the interior?"

"Yes, Miss Miranda."

"And the interior color?"

"Purple as requested, Miss Miranda."

"Good. Then you should have nothing to worry about then…"

Jeff winced internally at the thought of her finding out about the plane's status…

"So here we are," said Jeff pulling up alongside the twin prop eight seat plane. "The exterior trim has been modified as per your instructions. We also made a mock up what the livery would look like if it was reversed."

"How much did that cost?"

"$15,000."

"Well your financial target just got extended by $15,000. One day Jeff you'll learn not to think and just do. Do you understand? Maybe I should just talk to your PA; at least she seems to understand instructions."

Jeff withered under the feral look Miranda gave him.

"For sure, Miss Miranda. It will be taken care of."

He quickly moved off the subject.

"Let's go inside so you can see the interior design."

Jeff decided to go up the stairs first, mainly as he had no intention of having a view of Miranda's backside and undercarriage that was barely covered by her outfit. She was wearing a khaki sand brown miniskirt with sand colored platform boots. Her US army style t-shirt with military tags around her neck was covered by a sand brown leather jacket.

The first time Jeff had met Miranda she was wearing a similar revealing outfit and he had been quietly aroused by this thirty-something woman; now he wanted to avoid looking at anything that reminded him of a black widow spider.

Jeff carried on. "We have installed a small galley, the toilet and also the fully reclining seats. We have made the seat reclining mechanisms electric that allows the seat to convert to a flat bed, but at an angle to take into consideration the angle of the plane in flight."

With that, he encouraged Miranda to try one out… the one seat he knew worked. The others had not been adapted yet.

Miranda was soon lying down fully reclined on the seat.

"You need more padding in the seat," Miranda said. "It's like lying on a plank of wood."

"OK, Miss Miranda. I will add that to the update modifications. I was thinking about having a thin mattress to put over the whole seat in case someone wanted to lie down."

"Jeff, how many times do I need to tell you? Don't think, just follow my instructions."

"Yes, Miss Miranda, for sure."

Jeff continued with the tour of the plane and an hour later he climbed down the stairs with Miranda following.

"So, that's the tour completed. Do you want lunch now, Miss Miranda?"

"Sure, I need the energy to go through the business plan."

With that, they climbed back in the golf buggy and headed to the factory entrance and the executive staff restaurant where Tom and Craig were waiting… for their turn to be humiliated.

The small talk over lunch was taken up with the team trying to keep Miranda talking about herself. They had found over the past six months this was something she had no issues in doing. The stories were always the same and they had got into the routine of nodding and laughing in the right places. To Jeff, it was clear Miranda was a person so wrapped in herself and believing the bullshit she was saying that outside influences were irrelevant. He was more and more convinced Miranda was suffering from pseudologia fantastica. He'd come across the condition when he'd been studying Law at UW-Madison and what he saw were very extreme symptoms of a pathological liar. There was no doubt she was a very intelligent woman but had become detached from the real world. Seriously, claiming to have invented Bluetooth but not having patented it as she didn't see the value in it…

As lunch was finishing Miranda stated she needed to use Jeff's office for some calls. Jeff escorted her to the office and gave the instructions to his PA that Miranda was not to be disturbed for any reason.

Miranda locked the office door behind her and made for Jeff's private bathroom. Laying her purse down she pulled out a small metal tin that contained her 'medication'. Carefully undoing a self-seal plastic bag she poured a small amount of the white powder onto an unfolded piece of aluminum foil. Taking out a $100.00 bill she formed it into a straw-like shape and, with her Bank of America Platinum credit card, she cut the powder into two lines. She snorted the first line up her left nostril and the second up her right. Sitting back on the toilet she let the warm sensation as the coke entered her bloodstream flood through her. In a matter of minutes the stress she had felt had completely left her and the familiar buzz of the high as the coke did its work was a welcome relief. She thought about Clarence and what a feeble excuse of a human being he was a typical maggot, but well-connected with the right dealers to ensure she got the best quality shit. When his usefulness came to an end he would have to have an unfortunate accident... no loose ends...

She was now in a better place to go through the bullshit she knew was coming over the next hours. Rheinlander Aircraft would never be successful with the current management team in place, but they served a purpose. They were providing a good outlet for her to legitimize other business activities and when the time was right would be the perfect company to write off a number of the huge debts that had come with other of her acquisitions. For sure it would leave the management team at Rheinlander bankrupt and probably homeless, but that was not a concern for Miranda. If they weren't so incompetent she might have allowed them the opportunity to at least keep their homes, but the fact they were continually lying to her to try and hide their failures was justification, in her mind, for cleaning them out...

Thirty minutes later Miranda unlocked the office door and walked into the boardroom.

"OK, let's get this show on the road…"

Three hours later, having tied the management team in knots and got them contradicting their own statements, Miranda had had enough. Not once during that time had she showed the emotional outbursts she had shown during the tour of the plane. The coke was doing its job…

Jeff could not believe the transformation in Miranda. He had seen it occasionally, but the extreme change today was more noticeable than ever before. There had to be something during those calls she'd made and received that had done this, unless there was medication involved. Jeff doubted the latter however he was going to check his office out closely when she left.

Miranda was back to her charming best at the end of the meeting. A pale looking Clarence joined them in time to carry her purse to the waiting golf buggy to take them back to the plane. The drive to the plane was carried out in silence. Jeff waiting for the final tirade he was sure was to come. Miranda, Gucci shades on, smiling as if she had no worries in the world. Clarence wishing he was back home already in the arms of Gustav who would, for sure, know how to make him feel better.

The buggy pulled up at the steps of the plane. Tyler had gone and had been replaced by Chuck, who clearly was not 100%, but it seemed to Jeff that the smile on Miranda's face was just that little more genuine seeing the change in pilot.

Clarence went up the stairs first to ensure all was ready for Miranda and thirty seconds later poked his head out the door.

"OK, Miss Miranda, whenever you're ready."

"Thank you Clarence, I'll just be a minute." Miranda turned to Jeff.

"So Jeff, when are you going to stop lying to me? Firstly, the business plan you presented is shit. A graduate trainee could see that piece of shit would not work. I'm not sure what you're trying to hide but do it again and you will regret it." The smile was still there but those feral eyes were back. "You should try and come up with something that doesn't have you going around in circles and contradicting all your arguments. Remember, I'm the nice one here. If I let you loose on the market they would eat you for breakfast, so quit the bullshit and get me a proper plan I can look at. I want it this time next week in New York. Got it?"

"Yes, Miss Miranda. Sure, I understand."

"Good and finally, before I go, I also expect to see video footage at the same meeting of all eight seats working with electronics and not just the demonstration one you got me to try out today... Oh, and you need to have footage of this actual plane flying."

With that, she turned her back on Jeff and walked up the steps. Chuck gave a small wave to Jeff and pulled the door to.

Jeff stood there in shock. How the fuck did she know the other seats didn't work and that the plane was not air worthy... She was either a lot smarter than he gave her credit for or she had someone in the know in the 527 employees. His mind was all over the place. He needed to get the plane flying, that was for sure. The seats were another challenge, he didn't have the cash to buy the new seats; they were $20,000 each. Maybe he could get away with doctoring a video... Then he thought of the real possibility there was a mole in the company. He needed to get HR to run a check on all the employees. He would start with staff and then work through the shop floor employees; surely it had to be someone on the staff. Jeff barely noticed the plane at the end of the runway and begin its journey down the tarmac. He only registered when the plane took off and flew directly overhead as it turned in the direction of the bitch's lair...

Jeff drove back to the factory and got his PA to call Tom, Craig and his HR Manager, Angie. When they were all in his office and the door was shut he started.

"OK guys we are in a world of shit. The evil bitch knows what's going on."

"Hey Jeff, watch the language" said Angie.

"Angie, fuck the PC bullshit and listen. That bitch has got a snitch working inside the company."

"How do you know that?" asked Angie.

"Craig, looking at the seats on the plane could you tell, without trying them out, that there were no working electronics?"

"No way Jeff, we rigged up dummy controls that looked just like the real one."

"OK, so what about the air worthiness of the plane? Is there anyway looking at a plane from the outside or inside – unless the cockpit was empty of switches and dials – of knowing if it is air worthy?"

"No way Jeff, you don't have to register with the general authorities until you are putting a plane in service. No way could she have known."

"So Angie, you got any suggestions how some bimbo with no aviation experience can, without looking, know the status of our latest project?"

"Sorry Jeff, you make a strong case, but what do you want me to do?"

"I want you to find the mole."

"Then what and how exactly?"

"The what, you don't need to know. The how, well it's HR's responsibility to know everything about the employees, so I suggest you do some investigating, asking around. Find out who may have come into money recently. Anyone acting suspiciously... hell I don't know, but you've got six days to find who the leak is."

Turning to Tom and Craig, Jeff said, "Guys, we need to come up with a plausible business case. She didn't buy any of it. We've got one week to come up with a plan that gets us back on track. Angie, you ain't listening to this part of the conversation, right?"

"Right Jeff, I'll start looking for the mole." With that she got up and left the office.

"OK, guys we're going to have to pull the cash from the pension fund. If we can get the cash from the first hundred orders by the end of the quarter we can replace the cash and get ourselves stable."

Jeff could see from the looks it was not sitting well with his old friends.

"Look, there are no other options. That bitch won't sink another dime into this business; in fact, she hasn't sunk any of her own money into it yet. The only money that has come in is from us and she has been taking a cut every quarter. At least if we do this we stand a chance to make it. We don't and we might as well close the doors on Friday."

None of them liked the idea. Many of the guys on the shop floor had been with the company for twenty-five or more years and were like Jeff, Tom and Craig. At an age where they were too young to cash in their 401(K) pension plans, but too old for anyone in the area to want to hire them. Besides which, Rheinlander Aircraft was the largest employer for a good 50 miles in every direction. There simply was nothing around that could take on all the employees of the company going out of business…

At 28,000 feet above Wisconsin, Miranda was very contented. She could just picture the look of shock on Jeff's face and the blind fury he would be in with the fact she knew all about the cover ups. She was sure that Jeff would start a witch hunt but also that he wouldn't find anything. One thing she had learnt was that desperation was a pretty good way to buy silence. Miranda didn't know who the leak was; she had been pretty clear to Clarence that she was not to be involved in the details of who and how, but he did have a knack of finding people's weaknesses. Clarence, from his side, had found the perfect candidate. Doing some digging on the key employees he had come across the perfect victim. His victim was single and a well-respected member of the company and the community. They were a high-profile member of the Pine Grove Community Church and the Crystal Lake Cub Scout Reservation. They were also a closet paedophile.

Clarence had been able to unearth hundreds of pornographic photographs of young girls on the victim's computer. Clearly his victim knew more about young girls than they did about computer security.

When Clarence called the victim via a routed call six months previously and explained what he knew it didn't take much persuasion for his victim to agree to the cash incentive to provide the information that was ultimately handed over to Miranda. Despite Clarence's fragile state as he sat in the plane he thought he'd done a pretty good job of keeping Miranda happy. She had a good supply of quality shit whenever she needed and a group of insiders at the companies Miranda wanted watching. He had heard the closing exchanges between Miranda and Jeff and could only imagine the panic Angie would be having as being the leader of the witch hunt which Jeff would put her in charge of. What a perfect candidate…

Wednesday, 8 June 2005

Imogen pulled out her cell phone and called Miranda.

"Good afternoon, Miranda."

"Good afternoon, Imogen. How's it going?"

"Well thank you, positive news for us. I can confirm that the Rheinlander Management Team has secured additional funding and that the requests you made are being implemented. The funding is partly coming from the local government, from the management team themselves and also from a couple of local banks. I have also confirmed that the management fees to MV2 have been increased to the required level. In summary the status of the management fee structure is MV1 is operating with $12,500,000 per annum, MV2 is now at $17,250,000 and MV3 is at $425,000."

"Excellent. Have they found our inside channel yet?"

"No, however I can tell you there was an unfortunate accident on Sunday involving the HR Manager. There was a gas explosion at her home in the early hours. It seems the gas cooker had been left on and the HR Manager had lit a cigarette in another room, well at least the remains of the body, had been found in another room."

"How unfortunate. Is Clarence aware?"

"Yes and he said he would take the necessary actions, whatever that means."

"Probably best if you and I don't know what those actions are. Did you manage to check the security server?"

"Yes, there was a cable that had come loose; you should be able to reconnect now. I have not been able to verify that yet I would need to do that at Headquarters."

"No worries. I will check and let you know. Good work. Are you heading back today?"

"Yes, I will be in New York tomorrow."

With that, the call ended. Imogen pocketed her cell phone and walked back into the meeting room to close the meeting, allowing Jeff, Craig and Tom to leave. She had been touching base with Miranda to ensure there were no other instructions.

Imogen was keen to leave also as she had been away for a couple of days and was missing Amanda and was looking forward to a night of high-octane sex.

As she took her seat on the Rheinlander plane she thought about how well things had worked out for her since her graduation. She had turned up to the company headquarters after the two weeks' vacation. The vacation had been perfect she had taken Amanda to Florida where they had spent the whole time locked up in a beach apartment and only venturing out occasionally for dinner. Imogen's concern about going to Harvard evaporated as Miranda had quickly put her in a senior position and told her she would have to study for her Harvard degree on a non-resident basis. Imogen could not have been happier with the decision. Not only could she stay in New York, but she was already earning $200,000 per year on the payroll and could afford to take care of Amanda. It had been hard work and long hours but she had managed the balance, coming out with her degree in Business Management.

Monday, 6 February 2006

"Officer Bayfield, I need you in my office now," came the voice of Police Commissioner Campolong down the phone.

"Yes, sir, will be right there." Officer Bayfield wondered what he had done wrong. He was sure his tracks were clear on his moonlighting activities and he had never used police equipment in the small private detective business he had been running for the past couple of years. After all, had to fill his spare time since his now ex-wife had taken off with his life savings and his kid, not to mention find a way to afford to retire.

Officer Bayfield knocked on the commissioner's door and walked straight in. Sitting at his desk Commissioner Campolong even managed to make the large desk look short. He was close to 230 pounds and stood at 6' 3", that is when he stood up, which was as little as possible. He was a real political animal and his interest in his staff went only as far as what his own personal gain would be out of it.

"How can I help, sir?"

"Let me introduce you to Mr. Burke. He is from the Department of Justice, Fraud Office."

Officer Bayfield tried not to look surprised or worried. He was trawling through his mind about anything that might have warranted them being involved with his activities. He could not think of anything but waited for the commissioner to continue.

"Mr. Burke needs to speak with you about a case you worked on a few years ago."

Officer Bayfield inwardly sighed with relief and walked over to shake hands with Mr. Burke.

"Good afternoon, Mr. Burke, exactly which case are you referring to?"

"Please take a seat and I'll bring you up to speed."

"Thank you, sir."

Once Officer Bayfield was sat down Mr. Burke

303

addressed him.

"OK, the case in question relates to a Miss Smith back in December 2002. She was involved in a road traffic accident with a snow plow where both she and the plow driver were killed."

Officer Bayfield thought for a second and then had a flash back to the scene he had come across and the sight of the lower body in the car. The devastation itself had not left any scars, but it had been the beginning of the end of his marriage. The fact he didn't make it home until the following day due to the report and then getting called out to a homicide, mixed with the fiery temperament of his ex-wife had made a poisonous cocktail of personal issues which proved to be the tipping point for his marriage.

"Yes, sir, I remember the incident."

"Good. I need to ask you some questions about the case. Do you remember the report you wrote?"

"Vaguely sir. I do remember there was little left of the driver – Miss Smith – and when I was at the pound I came across some memory sticks and an envelope containing a report on a stake out and execution."

"Very good. I want to focus on the report you found and read. Firstly, are you sure the report came from Miss Smith's vehicle?"

"Being totally honest, I cannot confirm that. The report and memory sticks were on a table in the pound warehouse on a table. The items on the table had been taken from the vehicles before I got there. The process is the pound team does the analysis of the vehicles and puts associated documentation or finds on a specific table with a vehicle license plate as the file reference. Could they have been mixed up? It's possible but unlikely. The system at the pound has been in operation since I joined the force and in this case, they were the only two vehicles in the warehouse at the time."

"Thank you, Officer Bayfield, very helpful. We investigated the vehicle and owner and it was registered to a Miss Smith but it was an alias. In fact, the license documentation was a forgery; a very good one, but a forgery all the same. Further investigation identified that the vehicle in question had, in fact, been stolen from Conroe, Texas. An attempt had been made to remove the vehicle identification number from the engine block, but there was enough of a trace left for us to put it together. It seems that Miss Smith was, in fact, an enforcer-come-assassin doing jobs for cash and leaving no trace of her real identity. Unfortunately, at the time of the initial investigation the records tied up and the body was cremated and the vehicle itself was destroyed so there is no opportunity to try and get a DNA match. Putting all this to one side, we followed up with the named recipient of the report. The gentleman in question had died and none of his siblings were aware of the report or reason behind it. We sent a report to our counterparts in the Caribbean and they did uncover the remains of a lady in the river confirming the execution took place. This proved the report was genuine. The only other question I have for you is did you view any of the data on the memory sticks?"

"No sir, I didn't. At the time I had no access to reviewing the data and just made reference to the data sticks in the report as initially I thought they were cigarette lighters."

"OK thanks, Officer Bayfield. We are not sure if they are related to the file or were a separate case the late Miss Smith was working on."

With that Officer Bayfield was excused from the meeting. He had no desire to be involved in any more follow up on a case which was, in his view, a simple road traffic accident. The activities of the people involved did not concern him. For sure, if there were other implications it was important to close out, but he had more important personal issues to deal with.

Friday, 9 March 2007

It was a pleasant 77 degrees Fahrenheit outside as Frank got up to go for his early morning walk. Like every day since he and his wife had moved to Seminole on the outskirts of Tampa in the Sunshine State he walked the same route. Getting up at 6am to avoid the worst of the heat and particularly the humidity he silently got out of bed and got dressed. He'd had a troubled night's sleep which he put down to heartburn from the mussels he'd had at The Red Lobster that evening. It had been a celebration with friends for his diamond wedding anniversary. He'd made an exception and drank alcohol – five Bud Lights – something he'd not done for the past eight years.

Putting aside the heartburn he decided to continue with his walk. He was sure he would walk off the sensation, if not he'd take some sodium bicarbonate when he returned. Silently pulling the front door behind him he headed out. Ten minutes into his walk and Frank knew something was not right. His breathing was difficult and he felt like his heart was racing. He stopped on the sidewalk and instantly blacked out, ending in a crumpled heap.

Sharon was looking forward to spending a long weekend at home with her partner Adam and their 6 month old, Jemima. They were out for an early morning walk as Jemima was in the habit of being up and awake by then. Sharon had just completed a four day on shift at the South Seminole Hospital and her shift had only ended at midnight. She was tired but happy as they walked towards the Lake Seminole Park. She had been talking shop with Adam who had alternative shifts to her to ensure Jemima wasn't given to child minders or worse still, Adam's parents; they were difficult going at the best of times.

Out of the corner of her eye she spotted a movement across the street at the edge of her peripheral vision. Turning her head she was not sure if she had seen something or not as the sidewalk had a raised verge and she could not see clearly.

"Adam, I just want to check something out across the street. I think I saw something or someone fall over."

"OK, I will wait here for you."

With that, Sharon checked and saw the street was empty before walking across. She walked slightly away from where she thought she'd seen someone fall over just in case it was something less innocent. She'd seen too many cases of people being tricked and ending up in hospital with gunshot or knife wounds and the occasional corpse. Keeping in Adam's line of sight she cautiously walked up the embankment and peeked over. On the other side, in the middle of the sidewalk lay a motionless old man. She tuned round to Adam and called over.

"Dial 911 now, we have a geriatric faller."

No sooner had Sharon called out Adam pulled his cell out and dialed. He was connected immediately and heard the familiar voice of Joyce in the control room.

"Joyce, hi it's Adam, we have a geriatric faller."

Adam gave the location details and hung up without another word. He knew the paramedic team would be there very quickly. Hopefully, he thought, it would just be a fall…

Sharon had rushed over to the old man and felt his neck for a pulse. Nothing! Her medical training kicked in and she started the process of resuscitation. She immediately started the drill for cardiac arrest. She turned the old man onto his back and then, locking her fingers together, she placed her hands on top of each other and set them in place over his breastbone. With locked arms she pressed onto the breastbone thirty times, counting out loud as she did, then she gave two breaths mouth to mouth, before going into another thirty depressions followed by two more mouth to mouth breaths. Sharon continued the procedure until the paramedics arrived and they took over the resuscitation process. They had arrived within five minutes of Adam's call.

The local police arrived within a minute of the paramedics and soon the area was cordoned off and Adam and Sharon were giving statements, not that they could add much. It seemed to Officer Peters there was no suggestion of foul play. He thanked Adam and specifically Sharon for their support and diligence and went about the process of completing the mandatory report and notification of the relatives.

The paramedics had taken off under flashing lights and siren for the short journey to the hospital and the waiting ER Team. Sharon had managed to get a pulse with her emergency cardiac arrest actions. It was weak, but there was at least a pulse.

Sharon and Adam continued their walk pushing Jemima in her pram; she had gone to sleep and missed the drama. Adam had agreed to check up on the welfare of the old man when he started his next shift on Sunday at midnight as Sharon was not due back until 8am on Tuesday morning.

By 11 am Frank's wife was starting to get worried. She had given up trying to get Frank to take the cell phone she had brought for him when he went walking. He said he didn't like new technology and had survived eighty plus years without it and wasn't going to change now. Frank had frequently met different people whilst he was out walking and didn't have a regular time to get back, except he was always back home by 10 am. She picked up the phone and dialed 911.

"Do you require assistance from law enforcement, medical professionals or fire fighters?"

"I need law enforcement please."

"Please hold whilst I connect you."

"Hello, this is Seminole Law Enforcement emergency, how can I help you?"

She explained to the lady on the phone about Frank's disappearance and was advised that officers would be put on alert to the fact and the operator took details to contact her back.

Officer Peters returned to headquarters to finish his

shift. It had been a pretty quiet morning and he only had a few reports to submit. There had been a burglary reported from a liquor store, a report of domestic abuse and the old man who had gone into cardiac arrest. He had completed the first two reports when he came across a message about a missing person. He did a quick cross reference and was able to place the two together. The old man who had the cardiac arrest was found on a route the missing person regularly went. Great, he thought. He was not finishing on time today, better give the wife the good news; hopefully he wouldn't be too delayed.

At 2.30pm there was a knock at the door.

"Good afternoon, Ma'am. I'm Officer Peters with Seminole Law Enforcement, may I come in please?"

Showing his ID he was let in.

"Is it about Frank?"

"Yes, Ma'am. Could we sit down please? Thank you. He was found this morning in cardiac arrest close to the park. He was treated by a paramedic that was out walking with her family who managed to re-start his heart, but with regret I have to inform you he passed away by the time he got to ER."

There was complete silence except the ticking of the second hand counter on the wall clock. There was for sure the shock, she knew it would happen one day it does to everyone, but Frank seemed so active it just didn't seem right, yet she remained calm.

"I know this is difficult, Ma'am. Is there anyone I can contact? I will unfortunately need to ask if you could accompany me to the hospital so we can do a positive ID."

"Yes, please give me a few minutes."

She went into the bathroom and wept as the shock kicked in. Ten minutes later she came out and found a telephone book and called Marjorie, her best friend that had moved to Florida the same time she and Frank had. Marjorie had lost her husband five years before and she had been there to support her. She knew that Marjorie would do the same for her.

309

Twenty minutes later the three of them were in Officer Peters' squad car heading to the morgue. An hour later, with all the paperwork completed and, verifying that it was indeed Frank on the slab, Officer Peters took the two ladies back and bid them farewell. It was the part of the job he hated the most and reminded him how fragile life was…

Saturday, 5 May 2007

Frank's funeral had taken place a week after his death. Marjorie had been a constant partner for the following four weeks and had been an absolute godsend. Without her she would not have coped. The grieving period had been particularly tough and had taken its toll. She needed to try and put some closure on Frank's death and had started the process of clearing out. There were only a few personal items she wanted to keep, but Frank had a study that really needed attending to.

A week into the process and she had barely made it past the study door. Each document she picked up and every photograph brought back a flood of memories and she allowed her mind to wonder. A month into the task and she decided to postpone for some other time in the future. It coincided with asking her to on a six month cruise taking in the highlights of Europe with her. Maybe when she got back she would get around to it. With that she pulled the door too and focused on what the cruise and Europe had to offer. Frank would have wanted that

Friday, 11 May 2009

The six month cruise had been followed by trips to see Marjorie's extended family. Ruby had spent little time in her Florida home and every time she did she had ignored the office. There would always be another day. The two years since Frank had passed away had gone so quickly, but things began to slow down after Marjorie had a fall the previous month and had been hospitalized. Ruby was unsure if Marjorie would be let back out as her health deteriorated rapidly after the fall.

Looking to get some new sense of purpose Ruby had decided to finally tackle to study. It needed to be done as she herself had been thinking for a while of moving into assisted living accommodation. She was not getting any younger and the time would come soon enough when she would need help with the real basics in line and didn't want to go the same way as Frank....alone

Ruby could see the wood from the trees when she came across some of Frank's old documents and fell across a bulky file from the trip he'd made to New York. She remembered how Frank had discussed this case and how he hated open cases. It brought a brief smile to her face as she thought about his mannerisms and decided to send the file to that Dr. Hernandez's office in New York he's spoken about. They might as well have it.

Friday, 11 May 2009

Rosie arrived in the office at 8.30am. She was on the big countdown. Only ninety-nine working days left until she retired. It still seemed a long way off, yet at the same time she was getting more and more nervous about the approaching date. It was not as though she didn't know what she was going to be doing. She had a very full calendar and was really looking forward to the two months she was going to be spending travelling around Italy and Spain, but it was going to be such a life-changing experience. Like for many people, the fear of the unknown was difficult to manage.

Walking into the office she had just made herself a coffee and prepared one for Dr. Singh. He had taken over from Dr. Hernandez nine months previously when he had retired. It was a huge challenge with him leaving. She had shed a lot of tears that day and although they stayed in regular contact it just wasn't the same. Her desk phone interrupted her thoughts.

"Rosie, you have a package from Florida."

"Really, Josh? I didn't know I knew anyone in Florida. OK, I'll be along later."

"Thanks Rosie, see you later."

With that she hung up and went back to making the coffee.

Two hours later Rosie happened to be passing the post room and stopped by.

"Hey Josh, so where's this package?"

"Right here, Rosie. Can you sign please?"

"For sure."

Making a squiggle on the relevant paperwork she collected the package and headed back to the office. Sitting at her desk she opened the DHL package, pulled out a sealed envelope that simply said Dr. Hernandez and also a large file. Leaving the file she opened and read the letter.

313

"Dear Dr. Hernandez,

I hope this letter finds you well. I have some sad news that my husband of sixty years passed away on 9 March. I have been going through his study and came across this file. I remember him talking fondly about you and about a specific case he came to see you about some years ago. I didn't know if this was important or not, but wanted to let you have it in case you had need of it.

If you are ever in the Seminole area of Florida, please look me up.

Best Wishes
Ruby Reed"

Rosie put down the letter and picked up the file. She vaguely remembered it and decided she would read it later to refresh her memory. She still had a stack of jobs needing to be done today and decided she would take it home to read. Putting the package to one side she carried on.

Sunday, 20 May 2009

It wasn't until the following week that Rosie had the time to read the file she had taken home. There had been so many different things she had to do for her Europe adventure she just hadn't had the time. Sitting on the sofa with her iPod playing on shuffle mode, a selection of AC/DC songs from the five albums she had downloaded, she started to read and began to remember the visit from Frank. He'd been a very nice man.

An hour later she had covered the complete file except for the contents of an envelope held in the back of the file with a paperclip. Taking the envelope she opened it and inside was a handwritten letter. The handwriting was legible but a little like she saw from the doctors when they were writing prescriptions. She had often wondered why, in the case of doctors, they just didn't type on the computer the prescriptions, clearly when they were at medical school handwriting was not a focus for them...

To whom it may concern,

I am not sure if anyone will actually read this letter. If it is being read it means that I am dead, which is strange to be writing in a letter but the unfortunate reality.

Hopefully this file has ended up in the hands of someone that can continue the investigation I started back in September 1975. The case was a tragic one for many different reasons and for me personally one I have to admit defeat on. As a law enforcer in this great country of ours I have always prided myself in being able to solve even the most challenging of cases. This was one of the few I never managed to close out. That is not to say the case should be considered closed, as I believe I know who murdered Mikey, but more proof is required.

A really great man, Dr. Hernandez, helped me immensely in 2001 piece together some significant information leading me to confirm my suspicions, but nothing that could definitively be used in a court of law.

I would be hugely obliged whoever finds this letter if they would pass it and the file to the Department of Justice, Criminal Division. I hope they have the resources and opportunity to follow up and bring closure.

With the information (and unfortunately, supposition, as I have not had the resource to prove out) I pulled together and the huge support from Dr. Hernandez I believe Mikey's killer was, in fact, his daughter. The whereabouts of the daughter are not known and she may not be alive. What I can tell you in that at some time in the late 1970s Mikey's wife and daughter likely changed their names after they moved to New York. If, by the time this file is found, the key suspect is still alive she could be one of this country's wealthiest people.

I apologize for putting this situation in front of whoever reads it and again, ask if it could be passed on so that potentially a longstanding murder enquiry could be closed.

Kindest regards

Frank Reed (Retired Sheriff Roan County)
June 17th 2001

Rosie re-read the letter two times before deciding to call Dr. Hernandez in the morning and get his take on the letters and file. Rosie always called him and it was always in the mornings as she knew he had taken to going to bed early since his retirement.

Putting the letter back in the envelope she headed to the fridge to get a tub of Ben and Jerry's Cookie and Cream Cheesecake Core from the freezer section and enjoy another half an hour of Brian Johnson belting out the tracks on *Black Ice*.

Monday, 21 May 2009

"Good morning, Dr. Hernandez."

"Good morning, Rosie and how are you this morning?"

Dr. Hernandez's voice sounded as youthful as ever.

"I'm doing very well, thank you and yourself? How is the gardening project going?"

"Yes, yes all is well here, which is more than I can say for the garden. We have an infestation of aphids that are destroying the rose bushes."

"I'm sorry to hear that, Dr. Hernandez. Do you have a cure?"

"I guess I could use a flame thrower," he said jokingly. "Besides that we are looking at different solutions but we have to get some results soon or I won't be winning any prizes, except the worst looking rose competition."

They both laughed.

"So how are things with you, Rosie? How's Dr. Singh getting along?"

"I'm fine, thank you. I have been putting the final touches to my Europe adventure in place. I must be honest, I am just starting to feel a little jittery about the unknown..."

"Don't worry about that. By the sounds of it you won't have time to think about it once you move on, and that is the important thing about retirement, staying busy."

"I know, Dr. Hernandez but it's such a big change."

"You need to come over this weekend and the three of us will have dinner and the good lady and I will soon set your mind at rest."

"Thank you, Dr. Hernandez, that would be wonderful. Let me know which day and time. Just before I let you go I want to ask your advice about something."

"OK, but if it's man trouble I am not sure I'm the best to help," he said laughing.

"No it's nothing like that! I got a parcel nearly two weeks ago from Mrs. Reed. You won't know her directly but she's the wife of Frank that came to see you about

317

those drugs that were purchased in New York. He came to see you eight years ago."

"Oh yes I remember him now, he was a retired sheriff. Nice guy."

"Yes, unfortunately he passed away earlier this year and his wife was cleaning out his possessions when she came across the file you and he had been working on. She knew the case meant a lot to him and thought it might be helpful to send it on to you on the off chance you could forward it to someone who might be interested in it. I guess she wouldn't have known you had retired and normally I wouldn't even have bothered reading the file, but the fact she had spent money she didn't need to, and he was a nice guy, I decided to take the file home and read it. It wasn't until I'd read the complete file that I found a letter Frank had written only a few days after you met him. He was hopeful that whoever received the file and read the letter would send it onto someone at the Justice Department."

"I'm sorry to hear he passed away. I do seem to remember the case and he did seem pretty confident about who the murderer was, but the linking proof was missing. Tell you what, I'll be seeing a couple of my friends from DOJ on Friday evening; we get together once a month for some serious gaming. Well we play poker and the maximum anyone has won is five bucks... Let's catch up on it when you come round this weekend."

"OK, Dr. Hernandez."

With that they said their goodbyes and hung up.

Sunday, 27 May 2009

Rosie arrived at 4pm and rang the doorbell. It was opened by Dr. Hernandez's wife who gave her a big hug and welcomed her. She said, "He's out the back in the rose garden."

"Oh dear, the aphid issue still?"

"Yes and he's investigating it like it was one of those cases he used to deal with. I am sure he can tell you exactly where the aphids came from... country... species... how they arrived here. I am sure he could and will write a paper on it one day."

They both laughed and Rosie headed to the back door and into a beautifully managed garden.

"Good afternoon, Dr. Hernandez."

"Ah hello Rosie, and how are you?"

"Doing well thank you, and yourself? I hear the battle between man and insect has not yet been won."

"Unfortunately not but I have a plan," Dr. Hernandez said, laughing. "Let's take a drink on the patio before dinner is served."

Seated on the furniture, Rosie admired the perfectly manicured lawn and the separated areas of the garden that Dr. Hernandez had designed so that in each direction you could be transported to a different part of the world. Rosie specifically liked the fragrant smells from the herb garden and always thought cooking tasted so much better with freshly picked herbs.

She and Dr. Hernandez made small talk before dinner was served and discussed what had been happening in the office and who was doing what and a little bit about Dr. Singh. Rosie felt that Dr. Hernandez was probably a little bit jealous that someone else was running what he had started, but that was only natural after the decades he had put into it.

He asked, "So, is everything finalized now for the Europe adventure?"

"Yes, I got the final hotel confirmation this week

relating to Rome. Apparently I am staying at a hotel that has a view of the Basilica."

"That sounds wonderful. You had better make sure you bring back loads of pictures, you're going to places I've often dreamed of visiting."

"What's really great about this trip is that I have managed to arrange to be met at every airport and port I am arriving at. It took some doing, but it was amazing how many people I have got to meet in the job and all those old contacts have gone out of their ways to take care of me."

"That's wonderful and I'll be a lot happier knowing you are being taken care of. Switching subjects for a minute, I spoke with Daryl and Craig about the file. They think they know the right person to send it to and asked that I give you Daryl's contact details so you could send it to him directly and he will then forward on."

"Thank you, Dr. Hernandez, that's most kind. I don't know if anything will come of it, but it's the least we can do. I brought the file along just in case."

"Would you mind if I read the letter from Frank?"

"Not at all."

With that, Rosie handed over the file she had opened from at the back cover where the letter was again paper clipped. Dr. Hernandez read the letter a few times and went back through his mind to the conversation with Frank and his thoughts about the murderer. Finally, he closed the letter put it back in the envelope, reattached it to the file and handed it back to Rosie.

"Well I guess we will find out if this has helped in due course," he said.

"How's that?" said Rosie.

"Well, if Frank was right, the murderer will make headline news on CNN, Fox, CNBC and Bloomberg, if not all TV networks. I guess we just need to keep watching the news."

The evening came to an end at 9.20pm with Rosie leaving with a plastic carrier bag full of herbs and a promise to send the file off the next morning to Daryl.

320

Wednesday, 24 June 2009

The sign on the outside of the building in Pontiac said "United Advanced Rolled Decor". Like many automotive companies in Detroit they had felt the punch from the global financial crisis. Their heavy reliance on the Detroit Big Three had for many years been their bread and butter, now they were the nails in its coffin.

Miranda had been toying with acquiring a number of such companies but settled on UARD as the CFO was actually pretty smart and also very cute. She could picture herself being sexually fulfilled by this guy. The fact he was married was of no concern. Money would get past that barrier, besides which, once she owned the company she owned everything and everyone.

The CEO had gone the day Miranda had brought the company. He had been a complete waste of space and his only contribution had been to burn the company's profits with two executive jets that he used extensively to fly to Europe in order to court the CEO's and Global VP's of the European car makers. He thought nothing of renting entire hotels for the weekend of the Le Mans twenty-four hours race to entertain the guests he picked up in his jets. That, along with the vintage wines, Champagne and the gambling debts... His firing had sent shockwaves, not just around the company but through the automotive industry. Here was an outsider, a woman, who was taking on the white male dominance of the industry. Either there were a bunch of ass lickers working for the company or they saw Miranda as a godsend. She came in on the promise of rescuing American jobs and rebuilding a broken society. In those desperate times, the vast majority of the automotive industry sector was working three day weeks at best and huge layoffs had already impacted millions of families from the OEM's, through the suppliers and their sub-suppliers to the retail industry where many small business had closed down due to a lack of customers.

For Miranda this was the latest acquisition that took her

financial empire over $5 billion on paper. Only she knew the true wealth. The secrecy of Matriarg Vennote was hers and only hers to know about. She was pretty impressed with the way Mr. Watson had built it up and how unfortunate it had been five years ago when he had died in that car accident. He really should have been more careful over having his car regularly serviced. Considering how big the Jaguar S-Type was, it was amazing how little of it had remained when the car had not been able to brake before it went through the Armco barrier before dropping three hundred feet. ID had been made on DNA taken from the driver's airbag as there was not enough left of the human remains from the scattered and burnt wreck pieces strewn over the valley floor.

"Welcome to UARD, Miss Miranda," said Brian.

He had smoothly stepped into the CEO role. The three letter acronyms after his name were longer than his surname… …MBA, PhD, CPA, and then there was the BA Business Administration, BS Economics and BS Finance… one thing Brian was not short on was qualifications…

"Good morning, Brian and how are you today?"

"Better for seeing you, Miss Miranda."

The sleek mannerisms and oozing of confidence was something that aroused Miranda in many different ways. Finally, here was someone she could consider close to herself in both intellect and capability. She was close to actually believing here was someone she could relate to, maybe a soul mate. Trust, no, that was a word that didn't exist in her vocabulary…

"So, what's the plan for today?"

"Well, I have built a plan to get this company back on its feet and be in a position in the next three to five years to turn your investment into a seven figure return."

"I can't wait to hear and see it. On a separate note, how's my apartment coming along?"

"The apartment is ready for you to move in. We managed to get the final pieces of furniture in yesterday and I've had the executive cleaners in overnight to make sure it's ready for today."

"I'm looking forward to you showing me around it later…"

The undertone from Miranda was very clear. Brian understood he was not going home, at least not until Miranda was satisfied. He'd better ring his wife and come up with some plausible excuse that was going to keep him out all night… Again.

Brian's business plan presentation hit the mark. Miranda was purring with delight by the time it was finished three hours later. She didn't need the coke fix, but decided it would help put her in the mood for the after dinner entertainment. Brian, having learnt about some of Miranda's mannerisms, had his Chief Commercial Officer, Carmelo, on hand to escort Miranda to and from the different offices and meeting rooms and specifically when she visited the ladies room. Diligently, Carmelo would offer his arm, holding Miranda's purse in her other hand. The fact that Carmelo was from southern Europe meant that holding Miranda's purse didn't faze him as it was common place for men to carry bags there. Carmelo didn't have the same charm and charisma as Brian; he didn't have the intellect to carry it off. However his southern Europe tanned, honed figure and accent made up for his intellectual gaps.

Miranda had locked the door to the executive's toilet at 4.35pm and went through the all too familiar routine. The coke soon hit her system and she was taken into that parallel universe that was lasting shorter and shorter each time. Never mind, at least she had an evening to look forward to…

Carmelo, diligently waiting outside, was not sure if he should be concerned or not. What was she doing in there? Who went to the toilet for twenty-five minutes? None of his business, he thought, and continued to guard the toilet door… he was just going to follow orders…

Miranda opened the door at 5.15pm and walked out

323

with a slightly glazed look in her eyes. Carmelo never noticed he was just glad to see the door open and carry out his task: get Miranda back to the boardroom.

"OK, Brian I think we're done here for the day. So, what are the plans for this evening?"

Miranda was hoping the Brian was not going to have the whole of his management team with him for dinner. She was hoping to get the evening started early…

"Well Miranda, I thought you would like to have a quick tour of your apartment and then I have a dinner booking for 7.00pm at Ocean Prime on Big Beaver."

"Really, Brian," Miranda laughed as her perverse sense of humor kicked in. "It's sounding better and better by the minute. I'm ready whenever you are."

Brian had picked up the innuendo immediately and thought should he retort with the fact it was actually Exit 69 off Interstate 75… He decided that it was best at this stage to humor Miranda by smiling back as recognitions of the innuendo.

With that the meeting was finished and Carmelo and the rest of the executive staff were dismissed for the day. There was a mixture of disappointment and relief. Some of those present who had yet to witness the two sides of Miranda were disappointed not to be able to kiss her ass over an expensive dinner. Ocean Prime was the place to be seen in Detroit. Minimum entry to be seen there was a Porsche Cayenne. Carmelo, on the other hand, was happy to see the back of Miranda. There were already whispers, around the company, he had heard about him being called Miranda's bitch and Miranda's lackey…

Brian pulled his Ford GT up to the entrance of the office block and got out to escort Miranda down the steps. The 600 plus horsepower V6 was growing in the background; a sound he loved to hear. *This could be interesting*, he thought, taking in Miranda's outfit. Today she was wearing a black leather miniskirt with a studded black jacket and black 6" stilettos she could barely stand on, let alone walk in. Miranda was a good ten years older than Brian, but he had to admit that she was not bad looking for her age and thought it could be worse. He could be spending the night with a complete dog.

He opened the passenger side door and Miranda turned sidewise to lower her backside into the bucket seat. Unlike a lady getting into a low car, Miranda didn't keep her legs together. As Brian helped her into the car he had full vision of the thong that Miranda was wearing and it not covering her vagina lips. *Good news*, he thought as he saw his dessert, at last it was a shaved pussy…

"So, here we are. Your apartment."

Miranda took in the details and was inwardly pleased. Clearly, someone had been talking with her HQ people. It seemed as though some people in her business empire actually did listen to her. The furniture was easy for to like as it was some of her own that she had had shipped from her New York home. The best of it would be by the end of the night she would be being paid rent by UARD for having her own furniture in her apartment. She was confident that Brian would be up to the mark on many things by the end of the night.

Miranda's luggage had already been taken into the apartment and unpacked by the lady from the Executive Staff Cleaning Company (ESCC) under the careful scrutiny of Carmelo, the only other person to have a key to the apartment. He had let her in and followed her around for the six hours she had spent there cleaning and preparing for Miranda's arrival. She hadn't even been allowed to set foot in the property until she had signed a non-disclosure agreement and filled in a questionnaire that was more thorough than an application form to work with kids. Photographs and fingerprints were also taken by Carmelo. ESCC had already been through a detailed investigation before they were taken on, including police checks of all the owners and potential employees who would be looking after the apartment and its contents. No detail had been too small to ignore. Privacy came at a price and if you had the money then privacy would be guaranteed.

As Miranda entered the apartment she found herself in a reception area with a hallway in front of her. To her right was a door leading to a lounge which was combined with a twelve person dining table. To her left a door lead to the gym and spa which included a Jacuzzi, steam room and sauna. The corridor led to a T-junction. At the end of the right hand of the T was a door to the kitchen which had sliding doors that allowed access to the dining area. At the end of the left hand of the T was a door to the master bedroom which had a 270 degree window and balcony view of the golf course attached to Forrest Lake Country Club. Three other doors off the top of the T led onto three double bedrooms all fitted with en suite bathrooms. Miranda thought it was worth every penny of the $20,000 per month rent, especially as the bill was being picked up by UARD.

Twenty minutes later Brian escorted Miranda out of the penthouse apartment and back to his GT. Miranda again entered the car the same way and Brian noticed that during the comfort break she had taken in the apartment she had seemingly forgotten to put her thong back on. He was pretty sure that she was naked under the leather jacket and miniskirt. He was smart enough to recognize the sign and thought he'd better duly acknowledge the fact during dinner…

It was 6.58pm and Brian pulled up at the valet drop point in front of Ocean Prime. One of the young livered valets rushed up to Miranda's door and took in the car for the briefest of moments before opening the door. For the briefest of time he stared at the exposed vagina of Miranda before averting his eyes and giving the customized welcome. He could not believe his luck. He got to park a racing car and he had an impressive view of some bimbo's pussy, maybe he'd stick the job for a few more weeks…

Brian threw the valet the keys and at the same time asked, "You ever driven a stick shift before?"

"Yes, sir," came the reply. "My pop used to race them

at Flatrock and he taught me to drive in his '85 MR2."

With that Brian offered Miranda his arm and escorted her into the restaurant lobby where they were met by a trio of smartly-dressed hosts. Before Brian said anything the hostess directly behind the lectern said,

"Good evening sir and madam. Welcome back to Ocean Prime. If you would like to come this way I have a private booth for you."

Brian was sure there was a look of familiarity from the hostess but could not immediately remember why or from where. He made a mental note to come back again soon, on his own, so he could try and work out over a drink where he know the hostess from, or more importantly, to find out more about the hostess…

Sat at their private booth Miranda and Brian ordered aperitifs of Bollinger RD 1973 vintage Champagne at $1,200.00 per bottle. Brian thought it would be good to get Miranda into the mood and ensured her glass was kept topped up. Two bottles were quickly consumed and then it was onto a 1995 Marylyn Merlot at $650.00 per bottle. By the time the main course plates had been cleared away Miranda was very relaxed and her head was starting to spin. She was relaxing in her chair when she felt Brian's right hand on her left thigh gently caressing it. Her immediate reaction was to open her legs to give him more access. Brian duly obliged and allowed his hands to wander gradually moving further and further up her thigh until he could feel the heat coming off her vagina. He gently tickled the top of her inner thigh and heard Miranda moan slightly. Brian allowed his fingers to move slowly and sensually to the right and gently moved them over her vagina lips. With the middle finger on his right hand he traced a line up and down over where the lips came together. Within a minute there was juice flowing from inside Miranda's vagina.

Miranda sat there trying to focus on Brian but closed her eyes and felt the first flush of a potential orgasm come along. She moaned again a little louder this time, but only contained in the booth itself. Brian continued to caress her vagina for a few minutes and dismissed the waiter who came to ask if they wanted dessert. Once the waiter was out of ear shot he gently inserted his middle and index finger into a now very wet vagina. Miranda stiffened for a second and then relaxed as she felt the gushing sensation as her first orgasm came along. Fuck me, she thought, it was good to have a man playing with her. Brian continued moving his two fingers up and down inside her vagina and then inserted them as deeply as the constraints would allow. Miranda shuddered and gasped with pleasure and relief. She opened her eyes and said, "You can stop that now, we can carry on when we get back to my apartment."

Brian pulled his fingers out and offered them to Miranda to lick which she took with glee.

"Waiter, check please."

The waiter came over and Brian pulled out his American Express Centurion Card and paid the $3,300.00 bill before escorting Miranda to the exit and the waiting GT. His only thought was he was going to need to have car valeted tomorrow before he went home. He didn't want his wife getting in and smelling stale bodily fluids…

Brian shouldn't have driven back to the apartment with the amount of Champagne and wine he had consumed, however he should be alright if he kept within the speed limits and made it back to Birmingham without getting pulled over. Pulling into the parking lot he pulled as close to the apartment front door as he could and then escorted Miranda in. No sooner had he closed the front door he pulled her towards him and kissed her lustfully. She responded in kind and soon his right hand was again under her skirt and fingering her vagina. He stopped briefly to pick her up and carry her to the master bedroom where he laid her on the bed, with her legs dangling over the side and went down onto his knees. Miranda's miniskirt had ridden up and her vagina was fully exposed. Brian immediately started licking her vagina and inserting his tongue between her vagina lips. His face soon became

328

covered in Miranda's juices and he could feel the warm wet juices covering his cheeks. His left hand wandered up to Miranda's jacket and unzipped it half way down before allowing his fingers to explore. He quickly found her right breast and a very erect nipple. He grasped the breast and started to play with it like it was a piece of kid's Play-Doh. Miranda was moaning loader this time, free to make much more noise than she had in the restaurant.

Brian had also become hard. His penis was pushing against his trousers to the extent that his trousers were starting to dig into his ass. Miranda raised her right foot and with the sole of her stiletto started to rub his erection through his trousers.

Brian continued to lick and insert his tongue until he heard a particularly loud moan from Miranda and again her body shuddered as she climaxed. He pulled away from Miranda and unzipped and pulled down his trousers allowing his erection to protrude out at a 45 degree angle. Pulling Miranda up from the bed he inserted his erection into her mouth and gyrated his hips whilst Miranda licked the end of his circumcised penis. Brian let go of Miranda's head as she began working on his penis. She took the whole length into her mouth and throat making gurgling noises every time it went into her throat. It was Brian's turn to moan and he thought about emptying his load down her throat but held back and allowed her to continue working. Miranda used her teeth to generate pain with the pleasure which Brian found uncomfortable but stimulating at the same time. He thought this would never happen with his wife, she was only ever interested in the missionary position…

Ten minutes later Brian pulled his erection out of Miranda's mouth and roughly turned her over so her ass was in the air. He kneeled down again and licked her vagina and asshole to make sure they were lubricated. He stood up and with knees slightly bent inserted his penis inside Miranda's vagina. Miranda let out a loud moan as the full length of his penis hit the top of her vagina. Brian gave a number of full thrusts before he started teasing Miranda by just inserting the tip of his penis into her vagina. He could quickly tell this teasing was driving Miranda to another orgasm and within five minutes Miranda was yelling, "Yes, yes, yes, yesssssss."

As Miranda felt the warm glow of the orgasm hit, Brian withdrew his penis and aimed it directly at her anus. He inserted it without warning and roughly. There was no teasing and he struggled to get it fully inserted but blanking out Miranda's screams of pain and pleasure he achieved the goal and then ass fucked her. Miranda soon gained control of her pain and, whilst she was being ass fucked, played with her vagina.

Fifteen minutes later Miranda was coming to the boil again. Brian was also getting to the point of ejaculation and pulled out from Miranda's ass, turned her on her back and straddled her on top of the bed and finished himself off by emptying his load over her face, hair and the bedclothes. Having ejaculated his load he stuck his penis back in Miranda's mouth so she could lick off the residue semen.

They both crashed on the bed for ten minutes before Brian got up and wandered over to a bottle of Champagne that Carmelo had left as a welcome gift for Miranda. Uncorking the bottle he poured two glasses and found Miranda in the en suite testing the water temperature in the shower. She seemed to be glowing in the aftermath of the sex and gratefully took the Champagne flute before pulling Brian into the shower.

In the shower Miranda said, "Brian, I think we can do some good things together. I've got a proposal for you. You bring off this business plan and there will be a seven figure bonus check in it. In return I want…" Miranda went on to detail a list of items where she would get monies from UARD. Brian did a quick calculation, Miranda would be pulling in at least $5,000,000 per annum from the deal but that could be offset against the fact they had got rid of the two jets… and there would still be some benefit to the company... and he'd get a $1,000,000 bonus... Not bad for a night sleeping with the boss...

They had doggy style sex in the shower whilst the hot water cascaded over them. Once they had satisfied themselves they washed each other off acting like adolescent school children before heading back to the bed and getting under the covers.

Miranda finally passed out from the mixture of alcohol and energetic sex. Twice more under the covers Brian had brought her to orgasm with a mixture of his tongue, fingers and hard penis. With Miranda passed out Brian needed to relieve himself and turned her over onto her front, lifted her ass in the air and ass fucked her again, this time releasing his load inside her. A good night present he thought with a smile on his face. He climbed off her and walked back into the shower to clean himself thoroughly.

Thursday, 25 June 2009

It was 4.15 am when he finally let himself out of Miranda's apartment and headed to the McDonald's on Elizabeth Lake Road. He needed a serious amount of caffeine to sober up and stay awake for the day. Going through the drive-in in his GT was not his favorite maneuver but needs must and then it was onto the gas station to pick up a four pack of Red Bull before he hit Starbucks in Auburn Hills when they opened at 5am. He wanted to get into the office early so he could change his clothes before anyone saw him wearing yesterday...

Miranda woke up at 7.05am and felt stiff and sore. She realized that the lack of exercise and fine living was catching up with her former athleticism. As she started to recount the evening a broad smile came across her face and she wondered what time Brian had made his exit. Picking up her phone she sent him a text that simply said, "Good morning."

With that she got out of bed and into the shower to get rid of the previous evening's sweat, body fluids and the smell of being in a used bed. By 8am she was dressed in a new revealing outfit ready for the flight back to New York.

"Juan where's my coffee?" Miranda said down the phone.

"Right outside, Miss Miranda. I'm waiting with the limo."

"OK, I'll be there in two minutes."

With that Miranda hung up, checked to make sure her purse contained the essentials and headed out of the front door.

Juan opened the limo door for Miranda and she got in before being handed her Starbucks coffee. Juan got in the front with the driver and they started the forty minute drive to Oakland County International.

Miranda checked her emails and got on the phone to various employees around the States and the rest of the world, not caring that there was a twelve hour time difference in China… They were paid well enough…

During a lull in the calls Miranda thought about Juan and the fact he had become a very able replacement for Clarence, whose untimely demise saved her from some potentially difficult questions but had also caused her a challenge in order to secure regular supplies of high quality crack. It had worked out well in the end. The fact that Clarence had, as part of his signing up to work for Miranda, signed a contract, in essence not just buying his silence, but also in case anything happened to him, leaving Miranda as the sole recipient of his will and testament. He had no living relatives, only the faggot he lived with. Miranda hadn't realized until Clarence's will had been read that he was, in his own right, a wealthy guy. She had inherited $6,000,000 of property in New Mexico, and due to the fact that the gas explosion had killed his faggot boyfriend also, Miranda had inadvertently also inherited a close to $2,000,000 bank account. She thought how careless it had been for the maintenance guy to do such a poor job. The owner of the maintenance company had ensured the fault was laid on the maintenance man himself and he was looking at a ten to twenty year stretch for manslaughter. The guy was a jerk anyway and no one would miss him. At the same time, the company owner pocketed the $15,000 in cash for ensuring the wrong component was given to the maintenance guy…

Miranda had been at the funerals and wept at the right time and given a speech about the need to protect the vulnerable in the country and that she was going to set up trusts and make donations to support single mothers in run down cities. Her first act was to make a donation of $1,000,000 to the local children's hospital. Another $5,000,000 would be used to set up trusts. That took care of the house she'd inherited. No need to go over the top; she'd keep the cash from the bank account…

Juan had come along following a conversation with a business associate in Mexico. He was well educated, very quiet, reliable and connected. Miranda also soon learnt that he also has some perversions. She had had him followed by a private detective to learn more about him and the file gave her enough information to know how to manage him. When he had the chance Juan used to live out his fantasies, being tied up, whipped and electrocuted with crocodile clips attached to different parts of his body. Miranda took him on the day after she got the report from the private detective and ensured his services by explaining she knew of his private activities and explained what he was going to be doing for her. She knew he would be able to secure the crack. He was, after all, the nephew of a senior figure in the Mexican government...

Juan from his part was totally scared of his new 'boss. Whatever she wanted he was going to make sure it happened. He lived under a total blanket of fear as to what she could do to him. The positives from his side though, was that she had a nice pad, was paid well and once a month she would tie him up and whip him. The electric shock treatment was for him a dual benefit. The sexual one was a side benefit he'd found whilst trying new methods to detox his body. He had the body of a male model, but was only too aware the looks would soon go if he overindulged and he was very driven by his looks. Whether he knew it or not, he was a masochist and was completely trapped under the spell of a sadistic owner.

The limo pulled up at the airport and the plane was soon taxiing towards the runway and the flight back to New York.

Friday, 14 August 2009

"Miranda, the closure is being announced today."

Imogen was on her cell phone standing in the lobby of the Days Inn and Suites hotel in Rheinlander. There was a distinct lack of a good hotel in the area, so Imogen had been, in her eyes, slumming it.

"Shit, how bad is the damage?"

"MV1 is the one taking the hit. It will have a knock-on effect across the complete profile. In essence, we are going to lose 35% of the income for the parent company. The implications outside of this are the state lawyers are already preparing litigation documentation claiming fraud based on financial mismanagement. I know it's of no relevance however the closure will impact 476 jobs in the company and estimated another 75 in the town. The mayor is being briefed at 9am in his office by the management team."

"You're right, I don't give a shit about the people. What's the assessment of the fall out?"

"Talking to the governor's office yesterday, the law suit being filed is for $250,000,000 in damages."

"That's bullshit. If it wasn't for me that shitty town would have been dead and buried five years ago. I knew I should have fired the complete management team and started again. Stupidly, I thought as they were supposed to be experts in plane building they might know something about it."

Miranda was starting to rant. Imogen was used to these outbursts, although she noticed they were happening more and more recently.

"Make sure there are no loose ends and get out of there."

"Yes, Miranda, I'll see you later."

With that Imogen hung up and headed out of the lobby to her car and the drive to the company. She wanted to get in and out before the announcement was made to the workforce. It was planned for 1 pm. Arriving at the security hut she was waved through and walked straight to the office she had been allocated. At 6am she was alone and decided to bypass the morning ritual of making herself a cup of green tea and getting on with the job in hand. Having gained access to the email master site she systematically went through with the search function and deleted all emails sent by either herself or Miranda. She also deleted any emails where either she or Miranda was in copy. This would at least stop the electronic traceability. She then went to the backup files she knew were stored in the safe and completed the same process. The only thing she couldn't change was the fact that the modifications to the files had been tracked to the current date and time. To at least try and confuse this, she changed the passwords to all the accounts so it would be highly difficult for anyone to gain access to the records. She was sure eventually a professional system hacker, who would be brought in, would be able to access but she banked on the fact that in that process the change dates would be lost.

By 7.30am the records had been fully altered and the backups returned back to the safe. She removed the latex gloves she had been wearing throughout the process and, packing her briefcase with the memory sticks containing the electronic copy of all the associated emails that had been deleted, she headed back to the car park.

There were a number of cars already in the car park and more coming past the security gate, but there were no sign of Tom, Craig or Jeff. She wanted to be clear before they arrived; she was sure it was going to be ugly at the factory today and intended to be back in New York before the action kicked off.

Saturday, 1 December 2012

Nela had arrived in the office early. She was there by
6.30am which normally she would have considered crazy.
It was a weekend and she worked long hours Monday to
Friday, but there was a special reason today. As she picked
up her drive through venti, skinny cappuccino with three
shots from Starbucks she contemplated why she was going
through the drive-thru as opposed to being in bed enjoying
a well-deserved lie in.

Nela admitted to herself that she had been very focused
on her career. Her two kids were, for sure, a very
important part of her life, but she was driven to ensure she
had financial security at a young age to make sure she
could provide the best for them. It was her justification for
the long hours however it was masking some real
fundamental issues in her personal life. Nela was thirty-
five years old and when, she made the effort, was still a
stunner. She had kept her shape even after the birth of her
children. She had not fallen into the trap of many of her
fellow mothers of hitting the junk food and turning obese
to compensate with the challenges of balancing a job with
raising her kids. Her relationship with her husband had
become more and more strained as they had started to live
separate lives. He spent hours after work playing on-line
computer games, often not getting to bed until the early
hours of the morning. On the surface they appeared to be
the perfect family, big house, two nice cars and kids doing
well at school and in various sports teams, but under the
surface it was quite the opposite. Over the recent months
she and her husband had been arguing. At first it was
minor issues, however over the recent months they had
argued over everything from who was emptying the
dishwasher or putting out the waste, to carrying out
modifications to their home. Nela had reached a point
where the spark had gone and she was not going to sit
back and do nothing about it. She was missing fun in her
life and she was going to find and have some. She was also

337

missing good sex. Her sex life had evaporated in the past six months and she was going to change that.

She had been promoted to Vice President of Treasury nine months previously and resultantly had a lot more exposure to the running of the business but also to the executive staff. In this new position she had gained new insights into the business, and opportunities to improve elements for herself. The reason she was at the drive-thru this specific Saturday morning and at this time was to address a couple of those areas. When she was promoted she had made that little extra effort to look smart and also sexy. The outfits had been a little more revealing and the heels had got a little higher. She still knew what it took to get the opposite sex interested. Waiting for her coffee to be delivered she looked in the rear view mirror and liked what she saw. Looking down she wondered if the skirt was a little short under the long fleece lined coat. No, she decided it was perfect for her plans for the morning. The V-neck sweater was showing just enough cleavage and the fact she was not wearing a bra aroused her slightly, but also it was done to make life a little easier later that morning. She had set up the Saturday meeting with her boss very carefully. There was a specific project she had been working on for him and had used the excuse there was no time Monday to Friday for them to spend the focused time needed to get to a consensus how to move forwards. She had discreetly and knowingly been flirting with him at work. Up to this point she had not thought about pushing it any further, but today was the day to make a breakthrough on that front. The meeting was set up for 8.30am but Nela wanted to ensure everything was in place before he turned up. She was not sure if there would be anyone clsc on site and was pleased to see only a scattering of three cars on the parking lot, none of which she recognized. Using the magnetic strip on her employee badge she walked through reception and into the darkened main office leading to her office with its window view. These offices werc prized possessions and were, for sure, seen as a differentiator between those that had made it and for those who worked in the cubicles, who clearly hadn't. Setting up her laptop and taking off her winter coat she headed to her boss's office to make sure the window blinds were angled to ensure that anyone outside could see as little as possible. When they were to her satisfaction she completed the same exercise in the boardroom. She wanted to cover as many options as she could, just in case…

Back in her office she read a few of the mails that had come in from China overnight before putting the finishing touches on the official project.

At 8.25am the desk phone in Nela's office rang.

"Good morning Nela, how are you this morning?"

"Exceptionally well than you, Brian, and you?"

"Perfect thanks, do you want to come along to my office?"

"For sure, do you want me to grab you a coffee on the way?"

"No, it's my treat. You take a venti, skinny cappuccino with three shots don't you?"

Nela was taken aback, he knew her Starbucks order. She'd never told him… how had he found out? A smile came across her face; he'd been checking her out. This morning looked like it was going to work out.

"Yes I do,"

"That's good. I picked you one up on the way in, hope that's OK?"

"Perfect, thanks Brian. I'll be along shortly."

With that they hung up and Nela picked up the paper copy of the presentation and her laptop. After a last quick check of how she looked in a wall mirror she had close to the door. *Not bad*, she thought and headed to Brian's office.

"Come in Nela, take a seat."

Nela walked over to the informal table with the high back leather chairs and sat next to Brian where he would have the best view of her legs and high rising skirt. Brian was casually dressed in a button down shirt and jeans. Nela noticed he was struggling to keep eye contact with her and she deliberately leaned over the table on a regular basis as if to point out something specific, but allowing her V-neck to expose more of her uncovered breasts.

The presentation had been going for fifteen minutes when Brian said, "Nela, could I ask you a personal question?"

"For sure Brian, what is it?"

"Do you want to have sex?"

There it was. Nela was not sure how the approach was going to happen. She had worked out that unless her picture of Brian was completely wrong he was not an animal and therefore would not force himself on her, but even still she was slightly surprised.

Nela uncrossed her legs allowing Brian even more of a view up her skirt and said, "Yes."

Brian went to stand up but Nela put her hands on his shoulders guiding him the kneel down in front of her.

"Eat my pussy," she ordered.

Almost like a scolded kid he knelt down and pushed her skirt up over her thighs to allow Nela to open her legs. He pulled her panties to one side and, pushing his face up to her vagina, started to lick her vagina lips. Nela gave a small moan and felt her vaginal juices starting to flow for the first time in a very long time.

Brian let his tongue part her lips until he felt she was wet enough down there to insert his index finger on his left hand. The combination of tongue and finger brought a more intense moan from Nela. Her erect nipples were pushing hard against her sweater and she sensed, more than felt, Brian's right hand reach up under her sweater playing with her left breast. Nela was not sure how long Brian was playing with her. She had lost any sense of time. It could have been a couple of minutes, ten, fifteen she didn't care, but for sure she could feel herself coming to an orgasm. She pulled on the back of his head as if trying to get his tongue deeper inside her. The more he licked and

340

sucked the more her hips were gyrating and the louder her moaning became. Then the barrier broke and she orgasmed. The release was electric. Her body stiffened as she climaxed and then shook as the sensitivity of the after orgasm hit as Brian continued with his finger and tongue actions.

Brian, when he was pushed onto his knees, had started to feel himself go hard. This was not exactly what he had planned, but was not going to allow work get in the way of sex. He was used to being the dominant one, but found the experience of being dominated arousing. He had willingly complied with the order of eating Nela's pussy and when she had kicked off one of her shoes and rubbed her left foot over his covered erection he could feel himself getting highly aroused. Nela had interchanged rubbing his erection with kicking his scrotum that had mixed pleasure with pain. The, at first uncomfortable, feeling had changed to a pleasurable pain that had the combination of teasing him, but at the same time stopping him from reaching an orgasm himself.

Nela pulled Brian's head away from her vagina and encouraged him to stand up so she could unbutton his jeans. Pulling them so they were around his ankles she knelt on the carpet and licked the pre-cum off his erection. Liking the taste she started to lick around the end of his penis before sticking it fully in her mouth and sucking, using her tongue to tease at every opportunity. She could feel his balls getting harder and withdrew his penis from her mouth and then slapped it hard. It had the desired effect. The pain stopped Brian from coming. She counted twenty times she repeated the process before allowing Brian to ejaculate his load in her mouth. Standing up with her mouth open she made sure Brian saw her swallow his cum.

"Mmmmm that tasted nice, now fuck me."

It wasn't a request, it was an order and Brian allowed himself time to recover by sticking his head between Nela's legs again after she had lain back across his desk.

He wasn't used to performing like that. Normally he brought a woman to orgasm, shot his load, and carried on with his day... this was different, way different.

Forty minutes later they were both spent. The carnal lust had been extinguished, at least for the time being. Both had experienced the wow factor and there was a sense this was not the end of the road for this particular affair. Neither felt a morsel of guilt about what they had done, in fact they were feeling more like teenagers experiencing the pleasures of sex for the first time. Once they were both dressed Nela decided to strike whilst the iron was hot.

"Brian, there is something I want to discuss with you."

"OK, you certainly have my attention," he said with a smile.

"It's about the monthly loan payments we are making to MV3."

"What about them?"

"Well, the thing is if we could delay them by two days, in essence transferring the day from Friday to Monday it could prove to be very beneficial."

"Beneficial to whom?"

"Well, the people that make it happen."

"What does beneficial mean?"

"I've looked into the different options and, in essence, it would clear between $10,000 to $20,000 per month in interest."

"And that would go where exactly?"

"Well, the way I have it figured to a certain CEO and VP of Treasury."

"That is an interesting proposition, maybe we ought to go grab lunch and go through the fine details."

"Sounds like a plan to me."

With that Nela left Brian's office and headed back to hers via the restroom to freshen up.

Monday, 2 April 2013

Miranda had received word that the lawsuit documents would be arriving imminently. She had received news in advance from one of her moles in the Department of Justice that the case was built around inculpatory evidence. The mole was not sure of the exact amount being sought but a nine figure sum was being rumored. Miranda was not bothered specifically about the value, it was more a small dent in her ego. How dare anyone question her business practice, capability or skill! She was immensely wealthy and knew that there would be a multitude of jealous people out there that would like to see her fail so they could step into the space she vacated. That would never happen, of that she was sure; she was much smarter and quicker to act than any of her supposed peers.

As much with amusement as anything else, Miranda opened the FedEx package and scanned the introduction. She was amused that the front sheet used was the same in any case, she had seen many of them in the past and much of it was just local state bullshit, basically letting those who received such a writ that there was this 'higher place' that was there to be looked up to and feared. Clearly, Miranda had not picked up on the to be feared and read the words of some very small-minded bureaucrats who, too many years ago, had been given a blank piece of paper and told to make up some words to portray a picture of how important they were. The interesting reading started on page five where the alleged list of her crimes had been detailed. She could tell from the individual charges exactly where the claims had come from and each of the associated business deals. She was pretty familiar with all the cases in question and saw nothing from the claims that would cause her any concern in court. Besides which, she had a team of very highly skilled lawyers who she knew would represent her interests and had handled many other cases before, and Miranda was sure, would be again in the future.

Her mole was right, it was a nine figure sum. The claimants were seeking $200,000,000 in damages, the biggest claimant being the shareholders in Rheinlander. The only small niggle at the back of Miranda's mind was the fact this case was being overseen by a judge from the Ohio Supreme Court who was a senior Democrat. In her opinion, Democrats were stupid do-gooder's who just allowed anyone into the country and basically, all their policies were completely wrong. They had no interest in making the US great again, they were only interested in being seen to be in the pretentious role of leader of the world...

She had more important issues to deal with the island she was purchasing and needed some focus.

Friday, 10 May 2013

The office was a hive of activity. Justice Shah was directing his team at a frenetic pace. This was an important case and everything needed to be perfect. The evidence was compelling even though a number of the witnesses appeared to have been scared off from providing evidence in court. That was definitely a point he would be following up during the trial. The big question that had been hanging since the team came together was whether the star accused would actually turn up to court. There had been a bet going inside the team and they were pretty split. Justice Shah was prepared for that eventuality, ensuring just the right level of pressure had been applied to the relevant office to make them aware that a no-show would significantly hamper their case and would be seen as a contempt of court, increasing the risk of guilt and the penalty that would be applied.

The evidence showed a blatant disregard for the people supposed to be being protected and this act of America first was, on the evidence seen to date, just that; an act and a deception. There were other leads that needed to be followed up on but the case with Rheinlander was compelling on its own. Judge Shah was looking forward to this case as he had followed with some 'interest'. He used that word, but in reality it was more contempt and disgust at the career of Miranda. In his opinion this was yet another example of what pure greed does to people. This was not about the American way of life; it was pure and unadulterated greed. It was absolutely on the same lines as the Enron scandal, maybe not on quite the same scale, but here it wasn't multiple people involved, it was a single individual who had simply raped businesses for personal greed, resulting in the destitution of thousands of what had been hardworking people.

In his mind, there were no mitigating circumstances from the evidence he had seen; Miranda was as guilty as sin. His view on the case, not that he would say in public, was simply that she would be found guilty and his only goal was to ensure that she paid the maximum price for the crimes. It was clear Miranda was a Republican and this case was going to be a show piece about the corruption at the heart of the Republican Party. They stood only for themselves as individuals, they cared not about the people they were supposed to represent. How many more mass shootings were going to have to be allowed before action was taken against the corrupt old white men running the gun lobbies?

Judge Shah was a Christian and a Democrat in equal measures and saw his doctrine as the only one. In many ways he was as extreme as Miranda, they were just complete opposites.

Monday, 17 June 2013

Brian had been expecting the call and the venom that the voice carried. Miranda was as far past livid as he had ever experienced.

"What the fuck do you mean you're resigning? There is no fucking way you can resign. I'll fucking take you to the cleaners you lowlife piece of shit. I've done everything for you and you pay me back by snaking off behind my back. Who the fuck would employ you anyway? When I find out I'll sue them as well…"

The ranting continued for ten minutes. There were expletives used that even Brian had no clue what they meant, it was almost that Miranda had developed an aggressive form of Tourette's syndrome and was clearly getting the energy from some fix she had taken before the call. And then it ended. Just silence on the phone. Brian was conscious of the noise from the air conditioning unit. He almost wondered if Miranda had wound herself up so much that she had passed out… or had a heart attack and was lying on the floor of her office…

Ten, fifteen, twenty seconds passed and then, "So you're going, huh?"

"Yes, Miranda."

"Nothing going to change your mind?"

"Miranda, you know it's not about money or financial incentives. You have been very generous on those fronts."

Brian wanted to keep the conversation civil – and as short as possible he had a lunch meeting with Nela to make – and knew the way to achieve that was to turn the focus of the conversation away from himself and get Miranda talking about herself.

"The simple fact is that you set standards I can't live up to. I honestly believe for the company to move forwards it can only do so with you as the CEO."

"Yes, you are right, I do have high standards and yes, you are right again, I am the only person that can effectively lead this company and make a success of it. I should have realized this before but it took your act of treachery to make me understand that. I had really high hopes for you, Brian."

"I know, Miranda. We did work on some contingencies in case things didn't really work out and the company is at one of those contingency points today. It is a logical change point and that is what has honestly driven the timing."

Brian wondered how much of the bullshit he was speaking she actually believed. Probably most of it, as in Miranda's eyes he was showing he was feeble in comparison to her skill and intellect. He carried on.

"From my side I don't have any firm plans. I have offers overseas and out of state but am going to take time off to decide what to do next. My contract says twelve months garden leave and I plan to take it and take a break and work out my next steps."

This last part was complete bullshit. He had already signed a contract with another Tier 1 and would spend the next twelve months working for them on a consultancy basis through an offshore company he had set up with Nela. Things had been developing very well on that front and had gotten pretty serious; in fact, it had been Brian that had brought up the idea of them going through the associated divorce processes and moving in together. Even as he was on the phone with Miranda, and his mind was turned to Nela he was distracted by the thought of their lunch meeting and felt a bulge starting to grow in his pants. Miranda brought him back to focus.

"Well, make sure you do. I have spies everywhere."

"For sure Miranda, so how do you want to play this? Do you want to make an announcement or should I prepare something?"

Brian knew Miranda would come up with the press release and it would be a mixture of self-praise and slandering Brian, but he didn't care. Miranda's reputation in the industry and in the business community as a whole was pretty well documented by now. Saviour of American jobs or evil bitch? Just depended on which side of the fence you sat at any point in time.

"I'll prepare it. Just make sure you have cleared your office by 4pm."

"No problem. I take it then I am formally released from my duties from 4pm today."

With that the phone line went dead and Brian smiled and then laughed out loud. He had pulled it off. With the phone line cut he stopped the phone recording which he was sure he would need to use as evidence at some point. He trusted Miranda as far as he could throw her, and with the pounds she had added in the past six months that wouldn't be very far. Putting the recording in his briefcase, along with a few other personal effects from his desk, he walked out for his lunch meeting.

As he walked out of his office he asked his PA to set up a conference call at 3pm for his executive staff team, telling her that attendance was mandatory no matter where they were in the world, and yes, wake them up if they are in China. With the instruction out there he walked out through the lobby and into the pleasant midday sun.

Miranda was scheming even before the call had finished. She was going to make Brian pay. How?

"Imogen, get hold of security and send them up to my office now."

"Yes, Miranda."

Imogen hung up the phone and put the call through to Jen, the head of security.

"Jen, Miss Miranda wants to see you now."

"No problems Imogen, did she say for any particular reason?"

"No, but I was listening to one side of a call she just has with the CEO at UARD, so my guess it will be related to that."

"OK, thank you."

Jen walked up the flight of stairs from her control room and lightly knocked on Miranda's office door.

349

"Yes?"

Jen walked in and said, "You wanted to see me, Miss Miranda?"

"Yes, Jen I need your support on a particular issue I have."

"OK, Miss Miranda just let me know what and when."

"I need dirt on the CEO at UARD."

"Do you want anything doing with the dirt when we find it?"

"No, let me deal with that when you find it."

"OK, Miss Miranda. Do you have a timeline?"

"Yesterday would be perfect, today would be OK, tomorrow would be late."

The feral look in Miranda's eyes was back and it was if she was staring straight through Jen. Jen had degrees in a number of subjects including psychology and recognized the signs of someone who was insane. Miranda was showing all those signs and traits, but the pay was good and Jen always delivered.

"OK, Miss Miranda I'll turn the team onto it now."

"Good."

With that the meeting was over and Jen walked out and past Imogen, wondering if she had inherited the same insane tendencies her mother had.

Jen walked down the stairs to her office and called together her team.

"OK guys we have a priority one program. We need to do an assessment on the CEO of UARD, so tasks will be per standard surveillance. Jay, you need to check phone records from both office and cell numbers. Adam, you need to track back through all video evidence. Amy, you need to get a tail established and daily reporting, any questions?"

There were none. They had carried out this type of surveillance on many previous occasions and they had all developed their own systems, contacts and data inputs to get the necessary results. They also had state of the art tools to doctor any information that was required, and should it get to that Jen would make the call on what the content of the doctoring would be.

With their instructions given the team went off to start their own investigations. Jen reckoned the first results, if there was anything obvious, would be with her within twenty-four hours. Knowing the capability of her team she went back to working on a separate job. It was, for her, a little more lucrative as outside of working for MV she had her own internet security business that had been made possible with the no expense spared approach from Miranda to electronic eavesdropping equipment. There were few systems Jen had yet to hack and the potential was pretty enormous. She had to have a contingency plan for when MV crashed, something she personally believed would happen as she witnessed from close Miranda changing almost on a daily basis heading downwards in an ever-increasing spiral. Miranda was losing touch with reality and was living more and more in her own bubble and world. It was a world Jen didn't want any part of, but the pay check was good…

Thursday, 20 June 2013

"Miss Miranda, I believe I have the information you are looking for."

"OK Jen, what have you got?"

Jen set a portable DVD player on the table in front of Miranda.

"This information is pretty recent. There was nothing else of significant interest pulled from video and audio pulled from UARD. The other searches have not as yet identified anything that could be incriminating. Clearly we could come up with other evidence if you want."

"Let's see what you have first shall we?"

With that Jen pressed the play button on the DVD player and a view of the Brian's office came up on the screen. The camera was hidden in a corner of the ceiling which gave a raised panoramic view. Brian was sitting at his office table working on his laptop but within a couple of seconds the door opened and in walked Nela.

"Come in Nela, take a seat."

The presentation had been going for fifteen minutes when Brian said, "Nela, could I ask you a personal question?"

"For sure Brian, what is it?"

"Do you want to have sex?"

"Yes."

"Eat my pussy" she ordered.

Jen stood to the side of Miranda's desk and discreetly studied her boss. During the video Miranda's facial features and body language painted a whole range of emotions from psychotic rage to sexual arousal. Jen's impression of Miranda was more and more confirmed. The feral look was back and she, at points, was losing control of herself. After twenty minutes Miranda dismissed Jen from her office. Jen went back to her office and switched on the camera feed she had installed in Miranda's office, first telling her team she was not to be interrupted for any reason and, ensuring the video equipment was working, watched Miranda as she continued to watch the video.

Jen was always cautious when she was watching the boss, but also was also conscious she may need evidence in the future of her boss's activity, just in case…

Ten minutes watching the live feed was enough to capture Miranda taking a fix. As the fix hit it was visibly noticeable the change in Miranda's body language. She was visibly more relaxed and the feral look in her eyes was gone. The amount of times Jen had captured this on video was now in the hundreds. She contemplated telling Imogen on many occasions but had repeatedly decided against this. It would, for sure, end up with her losing her job and, knowing Miranda, a brutal and ugly law suit. With a sigh, Jen took the DVD from the recorder, added a reference with date and time tracker and put it with the others in her safe.

"Imogen, come to my office now."

"Yes, Miranda."

With that Imogen closed her cell down and headed up the two flights of stairs. Knocking once on the door she let herself into Miranda's office.

"How can I help you?"

"I want that slut from UARD fired today."

"Which slut exactly?"

"The one on this video," Miranda said as she threw the disk across the table. "You can watch it later. I am sure there is more to it than this. Gross indecency for a start, but I want to ruin her reputation. Get this out on all the revenge porn sites. Find out if she's married with kids. If she is, get a copy to her husband. If she has kids get the video to parents of the kids' friends and the school governors. She wants to abuse me, well let's see how she fucking likes it. Now get on with it."

With that the meeting was over. Even Imogen was shocked with the instruction. Ruining someone's reputation was one thing, but bringing their kids into it, that was low even for Miranda. Imogen had also witnessed the change in her mother. It seemed the more she felt threatened, the more extreme her reaction was. She was resorting to more underhand tactics to get what she wanted than following any kind of rational thought or action. Maybe the upcoming lawsuit was worrying her more that she was telling. Imogen was sure the video was about 'some slut' having sex at the UARD facility, but why would Miranda have a particular issue or interest in that? She would just have to watch the video and figure out how she was going to destroy whoever's reputation it was, but she drew the line with the kids…

Wednesday, 7 August 2013

Rosie was sitting outside the café made famous by the fight scene with Drax's henchman Chang from the James Bond film *Moonraker*. As a Bond follower and somewhat aficionado her current trip around Europe was actually a homage to the different film locations. The orchestra was playing outside to the midday tourists wandering around Piazza San Marc and the table service charge for the privilege of soaking up the atmosphere, in her eyes was excessive, but a necessary part of the experience.

Rosie was happily basking in the 86F heat with her floppy hat protecting her from the blaze of the sun. A gentle breeze was blowing up the Piazza from the sea. Immersed in the moment, Rosie was interrupted from playing over the moment Chang got thrown through the clock window to the sounds of the aria *Vesti la giubba* by the buzzing of her smart phone. Since getting this as an extravagance to herself she had become an internet junkie. Sighing slightly she thought she should try and find a therapist to help wean her off the device; she had nicknamed it 'crackberry', as it was, she was sure, as addictive as the drug… She picked up her device to see it was simply a message from CNN giving an update on the Edward Snowden Russia asylum situation. She had very mixed feelings about that situation but deep down he was a traitor and made her feel somewhat uncomfortable about being an American travelling abroad, although all the people she had met made her feel very comfortable and safe. Ignoring the orchestra playing in the background she opened the CNN app and scanned through the different news stories. Five minutes later, as she was about to close the app, she came across the news about the pending trial of one of America's most influential women. She read the article a couple of times and her mind went back to the case that Frank had brought up with Dr. Hernandez and wondered if this had anything to do with this case.

Closing her app down and turning back to the orchestra playing she made a mental note to follow the story.

Tuesday, 22 October 2013

It was another bitterly cold day. Temperatures would struggle to get above zero and the wind chill factor killed off any hope of it feeling anything other than ugly.

Judge Shah had not had a good night. No matter how he had tried, sleep eluded him. Today was judgment day in the case of Matriarg Vennote and the disastrous outcome that had befallen Rheinlander Aircraft and the local community. Despite the best efforts of his team at the Justice Department there was not enough solid evidence to clearly convict Matriarg Vennote and specifically, its evil owner of the collapse of the company and the resulting collapse of the local community. The suicide of the Human Resources manager did not sit well with Judge Shah, he was sure there was still more to it than that, but time had run out. His options were limited and with a sigh he opened the front door and was welcomed by a blast of frigid cold wind.

The Miguel Antoinne suits were on display as Judge Shah entered the courtroom. There were three of them representing Matriarg Vennote. The smug expressions on their faces reeked of the superior confidence they held that clearly came from being part of the most exclusive of law firms in New York. They were slick and slippery. They had used all the tricks in the book to defend and deflect the charges for the past month and believed today was just a formality. It would be a good payday for them and they were probably working on what luxury they would spend their fat bonus on. It made Judge Shah even more angry as he took his seat and considered the plight of the normal people who were now 'living the dream' of poverty due to the greed of Matriarg Vennote, its owner and these leaches.

The court was called to order and Judge Shah started his summation…

The summation went on for a good thirty minutes before Judge Shah came to the conclusion of the court.

"Ladies and gentlemen, with all the information presented I have reached the conclusion that at this point it is not possible to provide a clear verdict. This trial will be dismissed with a re-trial to take place at a date and time to be advised."

So there it was, the killer punch he had wanted to deliver was not possible, and the re-trial would only help if more information could be uncovered. It was not a satisfactory situation for anyone, except the suits from New York. He could visualize them rubbing their hands together in glee as they were on for another good pay day. For sure they would appeal against the decision however that would be easy to quash and push forwards with the re-trial.

With that Judge Shah dismissed the court and went off to his office to do the case review with his team so they could analyses, complete a lessons learnt exercise and decide what needed to be done differently for the next case, if anything.

Thursday, 3 July 2014

"OK guys. Is everything ready?"

The calls of "Yes" came from the thirty people in the room.

"OK, let's open the doors and get this show in the road and let's have some fun."

With cries of "Yes, boss" the team exited the amphitheater to take up their stations around the conference.

Curley stood by the lectern for a few more seconds watching his team heading for their stations, exceptionally proud of them. They were an eclectic mix of different nationalities and personalities, but every one of them was focused on the objectives and, in their own ways, all contributing to the goals. Curley did one more take to make sure his microphone was switched off before heading up the steps of the amphitheater to start the meet and greet process and the shaking of hands of some five hundred people that were due to attend the diversity event or as it had been nicknamed 'Speed Dating'.

The guest speaker was not due to arrive for another hour, however the fact that Miranda was attending had swelled the attendee list and it had been necessary to restrict the number of attendees from different companies to a maximum of two from each company. It was not the first time this event had taken place but Curley was still amazed at the draw of Miranda. Working with her and seeing her on a pretty regular basis had shown him the side of Miranda no one in public ever saw. Because this was one her pet projects it seemed she kind of liked him, it certainly was something that played into her ego as a defender of American jobs and diversity was something that was uniquely American. In the rest of the real world it was just a reality of life that you don't prejudice people because of color, race, age, sex or any other region... and just because you served in the military didn't give you the right to expect people to give you work... Was there more work that needed to be done, for sure, but to expect to have 10% of your spend with diverse companies was really BS and, more importantly, doing quite the opposite of rescuing American jobs, it was encouraging more people to offshore and set 'the wife' up as a diverse company so as to claim the associated benefits and plaudits. It was really hypocritical but, as with many things, it was part of a game and Curley was going to make sure that UARD was focused to deliver the goals and achieve the objectives…

The reception area soon became a bubbling cacophony of noise as the visitors went through the registration process and made initial contact with their associated blind dates for later in the conference. A few just helped themselves to the refreshments and headed to the amphitheater to get the best seats. There was a large group that literally travelled from one event to another and Curley was sure they had a ranking system like the football league where they ranked the events they attended. He was sure this event would be close, if not at the top. What gave the best rankings went around food, refreshments and the speakers involved. This event had a reputation of ticking all the right boxes.

An hour later the majority of visitors had registered and the reception area had quietened down somewhat when Curley went out to meet the guest speaker. The SUV pulled up outside the front door of the conference center and he opened the passenger front door ensuring he didn't lower his eyes as he knew doing so would put him off wanting to eat for some considerable time.

"Good morning, Miss Miranda."

"Good morning, Curley, how are you?"

"Exceptionally well thank you and yourself?"

"Looking forward to today," was the reply as Miranda exited the car. Today's outfit confirmed Curley's fear and was grateful he had retained eye contact during the exchange. The mini dress was, as usual, obscenely short and the heels were a good 6 inches. Offering his arm he walked her up the stairs to the reception area when, almost like a switch had been thrown, the whole area went quiet. It was like the president had walked into the room. Cameras started to go off as the guests in reception started to take photographs of Miranda. Curley went along with the show, dreading the inevitable requests from a considerable number of the attendees who would want a personal introduction to Miranda. The only other thought going through his mind was in four hours' time his life would return to normal and he focused on hitting Starbucks… and a smoke.

Keeping a discrete distance behind Miranda was Juan in his official role of 'the purse carrier'. The procession walked through the foyer towards the auditorium with Miranda doing a perfect imitation of a Tina Turner walk with gushing comments coming from faceless attendees as she staggered past.

Curley escorted her to her seat at the side of the auditorium closest to the lectern and next to the reserved seats for the privileged ass lickers who immediately started fawning over her. Curley excused himself and went in search of some of his staff to ensure they were on time.

The auditorium filled to a point where it became standing room only and Curley went to the lectern and switched on his microphone.

"Good morning, ladies and gentlemen. Welcome to, as our special guest calls this, our speed dating event."

There was laughter from around the room. Curley continued.

"So firstly a warm welcome to you all and before we start the dating process a small introduction."

With that, Curley hit a key on his laptop and the projector came to life projecting onto the 30' square screen behind him with a preloaded ten minute video. The video started.

"Miranda, the savior of American jobs, the protector of American dreams…"

Curley sat down, switching off to the video. He had

seen it so many times he could almost do the voice over word for word. One person after another came on the screen praising the energy, efforts, work ethic and basically one after another kissed that cellulite ass, big style.

As the video came towards the end the dry ice machines placed either side at the front of the auditorium started up. The video started to reach a crescendo with comments and music coming over like a cult brainwashing session. Curley by this time was back at the lectern and on cue.

"Ladies and gentlemen, please welcome our special guest, Miss Miranda."

As Miranda stood up the room exploded in cries of adulation, stamping of feet, cheering and applause. Curley stood next to Miranda, convinced he had crossed into a parallel universe. The closest thing he could imagine would be one of those election events where the crowd was either given access to free weed or alcohol… or both and had been built up like a steam engine before the brake is taken off.

Ten minutes later the noise level in the auditorium had subsided to a level where Miranda could actually be heard using the microphone she was wired up to and brought the cultees to order.

Curley discretely moved away and, standing out of the light but facing the audience, had a number of thoughts. How was he going to follow the She God, was the introduction beyond even the bizarre, did he have time to sneak out and grab a smoke… Signing internally he waited for the speech had hear a hundred times before to be delivered as only Miranda could

Thirty minutes into the rambling Curley gave Miranda the five minute notice gesture, which prompted Miranda to throw in a few comments about her minder telling her she had said enough which brought raptures of booing.

Fucking great, Curley thought to himself, *here I am in a fucking cult meeting with the baying cultees wanting my*

blood. Shit, it wouldn't be so bad if she was paying top dollar!

Miranda only ran over by ten minutes which Curley thought was pretty good as previously she had ranted on for literally hours. As the applause and cheering died down Curley switched on his microphone thanking Miranda for her inspiring speech and tried to steer the cultees back to what the event was really about. Thankfully, Miranda only sat through the next thirty minutes before exiting from a side door with her official purse carrier in tow.

Tuesday, 29 September 2015

"What the fuck is going on? Do any of you imbeciles know anything about this company, or how to run a business? Clearly not. Whose fucking idea was it to hide the results from me? Tell me now or I'll fire all your asses. I knew I'd have to do all your jobs myself, you are all fucking incompetent…"

Miranda was ranting. She was wound up and was going to make sure the people in front of her suffered. Firing them would be too easy; it wouldn't be hard enough on them. She knew most of them would love to be fired to get out and bring some pathetic legal claim against her for compensation. Clearly they were too dumb to understand the wording in their contracts. She had them where she wanted them… scared.

"Where are those fucking numbers you committed to?"

The gathered group was shrinking in their chairs. Most of them had taken individual abusive phone calls over the weekend and were waiting for each other to speak up. It was a game of brinkmanship. Who could hold out the longest. Each hoping Miranda didn't focus on them first. At least then they would have the opportunity to join the bandwagon of turning the attention from their areas. All knew this was coming as the whole budget process was just a facade of pushing off the inevitable to a later date. Today was, in essence, judgment day…

"Who's going to explain where my money is?"

There was another reason Miranda was ranting. Payments to a number of the shareholders were due and she was banking on this coming from UARD. If these shits didn't turn up with the cash she had a major headache. The court cases were starting to stack up and rumors from her inside information was the DOJ was preparing the next case and it was a big one… one billion dollars! If she could get by with the current payments she could buy enough time to clean up and clear off to her island and retire…

"You have exactly forty-eight hours to get the cash, otherwise you will be paying it personally. In case you don't think that's possible, check your contracts. If you don't believe me, check your contracts…" With that, the gathered executive staff members were dismissed and it was a mad rush to the office door to escape…

With the office door locked, Miranda sat down and pulled out her special box and set about the task of calming herself down…

Thursday, 25 August 2016

Three long years had passed, but the wait was going to be worthwhile. The evidence collected had grown and was now filling the three tables that were going to be waiting in front of Judge Shah. The original case had dragged on, but a new case had been brought by separate 'partners' of Matriarg Vennote. This case was targeted at $1,000,000,000 and, from the investigation and research from his team had built up, a complex web or deceit, lies, blackmail and homicide. Matriarg Vennote's defense team had changed twice in the preliminary stages leading up to this trial and it was rumored that Miranda had been plowing $3,000,000 a week to cover her legal costs.

As Judge Shah drove to the courthouse sipping his venti Americano in the morning rush hour traffic his mind wondered who the poor bastards were that were slaving away to pay off those costs. He was sure the funds would not be coming from Miranda's personal accounts. He made a mental note to ask the question, not that the lawyers representing Matriarg Vennote would know or care, but he was going to make a point out of highlighting the irony of someone who claimed to fight for American jobs wasting all their hard work and putting more American jobs at risk.

The temperature was already increasing outside and it was forecast to be up to 94F. As Judge Shah crawled in the morning rush hour traffic he thought of the irony. It was his intention to ratchet up the heat on Matriarg Vennote and its owner over the next weeks and months. He didn't really care how long the case went on; his goal, though, was to get the case closed before the election. He didn't want to leave any stone unturned and he was determined to get all the sordid details out into the public domain and make sure justice was done.

As he pulled into the parking lot there were already signs this was not a normal day at the office... courthouse. Close by, a number of news vans with their crews were already setting up. As he pulled into his parking space he didn't see anyone fameous amongst the gathering news hounds and he slipped into the building by a side door without being accosted for an interview. The case was not due to start until 11.00 am, so he still had a number of hours to go through a final briefing with his team. As he sat at his desk he could feel a sense of history coming. He was determined his name would be famous for being the defender of the American people and the stage was now set. He was intrigued to see which 'suits' would turn up to defend the indefensible, maybe ones realizing it was a lost cause, but knowing they were in for a good cash injection for the business... And, for sure, for themselves for as long as the case went on. Three million dollars per week, or a portion of that, sure would cover a decent new condo in the Bahamas...

His mind wandered to the question of what exactly the 'American Dream' really meant or stood for. It was seriously ironic that the drive to make money over everything else was nothing more than greed, inevitably involving corruption and creating ego personalities that believed they were above the law and in reality, the planet they lived on was not the one the average person could ever understand. It wasn't about making the country greater, it was purely about self-interest and overindulgence. The epitome of this was the reason he was in court today. The reality of 'living the dream' was seen in the 2008 financial crash.

"Good morning, boss."

The greeting shook Judge Shah from his mind wandering and back to reality.

"Good morning, Meghan and how are you today?"

"I'm doing great, thank you. I managed to take in the new show last night. It was cool."

"Excellent, you must send me a quick review so I don't have to go and see it myself... and pretend to my golf partners I'm educated and sophisticated."

They both laughed and Meghan headed out of his office

to do the morning coffee run in the canteen.

By 9.30am the team was gathered in the conference room.

"OK, let's go through this one last time." Meghan was at the front of the conference room with her laptop projecting wirelessly.

Each one of the twenty staff members around the conference table stepped in when their element came up for review. Judge Shah realized at that moment this team had come a very long way since that first trial in 2013. The level of maturity and subject knowledge had grown dramatically. Sure, some of the original team had moved onto new opportunities, but the core was still together and had become a well-oiled process. Each knowing where their tasks and responsibilities began and finished, each backing their peers up. He couldn't help have a small wry smile.

"Something wrong, boss?" Meghan enquired.

"Not at all, I was just sitting here and thinking how impressive this team is. Now let's go and kick ass."

With that the meeting adjourned to get ready for the start of the case.

Monday, 31 October 2016

Miranda's destiny appeared to be hanging in the balance of the election next week. Things were not looking good. According to the polls the Clinton bitch looked like she was going to get in and that would be shit for her. She had already made plans to leave the country as soon as the results announcement was made, in case Trump failed. She knew he was full of shit but he was, at least, the best opportunity she had to keep out of jail.

Miranda had some back door channels into him and had been working outside known communication channels to make sure he could be successful. The WikiLeaks and Russia connection could never be linked to her, she had made sure the path was covered, but it was the least she could do to secure her own freedom…

The lawsuits continued to appear, but it was the one with that bastard Judge Shah which concerned her the most. The verdict was due out anytime and the re-trial had turned up many new ways that Miranda could by taking a one way ride to a correctional institution for the rest of her natural life

Tuesday, 8 November 2016

Miranda was worried. It was somewhat of a new experience. The net was finally drawing in; a day she had thought would never arrive was now looming. She had always pushed such thoughts to the back of her mind, almost deliberately ignoring the inevitable fact. The past was coming back to haunt her, now it was getting closer. The enormity of what lay ahead was threatening to explode and it was driving her literally insane...